The Book of Summer

ALSO BY MICHELLE GABLE

A Paris Apartment
I'll See You in Paris

The Book of Summer

Michelle Gable

ST. MARTIN'S GRIFFIN NEW YORK

This is a work of fiction. All of the characters, organizations, and events portrayed in this novel are either products of the author's imagination or are used fictitiously.

www.stmartins.com

Designed by Anna Gorovoy

The Library of Congress has cataloged the hardcover edition as follows:

Names: Gable, Michelle, author.
Title: The book of summer : a novel / Michelle Gable.
Description: First Edition. | New York : St. Martin's Press, 2017.
Identifiers: LCCN 2017001070 | ISBN 9781250070623 (hardcover) |
ISBN 9781466880955 (ebook) | ISBN 9781250153173 (international edition)
Subjects: | BISAC: FICTION / Contemporary Women. | FICTION /
Family Life. | FICTION / Historical.
Classification: LCC PS3607.A237 B66 2017 | DDC 813/.6—dc23
LC record available at https://lccn.loc.gov/2017001070

ISBN 978-1-250-13740-1 (trade paperback)

Our books may be purchased in bulk for promotional, educational, or business use. Please contact your local bookseller or the Macmillan Corporate and Premium Sales Department at 1-800-221-7945, extension 5442, or by email at MacmillanSpecialMarkets@macmillan.com.

First St. Martin's Griffin Edition: May 2018

10 9 8 7 6 5 4 3 2

For
Paige Virginia
and
Georgia Anne

The Book of Summer

1

Island ACKtion

CLIFF HOUSE A GONER?

May 15, 2013

Rumor has it the quintessential Nantucket manse known as Cliff House is days from falling into the ocean. A heartbreak, to be sure. It's the only original and complete pre-1978 building left on the northernmost portion of Baxter Road.

For anyone living under a seashell, the home is all the way over in Sconset, atop a bluff and a few beats from Sankaty Head Light and the famous golf course where you can find a certain hoodied NFL coach swinging his clubs.

Besieged by decades of erosion, Cliff House is a lovely old place that has aged a century in the past year alone. There was Hurricane Sandy last fall, followed by the cruel February blizzard, and a ruthless nor'easter in March, which brought winds exceeding 90 mph. In only eight months, Cliff House has lost over fifty feet of bluff.

As most know, town shaker Cissy Codman owns Cliff House. Cis claims to have some tricks up her sleeve, sand recycling and barricades and such. And while we're obsessed with Cissy and her tricks, whatever grand plans our favorite Sconseter has devised must be okayed by a bevy of local and state interests. By and large, islanders don't want the barricades. The Summer People do. And Cissy Codman is a little bit of both, living here mostly year-round but being a Bostonian at heart.

They say hope is gone but we at *Island ACKtion* find that a hard pill to choke down. If anyone can save the bluff, it's Cissy. No doubt, she'll move heaven and earth to get what she wants. Let's pray the earth doesn't move first.

Stay tuned, Nantucketers. This fight isn't over. Personally, I'd put my money on a spunky sexagenarian who never seems to sleep.

ABOUT ME:

Corkie Tarbox, lifelong Nantucketer, steadfast flibbertigibbet. Married with one ankle-biter. Views expressed on the *Island ACKtion* blog (Twitter, Facebook, Instagram, et al.) are hers alone. Usually.

2

Saturday Afternoon

Only Cissy Codman would pick someone up at the airport on a bike.

"Bess!" she hollers, pedaling up. "Elisabeth!"

Cissy is in her standard uniform: khaki shorts, denim button-down, beaten-up Keds. Her hair is tucked into a Red Sox baseball cap.

"Oh, Bess, you are beautiful!" she says, and then annihilates her daughter with a Cissy-grade hug. Vigorous. Aggressive. Almost punishing. "I expected so much worse, given the divorce."

"Pending divorce. And Mom? A bike?"

Bess is too flummoxed by the mode of transportation to grouse about any backhanded compliments, which are a Cissy Codman specialty. Bess is used to them, and to the bike as well. None of it should come as a surprise, yet Cissy always catches her daughter off guard.

"Do I need to rent a car?" Bess asks, and wheels her suitcase out into the sunshine.

She shades her eyes with one hand.

"Don't be ridiculous," Cissy says. "This is Nantucket, not LA."

"Okay, but I live in San Francisco, which is four hundred miles from Los Angeles and basically like living in a different state. Also, you realize we're at least five miles from Cliff House?"

"Just over seven," Cissy says. "I have a basket on my bike, though!"

Bess glances down at her suitcase. It fits in an overhead compartment, but definitely wouldn't in the weather-beaten wicker box dangling from Cissy's handlebars. Not to mention, Milestone Road is one boring, interminable shot out to Sconset. To bike it without luggage is hassle enough.

"Cis, do you really think I can fit this . . ." Bess gestures toward her suitcase. "Into that?"

The bike basket is so lacking even the Easter Bunny would complain.

"I didn't expect you to bring so much," Cissy says.

"Oh, Mom."

Bess leans in for a second hug. The first one came at her so fast she didn't have a chance to hold on.

"It's great to see you," she says. "I'm glad a few things never change."

Bess pulls back.

"I love that you think you can drive the entire world on those scrawny legs of yours," she says. "But, seriously, we need to explore other options."

"Who raised such a princess?" Cissy asks with a grin. "Sheesh. Too much time in California. I can't even tell you're from New England anymore."

She latches on to Bess's suitcase and tromps out toward the street—guiding the luggage with one hand, her bike with the other.

"I can carry that!" Bess calls.

Cissy quickens her pace, the curly, salty blond ponytail bobbing through the hole of her hat. Bess flattens her dark, straight bangs, as if in response.

"I'm not sure why you're here," Cissy calls over her shoulder, "so far in advance of your cousin's wedding. Don't get me wrong. It's great to see you. But aren't you supposed to be working?"

Yes. Working. That's exactly what she should be doing. It's the same argument Bess made when her father called.

"Well, Dad says . . ." Bess starts.

"Oh please." Cissy makes a snort-puff sound. "Your father exaggerates as a rule. He probably did his best to raise your hackles, to make the situation seem irreparably dire."

Bess shakes her head. "Dire" is one word. "Catastrophic" is another.

"Elisabeth, you have to drag your mother out of that house," he'd implored only seventy-two hours before.

"Why can't you do it?" Bess had asked. "She's your wife."

"Please. She stopped listening to me years ago. You're the only one who can help."

Though it sounded suspiciously like a compliment, it wasn't one at all. No, Dudley doesn't believe his middle child capable of swaying one very stubborn and immovable matriarch. His faith in Bess is more practical, rooted in his daughter's ability to show up on short notice, at least compared to her siblings. She's no Clay, the big brother, who works a gajillion hours a week at their dad's hedge fund and has two young kids and a demanding, nine-months-pregnant wife who makes a full-time job of issuing summonses and demands.

Neither is Bess like last-born Julia, known almost exclusively as "Lala" owing to a multiyear inability to pronounce her own name. Sweet Lala is in the Sudan helping refugees, because baby sisters with Harvard degrees and privileged upbringings can do that sort of thing. In sum: Lala has nothing to prove.

"I can't fly cross-country right now," Bess told her dad. "I have to work. To get all of my shifts covered would inconvenience multiple people."

Not to mention that her personal life is in a state of bedlam, though Bess did not disclose that to him.

"I'd love to help," she lied. "But it's not feasible. Have you tried Clay or Lala?"

"Absolutely not. I'd never ask either one."

"Of course you wouldn't."

"Aren't you going to be on-island at the end of the month anyway?" he asked. "For Felicia's wedding? Leave earlier."

"Dad, I'm a physician. I can't just bail."

"Don't you work, like, three days a week?"

"Three *shifts,*" she said. "Which are longer than an average workday."

"You work in the ER."

"The ED. It's really more of a *department* than a room."

"Whatever."

Her dad was getting frustrated, as Dudley Codman was prone to do when things weren't going his way. The man was loud and intimidating, like a dictator or the head of a drug cartel. But it all unraveled when somebody crossed him.

"Elisabeth," he said with a beleaguered sigh. "Have another doctor cover for you. No one plans to see you specifically. Don't random people just show up with a stab wound or whatnot looking for anyone with a pulse?"

"Also a medical degree. And we have precious few stab wounds. But I get what you're saying."

On some level, her father was right. It is simple to trade shifts, and unlike her colleagues, Bess isn't opposed to working holidays. In fact, she prefers it. She likes doing people favors, plus emergencies tend to be better during times of celebration. There aren't so many drug seekers and paranoid moms.

"I'm already taking off Memorial Day weekend," Bess told him, counting backward in her head.

If she did as asked, she would arrive ten days earlier than planned. That was no kind of option.

"And finagling time off for Flick's wedding was a major coup," she said. "They sort of expect me to work holidays."

"Why? Because you're a divorcée?"

"Almost-divorcée. And it's not quite that blatant. But, yes."

"Listen, I don't have time to argue," he said. "You'll go to Nantucket, help your mother pack, and drag her out of that crapshack she calls a home. Now, if you'll excuse me, one of my companies is about to release earnings and I'm positive they're going to post a miss."

"Dad, I'll talk to her when I'm there. I'll call her tonight! Surely nothing will happen between now and—"

"Listen, Bess," he snapped. "If you don't go, your mother will end up in a pile of rubble on the beach."

"Jesus, Dad."

Dudley's intrinsic mobster was leaking out.

"We'll spend months trying to sort out which pieces are bones," he went on. "And which are rocks."

And then the line went dead.

So, "dire"? Yes, he made it seem quite dire, right down to the shards of bone.

"I don't know, Cissy," Bess says now, once she catches up to her mom, a sixty-five-year-old lady who can outrun her three kids and probably half of the Nantucket High track team. "Dad made it sound pretty treacherous."

"If it were that bad, don't you think he'd be here?"

"He says the house is going to fall over the bluff."

"As if I'd let that happen."

Cissy jams her fingers into her mouth and emits a sharp whistle. Two terrified seagulls flap away from their telephone-pole nest. She whistles again, and then juts her thumb out toward the road.

"*We're hitchhiking?!*" Bess yelps.

"Don't be such a pansy."

Bess stands openmouthed, a bead of sweat crawling down her back. *There goes Cissy Codman*, folks driving by must think. *Up to her usual antics.*

Bess's mother is famous on that island. No, infamous. When Bess returned to the island to finish high school, Nantucketers almost seemed surprised that Cissy was something more than a municipal agitator.

"My mom will be here in thirty minutes," Bess might say.

"Your mom?" was the reply. "You mean Cissy?"

"My mom wanted me to drop this off."

"Who's your . . . Oh, ha ha ha. Why didn't you just say Cissy?"

And so Bess started just saying Cissy. It was a joke, but then it stuck. Her mother didn't seem to mind, or even notice.

"Cis, let's rent a car," Bess says. "Obviously no one's keen on picking up a couple of grifters and this isn't exactly a thoroughfare."

"Have a little patience, why dontcha? Honestly, Bess."

Bess sighs, though a smile slips out. God, she adores that crazy woman. Bess fixes her eyes on the horizon. A few cars motor by, then nothing. She grows hot and impatient. How much longer will they wait? Alas, fortunately or unfortunately—Bess cannot decide—a white, wood-paneled truck appears in the distance. It approaches and then rolls to a stop.

"Is that . . ." Bess says.

"Just friggin' fabulous."

Cissy drops the bike and then the suitcase.

"Go to hell, Chappy!" she screams, and raises both middle fingers.

"Mother!"

"Polished as ever," the man says, and leans across the passenger seat to leer at them through the open window. "What a mess, eh? Well, Bess. Welcome home."

"Thanks," she mumbles.

"Here, hop in."

"This is fucking perfect," Cissy grouses, but she throws the luggage and bike into the back nonetheless. "I guess you're the only option, on account of my daughter's baggage situation."

Baggage situation, Bess thinks with a smirk. How painfully appropriate.

"Are you even allowed to drive?" her mother asks the man, their neighbor Chappy Mayhew, as they rumble away from the airport. "Don't you still have that DUI conviction on your record?"

Chappy laughs and shakes his head. Bess can't help but smile. Yep, she's in Nantucket all right. Or, as Cissy would say, it's "just fucking perfect." Welcome home indeed.

3

Saturday Afternoon

"So how ya been, Doc?" Chappy asks as they splutter toward Baxter Road, Bess wedged between him and her mother.

Cissy has her eyes closed and her head pressed against the frame of the car. She keeps emitting small burps, as if she might be sick.

"Fine," Bess answers curtly. "I'm just dandy."

"So what brings you to our lovely island all the way from California? Far as I can remember, you haven't been round since your wedding. And that was, what? Two years ago?"

"Four," she says.

Chappy whistles.

"Wow. That's a long time away from your mom."

"Give it a rest, Mayhew," Cissy says. "She visits us in Boston and I go to San Francisco at least once a month."

"You do?" Bess says, and cranes her neck to look at her.

"Anyway, mind your own damned business."

"Wouldn't that be a treat?" he says with a snort.

It would be tough for Chappy to mind his own damned business, given that he lives in the gray saltbox directly across from Cliff House. Within shooting distance, as Cissy would say, with some degree of cheer. Chappy's been their neighbor since before Bess was born, and even if they didn't live so close, Cissy Codman is impossible to ignore, with that incessant biking, her town-meeting intrusions, and the general propensity to raise hell.

In short, Cissy and Chappy are natural enemies. He: a grotty local, the last commercial fisherman on the island. She: an indulged off-islander trying to screw with the ecosystem and therefore his livelihood. Of course, as Cissy has lived in Sconset (mostly) full-time for over twenty years, she considers herself a local through and through. But the real locals don't necessarily agree. She is not *from there*, after all.

Cissy doesn't help her cause with the Back Bay townhome and tendency to abscond to Boston at the first snowflake, not to mention the millions she collects in bluff-restoration dollars among her Summer People squad. They are saving the shoreline, dontcha know? To benefit residents and visitors alike. Why, they're downright heroic!

True Sconseters aren't buying that claptrap, though. In their estimation, off-islanders don't care about Nantucket. They care about their fancy summer homes. It's their own stupid fault, too. Locals never would've been so idiotic as to build directly on a bluff.

"Minding my own business," Chappy says, "would be a dream come true. Ya know, you two are pretty feisty for hitchhikers. I'm only gonna pick up dirty hippies from here on out."

"Sounds like a plan," Cissy grumbles.

As they drive along in achy silence, Bess wonders if they should've biked after all. She has no real beef against Chappy, other than his salty demeanor, but being cordial feels like a direct betrayal of Cissy. Plus, his truck seems to lack shock absorbers. Bess swears her bones are clinking together.

"I assume you're here to pack up your mom," Chappy says at last. "Yank her out of that house."

"Something like that."

"The fight's not over," Cissy reminds them both. "If I have to go down, it'll be swinging."

"Oh brother. Lady, I know you see this as a battle royale, an us-versus-them smackdown . . ."

"How many times do I have to tell you? There is no us or them. It's we! I'm one of you. I live here! We want the same thing: a better Nantucket."

"A better Nantucket?" Chappy says, and rolls his eyes. "Better for you. Using your golf-ball money to keep property values sky-high and screw with the environment in the process. I mean, really. Just buy another damned house, why don't you. Or better yet, go back to America."

Bess smirks. The hallmark of a true Nantucketer. He views Boston as "America" and the island as something else entirely.

"First of all," Cissy says, "that is my *home*. I don't want another one. Secondly, we sold that company ages ago, as you are well aware. Thirdly, golf balls were the very least of it. My grandfather started his company by reconstituting rubber scraps into usable material. In other words: recycling. Before it was fashionable to do so."

"Meanwhile, he had a factory on the riverbank, spewing God knows what into the Acushnet."

"That's quite enough."

"So this is fun," Bess pipes in.

"Listen," Chappy says. "I don't much care if your family got their wealth saving orphans or trading them on the black market or in some other way. I don't care and God doesn't care. Not even ballsy Cissy Codman and her sacks of cash can fight the hands of time."

"Ballsy. I appreciate the compliment, really I do, but you already gave this strikingly unexceptional speech two nights ago. We have a plan. Hell or high water, fire or brimstone, I'll get this done."

"There'll be high water all right."

"In conclusion, as I've said so many times before: Fuck off."

"All right then. You keep your plans. I'll stay on the side of Mother Nature and of God."

Chappy cranks the wheel hard left and steers them into his driveway. Bess can almost feel the strength and size of Cliff House at her back. She realizes then that she didn't even glance its way as they passed. Four years. Chappy is right. It's far too long.

"Here we are," he announces, unnecessarily.

Bess takes in a sharp breath.

"Well, thanks," Cissy says as she leaps out of the cab. "I suppose."

She heaves her bike from the truck bed. Meanwhile, Bess takes her time in disembarking, first scooting across the cracked leather seat before ultimately sliding down onto the ground.

"Stop dawdling!" Cissy yips.

Bess hears the bike's wheels crunch on the gravel.

"Good grief, you've turned into a bona fide Californian, haven't you? Heaven help me. *Hang loose brah.*"

"I've literally never heard anyone say that."

Dr. Bess Codman is indeed dawdling. What she's afraid to see, not even Bess understands. A lot can happen in a thousand-plus days. Perhaps the home will be as wrecked and keening as Dudley described. Or else it'll be the same old place, the house even *she* lived in year-round, for a while, after her life had gone to shit. In other words, the glory days. It's funny what amounted to problems when you were sixteen.

Alas, Bess can no longer stall, particularly if Cissy has anything to say about it, which of course she will. And so with both eyes squinched closed, Bess shuts the car door. She inhales and twists her torso to the left and then to the right. At last Bess reopens her eyes. She lets her mind swallow the scene.

And there it stands: the inveterate Cliff House. Large. Gray. Shingled. Surrounded by a massive privet hedge. Looking almost like it did before.

"Oh," she says aloud.

Maybe this isn't so bad.

Bess takes a few steps forward, and more after that, her knees shaky beneath her. As her toes touch Baxter Road, Bess realizes that although the home resembles its usual self, the ocean seems closer than it's ever been.

She shuffles onto the white-shelled drive, suitcase dragging behind her. To the left is nothing but a view of the Atlantic. There were once two guest homes in that spot, and Bess expected to see at least one. Cissy told her that "Overflow" was lost about a year ago, but now "Family Room" has vanished with it. To the right looms Cliff House itself, secure for now behind its hedge.

Bess exhales and walks farther up the drive, past her mother's ancient Land Rover Defender, plastered as it is with bumper stickers from her kids' colleges. Cissy's "ACK nice" sticker had been covered up—by Chappy—with an "ACK naughty" one instead. ("Oh, Chappy Mayhew wants naughty?! I'll show him naughty!") Bess chuckles, thinking a truck like that beats the heck out of a basket and a bike. Sometimes her mother is in tight supply of that good New England sense she yammers on about.

Suddenly Bess notices the flagpole, or, rather, the lack of one. When she pictures Cliff House, her mind begins with only three things: a big, gray house, the privet hedge, and Old Glory fluttering above it all. Bess abandons her suitcase and rushes through the hedge's arbored gate and into the side yard.

The flagpole is in fact gone. So are the tennis courts, the outdoor shower, and the storage shack. All of these things, and more, turned to air. Bess's breath goes thin.

"Jesus," she gasps.

Cissy is a tenacious old broad, but Chappy Mayhew is right. It's time to give up on Cliff House. There's already too much they'll never get back.

4

Saturday Evening

They stand on the back patio, the last of the day's sun stretching across the Atlantic. Though the view is magnificent, Bess's stomach roils and churns. Her insides are nothing but roller-coaster drops. The excessive winds don't help.

"Cissy," she says. "We can't stay here."

Vanished. Cliff House has disappeared.

The building itself remains, for the moment anyway, but gone is the lawn where Bess got married, where so many before her wed, including Cissy and her grandmother Ruby. Ruby's vegetable garden has also evaporated, as well as the public walking path behind it.

Gone also is the pool, once set in the grass, a rectangle of blue with a single white border around it. Gone is the volleyball court Cissy ambitiously installed though it was the one sport the family never played.

The outdoor shower, the flagpole, the bike and board shed: gone, gone, and gone. Even their remarkable privet hedge, tended to for generations and photographed for magazines and tourist brochures, is dead and brown in the back. How could it all look okay from the road?

"This isn't safe," Bess says.

If she walked ten feet forward, she'd reach the end of the patio, where steel edging is exposed. A cell phone dropped in that very spot would fall several stories onto the rocks below. As the wind howls through her, Bess wonders if she's in danger of tumbling over the cliff herself. The gusts are strong that far up on Baxter Road. Within minutes she has sand in her teeth and on her skin.

Bess's throat prickles and it has little to do with the sand she's inhaled. She understands Cissy's reluctance to let go. It's about the house, yes, but also their family. In the early twentieth century, Bess's great-grandmother Sarah Young longed for a home their brood might retreat to in the summers. Her husband, Philip, was an MIT-educated scientist who devised a way to process reclaimed rubber. His invention built a fortune and it built his wife the house of her dreams.

Sconset, seven miles from Nantucket Town, has never been the most fashionable part of the island. Back then it was riddled with artists and seamen and new-money types like the Youngs. But Sarah adored it on sight, even more so when she and Philip made the one-mile trek up Baxter Road. With a single glance at the unadorned bluff, she envisioned lawn parties and orchestras and ragtime performers playing into the night. Her family would grow up there, Sarah decided. Whatever happened in the months before or after, each year would be anchored by a summer spent at Cliff House.

Bess's heart breaks to see it end up like this.

"We have to leave," she says, shimmying off the encroaching nostalgia. It's time to get practical. "Dad mentioned he sent over some empty boxes? Let's start packing. It's funny, I never realized I was afraid of heights."

"Bessie, I acknowledge it seems a little . . . dicey?"

Bess turns toward her mom, mouth agape.

"If by dicey you mean lethal, then I agree. Your plumbing is sticking out of the bluff!"

"Yes, well, we've had a streak of bad luck between Hurricane Sandy and then those ghastly winter storms," Cissy says. "We still had half a pool at Christmastime! But there's no immediate threat."

"Have you looked?" Bess says, pointing. "Right there?"

"The weather has stabilized and the veranda is quite expansive . . . I can stay on for at least a little while."

"No. Not happening." Bess waves her hands around, as if trying to make the situation disappear. "I'm not losing my mother to erosion. 'Here lies Caroline Packard Codman. Expired of stubbornness and not knowing when to quit.'"

"I recognize the need to relocate at some point. But in three days they're voting to approve—"

"Or not approve," Bess reminds her.

"Fine. On Tuesday they're weighing in on the revetments."

"And that makes a difference because . . . ?"

"Revetments work brilliantly on Martha's Vineyard! Heck, the entire Jersey shore is one massive beach nourishment project. Once the revetment plan goes into place, I can focus on my own predicament. It's not about me, you know. Despite what Chappy Mayhew claims."

Bess ogles the bluff. Either her eyes are playing tricks or rocks are right then rolling down onto the beach. Bess goes to steady herself on a railing but reconsiders. Who knows what kind of house of cards they're dealing with? One wrong move and, well, Bess won't have to worry about her imminent divorce anymore, or the problems that follow.

With an exhale, Bess takes several steps back.

"Why are you staying here?" she asks. "You can fight this same battle from somewhere else."

"This is my home, Bess."

"I get that, but . . ."

"Beyond that, I have my reasons." Cissy sniffs. "Listen, after the meeting, I'll pack up. Promise."

"You promise? *Real* promise? Or Cissy squidgy, room-for-movement promise?"

"Very droll. I *promise*. Come Tuesday, I'll move."

"Okay good." Bess's shoulders slacken.

"Cliff House and I will both move."

Cissy turns on her heel and brushes past Bess, cutting a mean path toward the outdoor bar.

"Excuse me?" Bess says as she whips around. "You'll *both* move?"

"I'm thinking we can push it back about seventy yards?"

"Push *what* back?" Bess asks, growing panicky once more.

"Cliff House, silly. We have a lot of front yard to work with."

"What?!"

"I need to get the engineers back," Cissy continues. "The golf club's granted an easement."

"So you're just going to . . ." Bess stutters. "Relocate the entire house?"

"It worked for Sankaty Head."

"A lighthouse is a tad easier to move than a five-thousand-square-foot home."

"You'd be surprised."

Cissy vanishes beneath the bar and resurfaces with a bottle and a glass. Like a rerun of your favorite show, she makes herself a vodka rocks. The backdrop is disorienting in its sameness. Here stands Cissy Codman on the patio at Cliff House, stirring drinks and mixing schemes. Bess can almost overlook the gawping Atlantic a few yards away.

"I can't believe *that's* where I got married," Bess says, and points to the clouds.

A headache is coming on.

"That was a great day," Cissy replies, beaming.

"Was it?"

"I can't wait to have weddings here again. I offered Cliff House to your cousin for *her* wedding." Cissy frowns. "But Flick turned me down. The Yacht Club, of all places. It's like she's taunting me."

"Flick is not taunting you."

With the mere mention of Felicia, Bess feels the undeniable creep of dread. Her cousin's wedding is on Memorial Day—a week from Monday. Will Bess have to stay on-island until then? "Play through," as it were? She has her shifts covered, but the time off is supposed to be for another reason altogether, a reason that does not include unexpected trips to Nantucket. Forget the time involved in going back and forth between two coasts, Bess is not exactly flush with cash. Divorces will do that to you. Especially ones like hers.

Bess shakes her head.

"Cis, no bride in her right mind would get married here."

"Cliff House has hosted countless weddings," Cissy says. "And the side yard is plenty big for the one Felicia is planning. She's only having fifty guests!"

"Don't take it personally. I'm sure Flick doesn't want to tussle with liability insurance or sorority sisters falling to their deaths."

"All of her friends are investment bankers and lawyers," Cissy says with a shrug. "A few less of them wouldn't hurt."

"Hilarious."

Bess tiptoes up beside her mom and puts a gentle arm around her shoulders.

"You have to admit, Cissy. This place isn't exactly event-ready."

"Oh, I know," she says, and forces a laugh. "I might be a little foolhardy at times but I'm no fool. Mark my words, though. Once we get the new measures in place and push the house closer to the road, Cliff House *will* be guest-ready once more."

Cissy turns to lock eyes with Bess. Tears gather on her lashes.

"A hundred years," Cissy says, voice quavering. "Next summer Cliff House turns one hundred years old."

"Wow, I didn't realize. But 1914." Bess pictures the bronze plaque by the door. "The math is there."

"I have a marvelous party planned." At once Cissy's eyes brighten and grow. "Just wait. We'll host a soirée to beat any this house has ever known. And there've been hundreds on this property. A thousand. I'll die before I let them take that from us."

"Okay, Mom." Bess has to bite her lip to prevent her own tears from forming. "I'll book my flights for the Centennial this week."

Cissy sighs and sets down her glass. She crosses her arms and surveys her daughter head to toe.

"You are beautiful," she says. "Out here. The light, the sea, the air. Cliff House, it makes everyone lovelier."

"Now you're just getting sentimental. . . ."

"No. Really." She smiles. "Your skin looks kissed by the moonlight. Your hair is tangled and lovely and wild."

"Tangled hair. Got it."

"That's a compliment and you know it. It's so much more relaxed and free than when you stepped off the plane. No one's hair should be that straight or that dark. You're working too hard at it, my girl."

Bess smiles back, taking the praise where she can get it. At least she's faking it well enough to be called beautiful when really Bess feels like a heap of food trash on a humid day.

"I'm working too hard at it?" Bess says. "This coming from a woman trying to save an entire shoreline!"

"I'm going to do it. Don't doubt me for an instant."

"You're the very last person I'd doubt."

Bess walks over to the fridge beneath the bar, where she finds an already opened bottle of Chardonnay. A week or a year old, there's no way to tell. At Cliff House you really never know what you're getting.

"But Cissy?" Bess says, and pops out the cork. "Can we make a deal?"

"I don't make deals. I prefer to get my way."

"Noted. But hear me out. I'll let you stay until your meeting on Tuesday."

"I didn't realize you were in charge."

"But after that . . ." Bess says.

She sniffs the wine and her belly rumbles. What the hell; Bess pours herself a glass.

"Immediately after the meeting," she continues, "you're moving out. Within twenty-four hours because I need specifics from you. 'After' is way too vague."

Bess takes a sip of wine and holds it in her mouth for a second before spitting it into a rosebush. Something isn't right. The taste makes her want to puke. She dumps the rest while Cissy quite literally looks the other way. It's one of the great things about Cliff House. You don't have to bring your nice shoes, or your manners.

"Fine. Whatever." Cissy slaps at the air.

"So as of Wednesday morning," Bess says, "it's good-bye Cliff House and back to . . . Boston, I guess."

"Boston is not my home," Cissy says.

"Then you can move to town. Or Tom Nevers. Anywhere that's not here. I don't like worrying about you. It makes me uncomfortable."

"Oh, Bess, you can't worry. And yes of course I'll take up temporary residence in town. I can't be *physically* in the house when they're moving it, can I? Though it does sound like fun."

"But, Cis, why are you here *now*? You've said you have your reasons. What are they?"

"I want to show that I'm committed. Determined. Like a true Sconseter."

"No one would question your commitment. You probably need to *be* committed but your dedication is unflagging."

"Har har," Cissy says. "My daughter is a doctor and comedienne both. How did I get so lucky? Elisabeth, if you want to stay in town, do it! I won't be the least bit offended. The Bradlees have plenty of room and they won't be here for days. I'll give you the key right now."

"Mom, I . . ."

"It's okay." Cissy places a hand on Bess's. "Your dad gave up on Cliff House long ago and I've managed splendidly on my own. We can pack during the day and at night you can stay at your cousins' place. Honestly, sweet girl, it's fine. Do whatever you need to do."

Bess closes her eyes. *Do whatever you need to do*. Typical Cissy Codman. The Chinese finger trap of moms. If only Bess didn't love her so damned much.

5

Sunday Morning

Sleep is a tough pursuit in a house about to slide down a bluff.

It's always been too drafty, that home, or too stuffy and warm. Central air was never contemplated, and so the family made do with ceiling fans and coastal breezes. But now, with each of these "breezes," Bess swears the house shifts, that she can hear the plink of patio bricks. When dawn at last noses its way through the shutters, Bess says a quick thank-you to the heavens, genuinely surprised to have survived the night.

"Good morning, Cis," she says, strolling into the dining room.

It's just before six and her mother has been up for at least an hour. Bess's dad used to joke that when the kids were newborns, Cissy woke *them* up in the wee hours instead of the other way around. "I like to keep busy," she'd say, in her own defense.

"Morning, love . . ."

"Whoa," Bess says, craning, peering over the flood of cardboard in the room. Cissy is standing but Bess can only see the top of her face, that curly and wild hair. "Dad wasn't kidding. He did send over a 'few' boxes. It looks like a recycling facility in here."

"What he sent were movers," Cissy says. "Which I refused. But they graciously left behind their supplies."

"Well, this is a mess," Bess says as she kicks a path through the room. Most of the boxes are gallingly weightless.

She leans in to give her mother a kiss.

"Should I ask them to come back?" Bess asks. "The movers? This is a pretty big job for a couple of unskilled gals."

Bess thinks of the rest of the home. Five thousand square feet filled with nearly a century's accumulation of knickknacks and personal effects. It'd been decades since Cliff House opened and closed with the seasons. This is a year-round place now.

"Who are you calling unskilled?" Cissy balks. "I was on the committee to move the lighthouse, you know."

"Yes. I know. We all do."

"And movers? Please. I'm not letting a bunch of strangers manhandle my belongings. Since when are you afraid of a little elbow grease? You're losing your good New England hardiness and it's breaking my heart."

Cissy flings a box into the corner.

"So," she says. "How did you sleep?"

"Great!" Bess chirps, on reflex, though it's a lie.

The bluff might've diminished but not the power of Cliff House, it seems. Something about the musty-salt scent of the rooms causes the magic to stick to Bess as surely as grains of sand are perpetually glued to her feet and toes. The place can make you forget what's really going on. Why didn't Bess return before now? Before it was almost too late?

"See?" her mom says. "Cliff House is as safe and peaceful as it's always been."

"But Cissy . . ."

"Not to fret, though! I've already begun packing, like the dutiful girl that I am."

"Major red flag. You haven't been dutiful a day in your life."

"You kids never give your old mom any credit."

Bess shakes her head.

"So where should I start?" she asks, hands on hips. Bess scans the room and within seconds spots a familiar object just out of reach. "Hey! Is that . . ."

As she leans, a sharp pain rockets up Bess's side. She pushes through it in order to get her mitts on a scrapbook perched at the far end of the table. Cramps surge through Bess's midsection as she lifts the book. It must weigh twenty pounds at least.

"The Book of Summer!" she says with a grin.

Bess rubs the crocodile-embossed cover. Dust sticks to her fingers. "Hello, you wonderful relic."

The Book of Summer is as old as Cliff House itself. From the first day of the first season, Sarah Young asked visitors and family members to record an entry, tell a brief tale of their Cliff House stay. It's a tradition as important as the view, or the once-great lawn, or the bunk rooms upstairs. As a girl, Bess loved combing through the paragraphs and photographs and the mementos tucked inside. Most people only signed their names, but even now, whenever Bess misses Grandma Ruby, she knows she can find her in the pages of summer.

"Ah, yes," Cissy says, wrapping a set of blue-and-white ginger jars. "The book, the book. The famous book."

Bess peels back the brown and crackled cover to find the inaugural entry, dated July 11, 1914, penned by Sarah Young herself. Bess's eyes scour the page, though she does not need to read the words. She memorized them long ago.

Even my wildest dreams didn't dare look like this.

Never could I have pictured the shingled, rambling novel of a home or me, reclined on its veranda, belly big as a stove. As massive as I've grown

I am but a speck on the wide expanse of patio, to speak nothing of the yawning lawn behind it, or the boundless ocean beyond. The great Atlantic reaches farther than my imagination ever could. At the horizon the heavens bow to meet it, as if to say "you take it from here." This must be what forever feels like.

Philip says Cliff House is for me but I see it otherwise. The home is not mine but a gift, to me and all who follow. We will hand it down to the next generation, and they the generation after. Our memories, our marks, our moments, they will linger for a while and eventually fade away, to make room for the new, just as it should be.

We will greet each summer with expectant delight, Cliff House the reward for the winter and the toiling away. The deed bears Philip's name but it belongs to us all. We'll invite friends, we'll invite family, and the friends of family. We will throw open the doors and shout, "All of you! Come stay a night or three! Leave your shoes in the basket, your worries outside the door. Together now, let's pour ourselves a drink."

In lieu of rent we will ask our guests to make payment via words in this, the Book of Summer. We'll do this so the memories will stick and so those who follow appreciate what came before.

Bess looks up from the book and toward her mother, who is aggressively boxing silver, slamming the forks and knives as if they've committed some great offense.

" 'And so I say,' " Bess reads out loud, " 'warm greetings, you beautiful Cliff House. So nice to finally meet you. Together we'll have a grand old time.' "

With a sniffle, Bess sets the book back down.

"What are you going to do with it?" she asks. "Take it back to Boston?"

Bess must convince Cissy that *she* should be the rightful owner of the Book of Summer. She'll need to get through Lala and Clay first, but they won't mind. What do they need with it? Lala doesn't even have a permanent address.

"Boston?" Cissy says. "Who mentioned Boston? Truth be told, I'm thinking of doing something with it for the Cliff House Centennial Celebration."

Bess sees the capitalization and bold print as her mother speaks.

"The Cliff House Centennial Celebration," Bess repeats. "That sounds like a proper title. Will there be T-shirts?"

"Elisabeth." Cissy peers over her glasses. "There are *always* T-shirts."

Cissy is right then wearing a Young Family Reunion 1984 windbreaker.

"So what, exactly, do you plan to do with it for the capital-'c' Celebration?" Bess asks.

"I'm not sure. The Book of Summer belongs to the people who've made memories here. I'd love to package up sections for those who've stayed, or their relatives."

"You mean tear out pages?" Bess says, heart galloping. "You can't deface the Book of Summer!"

"Oh, Elisabeth," Cissy chuckles. "What do you propose, then?"

"Let me take it home."

Cissy pivots her gaze in Bess's direction.

"Beg pardon?"

"I want to keep it. I'll check with Lala and Clay, of course, but I'm sure they won't mind."

"Let me get this straight. You want the Book of Summer to live in *Cal-i-for-nia*?" Cissy drags out the syllables, top lip curled as if she were talking about a venereal disease, or a Republican. "You honestly think that's a good idea?"

"Well, it's certainly preferable to have it stay within the family versus getting ripped up and distributed to a bunch of randoms. Grandma Ruby would roll over in her grave!"

"Most definitely," Cissy says. "But my mother has been in a constant state of rolling over for years."

"She wasn't *that* prim, or judgmental."

"Please. You know Ruby Packard's favorite adage. 'A woman's name should only be in print when she's born, when she marries, and when she dies.' The past few years I've been in the local rag more than Bill Belichick."

"I should have it," Bess insists again, flicking through the pages. "You can cut me out of the will entirely, but leave the book to me."

"Who says you're even in my will?"

She stops on a page, her eyes watering with one glance at Grandma Ruby's telltale boxy scrawl. How Bess loves that woman, strongly and still, despite the twenty years that have slipped by since she died. Bess attended one of the most prestigious boarding schools in the nation—for a time, anyway—and her most salient memory of Choate was when Cissy called to say Ruby Packard was no more.

It wasn't until that moment, or perhaps even later, that Bess realized she admired her grandmother. Ruby was so different from Cissy, a much-needed balance to her hell-and-fire mom. Bess loves Cissy greatly, but she's exhausting. Ruby was an antidote, a counterpoint. Of course, this was the least of her.

"Let me tell you something about your mother," Grandma Ruby said oh so many times. "Whenever the young people gathered for a football game, Cissy was picked first, before any of those Kennedy schlubs. She is infinitely more Kennedy-like, too, smarter and sportier than all of them combined. They're more teeth than brains anyhow."

The party line was that Cissy should've been a Kennedy. Never mind her penchant for rabble-rousing; she actually looked like one, with the hair and the smile and, yes, all those teeth. The "Cissy Kennedy" quip was never quite a commendation, though, coming from Grandma. Ruby appreciated their grit, but was largely "not a fan." Their patriarchal nature needled her. The men in that family called the shots.

"This is a house of women," she used to say. "Cliff House is ours."

Ruby Packard, an early feminist in her quiet, iron-walled way.

"Here's one of my favorites," Bess says, turning to an entry from the summer of 1939.

She clears her throat, trying to dislodge Grandma Ruby's Boston Brahmin, Thurston Howell the Third, delightfully snooty Katharine Hepburn inflection.

" '*Lahst* night,' " Bess reads, giving it a try, " 'when Sam and I were on the *beach*.' "

"What is that voice?" Cissy narrows her eyes. "Are you mocking your grandmother?"

"No, it's just . . ."

Bess shakes her head. She's never had a flair for accents. At Choate they gave her a dialect coach for the one line she had in the spring production of *Pride and Prejudice*. She truly was that wretched. So instead of trying to re-create Ruby's cadence, Bess reads on in her ordinary, unremarkable, untrainable voice.

6

The Book of Summer

Ruby Genevieve Young
August 10, 1939
Cliff House, Sconset, Nantucket Island

Last night, when Sam and I were on the beach, I was sure he was going to ask for my hand. Absolutely positive! A million butterflies strummed against my chest as we strolled along.

I did recognize the possibility that he might bungle the situation, or have a hard time getting round to it. Sam can be timid, downright shy at times, which is but one reason I love him so—that faint blush and stammer are wildly endearing! When a gal has brothers forever knocking her upside the head, she comes to appreciate those with a more delicate disposition.

So back to last night. We were partway down Sconset Beach. The sun had set but our path was well lit thanks to the golden misty moon and Mom's soirée on the bluff above. She'd strung five hundred lights between the trees. A veritable star-shine heaven over the back lawn. The noise and mirth from the guests shone even brighter.

"What a night," I said to Sam, trying to sound encouraging. "It's like anything could happen, as though there's no limit to what's possible."

I squeezed his hand extra hard.

"Ruby," he responded at last.

I beamed with gusto, stretching my face to near-collapse. Then I braced myself, waiting for the knee and the ring. It promised to be a good hunk of ice, too. The Packards have quite a lot of money and wouldn't mind me saying so.

"Sam . . . ?" I said, blinking.

Get on with it already!

"This world is changing," he said.

"Yes! Yes, it is, my love!"

"I have no doubt," he went on. "The problems in Europe will become ours."

Europe? What the dickens did Europe have to do with us?

"The entire world will soon be embroiled in this fight," he continued.

I started to speak, intent on pointing out that talk of war was just about the least appropriate topic to broach on a romantic walk, when, all of a sudden, a man came sprinting down the beach, screaming like an Apache.

While Sam was startled, I remained unplucked. It was my brother. He had on Daddy's clothes and a fake beard.

"My wife!" he shouted, ranting, chucking golf balls at us both. "Get away from my wife!"

Playacting, a gag, a Topper special to the hilt. There isn't a night so perfect my baby brother can't ruin it with one of his tireless pranks.

"Get lost, creep!" I said as Topper ranted about his alleged wife—me—who was stepping out behind his back.

"It's only my brother," I then told Sam, who looked stricken and scared.

"But . . ." he sputtered, eyes jockeying back and forth between us.

"He's easy to recognize, what with that gangly height, not to mention the blasted camera forever bobbing from his neck."

"Gangly?" Topper said. "I prefer to think of myself as stately. Possessing an immaculate and powerful presence."

"I'm sure you do," I said with a snort.

"You two," Sam grumbled. "I can't fathom the depravity . . ."

Depravity? Forget the romance, now my beau was red-faced and cheesed.

"Oh, Sammy, everything's fine," I said. "You know Topper. He likes to play the fool. And he's quite accomplished to that end."

Topper lifted his camera. Click. Right in Sam's face.

Well, you would've thought he walloped him upside the head. Sam unleashed a squall of curse words, then turned and stormed off down the beach.

"Swear to the dickens!" Sam called as he tromped away. "You two must've been raised in a zoo! A monkey exhibit! Someplace where a suitable evening can't be had until someone throws his feces at a guest!"

My mouth fell open. Topper and I locked eyes. Then my brother collapsed into a fit of laughter on the damp sand.

Instead of following Sam, which would've been the shrewder course, I chewed out Topper something fierce. By the end of it, though, we were both in stitches. He does a spot-on impersonation of not only fake double-crossed husbands but also stupefied real-life boyfriends and feces-hurling primates. (Oh, Sam! If you ever read this, please forgive me! It's only because you're such a doll that I can excuse his boorish behavior in the first place.)

Alas I fear we might be done for, kaput, Sam and me. There is only so much Topper someone with manners can take. Though they were friends once, something happened about the time Sam left for Princeton. A lack of some understanding, as each of them tells it. Two different people, is what they mean. If either boy reads this, please clue a gal in. And set aside your differences for a person who loves you both.

In any case, I'll insist my brother fix this situation. If he can't, well, he'll need to find me a new man since he's the one who constantly chases them away. If I ever hope to get married, I should probably keep that particular monkey in his cage.

Yours sincerely,
Ruby Young

7

Sunday Morning

Bess sets the Book of Summer back onto the table.

"I can't imagine Grandma Ruby making a joke about feces," she says with a chuckle. "I just can't. She's too civilized for that."

"Really the joke was more my father's," Cissy says. "And Topper's. But your grandmother was not short of moxie."

"Self-controlled moxie," Bess says. "It's funny. Ruby always called Topper by his real name. So there is Robert, or Topper, and Grandpa Sam. Her other brother P.J."

"Walter, too," Cissy says. "He was the middle brother who died as a teen."

"For a 'house of women' there sure were a lot of dudes."

Cissy gives a halfhearted smirk.

"Well, the dudes they come," she says, eyes cast toward the floor. "And they go."

Bess could nearly hear her grandmother's voice. *They come and they go . . . and a house of women it remains.*

True enough, Bess thinks. It is only women sitting in that dining room, the two people left clinging to the house, as the house itself clings to the side of a bluff.

"The guys usually can't hack the tough stuff," Bess says. "That much is true. But at least Sam wasn't scared off despite Robert's—Topper's—best efforts. And thank God for that or you and I wouldn't exist."

Bess doesn't remember Grandpa Sam, or even much about him. He died of a head injury when Bess was young. A head injury, she'd later learn, incurred after falling through a window while drunk.

His death was enough of something, an embarrassment, or shame, or heartache, that he was all but vanquished from the family lexicon. Whenever he did come up, the name was new and strange and tricky to place. *Sam? Who was Sam again?* There are random nonrelatives from the forties whom Bess can more swiftly recall. Mrs. Grimsbury, for example. Some so-called cousin or aunt who lived in France.

"You know, you never talk about your dad," Bess says as she thumbs through the book. "I was young when he died, but you were an adult, a mom even."

"That I was," Cissy answers with a nod. "There's not much to say. He was a sad and troubled person."

"Which usually means there's a lot to say."

"Well . . ." Cissy exhales. "You're probably right. He was a very sweet man, just as Mom said. I wish we could've . . ."

She lets her voice wander before picking it back up.

"When someone offers help," she says, "it can seem like criticism. In other words, you're doing this wrong. My father hated . . ." Cissy shakes her head. "Sam Packard was terribly *critical* of himself. We were trying to be delicate, Mom and I. Too delicate, as it turned out. We weren't . . . we didn't have . . . things were different then. Plus, he was never an angry drunk, only a very sad one. I guess we thought we could love him back to health."

Bess bobs her head in response, unsure what to say. Her own father is not the overly emotive type. He never coached any of their teams or told amusing stories at the dinner table. Her brother calls him Clockwork Codman. He punches in, he punches out, he does what's asked.

But Bess always wanted some indefinable "more" from the man, a realization made in the last few months, during a perfunctory stab at marital counseling. The shrink tried to tease out some daddy issues on which to pin their problems. In the end, the issues weren't deep enough to explain why Bess ended up in that place. And now she feels ashamed for talking about Dudley like that, at $200 per hour no less, when he is basically fine, as far as dads go. At least he's not a drunk.

"Poor Grandma," Bess says as she glances out the window.

The skies are clear but the fog is leaking in. Bess's phone indicates it's supposed to drizzle by nightfall. A light rain isn't exactly Hurricane Sandy, but Bess cringes to think of more weatherly abuse being inflicted upon Cliff House. The vote is the day after tomorrow. Surely the home can survive until then.

"And poor Cissy," Bess adds, looking back at her mom.

"Poor me nothing. I was cared for. I was loved. As for your grandmother, she had enough mettle to get by."

"Yeah, this family is lousy with mettle," Bess says. "I really miss her sometimes. Is that weird? She's been dead for a greater portion of my life than she was alive but sometimes I can actually bring myself to tears just thinking about her."

"Not weird at all," Cissy replies with a distracted sniff.

"I really looked up to her."

"Mmm-hmmm."

Cissy hoists a box from the table and thumps it, loudly, onto the ground, a signal she is done with the conversation. She can be so darn cagey about Ruby, the end of her rope quickly reached. Moms and daughters. Did it always have to be that way?

"So, the divorce," Cissy says, apropos of nothing. Not that segues are her style. "You're still doing this?"

"Yes, Mother. I am 'doing this' and, really, it's all but done. We have a few details to work out, some papers to sign, and then the marriage is legally over."

Cissy frowns.

"Mom . . ."

"But you seemed to really love each other," she says. "Brandon was so helpful. So protective of you."

At once Bess remembers Cissy's first visit to their home in San Francisco. Dudley stayed behind, characteristically neck-high in yet another "earnings season." Bess was relieved: only one parent to impress with her adulthood and new fiancé instead of two. Cissy was an easier sell, though only by degrees.

Bess had big plans to welcome her mother to San Francisco with a meal featuring only Northern California cuisine. Oysters. Dungeness crab. Fresh sourdough. About a quarter of the way through cooking, Bess realized she had no butter, not to mention a scarcity of Chardonnay. Things spiraled from there. What the hell was she doing? Bess had never been a decent chef, and a Nantucketer was hardly going to be impressed with fresh fish. She should've opted for Rice-A-Roni, "The San Francisco Treat."

"This is a disaster!" Bess said, fighting tears of frustration. "I don't even know what I'm doing! Dungeness crab? I burned a Lean Cuisine last night!"

At the time, Cissy was due back from a walk. Or else she wasn't. Cissy was known to stroll for hours.

"Stop," Brandon said as he entered the kitchen. "Stop. Just calm down."

He pried a wooden spoon from Bess's grasp. Also a cheese grater, though there wasn't any cheese nearby.

"Go read a book," he ordered.

"I have to finish dinner!"

"I'll take it from here. You relax."

So Bess let him complete what she'd started.

The dinner was okay, nothing fantastic. But it was more than edible, a better feat than Bess could've pulled off. And that Brandon stepped in rendered the meal perfect, in the end.

You seemed to really love each other.

"Yes, it seemed that way," Bess says now, in the dining room of Cliff House.

She rips a piece of tape from its roll.

"Are you sure, sweetheart?" Cissy asks. "Absolutely certain that you want to go through with it?"

"Yes. One hundred percent," Bess says, and means it. "I know what you're thinking. The first divorce in the family, the black sheep, et cetera. But there's simply no other option. I'm sorry. I'm sure you're disappointed. And believe me, I am, too."

"Disappointed? Please. I couldn't be prouder of my Bessie if you cured cancer."

"Well, I hope you'd be a *little* prouder of me if I cured cancer."

"Professional accomplishments," Cissy says, and blubbers her lips. "Who gives a crap? And, by the by, if you think *you're* the black sheep, you're not paying attention."

"Either way, there's no going back."

No going back. Bess's side twitches. She tries to rub it away.

"Okay, my dear," Cissy says. "I hear you. But I do think it's better to talk things through with someone who loves you."

"Thanks but I'll pass."

"I still don't . . ." Cissy shakes her head. "I'm sorry, but I still don't understand why you're getting divorced. Is there a specific reason?"

Bess hesitates. Yes, she has a reason or twelve. Most of them she can't mention to her mom.

"At its simplest," Bess says finally, "he's not the person I thought I married."

Then again, maybe he is and Bess should've seen it coming. There were signs. She couldn't say there weren't signs, emergency meal preparations notwithstanding.

"Not who you married?" Cissy answers with a small grunt.

"They never are. Your grandmother could've told you that. But just because . . ."

"Mom." Bess gently smacks the table. "I'm serious. I don't want to talk about it. I'll only get upset or angry and I'm so tired of feeling both of these things. One day I'll tell you the full story."

"Fine." Cissy scoots around the table to give Bess a hug. "And since you called me 'Mom,' I suppose you mean business."

"Oh yeah, I mean business. Big business."

"All right, Big Business," Cissy says, checking her watch. "I'm off for a jog. I'd ask you to join me but . . ."

She shrugs. Although Bess is a decent golfer and a crack tennis player, the family knows she never exercises in vain. Or, as Lala likes to tease, Bess doesn't want to sweat if no one's keeping score.

"Should we squeeze in nine holes later?" her mom says.

"Sure. I'd love to."

"Okay, sweetums." Cissy gives her a slap on the rear. "Don't get into any trouble while I'm gone."

"Thanks, Cis," Bess says as her eyes dart out to the patio. The fog is already thick, rolling in with greater force. "I'll try to keep myself alive."

"Very funny."

"I'm not joking."

Tuesday can't come soon enough.

The Book of Summer

Ruby Genevieve Young
July 19, 1940
Cliff House, Sconset, Nantucket Island

The last cigarette has been smoked.

The last car has puttered away.

Mother's bedroom door is closed. Even Topper has worn out his shenanigans and is holed up in the boys' bunk room.

And here I sit, at my desk, the windows thrown open and the sound of the waves crashing nearby. It's my last night as a single gal, twelve hours until I'm a married hen.

Tomorrow at exactly eleven o'clock in the morning, I'll stand beneath the pergola, white wisteria dangling overhead. Sam and I will exchange vows and voilà, I'll transform from Miss Young, Philip Young's only daughter, into Mrs. Samuel Packard.

"You'll always be a Young," Daddy says. "More than a Packard, to be sure."

I suppose in some ways, yes. But not in the way of Topper and P.J. It's different for girls. As much as I'll be proud to carry Sam's name, that's Mrs. Packard to you, *I'm still losing some part of me. It's nothing but change from here on out, I suppose.*

"Don't worry, petal," Daddy says whenever I anguish over any little thing. "It'll all work out in the end."

And you know what? He's been right thus far.

So tomorrow, when I'm anointed Ruby Packard, after the luncheon, and the toasts, and the jitterbugging on the patio, Sam and I will hop into a car (a black Mercedes-Benz Roadster) and zoom off toward the airport where we will board the late plane to Acapulco.

Two weeks in the Mexican sun and then it's back to Boston, where Sam will chair Daddy's newly minted Golf Products division. He has no interest in dentistry and it seems this is the only family spot being offered to him. Alas, nothing to brood over, as there's plenty of room for Sam at Young Processing Co. Who knew a bunch of old guys stomping about with sticks in their hands could generate such a gold mine? Sammy doesn't seem notably buzzed by the prospect, but he's not keen to play.

Whenever I start to spook about the changes I remind myself that a year from now we will be back at Cliff House. Mother and Daddy. My brothers. Sam and me, with (hopefully) Sam Junior already on his way. The summers, at least, will never change, other than a couple of new people along for the ride—God willing.

And with that, I am, for the final time,

Yours truly,
Miss Ruby Genevieve Young

9

The Book of Summer

Samuel Eugene Packard
July 20, 1940
Cliff House, Sconset, Nantucket Island

The Legend of the Golf Ball
-OR-
Rubber Man and the Dentist

Many years ago, a decade almost, two men met up at the club in Sconset as they were wont to do several times per week, June through August every year.

One was a skinny fellow, a scientist by training but a businessman by trade and sheer doggedness—now a honcho of some repute. He'd founded a rubber-processing operation, selling to industry. The top producer for a time.

The other man was bigger, brawnier, a former Harvard linebacker whose middle had somewhat gone to pot. He was a dentist, an entirely new profession amid his family. They had been stock speculators previously, which worked well until it rather didn't. Now the family sneaks by on its old prestige.

So on this particular day, these two men, both fathers with a passel of kids between them, grabbed their sticks, and headed to the Sankaty Head Golf Club.

Things started out most inauspiciously, for the Rubber Man at least. He was the superior player and thus more prone to golfing discontent. As for the Dentist, any shot not destined for a bunker or the Scotch broom was dandy by him.

By the sixth hole, a straightforward job, the morning had taken a sour turn. The Rubber Man missed a very makeable putt, by his standards anyway. Enraged, he launched his putter into the brush, followed by a seven iron toward some other gent's caddy. After completing his tantrum, Rubber Man picked up the offending ball from where it sat on the green.

He held it to his eyes.

"The core is off-center!" he shouted. "I hit that ball expertly!"

"Is it the lie of the green?" the Dentist suggested.

It sounded right anyhow.

"No, no, no," Rubber Man said. "It's the ball. I'm gonna slice this bastard open and take a look inside."

"Or you could x-ray it."

"Come on," he said with a scoff. "Where am I going to find an x-ray machine?"

"I have one," the Dentist reminded him. "I've used it to study your teeth."

"Hot damn! You're right. Sometimes I forget you're a tradesman, too. Come on, let's go."

Soon Rubber Man and the Dentist were ensconced in a Packer, motoring toward Boston. Once in the city, the Dentist unlocked his office, making a liar out of its "closed for two weeks" sign.

They fired up the x-ray machine. To the Dentist's vast surprise, though not at all to Rubber Man's, the golf ball was the problem. Its core was off-center, oblong and tilted.

By the next summer, Rubber Man had patented a cross-winding machine, which created a perfectly round core. And just like that, his company began manufacturing golf balls along with the swim caps and water bottles they'd resorted to when rubber prices fell. A few years later he'd use this same machine to develop the "dead center" ball. He'd name it "Titleist" for all the titles its users would surely win.

"I never thanked you for that," the Rubber Man said, years later, on that same sixth hole at Sankaty Head. By then one-fourth of U.S. Open entrants used his Titleists. "You suggested the x-ray machine and in effect improved both my golf game and my balance sheet. The former immeasurably more important than the latter, of course."

"Speak nothing of it," the Dentist said, stumbling.

His old friend was not known for his compliments or a tendency to give credit where credit was due. He may have been a scientist-turned-businessman but he lacked the smooth glad-handing of the type.

"Yesterday I transferred ten thousand shares of Young Processing Company into your name," Rubber Man told him, matter-of-fact.

"Much obliged," replied the Dentist, as yet unsure whether this gesture was generous or miserly to the extreme. What did ten thousand shares mean, really?

"It's unfortunate you're too elderly to have more kids," the Dentist said, joshing for the most part. "Or I might ask that you name one in my honor. It only seems fair."

Rubber Man laughed.

"Well," he said. "I am too old for babies. Grandchildren, perhaps. Something to consider when the time comes."

"Swell idea. Alas, your children might not appreciate having to name their offspring after their father's golfing pal. Not to mention future spouses' opinions on the matter."

"Ah," Rubber Man said with a wide grin. "There's a solution to that. My only daughter goes to your oldest son." He jabbed his club into the ground. "And so it is decreed."

And wouldn't you know? Some years later, on the lawn of the great Cliff House, the only daughter would go to the oldest son after all.

Whether this "deal," however made in jest, sealed the fate of this young couple, we shall never know. But one thing is certain. The Dentist's son will be forever grateful for a universe that befitted him with such a spectacular gal.

10

RUBY
July 1940

"So you'll really go through with it?" Topper said. "The hitching?"

He was supine on Ruby's bed, lobbing a baseball from one hand to the other.

"Why wouldn't I go through with it?" she asked.

Their mother would have a fit, seeing Topper in Ruby's room while she was in nothing but a panty girdle and a bra. But Ruby didn't have a sister, and her nearest brother, ten months younger on the nose, was the next best thing. Not that Topper was at all girlie, especially with his sports playing and skirt chasing, but he was doggone skilled at humoring his sister and pretending they were interested in the same things.

"I don't get it," Topper said. "Why, exactly, are you marrying him? Because I can't really figure it out."

"What's there to figure out? It's quite simple, really. I love Sam. He's kind, and smart, and devastatingly handsome. All the usual reasons."

"Are those the usual reasons, then? I'm glad to have you around to tell me."

"I do what I can."

Ruby stood and walked over to her dress, which hung from the pink wardrobe in the corner. After giving it a thorough glare, she took to patting it down. Forty yards of silk taffeta. Lord almighty, it looked like a hurricane. The blasted thing could've swept up Dorothy and taken her to Oz.

"We want the same things," Ruby said. "Sam and I."

Topper froze, holding the baseball to his chest.

"Huh," he said with a faint chuckle. "I guess you do. You *want* to want them, in any case."

"That doesn't even make sense," Ruby said, and rolled her eyes. "Babble all you want, but despite your best efforts, the hitching will commence at eleven."

Topper snorted and took to throwing the ball against the ceiling. Clonk, clonk, clonk. Mother would appear at any moment, materializing like a chimera and sporting a sour-lemon frown. Ruby glanced out the window toward the orchestra practicing in the distance. They had a fair length to go until they were fine-tuned.

"I'm not sure about this thing," Ruby said, turning her attention back to the dress. "There's quite a lot of taffeta."

"I thought that was the point? Anyhow, you're stuck now. You should junk the hat though, Red. Not flattering a'tall."

He called her this, Red, despite hair that was golden like the summer sand. She was strawberry blond as a young child, but mostly it was a play on her name. Red, as in Ruby Red, though she was never as colorful as that.

"What do you have against him?" she asked.

"Who? The hat?"

"Yes, the hat," Ruby said, and rolled her eyes again. "I've named him Pete. He's quite the fella. I meant Sam, you dope."

Topper sniggled.

"What's the rub?" she asked. "You two used to be grand pals."

"I wouldn't go that far. Listen, I have nothing against your fella. Sam's a fine man. Attractive. Unobjectionable. That, dear Red, is the very problem."

"That he's attractive and unobjectionable?" She arched a brow.

"You need someone with more . . . gusto."

"Gusto."

"A little fire!" Topper said. "Some verve."

"Right-o. A person to match my wildcat nature."

Fact of the matter: Ruby was a damned straight arrow. Sure, she possessed a spicy tongue and had committed a few petty crimes in her day—the nicking of cigarettes and hooch while at Smith—but mostly Ruby listened to her parents, used her manners, and never went too far with any boy. Everyone found her universally delightful, a gem of a gal.

"I really should be with someone who causes a scene," she added. "It'd be the primo fit."

"Precisely, dear sister," Topper said with a wink. "You've been too good, too protected, too damned cloistered in your ivory tower. You need someone to pitch a curveball atcha."

He demonstrated with the ball in his hand, which thwacked against a ladies' tennis trophy sitting on a high shelf.

"Ivory tower?" Ruby barked. "Hardly! Look around. The toilets at Cliff House only work half the time."

"Yes, yes, you're quite roughing it in your summer home. I'll ask Mummy to take up a collection at church."

"You're a real gagster. Golly, it'll be a nice change to live with a well-mannered gentleman for once."

Ruby's thoughts drifted back outside, where glassware clinked and groups of men bustled about the grounds. Her eyes flicked down to the long, white table that divided the lawn in two. Three dozen small, round tables flanked it, their umbrellas spinning and dancing in the wind.

"Here's the thing," Topper said as Ruby glanced back toward her dress. "Sam's a swell guy but it's like he's following a script. You need someone more . . . his own man."

"Sam is very much his own man," Ruby said, though did not strictly know.

"Ruby!" said a voice from the hallway, a caw followed by three sharp pecks on the door.

"Oh brother," Ruby muttered.

It was P.J.'s new wife, Mary. A real cold fish that one, an utter snore.

"Ruby!" Mary warbled again. "Mama Young sent me to check on you."

"I'm *fine*. Almost ready."

"Lovely! Have you seen Robert?"

Topper pressed a finger to his lips, all the while chortling behind it.

"Yes, he's in here," Ruby said. "Helping me get dressed."

"*Ruby Genevieve!*" Mary screeched. "That is sickeningly inappropriate. I just . . . I don't even . . ."

"Then don't."

"I can't!"

Mary huffed and stomped several more times before turning on her toes and marching back to "Mama Young."

"That woman," Ruby growled.

"Oh she's not so bad."

"Actually, she is the very worst."

With a sigh, Ruby slipped her wedding frock off its hanger and tried to wade through the froth to find its center.

"I'm sure Mother wants to help you with that," Topper said. "You being her only daughter and all."

"Probably."

Ruby wiggled it up toward her chest, then over her shoulders.

"We are a sorry lot." Topper tossed the ball one final time. "This family. Poor manners. No decorum. Thank God money covers most ills."

11

Monday Morning

For the second day in a row, Bess wakes up in a blind panic. And her first thoughts aren't even about the cliff.

Not that the rapidly eroding bluff isn't terrifying. It is and very much so. On some mornings, the fog is too dense to see the veranda. As a little girl, Bess would sit in her window and gaze into the white, pretending she was a princess in a cloud. And while the haze is thick this morning, the very best of princess dreams, Bess can see straight past the edge of the yard and down to the shoreline. There is no space left for make-believe.

Alas, it is not impending doom that brings Bess the initial wave of heart-knocking nausea but the date itself, glaring up from her phone.

Monday, May 20.

Cissy's meeting is tomorrow; Flick's wedding in a week. In between, two women must move the contents of a house. Bess is a damned good procrastinator, a near-expert embracer of denial. But even she has to acknowledge that there won't be a return trip to California. Which means Bess must address Wednesday through Saturday, and the meetings and appointments waiting for her back in the Bay.

"Crap," she says, scrolling through her calendar. "What am I going to do?"

The question applies to so many things.

Suddenly, the door pops open and claps the far wall.

"Cissy!" Bess yelps.

She socks the phone against her chest, as if Cissy might see the screen.

"How about some privacy?!" Bess says as Cissy hard charges in, an empty box between her hands.

"Gimme a break. What do you need to be so private about? I pushed you out of me, tore myself from stern to bow."

"That's lovely. . . ."

"So your flimsy getup is hardly worth noting. You look great, by the way."

Bess glances down at her camisole and underwear. *Great?* She doesn't feel the least bit so.

"Thanks," she mumbles nonetheless.

"Let me know if there's anything in this bedroom you'd like to keep," Cissy says, yanking open the door to the pink wardrobe, which, come to think of it, has been in that same corner Bess's entire life. "Let's see. What relics has Bess Codman abandoned in here? Cap and gown . . . letterman jacket . . . wedding dress."

"Ha!" Bess yaps. "Feel free to let the dress fall over the cliff."

"Don't be so negative. Maybe you'll have a daughter one day who'll want to wear it. Vintage, you know."

"Too true. Who doesn't love the nostalgia of a failed marriage?"

"What about these?" Cissy asks, reaching for the top shelf.

She removes four yearbooks, two from Choate, and two from Nantucket High.

"You can ditch those, too," Bess says.

"You know what?" Cissy flings them onto the floor, where they land with a thud. "I'm going to hang on to them. Just in case. It's not like you could ever get them back."

Cissy roots around the wardrobe for several more minutes, casting a flurry of apparel, scarves, and questionable forms of millinery across the scuffed wood floors. Evidently Bess wore a fedora at some juncture. She doesn't remember it at all.

"Oh!" Cissy exclaims in a burst and without warning.

She twirls around to face Bess.

"You will not believe what happened earlier this morning!"

"All right . . ." Bess says, cautiously.

Cissy's "you will not believe" could be anything from spilling her coffee to accidentally rescuing a seal pup from the jaws of a shark.

"Chappy Mayhew," her mom says. "The bastard encroached upon my property!"

"Um . . . er . . . what?"

"He *claims* he was just fetching the paper. That it was thrown onto my driveway by mistake. Likely story! Benji Folger is the paperboy and he's a Little League pitcher, a stellar one at that. I've watched three and a half of his games. There's no way he'd miss his target."

"Okay . . ."

Bess walks over to her suitcase and extracts a pair of sweatpants. She'd gone to unpack last night but decided not to bother. They'll be moving on soon. Bess can't fathom that she'll never unpack at Cliff House again.

"That Chappy Mayhew," Cissy says, still at full rant. "The nerve of him! If only his balls were actually as big as he pretends they are."

"Mother! Enough! And unless he did something wrong, I'm sure it's well within his purview to wander across the road."

"I saw him hock a loogie onto my roses."

"Cis, I get that he rankles you. That family's always been unnaturally egotistical. . . ."

"They're a bunch of smartasses, is what they are."

"Agreed," Bess says with a nod. "And I appreciate all you're trying to accomplish with the beaches and the revetments, but the man has his own concerns. Chappy is worried about his livelihood. You can't fault him for that."

"Actually I can fault him for that because it's a bunch of horseshit. As long as there are tourists on Nantucket, Chappy Mayhew will have a steady stream of income."

"How's that?"

"Our entire restaurant industry thrives on the lore of the last remaining fisherman. They'd dump a boatload of bass into the Yacht Club swimming pool, just to be able to say the fish is locally caught. That man isn't worried about his job. He just likes to piss me off. Chapman Mayhew can smooch my flat, white, wrinkled fanny."

"All right, Cis," Bess says with a sigh. "I haven't had the coffee yet to deal with that mental picture."

Bess slides one leg into her sweatpants (red, faded, Boston College; fifteen years old), and then the other. She hoists them over her hips, loosening the drawstring as she goes.

"Speaking of," Cissy says. "I need a favor."

"A favor? Related to your fanny? Thanks, but I see enough derrières at work."

"Stop with the jokes, Dr. Codman. Are you helping me or not?"

"Always, Cissy. I'm forever at your disposal."

"Exactly what I'd hoped. All right, my dear. Here's what I need you to do."

12

Monday Morning

Bess must be suffering some off-brand, New England version of island fever, because she's inexplicably agreed to play accomplice in one of Cissy's harebrained schemes.

"Sure, Cis," she idiotically said. "Whatever you need."

Sometimes Bess forgets that hers is not an ordinary mom.

As she crosses Baxter Road, Bess tries to script an introduction that doesn't sound batshit insane. Chappy Mayhew is insufferable by nature but she's about to hand him a blank check for mocking.

Why? Why is it so damned hard to tell Cissy no?

With an inhale, Bess nudges open the gate and walks toward the front door. She is at once charmed by the quaint fishing shack. The place is all Sconset enchantment with its weather-beaten, splintered face, the picket fence, and the roses, which are just beginning to bloom. By summer's end, the cottage itself will be blanketed in bright pink flowers. It will also have a panoramic ocean view, once Cliff House falls out of sight. Some bastards have all the luck.

Bess knocks, quickly, with a rat-a-tat-tat. It's feasible that no one is home (oh please, oh please) and she can crawl back into bed. Alas, to her great dismay, clomping footsteps answer Bess's call. The door opens before she can escape.

"Listen, Chappy, I'm sorry to bother you, but you know how Cissy is. Here's the thing . . ."

Bess releases every last molecule of oxygen from her lungs and glances up, face flaming. But it is not Chappy Mayhew standing before her. It's worse.

"What the hell?" she squawks, with unnecessary volume.

Bess clears her throat and lets it fall to a whisper.

"Do you *live* here?" She drops the question from the side of her mouth, as if it's a secret and there are curious ears nearby. "You live with your dad? *Still?* Or did someone kick you out? Oh, this is sad."

As the man belts out an all-too-familiar laugh, Bess blushes ever more furiously. Of course. Of course he'd answer the door. Tall and tanned and sandy and perpetually unbothered: Evan f'ing Mayhew, in the radiant, windburned flesh.

"I see you've inherited your mother's social graces," he says with a grin.

"I didn't mean to . . ."

"I'm here to build a bookshelf for my dad. Oh man." He chuckles again. "I can hear Cissy now. *Chappy Mayhew knows how to read?* I walked right into that one, didn't I? It's great to see you, Bess. Please. Come in."

Evan steps out of the doorway and makes a sweeping motion with his hand.

"Thanks," she mumbles.

Bess fiddles with her hair as she skulks through the entryway. She really should've done more than whip it back into a ponytail and flat-iron the hell out of her bangs. She also should've worn contacts, or at least something other than glasses so old they make Bess seem like she's going for that hipster, "pre-cool" look typically associated with unicycles and twisty mustaches.

"Well, good to see you and everything," she says, following Evan into the kitchen.

God bless it, she is wearing sweatpants. Purchased in the late nineties.

" 'Good to see you and everything,' " Evan says, never missing a thing.

He opens the fridge.

"Oh, Codman, I miss that mushy streak of yours. Beer?"

"It's ten o'clock in the morning."

"Light beer?"

"Tempting, but no."

"So . . ."

Evan rests his back against the counter. He crosses one disturbingly muscled arm over the other and gives Bess a thoroughly invasive visual head-to-toe. Meanwhile, Bess wants to shrink into the corner, or disappear behind her bangs, which is the exact point of them.

"Let me apologize in advance," she starts.

"No apology necessary, but I am curious as to what errand of mischief brings you to my father's doorstep. Given your apparent shock in seeing me, I can't really flatter myself into thinking you've come to pay me a visit."

"Uh, no."

Bess snorts, eyes glued to the floor. Staring at Evan Mayhew is like looking directly into the sun: awful, beautiful, and damaging at the same time.

"I'm an emissary of my mother's," she explains.

"Emissary or adversary. When it comes to Cissy Codman, a person can only be one of the two."

"Oh, come on, she's not that bad."

"Bess, your mother is terrifying."

"She's not terrifying."

Bess looks up and feels the burn of Evan's dark brown eyes. He surely knows about the divorce. He probably cackles about it behind her back. Then he goes to bed with some sort of wife or girlfriend or a rotation of models.

Then again, the more likely scenario is that he doesn't think of her at all.

"Cissy is . . . spunky?" Bess says. "A go-getter."

"Didn't she once shoot Michael Kennedy in the kneecap?"

"It was RFK Junior and it was an accident. She said he deserved it."

As Evan laughs, Bess stiffens. No. Uh-uh. No way. She will not allow herself to relax into that easy, distant sound.

"Yeah, so my mother issued a TRO against your dad," Bess says, murmuring, letting her voice get lost in the light streaming through the kitchen window.

"Beg pardon?" Evan leans toward her. "She issued a what?"

"Temporary restraining order," she says, louder this time. "I'm supposed to make sure Chappy received it."

"Oh yeah." Evan laughs. Again. Again and again. "He got it all right, as your mother is well aware. She watched the whole thing from the captain's walk."

"The *captain's walk*?" Bess says with a quack. "It doesn't even have stairs anymore. How'd she get up there?" She shakes her head. "Forget it. I don't want to know. Good God, Cliff House is going to be the death of me."

"Only if you're not careful. So, why are you here? When your mother already knows about the TRO?"

Bess sighs.

"The thing is . . . the problem, you see. Chappy violated it this morning. Allegedly."

Bess holds up air quotes long after the word has been spoken.

"Allegedly." Evan smirks. "How so?"

"He sneezed or farted near the property or something," Bess says with another sigh. "Anyway, I'm not here to quibble over the details and I fully recognize the ridiculousness of the situation. But your dad is very obstinate and peevish . . ."

"*He's* peevish?"

"Yes. Very much so. Hear me out. Cissy and Chappy, they have their little repartee, their back-and-forth."

"That they do. . . ."

"Their saucy insults and middle fingers." Bess lifts one, as if to demonstrate.

"Bess Codman, you're cute as ever."

"But it's a dance," she says, ignoring Evan and speaking as fast as her mouth will carry her. "And the more he antagonizes her, the more she digs in. I'm trying to compel Cissy to *leave* Cliff House. In case you haven't noticed, it's about to fall into the ocean."

"All of Nantucket has noticed. I heard *Vanity Fair* is writing an article about it."

"Fantastic. And my grandmother weeps from the heavens," Bess says. "Anyway, here's the problem. I want Cis to leave but the more your father keeps sticking in her craw, the more she's going to stick around here."

"Cissy has a lot of craws."

"Yes, she's a real craw machine. Swear to God, Evan, if your dad was simply nice to her, if he treated her with a crumb of kindness or respect, she'd get bored and leave. Isn't that what everyone wants? Cissy would be out of Chappy's hair and I wouldn't need to organize a funeral. As much as Cissy torments your dad, he doesn't want her dead. I don't think so anyway."

"No," Evan says. "He would not want that at all."

"Can you just convince him to, I don't know, step away from the fight? At least until I get her out of the house? *Please?*"

"All right, Bess," Evan says, eyes softening, the playful spark falling right out of them. "I don't know that he'll take advice from me but I can sure as hell try."

"Thank you." She exhales. "That's all I ask."

As they stand stiff and silent, Bess notices the reflection of her sweatpants in the oven door. A sudden wave of dizziness overtakes her. What must she look like? Evan saw her in that very kitchen, in those very pants, a thousand years ago, back when Bess had the youth to make it seem like a casual outfit choice instead of the very definition of "giving up."

"So, I'd better—"

"It's been awhile, Bess," Evan says, his voice like velvet. "How long?"

"Four years," she answers with a sharp nod, as if confirming to herself.

"Since your wedding, then? Am I right?"

Bess nods again but won't catch his eyes.

"Four years," Evan says. "That's quite awhile. Guess you didn't miss this place."

"Are you kidding?" She looks up. "I've missed it with every speck of my being. Sconset is a dream. The ocean. The sand. The wild roses and honeysuckle and bayberries on the dunes. There's nowhere like it in the world."

"Wow," Evan says with a dry laugh. "They say Sconset is a place folks get sentimental about but I didn't think that'd apply to Dr. Bess Codman."

"Don't even start with the 'doctor' stuff."

"I have to say, you weren't so enamored with the lilacs and bayberries when Cissy dragged you back here to finish up high school with all of us barbaric islanders."

"Yes, poor me." Bess rolls her eyes. "Don't let my teenage surliness fool you. It's what I wanted."

"Uh, I thought it wasn't your choice? If I recall, you were kicked out of boarding school."

"Was I?" she says with a jokey shrug. "I don't quite remember it that way. Well, it's been real, but I'll let you go."

Bess pushes off from the counter, as if she needs the extra momentum to get out of that house.

"Thanks, Evan," she says. "For not being a total jerk about this. Okay. See you later."

She turns to go.

"We had fun, didn't we?" Evan calls from where he stands, fixed against the cupboards.

Bess pauses and then peers over her shoulder.

"We did," she says. "On the other hand, Nantucket can screw with your memories."

"Listen, do you have anywhere to be?"

"Me?" Bess spins back around to face him. "Right now? This morning?"

"This very minute."

"Aside from dragging my mother from her home? The answer is no, I have exactly nowhere else to be."

Well, she has somewhere to be, but it would involve a flight to California.

"Wanna come to my jobsite?" He tilts his head toward the door. "I have a construction gig down the way."

"You want me to visit your work?" Bess scrunches her forehead. "Doesn't that seem a little . . . ?"

"Calm down, Danielle Steele. I'm not going to put the moves on you. I may be dense about a lot of things, but I never make the same mistake twice."

"Gosh thanks," Bess mumbles. "You've made me positively weak-kneed."

"Do you want to go or not? I think it's a place you'd like to see."

"Sure. Like I said, I don't have anything else to do, other than stare off a cliff and reflect on my own mortality."

"Perfect." Evan claps a hand on her shoulder. "Trust me, you'll get a kick out of this. And it should stir up a few memories."

"Oh Lord. Memories. Well, make sure they're only the good ones. The bad ones I plan to leave out on the bluff."

13

Monday Morning

They stand on a concrete slab beneath the outline of a not-quite-a-house.

"*This* place is supposed to ring a bell?" Bess says, and knocks on a frame. "A house so new it's not even built yet?"

Though Bess pretends otherwise, she understands exactly where they are.

This plot of land once contained a fishing shack called Hussey House, a chunk of abandoned heaven that served as center stage for all manner of teen naughtiness. Hussey was one of Nantucket's original founders, but whether the family ever owned the property or the name simply seemed fitting for the stuff kids got up to there, Bess never knew.

"Elisabeth Codman," Evan says. "You don't recognize it? Damn. That hurts. I thought I'd left at least some kind of mark on your formative years."

Some kind of mark. That's one way to put it.

"Fine," Bess says, and walks to the edge of the foundation. "I remembered it on sight. How could I not? Codfish Park. You bastardized my last name as a result. Lizzy Codfish. What a gal."

She grips the sides of a doorway and leans out over a twelve-foot retaining wall.

"Be careful," Evan says. "You're a couple stories off the ground. We built up the pad to keep the house out of the flood zone. Can't screw with Mother Nature on an island outpost like this."

"Ha! You don't say."

Bess pushes herself back into the home, gaze still fixed on the beach across the road. With that view, and Evan's voice behind her, the years crash back onto her with the force of a nor'easter. Bess closes her eyes and pictures the people and the parties. She can smell the driftwood bonfires; see their flames dancing in purple and in gold. And Bess can still feel Evan, his arms wrapped around her waist.

Bess's eyes begin to sting.

"Are you okay . . . ?"

"It's so sad," she says, quickly. "That Hussey House is gone like all the other shacks. Soon there won't be any left. I hate seeing the new places scattered around, like pockmarks, so overt with their cedar shingles not yet turned to gray."

Evan nods.

"Sorry," she says. "I know it's your job. . . ."

"It *is* my job," he says. "And thank God for people who need more than one home. But I hear you. It used to be that this island was a place for escape. Now it's a place to be seen and it's losing more character by the day. Sconset started so modestly—a cluster of huts for the fishermen. They weren't even homes, really, just shelters to protect against the weather while the men caught their cod and bluefish. They had no floors. No kitchens. At least until the wives came for a visit and decided to stay for good."

"Really?" Bess turns back toward him. "I never knew Sconset was a down-and-gritty, boys-only kind of place."

"Of course you didn't. You're an off-islander. *Feed me,*" he says in a first-rate Cookie Monster voice.

Bess thinks that he must have kids. He's not married, she knows that much. Or, at least, he doesn't wear a ring, a detail Bess hadn't realized she'd noticed.

"'*Feed me*'? I don't recall demanding food."

As soon as she says it, Bess's stomach growls as if it's pulverizing gravel. That body of hers, betraying her once again.

"What happened after that?" Bess sputters, pressing into her stomach to shut it up. "With the fishermen and their shacks?"

"Well, like I said, the women showed up and complicated everything," Evan says with a wink. "As expected."

"Or, they made life inhabitable." Bess winks back. "As expected. Well, don't tell Cissy I didn't know that tidbit. I've worked hard to become the second-favorite child. She'd demote me in a blink."

"Aw, don't fret. You can't be expected to know Nantucket's rich history. You're an off-islander, here to rape and pillage."

"Oh, Christ." Bess rolls her eyes. "Lest you forget, I graduated from Nantucket High, same as you. And there was never a shack on our land, so my ancestors didn't contribute to the degradation of fair Sconset."

"Obviously there wasn't a shack on your property. Locals aren't dumb enough to build on that bluff."

"Wow! That hurt!" Bess says, though he's not wrong. "At least buy me a drink if you're going to fuc—Never mind."

She shakes her head and snickers to herself.

"Come on, you have to finish the joke. Buy you a drink if I'm going to, what?"

"You know what."

"Rhymes with 'duck'?"

"You were right about the memories." Bess shakes her head again, laughing, trying to move on. "Suddenly I'm back in high school getting teased and harassed by you. I'm curious. Did the Husseys ever actually own this land? Or is it something some doofus concocted because it seemed apt?"

"It really was in a Hussey's hands. Back in the 1800s, Ebenezer Hussey bought the place for thirty pounds of cod."

"I'd sell Cliff House for less if I had any faith in my ability to get Cissy out of it."

Bess exhales and sits on a nearby stack of wood. She is suddenly dead tired, bone-dragging spent. Cod or no cod, her head feels like it's swimming with it.

"Are you okay?" Evan asks. "You look a little peaked."

"I'm peaked all right." Bess braces herself against both knees. "It's been a helluva few months."

"Oh yeah? Anything specific?"

"I'm getting divorced."

"I heard something along those lines."

"That's why I feel like total shit," she says. "One of the reasons anyway."

Evan's head moves to some imperceptible degree. Bess studies him for a solid twenty seconds, waiting. He gives her nothing, which is exactly what Bess would predict. Evan f'ing Mayhew. Aged sixteen years but hasn't changed a day.

"Any day it should be finalized," Bess goes on, suddenly hot and sticky beneath her arms. "We're just squabbling over investments and furniture now. I'm letting him keep the house. Seems easier that way."

Still, Evan doesn't say anything.

"I know what you're thinking!" she chirps, returning to her schoolgirl self, desperate with the need to fill every gap in conversation. "What fool would let this fox out of his clutches?! Look at me!"

Bess gestures toward her sweatpants, her braless tee. She should've gotten a boob job back when Brandon suggested it. She'd been indignant at the time—she's a doctor, for the love of God!—but the man had a point. Her breasts, they are not so great.

"Bess . . ." Evan says, and reaches for her hand. "I'm sorry?"

"You're sorry? Question mark?"

"If you need me to be sorry, that's what I am."

"You should write for Hallmark with that level of inherent sympathy. How compassionate."

She is thoroughly vexed but the comment is so Evan. The very worst of him, as a matter of fact.

"Lizzy C."

Bess lurches. *Lizzy C.* His old nickname for her; he was the only person to ever use it. She wishes he'd knock it off.

"I didn't mean—" Evan starts.

"Thanks but don't bother with the 'sorry's. It's really for the best and I don't have a shred of regret. About the divorce, anyway."

"That's what I suspected, which is why . . ." Evan shakes his head. "Here's the deal. What's his name? Your ex? Brian?"

"Brandon. You don't remember his name?"

Then again, why would he?

"Brandon," Evan repeats. "Yep, sounds like a douchebag all right. Listen, I don't know much about him. Or you anymore, for that matter. But as for Brandon, I only met him twice. Once at your wedding, and once when you trotted him out to some party at the Yacht Club."

"Did I really bring him only twice?" Bess says, trying to remember.

Though they never made it to Sconset during their four-year marriage, they had dated for two years before that and met further back still, when they were both at Stanford, Bess for medical school and Brandon for business. No, it must've been more than twice.

"Are you sure?" Bess asks, mostly to herself. "Twice?"

"I can't be *sure*. It's not like you kept me apprised of your comings and goings. Plus, I was in Costa Rica for a while. You could've visited a hundred times in those years."

"Probably not a hundred."

Costa Rica. Bess feels a kick to the gut.

"Look, maybe I'm wrong," Evan says. "Even if I was around, you'd hardly want to introduce Mr. Fancy-pants to your random townie ex-boyfriend. Best to keep the locals on the down low."

"Please," Bess says, and lets her eyes skip away. "I told him plenty about you. Plen-ty."

Evan doesn't really think that, does he?

Evan doesn't truly believe that he is some boyfriend from the closet of the unmentionable and denied? Bess has those types from college, to be sure, but her only remorse about Evan is in how it ended. Or didn't end. Or whatever it was that happened.

Bess chose Boston College for undergrad because it was closest to home, and therefore closest to him. She thought they had some unspoken agreement, but then Evan left. He went to Costa Rica for a summer, which turned into six years once he found a native to shack up with. The woman was Latin and glorious and sent a ripple of envy through every male who'd been bred on the island. Son of a gun, Evan Mayhew leapfrogged them all.

When Evan showed up at Bess's wedding, she wasn't sure if he'd come on a plane or from across the street.

"Oh no, he's been back for years," some now nameless and faceless Nantucketer told Bess as they waited for refills of wine.

"What happened?" Bess asked whoever it was.

Meanwhile, where was Brandon, Bess's new husband? Who the hell knew. The important question was: Why did Evan leave Costa Rica and did he bring the girl?

"Dunno," the person replied.

"I have to admit," Bess says now, at the construction site, the wind stirring up the sawdust around them. "When discussing high school boyfriends with the girls on my freshman hall, 'random townie' ranked as the best by far."

"Well, duh. Especially once they learned you were serenaded at prom."

"Ah, yes. In front of the whole school. Actually that almost disqualified you."

"Hey," Evan says, pretending to be outraged. "That was the most romantic thing I've ever done!"

"How sad for you. I don't mean to sound ungrateful." Bess puts a solemn hand to her chest. " 'Gangsta's Paradise' is very romantic. I've grown awfully tired of hearing it at weddings though. I mean, come up with an original first dance song already."

"Cut me some slack. I was an eighteen-year-old kid. That was my way of showing affection."

"And it was very cute," Bess says. "Initially. But after the song ended, you and the rest of the baseball team broke into the 'Macarena.' So forgive me if I wasn't swooning."

Evan laughs.

"Okay," he says. "You have me there. The 'Macarena' is terrible. Well, I can tell you one thing. That Brandon douchebag never sang 'Gangsta's Paradise' to anyone."

"Safe assumption. So that's why you didn't like him? He was deficient in Coolio appreciation?"

"Yes. That. Also because, from the moment I met him, I knew he wasn't good enough for you."

"Brandon?" Bess is puzzled. "Seriously? He's an asshole once you get to know him, but on the surface . . ."

Brandon wasn't all bad. Not in theory, anyway. Bess has standards. She fell in love with *something*. There was his over-the-top-gentlemanly stuff, for one. He made the bed the first time he slept over. While Bess showered, he snuck out and bought not only breakfast but a week's worth of groceries. Never mind the chores; there were the notes he left in Bess's purse. Once a week, at least.

You looked beautiful this morning.

I couldn't sleep. I kept looking over to make sure you were still there.

Don't make plans tonight. I have a surprise.

He always kissed her before leaving for work. And if he somehow forgot, Brandon would drive all the way back to right this grievous wrong. Sometimes he came back anyway, ten, twenty minutes having passed.

"But you said good-bye!" Bess might've laughed.

"I needed another kiss. And I love that look on your face, the surprise when you were sure I'd already gone."

Brandon could be so loving. So protective. So overly concerned with Bess's whereabouts. At least a half dozen times he showed up at the hospital because Bess wasn't home and he was worried. Admittedly, that was a bit creepy in hindsight, but Bess was too swept up to question it.

"On the surface, what?" Evan asks, and lifts a brow. "Listen, he's pretty and all. If you're into that kind of thing. But I remember thinking, whoa, that guy does not deserve to be here. He shouldn't even be at the game."

"But why? That's not what you . . ." Bess starts, trying to shake off the confusion. "Okay. So in your grand total of two times meeting Brandon, what, exactly, didn't you care for? And P.S., you could've mentioned something."

"He has jerk hair," Evan spits out.

"Jerk hair."

"It was too styled. Plus, he had this vibe . . . like he's a shyster or something."

"A shyster?" Bess chuckles. "That makes him sound far cleverer than he really is, like his dickishness is intentional and not simply part of his DNA." Bess mulls this over. "Although, I did once bust him Googling 'romantic gestures.' Now I can't decide if that's sweet or 'psycho to the extreme,' which was my cousin's take."

Evan laughs in return.

"I don't know if it's psycho," he says. "But it's not normal. Did you ever recognize any of the alleged 'romantic' moves?"

"Oh yeah, all the time." Bess sighs. "I should've listened to Cissy. Never trust a guy who didn't play a team sport."

"Not a jock, huh? Well, between that and him being a techie type . . ."

"You remember he's a techie type?"

"I have this mental picture of him hunched over a computer, all pale and sickly and wheezing on an inhaler. It's a pretty awesome visual."

"As much as I like the concept," Bess says, "Brandon is not pale or sickly. He plays golf and racquetball and his lung capacity seems to be in excellent shape."

"Because of golf? Can you even break a sweat doing that?"

"You can. There's also his proliferate sex life."

Evan flinches, and so does Bess.

"Crap," she groans. "I can't believe I just said that."

Dear God, how far over the line has she just leapt? This is the problem with Evan Mayhew. It always has been. He's either poking at Bess, or making her feel way too much at home.

"Ugh," she says with another groan. "Forget it. Let's never speak of this again."

"A little hard to forget," Evan responds, slowly. "As for the sex, you must not be talking about yourself as you sound pretty pissed off for someone getting a lot of action."

"Well, we had sex *sometimes*. We were married after all."

"But the bastard had a girlfriend," Evan finishes for her. "What an asshole."

"Oh, I don't know that he had a girlfriend per se."

"Then why . . ."

"I was referring to the prostitutes."

And bam, just like that, a second admission slips out. A bigger one this time. Bess smacks a hand over her mouth, though it is far too late. But, really, her mistake is no surprise. When it comes to Evan, she is guaranteed to overstep, overexplain, over-Bess or "Bess up" in some irreparable way.

14

Monday Morning

"Prostitutes?" Evan says as Bess burns with regret. "Prostitutes?"

He is the second person Bess has told about the specifics of the divorce, the first being her cousin Palmer, who remains in a state of disgusted disbelief. Bess isn't even sure Palmer buys the story, or knows exactly what it means. After all, Bess had to explain that the term "working girl" didn't refer to a lawyer or a banker. It's as if Bess enjoys torturing herself. Palmer was bad enough. But Evan might never look at her the same way again.

Deep down, Bess knows it's not her fault that Brandon was such a snake. But, let's be honest. When a famous guy is outed for hookers, everyone wants to know about the wife. If the missus isn't beastly, or frigid, she is at a minimum very, very dumb.

Well, that sucks, Bess imagines Evan saying. *But you did marry the guy.*

"You mean actual hookers?" Evan says instead. "Or are you just being pejorative?"

"That SAT prep class helped after all. No, I am referring to real and bona fide workaday, wage-earning whores."

Bess exhales, and is surprised by the quick rush of relief. It feels good to tell Evan her secrets. It always has.

"Yep, Brandon likes himself the fancy ladies," Bess says. "Working girls. Hookers. Escorts, if you want to get 'classy' about it. He claims they were high-end call girls, as if that makes it any better. That's why I'm getting divorced. More clear-cut than most splits, I'd venture. But don't mention it to Cissy. She has no idea."

"Of course I won't tell Cissy. Jesus, Bess. That's so jacked up. How'd you find out?"

"He was embroiled in a lawsuit with his former partner," Bess explains. "Intellectual property rights. Who owns what code. The partner believed he was getting fucked and fucked Brandon in return. I'm not sure how it became a threesome, as I am certainly part of the screwing. In the end, though, I'm glad it happened, even though it's beyond painful. A fondness for hookers is something you should know about your spouse."

"Jesus," Evan says again. "Was he at all apologetic?"

"He made a good show of it. At least until I said there was no getting past what happened. Then he really let me have it."

Bess braces herself for the words she can still hear, words that stung far worse than finding out about the prostitutes in the first place. That's when Bess told her lawyer: Hurry up and settle, mediate, divorce. ASAP. It was like escaping a house fire. Grab what's important. Get out in one piece. She did not want to see his face again.

"What a shit-for-brains," Evan says. "He obviously has some sort of mental condition or personality disorder. God. Those poor prostitutes."

"The *prostitutes*?" Bess can't help but laugh. "I'm glad you're focusing on the correct victims in this story."

"Whatever." Evan flicks his hand, as if batting away the thought. "I'm not worried about you. You have loads going for you. Those hookers were already damaged. Now they're scarred for life."

"Well, his penis is very small." Bess smirks. "And he's a pretty wretched kisser. Too dry-mouthed. If I had to screw someone to make a buck, Brandon would not be my top choice."

"Huh," Evan says, eyes still blinky and surprised.

"So. Yep. There ya go. Hookers, the ultimate deal-breaker. A tip to take with you into future relationships."

"Bess." Evan makes a face. "I would never."

"I know. I'm just trying to be funny. As you've gathered, I'm quite good at it."

"Can I ask you something?" he says, brows crunched. "Why haven't you told your mom? You guys are so close."

Bess considers this.

"I don't know," she says. "Cissy and I *are* close but it's just . . . she's a tough broad, that mom of mine. You never know when you're going to step on a land mine with her. That's why it's usually best to stay up here."

Bess raises both hands to eye level.

"Uh. Yeah. Tough broad. That is the very definition of Cissy Codman. But, you're Bess. She loves you more than she loves anything. Even that house."

"I wouldn't go that far," Bess says with a snort. "The thing is, her judgment is already emanating at me and she doesn't know the half of it. She keeps asking if I'm sure about the divorce."

"What could she be judgmental about?"

"I'm giving this family its first broken branch on the whole damned tree. I am the middle child, though. So I'm the right person to play family pariah."

"Wait a minute." Evan shakes his head. "Aren't your parents . . . I thought they were divorced?"

"What?" Bess laughs. "Divorced? No. Not at all. I mean, my dad never comes to Cliff House and Cissy's rarely in Boston." She laughs again. "I'm not suggesting they have some grand love affair for the ages or anything. They basically tolerate each other."

"Sounds very romantic."

"Cissy isn't the romantic type."

Bess tries to stand. Her left foot has fallen asleep and so she stumbles on the way up. Evan gives her a steady arm.

"Thanks," Bess says, as the blush creeps across her cheeks once more. She is suddenly woozy. "I'll let you get back to work."

Evan keeps his hand at her elbow, guiding her down the dirt path.

"Yeah, I should do some work today," he says. "This might surprise you, but people get very hostile when they think their contractor isn't keyed in to every nail and two-by-four. I'll drop you back at Cliff House."

"Drop me back at Cliff House," Bess repeats, as the rocks and pebbles roll beneath her flip-flopped feet. "That might be the last time someone says those words to me."

"Wow, betting against Cissy Codman? That's a bad sign."

"You've seen the bluff, right?"

"I have," Evan says. "And despite my father's very loud opinions on the matter, I wish it could be different, I really do."

"Me, too. And thanks."

Bess pauses. Squinting, she stares out across the Atlantic.

"I haven't been to Sconset in forever," she says. "But there was always a comfort in knowing Cliff House was waiting for me. Like a backup plan. When my marriage went to shit, my first instinct was to quit my job and hide out here. I'm way too practical for that, but it sounded good at the time."

A few tears slide onto her cheeks.

"Aw, man," Evan says. "Don't cry. Please. I've never been able to handle it."

"Yeah, I remember." She smiles through the wetness. "I can't believe it. No more Cliff House. No more summer."

"Oh, Bess. Summer will come. Cliff House or not."

"It doesn't feel that way."

"Hey! Monday is Memorial Day. And whaddya know, Cliff House is still around. Your old shack has her chance. The season hasn't even started. There's an entire summer left to go."

15

The Book of Summer

Mrs. Philip E. Young, Jr.
May 16, 1941
Cliff House

Mother Young tells me I must write in this book, as summer's first visitor, even though I don't understand how Philip Young, Jr.'s wife can be classified as guest. Alas, I am nothing if not compliant so here goes.

We arrived on-island this morning: Mother Young, Ruby, me, and Mrs. Grimsbury. Mother Young and Ruby took immediately to opening Cliff House for the season. This involves removing drop cloths, dressing the beds, turning on the plumbing, restocking the kitchen, and, as I've learned, a litany of complaints from Ruby. Tugging plywood off the windows is apparently the universe's most laborious task.

As a newly pregnant Madonna-to-be, I'm unable to assist with the preparations. We've not yet had the pregnancy medically confirmed but I am certain there's a baby growing inside. I look forward to the importance, the meaning this small person will bring to our lives. As the wife of the family's eldest son, I can't take any chances, lest I cause harm to the heir of the Young fortune.

"The heir?" Ruby quacked when I refused to drag patio furniture to and fro. "Lady, you've got the wrong family."

Then she tee-heed for ninety seconds straight. I don't understand her at all.

And that's Cliff House as I know it so far this summer. What else do folks write in here? Let's see. Today the weather was fair, around sixty-two degrees, with a pleasant breeze. Tonight there's a dance at the Yacht Club. I've switched from Parliaments to Chesterfields. The weather tomorrow is supposed to start out a bit foggy, clearing by lunch.

Best regards,
Mrs. Philip E. Young, Jr. (Mary)

16

RUBY

May 1941

What was Daddy thinking? Ruby could kill the man! Just kill him!

Not literally, of course. But, still. Of all the crummy notions, he picked this one.

"Gas masks!" Ruby said to no one in particular as she yanked a drop cloth off a settee. "Horrific!"

From golf balls to gas masks, in a snap.

As if Sam (and Topper) weren't keyed up enough about the blessed skirmish, that warmonger FDR announced mandatory conscription approximately three minutes after Sam and Ruby returned from Acapulco. A peacetime draft. Didn't that just beat it all? Sam's number had not yet been called, much to his never-ending dismay.

"Perhaps I'll sign up," he said—nay, threatened—thrice weekly. "They need good men."

"Darling," Ruby responded, her face flat while her heart thwacked. "This will be a long battle yet. If you're meant to go, you'll go."

Then she'd excuse herself and spend the next hour kneeling in the closet, begging God to spare her sweet husband. It's as though he wanted to be some sort of hero. Baloney. A good man, that was the hero Ruby admired.

To make matters worse, a few weeks before they were to open Cliff House, Daddy announced a change to his business. Young Golf Products would cease the manufacture of golf balls and focus its facilities on gas masks. With one fell swoop, Daddy ruined the summer before it began. Swear to peaches, if a single gas mask found its way to Sconset, Ruby would hurl it right off the bluff.

Cliff House was peace. It was calm, a retreat from the real world. In Sconset, life glittered like the Atlantic beneath the sun. But now the men would toil away in the city during the week and bring to Sconset if not the masks themselves, visions of defense equipment coming off the line.

Ruby tried everything: reason, threats, and good old-fashioned crying. But Daddy remained unswayed.

"It's only temporary, petal," he said, just last night during their family's final meal in Boston before decamping for the summer. "We must do our part."

"Must we?!"

"Hear, hear," P.J. cheered.

"That's the way, Pops," Topper said. "You shred it, wheat."

Ruby gave him a swift kick to the shin.

"It's a man's duty to support his family," Mary reminded them all. "And a woman's duty to support her husband's occupation, whatever that might be."

As everyone nodded in agreement, Ruby rolled her eyes and then promptly received a sharp glare from her father. Her impertinence amused and charmed him—to a degree.

"If you ask me," Ruby's mother said about the change, "this is a jolly good arrangement. Better a contract with Uncle Sam than with a sporting-goods store that could be broke by next Tuesday."

They'd gone through plenty of that a decade ago, if you please. Mother was right. The economic decline was certainly no costume ball. So Ruby shut her trap for the rest of the meal, even as she simmered inside.

Now they were at Cliff House, the women anyway, opening the home for the summer. Ruby experienced none of her usual thrill, the giddy anticipation for the next one hundred days. The cloud was thick, the doom too real. She tried not to imagine next summer, or the summer after that.

"*We must do our part,*" Ruby groused as she polished a floor radio. "I've got it! Let's get ourselves killed for someone else's problems!"

"Oh Ruby!" Sarah Young said from somewhere upstairs. "Are you still down there? How's it all coming?"

"Yes, Mother! I'm down here. It's going splendidly. Working myself to the bone!"

Ruby looked toward a box on the floor and the twenty or so porcelain figurines left to unwrap.

"Have you started on the dining room?" Sarah asked.

"Not quite yet."

Ruby sighed. Nothing was ever fast enough.

"Soon, though!" she added, already beat.

"Thank you, dear! Couldn't do this without you!"

With a smirk, Ruby pulled back the floral drapes, whipping up torrents of dust along the way. Mother couldn't do it without her indeed. As she had so many times before, Ruby wondered why the boys (or, rather, *the men*) weren't there to assist, why the opening of Cliff House fell to the women.

In fact, *everything* at Cliff House fell to the women. Not just the unpacking but every day, all day, all summer long. Through it all, the men came and went like important guests of a finely run, excessively accommodating hotel. But, really, Cliff House was *their* home, Ruby thought. The women's, more than the men's. It was their work. Their fingerprints. Their soul.

"Aw, Ruby Red," she could almost hear Topper tsk. "Sorry you have to labor a single smidge in your otherwise gilded lifestyle. Must be a real grind! You poor lass!"

Then again, Topper considered golfing in light drizzle a monumental achievement, so he was in no position to pass judgment on residents of Easy Street. He was the doggone mayor of Snazzy Town.

"How's the view for ya, gents?" Ruby asked aloud, rubbing the salt and grime from the windowpanes. "And the veranda? Has it been properly swept? Yes, please do! Continue to drop your cigarette ashes about! No need to hassle with a receptacle. There's always someone to sweep it up!"

"Ruby?" said a voice, a pinch to the side.

"God bless it!" Ruby jumped, and then turned to the doorway. "Applesauce! Mary Young, you scared the dickens out of me."

Her sister-in-law looked wan and mildly depressed, as was customary. Ruby was a touch wan and depressed herself.

"How does Sam stand such rough language?" Mary said.

"He taught me all the best curse words, dontcha know?" Ruby joked.

"Life's such an endless gas for you, isn't it? When will you ever get serious?"

"I'm as serious as they come. So, what are you up to, Mare?"

Not opening Cliff House, Ruby hastened to add. The previous year Mary had been of moderate assistance, but now that she was pregnant—a new "scion," she claimed—it was all convalescing and complaining so far. And Ruby had her doubts about the alleged baby. Mary displayed none of the usual pregnancy signs and anyway the woman seemed about as fecund as a coal mine.

"Can you imagine sticking your pecker into that broad?" Topper once asked a pal, accidentally within earshot of Ruby. Her brother had been three deep in his favored whiskey-and-whiskey cocktails. "The damn thing would snap like a twig."

Ruby made like a respectable society bird and promptly jumped to her feet and slapped her brother on the cheek. But, facts were facts. It was the most vivid description she'd heard of another human. And despite her knowing very little about *peckers*, it seemed accurate to boot.

"Just wanted to check on you," Mary said as she leaned into the doorjamb, winded with indignation. "Before I catch up on some correspondence. The work never ends! By the by, Mrs. Grimsbury has put tea out on the veranda if you care to partake."

"Swell," Ruby replied, eyeing Mary's midsection and noting it was wooden and flat as ever. "Alas, I don't have time for sipping tea. There's a house to be opened. But I do hope you enjoy reclining on the very lawn furniture I dragged from the shed last night!"

"No need to be testy."

"I'm only ragging you. The tea sounds lovely but I'm short on time. Give Mrs. G. my regrets."

"All right," Mary said with a shrug. It was the most physically demonstrative she'd ever been. "No tea. Suit yourself."

As she pit-a-patted out of the room, Ruby shook her head. Good Lord, her brothers had horrible taste in women. They were lucky she brought Sam into the fold. Their gene pool was going to require some degree of help.

The first night at the club: always with a ten-piece band, the same man and woman at the mike. Both of them were Negroes. A couple, or maybe not. Either way, as the party reached its peak, they were marching the saints right on in.

"What a night! What a night!" Sam said, puffing on a cigarette and drinking like a horse.

He was grinning like a loon, too, his face glossed with sweat. His hair, hours ago slicked back, now dipped in chunks across his forehead, the ends kissing his thick black lashes.

"You said it." Ruby moved onto his lap. "An utter kick."

She grabbed the cigarette from between his fingers and took a puff as he kissed her neck. Ruby pictured people gasping. Mary would be notably horrified—that is, if she weren't out on the floor. How Ruby's sister-in-law could justify a day of convalescing followed by a night spent jitterbugging was a mystery for the ages. For all her manufactured propriety, Mary sure liked to play by her own rules.

"Sitting on my lap?" Sam teased. "In front of all these people?! You're bad business, Mrs. Packard!"

Ruby giggled and nuzzled a spot where her husband had neglected to shave.

Remember this, she wanted to say. *Remember how happy we are. If you go to Europe, it could be a year before we see each other. More. It's possible we might not meet again until we're on some other plane.*

"My wife, scandalizing the club like she's on a mission," Sam said, and shifted awkwardly.

"Please! We're married!"

Ruby locked her knees together and batted her eyes.

"I'm just an innocent island girl," she said. "A near-Quaker, like the ones who founded this place."

As Sam leaned in to kiss her again, Ruby beamed. God, she was happy. So deliriously happy.

Oh, the night had the potential to end badly, it did. In two hours Sam might be passed out on the marital bed, or making sick in Mother's roses. But Ruby loved him even more when he was like this, filled with light, not ruminating on battleships or gas masks or that awful Hitler and his bombing planes. This Sam reminded her of the one she'd known since she was a girl.

"Come, my love," he said, boosting Ruby to her feet. "Let's take those hooves for a spin."

"Saaaam . . ." Ruby said, protesting a little.

Her knees ached, her ankles keened. That iron lawn furniture was no joke and she'd moved it all herself. But Ruby followed him nonetheless. Sam was the most splendid dancer. Whenever his shoes began to bop, the room split in two. Everyone wanted to watch him move.

"Long day, my darling?" he asked, detecting the crackle in her ankles as he spun her about the floor.

"The longest. I think the furniture reproduced while we were away. There are more pieces than ever. And the plumber was three hours late to turn on the water! All the while, Mother barked orders and Mary didn't lift a single craggy talon."

Sam tipped his head back and laughed.

"Oh Mary," he said. "Good old Talons Magee. Well, now, what can you expect from Mrs. Philip E. Young, Junior? She's gestating a future scion of industry in that steel belly of hers. And steel never bends."

Sam twirled Ruby once beneath his arm, and then again. She was dizzy from the dancing, and the champagne, and the attentions of her very own Cary Grant. Lord, was Sam ever a dreamboat. When you'd known someone most of your life, it was easy to forget.

"Well, Mrs. Packard," Sam said after sending her toward the floor in a most beguiling dip. "Sounds like you've worked the feathers right off your tail. But here you are, dancing with me. And you've cleaned up rather well, it should be noted."

"Oh I try," she said. "All for my special man."

He gave her a few more whirls and Ruby's insides soared straight to the heavens. Soon the band changed its tempo, "God Bless America" on the docket. Ruby checked the clock on the far wall. Dang it all to hell. The party was about to end.

As if reading her thoughts, Sam frowned. But when Ruby looked over her shoulder she realized it was not the clock causing him to glower but her brother, marching straight at them.

"Hello, lovebirds," Topper said, affecting a drawl. "Mind if I have this dance?"

"I'm grateful for the offer, but you should dance with your sister," Sam said.

"A real cut-up, this guy." Topper offered Ruby his arm. "Shall we?"

"Do you mind?" Ruby asked her husband.

"Of course not. Dance on, you two."

Sam made a circular motion with his hand and Ruby smiled in thanks. Perhaps the chilliness she saw between the men was squarely in her mind.

"You kids have a nice trot," Sam said. "I'll be enjoying a smoke near the valet."

Though he smiled, Ruby noticed that his eyes seemed lost. The brewing of his inner jingoism, no doubt. Ruby watched as he walked off, singing along to the band.

Stand beside her, and guide her, through the night with a light from above.

"What's the matter, little sis?" Topper said, and placed a hand at the small of her back. "Blue to be with second place? Listen, I'm no Ducky Shincracker like your boy Packard, but I can cut a rug or two."

"So you claim," Ruby answered, casting eyeballs about the room.

She watched Sam brush against a potted palm and then slide through the door.

"You seem to be having a lovely night," Topper said, gently leading her to the beat. "At least until I showed up."

"It's been wonderful," Ruby said. "Before and now. We're having a blast. Sam is in a great mood. It's fab to see."

Topper cocked an eyebrow.

"Sam's in a great mood. As opposed to . . . ?"

"I didn't mean it like that." Ruby shook her head. "It's just that Sam can be so serious. Moody."

"That he can," Topper said with a nod.

"It's nice to watch him reveling in the night, having a drink, dancing. He's been so worried, lately. Hitler. This war. It's not even our war. He's distraught over nothing!"

"Nothing?" Topper threw her a strange look. "Whaddya mean he's upset 'over nothing'?"

"The war in Europe . . ."

"Listen, darling, that ain't nothin'."

Topper took to dancing again, this time more slowly, deliberately, a subtle shift between his feet.

"I know," she said. "It's a war. And now there's conscription. But it's over *there*."

She jerked her head, though it was not in the most accurate direction. Essentially she was aiming toward Boston.

"Yes," Topper said, his brow darkening. "It's 'over there.' For now."

"It's like he's infected everyone."

"Who? Hitler?"

"No! Why would I bring up Hitler on a night like this? I meant Sam!"

"Whoa, girl," he scoffed. "'*Infected*'? Don't you think that's a mite hard-nosed?"

"I didn't really mean infected, per se."

"I agree with your husband," Topper reminded her. "We need to get involved in this war. Am I infected, too?"

"Well, that's different," she said. "You're still in college."

"What's that supposed to mean?"

"I'm sure at Harvard it's the very fashion to . . ." Ruby shook her head. "The thing is, Daddy's started making gas masks and even Mother is in the blue moods about it all." She lowered her voice to a whisper. "She's thinking of joining the Grey Ladies."

"No!" Topper let out a fake gasp. "Do-gooding and Bundles for Britain?! Say it ain't so! We cannot have that kind of philanthropy in our family. We might earn a reputation for being kindhearted!"

"Hilarious." Ruby gave him a swat to the shoulder.

"This war, Red. We can't stay out of it forever. By us I mean the United States. I mean you, I mean me."

"Don't get any ideas."

"I'm going over," he said. "If I'm not drafted, I plan to sign myself up."

"Topper! You can't! Mother wouldn't survive it. I wouldn't!"

"It's a matter of time, the only question being . . . do I go the army route, or do I climb aboard a ship?"

"This isn't funny!" Ruby yipped. "Of all the nights . . ."

"I have to go, Red. It's the right thing to do."

"But this war isn't ours to fight!" Ruby looked up at him, a crick already forming in her neck. At six-four, Topper had a good foot on her. She spent ninety percent of their time together with her face tilted toward the sky. "Lindbergh says they're making the same mistakes from the first war. You're going to risk your life for that?"

"Dear God. Don't even talk to me about Lindbergh." Topper pretended to spit.

"We were tricked into coming to people's rescue and lost fifty thousand men in the process! Not to mention we don't have the power to defeat the Axis right now. A suicide mission is what it is."

"You sound like Chuck Lindbergh sure enough. That's not a compliment, by the way."

"What do you have against Lindbergh?"

"He's practically a German. Folks call him the 'number one Nazi fellow traveler.' And he supports racial purity! That's eugenics, Ruby. In case I need to spell it out."

"I don't agree with him on that front. But he's a patriot! And he's been through so much."

"He's handsome and had a baby kidnapped. Sorry, Red, that doesn't make him right. And don't get me started on that wife of his."

"Anne is delightful," Ruby said.

She'd met her once, back at school. Anne Morrow was a Smithie, too, and had made an appearance on campus, enchanting every last one of them.

"Mrs. Lindbergh is so lovely and strong despite the tragedy," Ruby said. "Why, if I were in her shoes, I'd never step out of my house."

"Doesn't give her the right to act like a cretin. For the love of God, Red, that book of hers is a Nazi handbook if ever there was one. The

Lindberghs. Christ. I'd welcome their insight even less than I'd welcome typhoid fever." Topper eyed the ceiling as if in contemplation. "Smallpox? Polio? A knife to the gut? All of the above?"

"I get it. You don't care for them. I just can't figure how muddling around Europe's problems does anything for us."

"You want it to do something for us?" Topper wrenched up his mug. "To begin, as it relates to Hitler, it's first stop Europe, next stop the world."

"But he's said he has no designs on this part of the globe. I read it in the *Times*. Your favorite rag."

"Well, if there's ever a man to take at his word," Topper said with a snort, "it's Hitler. Just ask the Austrians. And even if he were being uncharacteristically honest, you can't . . . It's not morally sound to be an isolationist anymore. I'm a little embarrassed you still have such ideas."

"Embarrassed? Ouch. And since when do you care about morals?"

Topper flinched as if stung, though he'd jabbed at her first.

"I'm sorry, I didn't mean . . ." Ruby started.

He shook his head.

"No. I know. It's fine." He sighed. "The thing is, Ruby, I'm a lover not a fighter."

"Spare me!"

"I don't like the thought of getting involved in some far-flung war any more than you do. But we can't keep burying our heads in the sand. Grievous atrocities are being committed. Last week, five thousand Jews were rounded up in Paris and shipped off to prison camps, to endure God knows what abuse. These places have death quotas, Ruby. Which they're besting several times over."

Ruby's stomach lurched. She clamped her eyes shut. The boy was far too fixated on every iniquity they printed in *The New York Times*.

"Topper, please . . ."

"You can't turn away, Ruby. That man—Hitler—he's pure evil. He must be stopped."

Ruby opened her eyes and nodded absently.

She didn't wholly agree with her brother, or with Sam, but Ruby understood Topper's heart. For a second she felt a ping, the urge to do more than complain or disagree. For all his claims that the woman was a fascist monster, Ruby quite concurred with Mrs. Lindbergh, who said that her heart wanted to help but her mind questioned the sanity of it.

"I suppose I can do something," Ruby said. "With the Bundles for Britain program. The Grey Ladies are in the thick of it. According to Mother, they've requested more hands."

Yes, Ruby decided. She could take to knitting socks and hats to be sent overseas. Though she wasn't in favor of the United States joining the fight, that didn't mean she couldn't support Britain and her allies. There was more than one way to think about this war.

"Bundles for Britain?" Topper said with an arched brow. "You're really going to join up?"

"Why not? You've said it yourself. I have an idealistic view of the world. My tinseled cocoon and whatnot. Time to get serious. I'm having too much fun."

"Aw, hell," Topper said with a forlorn sort of head tilt. "Ruby, you're a doll. Bundles for Britain sounds swell but don't listen to your baby brother. I'm full of bunk ninety percent of the time."

"That is definitely true."

"Forget serious, Red. You keep your sunshine. You stay in that cocoon. Everybody loves the la-la girls. In New England you're the rarest kind of bird."

17

Island ACKtion

CLIFF HOUSE UPDATE: CISSY C CALLS REINFORCEMENTS

May 20, 2013

As I informed my ACK squad a scant five days ago (click here for the full article), though the building still stands, for all intents and purposes, the legendary Cliff House is *finit*.

The Baxter Road behemoth has been the site of some of the island's most festive and famous shindigs. According to hospital records dug up by my intrepid intern, a total of seven Kennedy-related injuries have been reported on the property over the years. Many more have not been reported. And one can only imagine the sexual misdeeds committed on-site. There's no telling whose DNA would be found if the dressing rooms that once surrounded the pool remained.

But the pool is gone, along with the dressing rooms, the lawn, the tennis courts (one clay, one hard), and most of the back veranda. The only thing left, really, is the home itself, one-quarter of a privet hedge, and a cantankerous owner still inside.

Don't misunderstand. Cissy Codman and her seldom-seen husband Dudley are not entirely out of options. Tuesday will mark an important day in the fight to save their home. That night, the Board of Selectmen will vote on whether to move ahead with Cissy & Co.'s controversial hard armor schemes. She's worked wicked hard on her quest and has even kicked millions of her own. Calls to Dudley Codman have gone unreturned, as per usual.

"It's not happening," says lifelong Sconseter and commercial fisherman Chappy Mayhew. "Her gimmick would cause havoc on a very fragile ecosystem. True locals won't stand for it."

To aid her cause, Cissy's shipped in one of her kids. It's the middle of her three children, Elisabeth Codman. Bess is an ER doctor in San Francisco and a graduate of Nantucket High School. She is the only one of Cissy's kids to have attended school on-island.

"I'm only trying to get her out of the house," Bess tells the *ACKtion*. "Seriously, Corkie, it's nothing more."

Way to play it cool, Bess. Way to lay low.

Stay tuned for news coming out of the Selectmen's Office on Tuesday. *Island ACKtion* will be live-tweeting the event.

ABOUT ME:

Corkie Tarbox, lifelong Nantucketer, steadfast flibbertigibbet. Married with one ankle-biter. Views expressed on the *Island ACKtion* blog (Twitter, Facebook, Instagram, et al.) are hers alone. Usually.

18

Tuesday Morning

"Well, well, well, the Bradlee girls are back on A-C-K," Bess sings, joke-style, as she glides through the side door of Tea Time, her cousins' house in town. "Alert the authorities."

Some might call Tea Time a compound—the Bradlees certainly wouldn't—but it has a front house and three guesthouses (aptly named "For Felicia," "For Palmer," and "For Everyone Else"), plus a pool, so it qualifies to Bess. Also, a former presidential candidate slash secretary of state has a place down the road and his is irrefutably smaller.

However.

"You can't have a compound in town!" Aunt Polly insists.

You can't have one in Sconset either, apparently. Or you can, but it won't last forever.

"Frick and Frack." Bess smiles, sauntering into the kitchen of the main house. "Together again."

Frick and Frack, or Flick and Palmer. Two sisters, two vastly different women, though close all the same.

Flick is tall, broad-shouldered, husky-voiced, and assured. She makes piles of money on Wall Street and has her own weekend home in Amagansett, in addition to "For Felicia" in Nantucket Town. Palmer is the little sister and Bess's closest friend. Delicate and blond, she is a former "mid-tier ballerina" who danced for some time with the Little Rock Ballet Company before chucking it all to get married to a guy with great hair and a country club membership.

"I never had to get a real job," she'd tell you in a delighted hush, never pretending she wanted it any other way.

Now Palmer teaches ballet to little girls in an Atlanta suburb, tots like her own cherub Amory, who is always either napping or sitting with her ankles crossed, mouthing the words to a picture book with her perfect pink lips.

Palmer has a sprightly, carefree, all-the-world's-a-dance vibe that would be utterly hateable if she weren't so self-aware, not to mention insanely nice. Everyone loves Palmer Bradlee, including and especially her husband, who calls her this, Palmer Bradlee in full, as if it's her first name or he's introducing a celebrity.

"Bessie!" Palmer says, giving her a fairy's hug: delicate, light, and smelling of flowers. "I'm so glad you're here."

"We thought you weren't coming until the wedding," Flick says, and marches to Bess's side. She wraps her in an athletic, wrestler's embrace. "What gives?"

Palmer shoots Flick a glare. Or, as close to a glare as she can get.

"What gives is a very good question," Bess says. "Long story short: Cissy's back at it."

Flick walks over to the coffeemaker and pours them each a cup.

"Cissy's *still* at it," Palmer corrects.

"Yes." Bess nods. "Still at it. And I've come to save the day. Poor Cis, right?"

"Jesus." Flick rolls her startling green eyes. "I love your mom, but come on. It's time to give up already."

"Everyone agrees. Except Cissy, of course. That's the problem. She believes that nothing or no one can match her will and determination. In fairness, very few can. Lala was born four weeks early but Cissy claims it would've been earlier if she hadn't 'held her in' for ten days."

"Goodness, I just love Aunt Cissy," Palmer chortles. "She is the best."

"This is not normal," Flick says gruffly.

"I agree but . . ."

"What kind of meds is she on?"

"Meds?"

"I think her dosage might be off," Flick says. "When was the last time your mother saw her shrink?"

"Oh, Felicia! You're such a Manhattanite," Palmer says with yet another charming giggle. "Aunt Cis doesn't have a shrink. She's a New Englander!"

"She needs one. I'm sorry but there's dedication and there's obsession and your mother's flown past both. She wouldn't talk to me for a month after I refused to get married at the house."

"Well, that's your own fault," Bess says. "You were already on shaky ground after buying that place in the Hamptons."

"Oh God, the 'eschewing of Nantucket' garbage!" Flick throws her head back. "I spent an hour explaining that I needed something closer to the city since I work approximately all of the damned time. Anyway, we have Tea Time. And here I am. Back. Getting married on-island and therefore not eschewing."

"Sorry excuse," Bess says with a smirk. "You could've at least gotten married at her house to compensate for the injustice. But instead you're 'mocking her.' "

"Yes. What was I thinking? Oh, that's right. I wanted my wedding venue to still exist when the guests showed up. Well, my dear cousin," Flick says, and taps Bess's hand. "All your mother's kvetching about the 'hundreds of weddings' on the lawn, and your marriage to Brandon will end up being the last."

"Felicia!" Palmer chirps as a tremor runs across her flawless face.

"I meant the last marriage at Cliff House," Flick hastily adds. "Not, you know, for you. Unless you want it to be."

"It's fine." Bess waves her away.

Suddenly a phone on the counter buzzes—Flick's, no doubt. Palmer always forgets to turn hers on or bring it in from the car. Messages collect for days before she thinks to check them.

"Shit," Flick says, studying the screen. "Oh fuck me. I knew I should've stayed a full week at the office. I'm working on this convertible debt offering . . ."

She punches in a number and then holds up a finger to "shush" Bess and Palmer, though Flick is the only one talking.

"The board says what?" she asks before stepping out onto the patio. "I thought they already approved it!"

The door swooshes behind her as Palmer turns to Bess.

"I'd apologize," she says. "But you know Felicia."

"Yep." Bess smiles. "That's your sister, through and through."

"I wouldn't have it any other way."

For a moment Bess feels an undeniable ache, that of missing her own sister, or what her sister should've been. Bess has never been as close to Lala as she's been to Palmer. Or Felicia for that matter. Never as close in terms of miles, or years, or even heart. She loves Little Julia, sweet Lala, but the seven-year gap sometimes seems like an entire generation. And in many ways it is. Bess certainly didn't have a phone in her backpack when she was in high school. She knows how to write in cursive.

"So how are you, Bessie?" Palmer asks, forehead rising in concern. "Are you doing okay?"

"Yes, I'm doing okay. Just barely."

Bess gives a tight smile as she fiddles with a blue-striped dish towel.

"Is . . . is it still true?" Palmer asks as she leans forward. "The . . . ya know?" She lifts her eyebrows three times. "The people?"

"You mean the hookers?" Bess asks. "Yup. That still cannot be undone."

Palmer gulps, as if hearing it for the first time. Her face goes even paler than porcelain, just this side of blue.

"It's still so shocking," she says.

Bess nods as she pulls her cardigan snug around herself. It's hard to fathom he's the same Brandon she fell for those six or so years ago.

They met at a party. Bess can't remember at whose house, but there were purple rugs and floor-to-ceiling mirrors involved. She spotted Brandon across the seventies-era monstrosity, he dorky-hot with his wavy sun-streaked hair, stone cheekbones, and black glasses. He'd spotted her in return and within seconds sidled up.

They chatted as young unattached people do—who are you, what do you do, who will you be—and then Brandon stopped short. He stared at Bess, curiously, as if someone had asked him to opine on a movie with decidedly mixed reviews.

"Well, nice to meet you, Brandon . . ." she stuttered, and began to back away.

"Wait."

He placed a hand on her forearm. Even today she remembers being surprised by the strength of his grip.

"This is going to sound silly," he said. "But coming to talk to you was calculated."

"Uh, what now?"

"I had to see for myself. I figured you couldn't be as smart as you are beautiful. Then I thought, well, okay, she's smart *and* beautiful, but she can't possibly be as cool as she is those two things. But, I was wrong."

"Um?" Bess said, blinking. "Thanks?"

He'd tease her about this later, mostly in front of other people.

I made this big romantic gesture, if I do say so myself. And she answered "um."

"One day," he said after Bess's fabulous display of graciousness.

"One day, probably within the year, I'm going to ask you to marry me. You'll say yes because you and I, we're meant to be."

Brandon was decisive like that, one of the things Bess appreciated most about him. Usually when Bess acted with such resolve it resulted in some sort of calamity.

"We will get married, Beth," he said.

"Bess," she told him.

"Either way." He shrugged. "Within the year."

After a great, long pause Bess replied deftly: "Okay."

Brandon took this as advance acceptance of his future proposal. A preapproval, if you will. Alas, Bess would never be sure what she meant by her reply. "Okay." It's what you say when you lack real words.

"I'll get over it," Bess says, to herself as much as to her cousin. "One day it will all be a bad dream."

Palmer doesn't nod. She's not buying it, not yet.

Outside, the winds are beginning to pick up, the drizzle turning to hard rain. Thank God the vote is tonight, because with every gust it feels like Cliff House is one inch closer to the end.

But the vote is tonight.

Which means it's Tuesday and then it will be Wednesday. If she were to look at her calendar, Bess would see all of tomorrow blocked off. She still hasn't canceled her appointment, but it's not a matter of simply rescheduling. Suddenly Bess wants to leap on the next plane. Or straight off the Sankaty Bluff.

"So, I'm going to change the subject," Bess says, stomach wobbling and turning.

"Understood."

Palmer gives her an ardent thumbs-up.

"Is everything set for the wedding?" Bess asks.

"Just about!"

Her cousin perks at once. Really, it's downright rude to talk to Palmer Bradlee about anything other than cake and tulle. Not that she can't handle it; it just doesn't seem right.

"Lala's sorry she can't make it," Bess says. "Flights from Sudan are hard to come by."

"At least Clay and Tiffany are coming!"

"You act like that's a good thing."

"Bess!"

"I love Clay. But Tiffany . . ." Bess rolls her eyes. "Luckily it's only for the day."

Tick, tick, tick, says the clock in her mind.

"You'd think by pregnancy number three," Bess goes on, "Tiff wouldn't be so dramatic. People do give birth around here. We have a legit hospital on Nantucket, believe it or not."

"Aw, she's just excited."

Yes, Bess thinks, her sister-in-law *is* excited. Excited about her ability to act like the empress of an enslaved land.

"So, what kind of turnout are you expecting?" Bess asks, and reaches for someone's half-eaten bagel. Flick's, most likely, as Palmer can't possibly eat carbs. "Cissy tells me the guest list is small?"

"*Was* small," Palmer says. "My sister is so entertaining. She keeps adding guests like she's throwing another ice cube into her lemonade." She hesitates and lowers her voice to a whisper. "There will be a lot of people from Choate. Is that . . . okay? Will you . . ."

"Listen, P," Bess says, shaking her head. "What happened twenty years ago is nothing. Rest assured, it's the very least of my humiliation and shame."

This is true, though it's a humiliation still. Bess can't admit this to her cousin, however.

"Well," Palmer says with a sniff. "You shouldn't have the smallest speck of shame about what happened with Brandon. He was a verbally abusive, controlling dickwad."

"Okay, he's a jerk. And I'm not sure I've ever heard you use the term 'dickwad,' so cheers to that. But verbally abusive? Come on. That's a tad excessive."

It's not the first time Palmer's sung this tune. She's been playing it for some time now and Bess cannot get her off it.

"In my opinion he was," Palmer says. "But either way, regarding the sex workers, he acted like a creep on his own. No assistance required."

She takes a sip of coffee, wrapping both delicate, spindly hands around an old, cracked Yacht Club mug, her fingers obscuring the little blue flag.

"We had fun, though, didn't we?" Palmer asks in her Disney princess voice. "At school? Before you left?"

"We did," Bess answers with a smile.

"'Door open, one foot on the floor!'" Palmer says in her best dorm-mother voice.

"Yeah, I think you're the only person who followed that rule."

"Or you *think* I followed it." Palmer blows Bess a kiss. "To this day Brooks can't understand why I have no modesty around the house. Sweetheart, I grew up showering with a hall of girls. Most of them all too willing to catalogue one's warts."

Her warts? What could Palmer possibly be self-conscious about? She is a ballerina sculpture, a perfect work of art.

"The one thing I remember," Bess says, "about coming to Nantucket after Choate was how blithely people ordered pizza. Wait, what? You just *pick up the phone and ask for food*? Don't we need to dangle someone from a window by their ankles?"

Palmer laughs.

"Geez, what we did for crappy pizza!" she says. "Remember when you joined the a cappella group?"

"Bad idea."

"The worst. Because although you have many talents, singing is not one of them."

"I was awesome at hand bells, though."

"No one is good at hand bells," Palmer says, still laughing, as Bess's belly fills with warmth.

Little Amory bounds in then, curls springing with each step. It's a wonder she can move at all, engulfed as she is in a frothy nightgown whisking around her like pink frosting.

"Bessie-boo!" Amory squeaks, running toward her. "You're here!"

"I'm here, Ammy. I'm here."

Bess clutches the little girl to her chest. As she nuzzles those curls, Bess inhales and feels a definite pull, a sense of yearning from a place unknown.

19

The Book of Summer

Patience Grimsbury
June 10, 1941
Cliff House

Mrs. Young asked me to write in this Book of Summer, which seems peculiar given my station, but she swears it's made for all.

The summer commenced in its usual way, the women fussing about, and ~~I have to go in and fix~~ naturally they're getting everything precisely right! I just fill in where I can! Mrs. Young and Mrs. Young, Jr., and Miss Young-now-Packard, they all have such a knack for making this grand house hum. I'm fortunate they let me be a part of it!

I'm waiting—any day now—for one of the younger set to announce her pregnancy. They are all trying, this I know. I hope this "Grey Ladies" enterprise doesn't hamper things in the womanly department. There's only one way to become a mother—focus on the endeavor wholeheartedly. Not that I know a thing about it, in the end.

Whether a baby or two will soon be on its way, I can't predict. But I do know one thing. This will be a summer for the ages. A summer to remember. I only pray that I can keep the whole thing ticking.

Dutifully,
Patience Grimsbury

20

RUBY

June 1941

It seemed like a lot of training for something so nonmedical. But after four monotonous weeks, Ruby was a certified member of the Red Cross Hospital and Recreation Corps, aka the Grey Ladies, Sconset branch. Together they knitted children's blankets and clothes and could upgrade to bandage rolling if all went well.

Ruby was pleased to help, even in this minor way. A gal could argue with the war, but she couldn't dispute outfitting displaced baby Brits. Meanwhile Mary took to it like it was her calling, and how. She delighted in the rigors of training, the long days spent at the Legion Hall, a fraternity of women united beneath a common goal. They were like a military battalion but with less threat of bodily harm, plus infinitely better attire.

"I never realized that other women could be so extraordinary," Mary confessed late one night, drunk on do-gooding and a little sherry.

It was quite the change of tack for her sister-in-law. To date Mary had approached everything with grim tenacity, even her own wedding. Her demeanor when she believed herself pregnant was precisely the same as when she found out that she wasn't. But with the Grey Ladies, Mary showed pep, some swing in her walk.

"We are nurses!" Mary trilled, repeatedly, on their first official day. "Isn't it grand?!"

They were on the veranda, Ruby working on an afghan as Mary knitted baby bunting.

"We are nurses!" she continued to sing while adjusting her jaunty nurse's cap.

"Not exactly."

"Oh don't be such a negative Nellie. We have the certification and pin to prove it. Helping the war effort. I've never felt so alive. Isn't this pure delight?"

"You betcha," Ruby answered, trying to join a new ball of yarn.

"Delight" was not the word Ruby had in her head. She was a little tired. And bored. And her fingers were already sore as the dickens. Plus, she was getting dizzy trying to concentrate so closely on the pattern.

"Hmmm," Ruby said, inspecting a dropped stitch.

If an afghan looked bonkers but still kept a person warm, was there room for complaint? Ruby chased the thought away with a blush. The Brits deserved nice things, too. Just as Topper said: a la-la girl indeed.

"These socks!" Mary held up a pair, knitted by some other Lady. "Are they not precious?"

"Sure are."

Ruby closed her eyes and pictured the British children, those who'd go on to receive the spoils of their work. Poor moppets. Snatched from their homes and spirited to the countryside to live with strangers. Ruby disagreed with the warmongering, but the little ones she could get behind.

"Don't be so glum, Ruby," Mary said, and stood. "You'll improve. Your output won't always be this terrible."

"That's not . . ."

"Do we have enough?"

Mary began lining up balls of yarn on the table. Twenty Grey Ladies were due at any moment. Though Mary and Ruby had been knitting all day, their efforts would continue past sundown. At least they'd have fresh blood. Even a zippy Mary was half a Mary too much.

"I think we have plenty to work with," Ruby said. "You've stocked us well."

"Goodness, isn't this delightful beyond words?" Mary assessed the scene, gobbling up the balls of yarn with her beady black eyes. "It's so much more fulfilling than playing tennis or acting with the Nantucket players!"

"Yeah, it's swell." Ruby sighed.

She'd dropped another stitch, damn it. Ruby was miserable at this knitting business. Plain awful.

"But I'm afraid I'll miss the tennis," she said.

"Ruby Packard, you're such an ingrate! I'll have you know . . ."

"Tennis?" said a voice, pure smoothness. "No one told me we'd have to miss tennis."

A woman walked up then. A right dish. She was a touch older than Ruby, or the same age. Her hair and lips were both fire-engine red and she wore polka dots and a wide smile. Ruby perked up at the very sight.

"Good afternoon!" Mary said, and swept across the patio to meet her. "Oh my! What a kicky outfit! Trousers even. I'm Mrs. Philip E. Young. And you are?"

"Hi-ya, Mrs. Young."

She curtsied, though Ruby suspected it was a gag.

"Miss Harriet Rutter at your service." The woman extended a hand. "You can call me Hattie. Pleased to meet ya."

Mary's own hand quivered as she returned the gesture. Trousers. Casual greetings. Oh the humanity. Ruby stood to rescue them both.

"Hello there, Hattie," she said. "My name is Ruby. Ruby Packard. Welcome to Cliff House."

"Charmed, Miss Packard."

"That's, um, Mrs. Packard," Ruby said, then cringed.

What did she care, Miss or Missus? This Hattie Rutter would figure it out soon enough. Anyway Ruby still felt like a Miss. She felt like a Young.

"All righty then," Hattie said with a wink, already in on the joke. She took a seat on the green metal glider. "*Missus.*"

"So, Miss Rutter?" Mary began.

"Please. Hattie."

"Are your parents Charles and Edwina Rutter? They've a place on Hulbert?"

"That's them." Hattie pushed off from a table with one foot, sending her chair ricocheting front to back. "Well, it's my father. Edwina's my stepmum. Nice lady but a bit of a snore."

As her glider continued to rock, Hattie glanced around sharply, deliberately, like a gopher poking its head from a hole. Then she closed her eyes and smiled. Her mouth somehow, impossibly, stretched wider. Hattie Rutter should've been in films. She'd light up the whole screen.

"What a perfect afternoon." She popped her eyes back open. "I haven't been to Nantucket in years. And Sconset even longer. It's beautiful here. So peaceful. I've missed it and only just realized."

"Yes, it's grand," Mary said, befuddled. She smoothed the front of her dress, pressing the area breasts would go if she had any to speak of. "So, uh, where do you summer?"

What Mary did not say: *You're a Hulbert Avenue sort, so why not there?* It was a posh address, smack in Nantucket Town, the pinnacle of swanky summer fun. Though but seven miles separated the two, Hattie's type deemed Sconset certifiable backcountry, nothing but fishermen and artist colonies.

"The majority of my schooling has been in Europe," Hattie explained. "Paris mostly, so usually I summer on the Continent. But Europe, you know, not so fashionable these days."

She gave a small hummingbird of a snort.

"When I do visit the U.S.," she went on, "it's usually the Cape. Mother has a house in Osterville with her new husband. Shabby place but with beaches for miles. Nothing like this outfit, though. You know how divorces are. They spread the green too thin."

"Er, um," Mary stuttered. "I hear Osterville is grand. And thank you for the compliment on my home."

Ruby's head snapped in her sister-in-law's direction. Since when was Mary the Cliff House emissary? Its mistress? "Her" home? Didn't that just beat it all. The last Ruby checked, both of her parents were still around.

"This place is a beauty," Hattie said. "Massive! It keeps going and going!"

"Yes, well, Mother Young has a grand imagination," Mary said. "And my father-in-law gives her whatever she pleases."

"The right kind of marriage, if you can get it."

"I suppose. Either way, they built the place from scratch, entirely at her direction. It's a nit overdone, but we enjoy it quite nicely."

Ruby rolled her eyes. Mary had spent all of three summers at Cliff House and was acting like she'd been there all along. Of course, she did have greater claim to it than Ruby, what with being married to Philip Junior and possessing the uterus that would harvest the heir to the family fortune. Whatever "fortune" might remain, that is, after the transition to gas masks.

"The house is snazzy as all get-out," Hattie said. "But what gets to me are these cliffs. So beautiful. Dramatic. At Points North we have a boring flat beach."

"I can see how that would be dull," Mary said.

"Tell me, though. How's the shopping around here? In Sconset or Nantucket Town? Since coming back from France I'm having a fiend of a time finding decent togs."

"You're worried about your clothing?" Mary said, her eyebrows spiked.

"A dame wants to look her best, right?"

"The shopping in town is fine," Ruby said. "Nothing spectacular, but adequate."

"Tell me, where do you buy your hats?"

"Our hats?" Mary said, and scrunched her nose. "What do you mean? We already have hats."

Hattie chuckled amiably and gave Mary a rap on the back.

"Oh, gals, we're going to have a hoot of a time. So, kittens." Hattie stood, hiking up her pants to expose slim and graceful anklebones. "Do we have one of those, whaddya call it, quotas? Let's kick off this show. The more efficiently we work, the more quickly we can have fun."

"Fun?" Mary said, utterly perplexed.

"Yes. You know, the stuff we get up to when the men are off-island? So, my new friends, show me where to start."

As Mary handed the girl a ball of white yarn, Ruby released a small smile. If the rest of the Grey Ladies were like Hattie Rutter, perhaps they wouldn't be so gray after all.

"Pardon me, Mrs. Young."

Miss Mayhew stood in the doorway in a simple beige dress. A glorified sack, really.

"And Mrs. Packard," she added halfheartedly.

Miss Mayhew was the latest addition to the household staff, hired by Mrs. Grimsbury to work directly *for* Mrs. Grimsbury because evidently their maid was in need of a maid herself.

"It's like I put something in order," Ruby overheard Grimsbury telling Daddy. "And the girls scramble it up again! I need some extra hands."

Ergo, Miss Mayhew. She was a local girl, plain as water, but nice in that Nantucket Quaker way.

"The guests are arriving," Miss Mayhew told them. "But they seem inappropriately early. Shall I make them wait? Mrs. Grimsbury is in a right fit about it."

"No one made me wait," Hattie said, and looked up from the bundles of wool in her lap. "Well, the old bird tried, but I sailed right past."

Miss Mayhew pulled an odd face, as if stifling a sneeze.

"Mind you, I have all the manners of a field cow," Hattie said. "So you shouldn't count me as a legitimate guest."

"Too true. Mrs. Young, what's your decision? About the early arrivers?"

"Oh, um . . ." Mary hemmed.

"For Pete's sake tell us who they are!" Hattie said. "Who's arrived? The fun ones or the dullards? Any of the lunkheads, make 'em wait."

Ruby tittered and turned her work. Miss Mayhew took in a sharp inhale, struggling to maintain her composure. Mrs. Grimsbury hadn't warned her about this.

"It's Miss Macy and Mrs. Brooks," she said. "But I really don't think . . ."

"Good grief, bring them out!" Mary said with uncharacteristic fire as she lifted from her seat. "Who cares if it's two o'clock or one fifty-three? For the love of puppies, there's a war happening."

"As you wish, Mrs. Young."

Miss Mayhew turned on her heels and padded back into the house.

"Sakes alive," Mary muttered.

As she sat back down, a strong gust hoisted up a chunk of coif. An impressive feat, given how doggedly Mary plastered it to the side of her face. Finger waves or corrugated metal, there really was no difference. Meanwhile, the very wind also kicked a mostly used ball of yarn into a nearby gooseberry bush.

"Whoops!" Ruby said, and rushed to retrieve it. "If not for the bush, we could've lost that one to the sea."

"More likely the tennis court," Hattie observed.

"Ruby Young Packard," Mary chided. "You need to take more care. We might be under ration soon. Wool doesn't grow on trees."

"Nope. Sheep, I think," Hattie said.

Mary shot daggers at them both. Here was the old Mary, pre–Red Cross style. Pigeons would soon start roosting on her shoulders.

"Mary, just sit down," Ruby said.

Her sister-in-law gasped.

"Oh brother."

"Ruby Packard, as I live and breathe," Mary said. "Look at what you've made! Blankets and socks and knit caps."

She bent to fetch one, appearing quite like a jackknife.

"These are marvelous."

"Well, thank you." Ruby blushed. "I still have room for improvement but at least I've accomplished something."

"Yes, buckets of room for improvement. But I'm tickled! All this time we've been so worried about you."

"Who's 'we'?"

"Oh, you know. Everybody."

Hattie glanced up.

"Worried about her?" she said, jabbing a needle in Ruby's direction. "*Why?*"

"Pish. No one's concerned."

"It's the war." Mary lowered her voice and plopped down onto a nearby ottoman. "Ruby was an isolationist as of last week."

"Not an isolationist," Ruby said. "And I haven't changed my views, necessarily. Dang it! I dropped a stitch! Again!"

"Isolationist, huh?" Hattie smirked. "I didn't take you for that kind of gal."

"Listen, I don't ascribe to one particular notion or another. I simply feel we should be cautious about the issues we get ourselves enmeshed in. More so when our involvement might result in casualties."

"Might result?" Hattie balked. "Might's gone clear out the window, doll. Just ask a European. Especially a queer or a Jew."

"That's quite enough of that talk, Miss Rutter," Mary said. "Let's just be glad that Ruby is finally seeing things in the correct light. I know her husband is pleased as pie."

"My husband?" Ruby said. "And how did you get his take? I don't recall you two exchanging much more than table salt."

Old Talon-hands, Ruby could almost hear Sam say. Her husband was inexorably polite, but Mary Young was not a person whom he could abide. A walking cadaver, he called her. All the charm of a lamppost.

"The information came to me secondhand," Mary said. "Philip met up with Sam and Topper for lunch last week. In Boston. Have you heard the latest? Topper's scratched the naval career concept. He wants to be an airman."

"Hold on." Ruby blinked. "Topper? And Sam? In the same room? Voluntarily and without my aid? This war's good for something, apparently."

"Heavens, Ruby! What a thing to say!"

Just then Miss Macy and Mrs. Brooks pattered out onto the veranda.

"Hello ladies," one of them said. "Your girl runs a right ship. Made us sign some sort of book. Thought she was going to ask for a piece of jewelry as a security deposit."

"That's Mrs. Grimsbury for you," Mary said. "Carries out her orders to the letter. Well, thank you for coming. There's plenty of yarn on the table. Help yourselves."

"So who's this Topper person?" Hattie asked as the women went to choose their yarn. "Lord, what a name. Let me guess, he's some kind of privileged milksop. Thinks the whole world is Harvard and summer homes. Wants to join the war because it sounds romantic but can't tell the difference between a foxhole and the crack in his rear."

"Hey!"

"That's about the gist of it," Mary said.

"Excuse me," Ruby snipped. "Topper is my baby brother. His real name is Robert. He's a senior at Harvard and he's smart and handsome and . . ."

At once an idea formed. A glistening, star-shine of a plan.

Topper *was* smart and handsome. And Hattie Rutter was ideal: gorgeous, well schooled, and with a sly side he'd not be able to resist. In sum, she was the exact kind of girl who could keep a fella from war, even Ruby's little brother, who never stayed locked on one broad for long.

That was the problem, Ruby realized. Topper was anxious for adventure because nothing tethered him to the States. He'd be graduating soon and didn't have a girl or any solid occupational plan. No wonder he wanted to fight. Poor boy needed some meaning in his life.

Ruby cleared her throat.

"Well, the first thing you should know about my brother is that he's handsome as the devil," she said.

"Acts like the devil, besides," Mary added. "And watch out because he'll snap your photo when you least expect it. Lord knows what he does with all the prints. I'm afraid to ask."

"Topper is a gentleman of the highest order!"

"Of the highest order?" Hattie said. "What a shame."

"Ruby can't see it," Mary said. "They're Irish twins, ten months apart, but are like rascally little brothers Mark Twain might write about. Now, if you'll please excuse me, I have more guests to greet."

"Nothing wrong with a rascally sort," Hattie said as Mary walked away. "But you'll need to do better than handsome. Come out with it, Ruby. You've got something cooking in that brain of yours, any fool could see."

"Well, yes," Ruby said, eyes sparking. "I do have a scheme starting to bubble. Here's what I'm thinking. The boys will be in town for the holiday on Tuesday. Why don't we grab a bite together on the first? All of us? At the club?"

"A bite, huh? I s'pose Mary's not on the guest list."

"Well, no. It'd be Topper. And you. And me and Sam."

"Wow," Hattie said, and whistled. "Are arranged marriages still in fashion? Who would've thunk it?"

"No, no, no!" Ruby said, blushing madly. "It's nothing like that. You're a cosmopolitan girl, anyone can tell. I merely suspect the pair of you would get on like wildfire. You're the two most interesting people on the entire blasted island."

Hattie was perfect for Topper, patently perfect!

She possessed the face and the sophistication, with a hint of an adventuress lurking inside. She was basically European, so the proof was right there. If they did eventually marry, Ruby would have to relinquish her title of "Red" to the true redhead in the family. It was a price she'd gladly pay.

"Okay, Rubes," Hattie said. "Why the heck not? I'd be pleased to join you and your brother for dinner. Sounds like a real gas."

21

Tuesday Evening

They'd sat for dinner at the Yacht Club, though Cissy hardly touched her plate.

Her small appetite is customary, a byproduct of the time and effort expended planning and scheming. Cissy's one of those people who proclaims, "I forgot to eat today!" And genuinely means it.

"Cis, are you sure you had enough?" Bess asks as they tromp along the road toward the Public Safety Building, where the Board of Selectmen meets. "It could be a long night."

"Oh, sure! Plenty! That sea bass smelled great, didn't it?"

"What about your clothes?" Bess says. "I'm not sure we have time to run home and change."

Cissy's in her chambray shirt and Red Sox cap and though this is her standard getup, Bess can't help but think her presentation attire needs a boost. Or else she looks fine and the problem is that Bess has enough jitters for both of them.

"Change?" Cissy says. "Why would I want to do that?"

"You look great, but I was thinking of something a little less . . . everyday? It's an important meeting."

"You don't say."

Decidedly peeved with Bess's fashion advice, Cissy accelerates.

"Mom! Hey! Slow down!"

Bess is about to get outrun, she's sure of it. The throngs of people don't help. It isn't even summer and there are already bands of tourists buying whale T-shirts and streams of twenty-year-old drunk dudes lurching out of bars.

"And what do you suggest?" Cissy asks as Bess puffs up behind her. "That I don a loud, colorful tunic and white jeans? No thanks. People know who I am."

"Can't argue with that."

"Not that you won't try."

Cissy stops in front of the Public Safety Building. Hands on hips, she surveys the two-story brick structure, top to bottom. As Bess joins her, she detects the distinct scent of . . . buffet?

"Do you smell something meaty?" Bess asks.

"What?" Cissy turns to her. "Oh, is it the lamb meatballs?" She pops open her knapsack. "I threw in a few, plus a dinner roll. This meeting might run long. I was worried you could get hungry."

"Lamb meatballs? In your purse?"

"Just trying to be prepared. You're so darn testy when you haven't eaten." Cissy wallops Bess on the back. "So. You ready to do this?"

"Do what? I'm simply along for the ride."

"You keep telling yourself that."

Cissy pivots on a Ked and takes three skips forward. Bess straggles up behind her and together they walk through the white wooden door and up the stairs to the second floor, where the meeting will be held.

It's a public hearing and the room is already packed with fifty or sixty Nantucketers, by Bess's estimation. The eight rows of plastic chairs are occupied and spectators have resorted to setting up small encampments throughout the room. At once Bess remembers how blond and pink Nantucket can be. It's a crazy place where a college kid and his grandfather can show up in the same outfit with zero embarrassment. And of course Cissy was right about the caftans.

As the meeting is called to order, nerves rumble through Bess's belly. Just along for the ride? Hardly.

"Hello," says a man, a pink-pants-wearer. "Today we're here to vote on the Sankaty Bluff Storm Damage Prevention Project. The proposal includes the construction of a revetment, a shore-parallel structure designed to protect the land behind it."

The man points to a diagram, which hangs from a nearby wall.

"The structure under consideration is a stone seawall that would extend forty-two hundred feet, or approximately three-quarters of a mile. The project's purpose would be to protect the homes and public infrastructure along Baxter Road and to preserve the historic residential community on Sconset Bluff.

"We have two scheduled speakers today. Mrs. Caroline Codman, president of the Sankaty Bluff Preservation Fund, and coastal geologist Morton Schempler. After they finish we will open the floor to questions and comments. Then we'll dismiss the public, and the Board of Selectmen will vote. Cissy, would you care to start?"

"I'd be delighted!" Cissy says, and jumps to her feet.

She scrambles to the front of the room like she's chasing after a tennis ball. At the podium, she tightens the ponytail poking out through her cap.

"Well, there's not a person in this room who hasn't heard me yammering on about preserving our beautiful bluff. But just in case, my assistant will pass out flyers detailing the pertinent information."

Cissy pauses. Blond and gray heads bounce about, trying to locate the flyers, though most have probably read them. After all, Cissy spent Easter weekend tacking one onto every door on the island.

"*My assistant!*" Cissy booms, and gives Bess a look.

"Oh, me?"

Bess pats her stomach as if the information might be on her.

"In my knapsack, dear."

"Okay. Got it."

Bess retrieves the flyers—which are meat-sauce-free, thank God—and stands to pass them out. Suddenly a body materializes beside her. Without asking, Evan Mayhew takes half the papers from her hand.

"Thanks," Bess mutters.

"And what do we have here?" Cissy warbles. "Even Chappy Mayhew's son is on my side!"

"Uh, I'm only helping Bess."

"Oh I'll bet you're helping her all right. Where's your girl—?"

"*Cis!*" Bess warns, and then waggles her fingers. "Get on with it. We'll pass out the sheets."

"Fine." Cissy exhales as Bess and Evan make their way around the room. "The other members of the Preservation Fund and I truly believe that the historical and natural beauty of the bluff can and *should* be protected to benefit future generations. Our mission is to do this in a scientifically sound and financially viable way."

"Hi Bess," people whisper as she wends her way through old classmates and teachers and Yacht Club pals.

"You look great."

"How's your sister?"

"Baxter Road is the very soul of the bluff," Cissy goes on. "And it's also the road that leads to the iconic Sankaty Head Lighthouse. The street is lined with historic homes and is a crucial part of the island's identity."

"How's the ER business?"

"Your dad still alive and well?"

"As the bluff continues to erode," Cissy says, fixing her glasses so they are more firmly on her face, "Baxter Road is in grave danger. In addition to threatening the homes that are the very fabric of this island's character, the erosion undermines the infrastructure of Sconset itself, putting at risk our water supply and sewage lines."

Bess drops off the last flyer with the manager of their favorite restaurant, the Chanticleer, and backs up against the wall, arms crossed. She watches Evan distribute the rest of his.

"On top of this is the decline in revenue," Cissy says. "Erosion has already caused the loss of over sixty million dollars' worth of property. Sixty millions' worth of this island's tax base. And the number is increasing as we speak. Every day we lose more cubic feet of our beloved land."

Bess's head jolts up. Every day? As in *all the days*? Cissy glossed over this key detail. Damn that woman. So good at what she does. Professional rabble-rouser and sneaky, sly fox.

"Nantucket is a special place," Cissy continues, "and Sconset is a major reason why. Picture the narrow lanes. The charm of the rose-covered cottages. Beautiful Sankaty Head Light. Not to mention the houses, the historic homes with stories to tell. Homes with family memories, *island* memories locked inside."

As Cissy's voice bubbles with emotion, Bess finds herself growing weepy-eyed, too. She pushes away her tears and looks up to find Evan watching her. Bess glances away, pretending not to see.

At last Cissy wraps up her speech with a few more mentions of "character fabric," followed by a slide show featuring the homes that could be lost if they don't act. She hasn't put Cliff House in the show but the Mayhew place is "best for last," which elicits a brief Cissy-Chappy fracas until someone removes them from the floor.

"My house isn't going anywhere," Chappy calls, his parting shot. "Except up in value when it has a panoramic ocean view!"

"I'm surprised you're paid by pound of fish, and not by pound of horseshit."

Checkmate, Chappy Mayhew. Cissy got the last word after all.

"Ladies and gentlemen, I'll be concise."

Geologist Morton Schempler appears at the podium, shuffling along like a prison warden or the losing football coach. It's evident he doesn't have the patience for town rivalries or neighbors with agendas. No thanks on shrill grandmothers, either. These people paid for a study, not a speech, and he's not keen to stick around.

"This revetment project is a horrible idea," he says, straight off, from the spot where Cissy stood minutes before. "You'll see on the screen dozens of projects that have used walls exactly like those proposed by the Preservation Fund. And every single one has failed. Hard armoring has been proven ineffective multiple times, in a variety of situations. All it does is give a false sense of security to property owners and create further deterioration of the surrounding beaches."

"Well, this is uplifting," Bess mumbles to Evan, who is now beside her.

He replies with a snicker, an almost-secret laugh, like he doesn't want to be caught.

"Constructs like these," Schempler continues, "protect only the land immediately behind them, with no protection offered to the fronting beach. Ultimately, this causes ever more erosion and you'd have to keep building more walls to buttress the beaches. The beaches would continue to worsen, therefore necessitating—you guessed it—more walls. It's a vicious cycle and the long-term costs would far exceed the funds of any public or private sponsors. I won't bore you with a bunch of scientific gobbledygook as the formula is really quite basic. Hard structures plus water equals no beach. Thank you for your time."

Morton folds up a piece of paper, then tucks it into the back of his Dockers before advancing straight out the door. He's not going to stick around, because what could anyone say? The look on his face is this: Either you're with him, or you're dumb as a seawall.

Approximately ninety seconds later, the selectmen dismiss the public from the meeting. Everyone files outside.

In front of the building, islanders exchange hellos. Cissy makes a snide comment about Morton Schempler's skin tone and throws her car keys at Bess. She'll hoof it the eight miles home, through the mist and the chill. She needs time to think.

Back at the Public Safety Building, away from the eyes of the townsfolk, the selectmen sit down to vote on the Sankaty Bluff Storm Damage Prevention Project, revetment version. They've promised to announce the decision by midnight. Bess doesn't even stay up, because the result seems clear. Poor Cis. If your own daughter won't buy what you're selling, it doesn't look good.

22

Island ACKtion

TOWN SELECTMEN KNOCK DOWN HARD ARMOR PROJECT

May 21, 2013

Well, damn it. Cissy Codman couldn't work her magic. There's a first for everything.

After a year's worth of work, a year's worth of research, and hired experts, and God knows how many millions of dollars, the Board of Selectmen struck down Cissy Codman's Damage Prevention Project by a vote of 4–1.

Both sides presented compelling cases. There was charm and history and storied homes on one hand, erosion on the other. The proposed measures will do more harm than good, a geologist told the group. And so the no's prevailed.

"Sounds like one seawall really means two, which means ten or more," says one selectman, who wishes to remain anonymous. "Where does it end?"

Where does it end, indeed. According to Cissy, not here.

"The battle isn't over," she says. "There are other options."

More options. Fantastic. Can we go back to reporting on celebrity sightings and white parties?

As for Cissy, rumor has it she will finally move out of Cliff House, within the next twenty-four hours no less. It's a temporary situation, she claims, until she has a chance to relocate the home a few yards off the bluff.

To date, we here at *Island ACKtion* have not expressed a viewpoint on the proposal but let's say this. We love living in a place where a fired-up Cissy Codman exists. But it does seem like the most logical conclusion was reached. RIP Cliff House. You will be missed.

ABOUT ME:
Corkie Tarbox, lifelong Nantucketer, steadfast flibbertigibbet. Married with one ankle-biter. Views expressed on the *Island ACKtion* blog (Twitter, Facebook, Instagram, et al.) are hers alone. Usually.

23

The Book of Summer

Harriet E. Rutter
June 30, 1941
The Venerable Cliff House

I found this darling book today as I brambled about Cliff House, waiting for Ruby to conclude some verbal dust-up with her little brother, the erstwhile "Topper." They were haggling about the war or some such. Those two. Like twins, without the telepathy or mutual understanding.

I've had grand fun ticking through these pages, reading about guests past. It's so quaint, so charming, so very New World. It makes me adore these people all the more. I hope they write in this book for a hundred years to come.

Anyhow, these days everyone's all a-flutter about the upcoming 4th of July theatrics. There'll be no fireworks this year, more's the pity, but I suppose enough bombs are going off for now. Instead they'll host some sort of water carnival and a sky parade. The paper said they plan to drop animals, clowns, and fish from a plane. Clowns from a plane? This must be a typesetter's error but oh how I pray that it's not!

The spectacle will be followed by a Yacht Club dance, which Ruby expects me to attend with her brother, provided tomorrow's dinner goes as she dreams. Oh that Topper Young. Poor kid. Rumor does paint him as a suave and handsome sort but I doubt he'll relish his big sister's assistance in matters of the heart. Either way, I'll make sure we all enjoy some fun this summer. That much I can guar-an-tee.

Until later, I remain, yours truly,
Hattie R.

24

RUBY
July 1941

As they sat in the dining room of the Yacht Club, Hattie Rutter glowed and crackled like a blaze. Her hair, her cheeks, her lips, all a fireball brand of red. She had on a dress, God love her, a maize Parisian number so impeccably tailored she'd make a military fella look a wreck. And beneath it all, breasts that were high and full like a moon over water. Ruby longed to quiz Hattie about the specifics of her foundations—she could do with a little perk-up herself—but it was too crass, even for the summer and the beach.

Plus, there were things more pressing than the pertness of one's breasts. For all of Ruby's talk about Topper's dash, his suave bewitchery, the man was seriously rough. Possibly hungover. Like he was going to capsize.

Topper's hair was greasy and matted, his face sweaty and pale. He spoke in the rambling, slurred manner of a drunken vagrant as he smoked cigarette after cigarette, barely letting one extinguish before taking flame to the next. Not even Ruby could ferret out the handsome devil within him and she always saw the best in her brother, as a rule. It was a wonder Hattie hadn't excused herself to the ladies' and wiggled out the window.

"I can't believe FDR still thinks we can stay out of this war," Topper said.

"He doesn't *think* we can, he *hopes* we can," Sam returned. "Two different things."

Ruby's husband and brother were pecking at each other like a couple of roosters. Something about the recently announced Russian invasion. Bolsheviks. Two equally hateful countries duking it out until their deaths. Ruby took a few slugs of her sloe gin fizz to stave off an encroaching headache.

"Nothing," Topper said, mindlessly tapping his fingers as he stared out at the harbor. "We're doing nothing. Bunch of yellow-bellied pansies."

"Speaking of yellow, what's that color you're wearing, Hattie?" Ruby asked, trying to direct the conversation back toward the prettiest dame in the room. "Would you call it a Naples yellow? It sure is nifty!"

She was awkward as hell, but Ruby had to do *something*.

"Huh." Hattie shrugged. "Never thought to check. I just call it my yellow dress from France."

"Well, you look sensational," Ruby said, and meant it.

Hattie Rutter's fashion sense was bar none, yet she always seemed desperately clueless about it. "My yellow dress," for Pete's sake. Hattie had a gift, an innate gift. Style spilled right onto her.

"Whaddya think, fellas?" Ruby asked. "Isn't Hattie just beyond?"

"Now's the time to strike," Topper said. "While Hitler's focused on Russia."

"*Boys*."

Ruby slammed both palms on the table and rose to partial standing. The men startled, and every adjacent party turned to stare. With a mad blush, Ruby slowly lowered herself back down. Mother would hear about this within the hour and likely have her head.

"Can you please," Ruby said between gritted teeth. "Can you please, for the love of all that is holy, shut up about Hitler and pay our new friend the slightest respect? Every man in this cotton-pickin' joint developed a puppy crush on her before the salads were out. What's wrong with you two? Communists and Nazis, when this stunner's at our table. For the love of God."

"Oh, golly, Ruby," Hattie said after a giggle and a gulp of gin. "You're sweet as hell, but you don't need to come to my defense."

"It's not about your defense. The point is . . ."

Ruby sighed. What was the point, exactly?

"I just wish these two imbeciles would stop jawing for a second and appreciate the scene that's in front of them."

"Honey," Sam said, and placed a hand gently on Ruby's knee. "I appreciate you like nothing else. No two ways about it."

"Yeah, Red. Don't take it so personal." Topper's eyes zipped all over the table, every which way but up. "Your friend's a real doll. A dish times two. Sorry, Miss Rutter. We're a mite single-minded at present. When the entire world is on the precipice . . ."

"Don't think a bug about it," Hattie said. "These are serious times."

Topper gave her a quick salute and turned to get a better shot at Sam.

"We can't wait around for Russia and Germany to destroy each other," Topper said.

"No use getting emotional about it, old sport. FDR will dip his toes into this pool, by and by. But we need to be rational. Measured."

"Measured?" Topper balked. "Wrong. We should send every goddamned tank, bomber, and able-bodied man overseas *tomorrow*. Hitler's already wiped out an entire generation. He's bankrupted the art and culture of Paris, London, and Rome. Fifty million people are starving, and that doesn't even count the ones dying in forced labor camps. How many more countries will we let fall? How many people will die before we step in?"

"I'm telling you, we'll step in," Sam said. "Eventually. But it has nothing to do with saving folks halfway across the globe and everything to do with saving ourselves."

"It must hurt to be that cynical and dead inside."

"Topper!" Ruby chirped.

"No, no, it's fine." Sam patted Ruby's knee again. "Your brother likes to shoot off. That's his entire persona. Robert. You have to understand, this is about dominance and clout. The balance of power in Europe is the very reason the United States has reached its superpower status. And now that it's threatened?" Sam blubbered his lips and took a drag of his cigarette. "We're all up shit creek. Even Thomas Jefferson once fretted about what might happen if Europe operated under a single hand. This isn't about ideals. It's about maintaining our strength. And any action that threatens our formidable military force must be carefully considered."

"Maybe to save the world we need to sacrifice our own."

"Honestly Topper," Ruby said. "Is this appropriate dinner conversation? Killing our countrymen?"

"You can't look away," Topper said. "Not even for a good meal, especially when others are going hungry."

Ruby glowered at him.

"Half the stuff they print about the starvation and labor camps is fabricated," Sam said. "Yellow journalism through and through, designed to tug at the heartstrings of impressionable students such as yourself. This country's education system is turning out a bunch of pantywaists."

"Good grief, Sam," Ruby said. "You only graduated two years ago."

"Don't get me wrong," Sam went on, ignoring his wife. "Things aren't peachy, but the papers embellish."

With a scoff, Topper chucked his napkin onto his plate, which was still piled with meat. Ruby went to remove the discarded linen but found it already mottled with gravy. She glanced at Hattie and detected the hint of a smile, one eyebrow ever-so-slightly raised. What must she be thinking? Nothing good. She hadn't said a word.

"Well, I've read," Ruby said, trying to remove the stains from Topper's napkin with the corner of hers, "the folks in the camps are being treated well. They're even allowed to observe their religious practices without harassment."

Topper snorted.

"I'm sure reports from Der Führer are as reliable as a drunk."

He turned back toward Sam.

"We are all of us humans in this world. We should protect each other, not worry about arbitrary lines drawn by dead men or our own preeminence. Hitler is pure evil. He must be eradicated."

"He is evil, I agree, but . . ."

"Stop it, you two!" Ruby barked, letting go of the last smidgen of pretense that the night could be saved. "We're supposed to be having a nice dinner but you blockheads ruined it. Bolsheviks. A war we're not even in. Hitler—at the dinner table! You boys are the worst! The positive end of good manners! Good Lord, Hattie, I am so very sorry. They are not normally this repellent."

"Aw, don't sweat it, Ruby," Hattie said with a chuckle.

She leaned over and snaffled a smoke from Topper's pack. Hattie preferred French cigarettes, always at the ready with a package of Gauloises, but a lowbrow American brand could do in a pinch.

"I don't mind talk of war," Hattie said. "It's more real than a Yacht Club romance, that's for certain."

"You shred it, wheat," Topper said in approval.

Ruby blushed furiously and set to attacking her salad.

"But I have a question for you, our dear and oh-so-educated menfolk," Hattie said.

She gave a cute smirk, and then sucked deeply on her cigarette. They all waited as Hattie exhaled over her shoulder, the smoke curling away in a seductive dance. As Ruby scanned the room, she noted every man in the place trying to catch a peek of this magnificent and rare bird.

"What about the Iceland rumors?" Hattie asked, honoring the table with her attentions once again.

"Iceland?" Ruby said, thoroughly flummoxed.

"Sorry if I sound ivory-tower about the whole deal, but I've been cut off from the real world these days, truth be told."

"That's exactly how it's supposed to be on Nantucket," Ruby groused.

Anyway, women weren't supposed to be so politically charged. At Smith the only ones who moaned about politics were the bespectacled, down-at-the-heels pinko types. The gals with no beaux and tragic hair.

"Why would we send troops to Iceland?" Hattie asked. "Seems like a real crummy place to me. What would Nazis want with it, if the gossip's true?"

"Iceland is a stepping-stone," Sam explained. "An important stop between Europe and the States, as the Vikings demonstrated."

"The Germans are Vikings," Hattie said. "Got it."

"But Hitler says he has no interest in our part of the world!" Ruby blurted out.

"Oh, Jesus H.," Topper said. "Ruby. Please stop taking Hitler at his word."

"It's not that I believe him, it's only that he must have his hands full so why . . ."

"His hands are full with Russia, which is why we should strike now!"

"A German occupation of Iceland would be highly strategic," Sam interjected. "The Brits have been stationed there but are moving their troops to the Continent. People think FDR is going to offer up some replacements. It'd be a way to aid Britain without jumping all in."

"Why can't he send troops to Iceland *and* to Europe?" Topper said. "We've got plenty of men in this country anxious to help."

"For example . . ." Sam said, gesturing toward Topper and rolling his eyes.

"You boys are aces," Hattie said with a cackle. "Big fun."

"Speaking of big fun!"

Dang it all to hell, Ruby wasn't going to give up yet. Hattie must've met some real charmers in Europe to withstand Topper and Sam for so long a stint.

"It's buckets of fun," Ruby said, "to watch Hattie play tennis. She whips that ball around almost as deftly as she can knit a pair of booties. We've entered the Independence Day tournament together. Won't that be a hoot? I think we've got a decent shot at top prize."

"Swell, swell," Topper said, lighting yet another cigarette, though one was still fuming and pinched between his teeth. "If we do go to Iceland, it just proves that we don't actually care about helping the Allies. We care about protecting ourselves."

"Nothing wrong with protecting ourselves," Sam said. "The initial deployment has to go *somewhere*. This is good as any."

"I'm sure Londoners and Parisians will sleep better at night knowing we're in damned Iceland, cutting up with Eskimos and so on."

"You're thinking of Alaska. And it's save ourselves first, sport."

Topper grunted and flicked his cigarette. It skittered into Hattie's shrimp salad.

"Robert!"

Ruby leapt to her feet. This time she didn't care who was watching.

"Your manners are abysmal! Mother would be horrified. I'm horrified. Hattie, Miss Rutter, I'm so extremely sorry. I'd offer an excuse but I can't think of a decent one."

"Ah, shucks, it's no problem whatsoever." Hattie plucked the butt from her plate with her perfectly manicured fingertips. "This is the most excitement I've seen at the Yacht Club to date. And if you can't get your hackles raised by a war"—she tucked the cigarette inside a napkin—"then you don't have a pulse to start."

"She gets it." Topper crooked a thumb in her direction. "The woman gets it."

"You're a good sport, Miss Rutter," Sam said. "And Robert over here is most sorry. Their mother wasted all her energy in raising the older three. Gave up when she got to the fourth. He was too much of a project."

"Sam is full of tommyrot, but I *am* truly sorry," Topper said. He extended an arm across the table. "Friends?"

"Friends." Hattie shook his hand and extinguished her own cigarette. "And no apology necessary. I quite enjoy a political tussle. But just so we're clear, Mr. Young. Robert. Topper. Whatever they call you. You keep mentioning London and Paris, but there is more to Europe than these two cities."

"Of course, but I . . ."

"And I'm alarmed that you don't seem to know this."

As Topper tried to mask his pale-faced, dropped-mouth look of shock, Ruby smiled. Hattie did not act like a Hulbert Avenue type at all. Maybe this night wouldn't prove such a bust. Maybe Topper had finally met his match. There was hope in their little crew yet.

The Nantucket High School band kicked off the parade.

Ruby felt a swirly thrill with the boom of the bass drum and the first tentative clangs of the instruments, most of them poorly played but darn spirited nonetheless.

All along Main Street and its cobblestone byways, from the red-bricked, white-pillared Pacific Bank at its head to the Rotch warehouse at its foot, people waved paper flags as American Legion floats rolled past.

Ruby and her family were smushed together on the sidewalk with hundreds of Nantucketers and off-islanders alike. To Ruby's left was Mother, to her right was Mary. Behind them stood Daddy, his presence tall and firm. He'd been ill, unsure if he would make the trip out. Poor man had been working like a beast lately, retooling his facilities to handle gas masks instead of golf balls.

As for the other boys, Topper and Sam and P.J., they were having a few preparade pops at the Moby Dick. They promised to show up before it was over, but any pledge by Topper might as well have been made in sand, mainly where whiskey was involved.

"What a sight, eh petal?" Dad said, and squeezed Ruby's shoulder. "Best Independence Day parade yet."

She turned to smile, squinting with the too-bright sun, the brilliance of the trees and moors and heather. They'd opened Cliff House weeks ago but finally it was summer.

"It's the tops," Ruby said, blinking into the sunlight. "An absolute A plus."

Daddy smiled and gave her another squeeze. Ruby turned back toward the street to watch as Lord and Lady Marley of England motored by. Their appearance in the parade had been Big News on the island, but who or what they were Ruby didn't exactly know. It sounded fancy enough, which was probably the very purpose of them.

Ruby glanced toward the opposite sidewalk in time to see Hattie stroll up. She was with a pack of girls, a couple of familiar faces, though no one Ruby knew personally. Hulbert Avenue dames, no doubt. Ruby and Hattie caught eyes and exchanged smiles and waves.

Hattie was still in that morning's tennis togs, but Ruby had changed into a shirtwaist dress, partly because of Hattie herself. When Ruby tossed on her tennis costume that morning—crisp white shorts and a tab-necked blouse—she thought herself pretty danged sporty-slick. She even gave a little strut for the benefit of her husband, who had been reading the paper on the veranda.

"Why, look at you!" Sam had said. "You're cute as a bug's ear."

Ruby left the house tra-la-la-ing and feeling nifty, at least until Hattie meandered up in a midi skirt, nipped and pinched in all the right places. The getup was somehow old-fashioned and modern at the same time, and most assuredly direct from Paris to boot. Très chic, Hattie Rutter's customary status.

"Ready for the semis?" Hattie had asked, and stubbed out her cigarette on a bench. "Let's blast them to Hades."

Their opponents stood on the other side of the net, gawping at the pair.

With chic playing the ad side, and schoolgirl playing the deuce, Hattie and Ruby won their match (7–6, 6–4) against the prior year's champs. One was athletic and violent, prone to slamming balls at opponents' bellies. The other was pretty but dim. On the beam but off the bean, as they said.

Hattie and Ruby were to face a new team in the finals at four o'clock. They'd miss the annual fisherman-postman tug-of-war as well as the various eating contests (doughnuts, pies, apples). But if Ruby had the chance at a trophy, by golly she'd go after it. Lord knew she'd never get one trying to take down a plate of pie.

"There's your doubles partner," Mother said, and leaned close. "She's quite the looker."

"That she is," Ruby said with a nod. "Actually, I've been trying to set her up with Topper. I think they'd make a smashing pair."

"Topper?" Mother screwed up her face. "Why, it's hard to think of him settling down. He just plumb doesn't seem interested."

"That's one way to put it," Daddy grumbled.

"Oh! Look!" Mary called. "Here come the Red Cross ladies!"

"The way I see it," Ruby said to her mom, "Hattie Rutter might very well be the one to lock Topper into place."

Lock him into a country, she did not add.

"Perhaps," Mother said. "But I would hate for my fiendish son to waste the poor girl's time. She must have a line of suitors a mile long."

"She does. But is anyone more dashing than Tops?"

"Philip Junior," Mary offered as she kept her eyes glued to the Red Cross float and its six-foot-tall papier-mâché hypodermic needle.

"P.J. is darling," Mother said unconvincingly. "Well, I'm anxious to watch the two of you cream the Coffin sisters at four, sharp." She wiggled her brows. "Those girls don't stand a chance."

"What about you, love?" Daddy said, and gave Mother a soft pinch to her side. "Surely you can bring home a trophy or two, just like the old days."

"Oh please. My tennis is rustier than the weather vane on our roof."

"No, I was thinking along the lines of . . . let me see . . . By Jove, I have it!" Daddy snapped his fingers. "The rolling-pin-throwing contest. I've seen you exhibit great skill in that department. The other night, when I came home late from work, for example."

"Malarkey," Mother said, giggling as she squirmed away from him. "I *brandished* the rolling pin. I didn't throw it. You interrupted my baking."

"Likely story."

"Who could blame me? You tinker in that factory fourteen hours at a go. I barely know what you look like in the daylight. How is it that we've had so many kids? Better check with the milkman!"

Mary turned around, her mouth fallen in horror.

"Mother Young!" she yipped. "I've never heard such a crude remark!"

"Because you married the boring one," Ruby said.

As both of Ruby's parents laughed, Mary took several very deliberate steps away from them.

When Ruby turned to look at Daddy, she noticed Mother clinging to his arm as tears puddled.

"Ma?" Ruby said, tentatively. "Are you all right?"

"I've never been better. This island. My family. Cliff House. It makes me full, finally and at last."

Ruby flinched. Her mother's mind had drifted to Walter, as it so often did. The second son had been Sarah's favorite. He was kind and handsome and whip-smart. Walter committed but one error in life, a first mistake that would also be his last. Late one night, with too much hooch diluting his blood, Walter Young drove a carful of girls into a tree a quarter mile from the Dartmouth campus. The girls survived but Walter did not.

It'd been five years and the family hardly talked about the middle brother anymore. But Ruby still saw Walter, every once in a while, lingering between her parents. Usually, though, his ghost stayed in Boston. No one brought thoughts of him into summer.

"Nantucket is the best," Ruby said, aspiring to keep her mother's spirits high. "I can't imagine life without Cliff House."

Mother smiled, though her eyes continued to tear.

"It's everything I dreamed of when I asked your father to build it." Mother's tears were streams now, the puddles moved on. "And you know what? It keeps getting better. Because next year we'll stand in this very spot, together. And the year after we'll stand again. Soon there will be babies in our home and at this parade, clutching American flags in their chubby precious hands."

Mother sighed and Daddy wrapped one arm around her.

"Sometimes I think the world is so scary and hopeless," Mother said. "And getting worse by the day. But when our family is together in Sconset, it makes me believe that in the end, everything will turn out precisely as it should."

"Well, here they are. Everyone please put your hands together for the Ladies' Doubles Champions of the Nantucket Yacht Club."

Topper clapped wildly and took a deep bow. He kissed Ruby's hand, followed by Hattie's, then whipped out his Rolleiflex. As Topper set his camera down, Ruby saw his eyes dawdle on Hattie, as well they should. She was a one-hundred-percent-certified knockout in a silk ivory dress with ruffles cascading toward the floor.

"Champs," Hattie said with a grin. Her nose was slightly sunburned. "That's us. But, shhhh, don't tell the rag mags. We don't want to get mobbed by the press or our hordes of adoring fans."

"Your secret's safe with me."

Topper flung the camera over his shoulder and placed a hand over his heart.

"And as for you, little brother," Ruby said. "You cut a dashing figure. I'm glad to see it's not all snips and snails and puppy-dog tails with you."

"Thank you, Madame."

He took another bow, and then flipped the tails of his tuxedo as if they were feathers.

"I can gin up okay."

Ruby exhaled, only just then realizing she'd been holding her breath. Gee whiz, Topper sure looked and sounded loads better than the last time they'd all been in that ballroom together. Ruby thanked her lucky stars.

"Alas my countenance could never match that of a one Miss Rutter or a Missus Packard," he said. "You two dames have already stolen the show and it hasn't even begun."

"You snake charmer, you," Ruby said. "Speaking of Packards, where'd my husband run off to?"

"He's chatting with the valet. I lost interest and wandered off to find you."

He reached into his coat.

"Care for a cig, Miss Rutter?" He extended an engraved silver case in her direction. "I picked up some Gauloises on your recommendation."

"Glad I could spread the good word." Hattie snagged one. "I admire a man who takes my advice."

Philip Junior and Mary strolled up then, looking agreeable if not both slightly put out. He was acceptably dapper and she was elegant, for an old stodge anyhow. It was amazing how half a decade could turn a pretty, white-gloved deb into an ordinary Boston low-heeler. Then again, Mary's heels had never been that high, even when she wore the gloves. But Ruby had to give it to her. Mary did look mighty swell that night, years shaved off her in a jiff.

"Holy Moses!" Ruby said, and gave her sister-in-law a squeeze. It was easier to have compassion toward Mary after a few swigs of gin. "That's some dress. Gorge as can be. Would you call that a wisteria blue?"

Maybe the gal had a bit of the va-va-voom in her yet.

"Er, um, I'm not sure," Mary said, straightening her skirt. "I suppose you'd know better than I."

"Hello, Ruby," P.J. said, and gave his sister a tin-man embrace.

He nodded toward Hattie, a bob of acknowledgment.

"Hello there," he said.

"You really are a hot numbah," Hattie said to Mary, and took a suck on her cigarette. "Simply de-vine. Thank God they haven't rationed our good fabrics like over in Europe."

"Not yet," Topper said. "It's only a matter of time."

"And how."

Hattie took another drag and Topper slipped her a wink of appreciation, a gesture caught by Ruby alone. She beamed at the two of them.

"Hey now," Topper said. "Whaddya say we shake a leg and head outside? The water carnival and sky parade are due to start."

"Three parades in one day." Hattie shook her head and laughed. "And a tennis competition. This is some kind of town. Buzz off, ya stupid war!"

"Well, actually," Ruby said. "The sky parade is in lieu of the traditional fireworks in respect for . . ."

"T'hell with all of it!" Hattie prattled on. "We don't need any of that wretched business marring our sweet island."

"No siree!" Topper said, joining in. "I personally would rather think about lights on a boat than Stalin's scorched-earth policy. Come; let's find a place in line. A bad spot would be the true tragedy."

He took Hattie's hand and led her outside. Ruby's heart lifted as if the hand was hers. Though they were bantering about the stupid war, they were clearly enjoying the party, and each other.

"Shall we go, darling?" P.J. asked, petting Mary's slender arm. "We don't want to get a sucker's seat and miss the show."

"Very well," Mary said with a sigh. "Are you coming, Ruby?"

"Ummm . . ."

Ruby glanced toward the door, surprised to be suddenly frowning. "Actually," she said, "I'll wait for Sam. We'll be out in a minute."

"Fine." Mary sighed again. "But don't ask us to save you a spot."

The water carnival was no joke.

Every boat at the club was decked out in red, white, and blue minilights. A band played from a flotilla in the harbor while searchlights bounced between the land and sky. Colored flares lined the shores.

"Golly, what a scene!" Ruby cried, leaning more tightly against Sam.

He stood behind her, arms secured around her waist. Every once in a while, he nuzzled her neck and hair.

"Get a load of all the people!" Ruby said. "They're dancing everywhere!"

"It's a scene and a half," Sam agreed.

With a smile on her face, Ruby picked through the crowd with her eyes. Surely somewhere in the middle of the festivities were Hattie and Topper. She grinned wider just to think of it.

"Oh, Sammy."

Ruby spun around to face him, tucking both arms beneath his.

"Isn't this night the tops? The laughter, the lights, the air itself. I'll never be able to breathe enough of it in."

She looked up at her husband, expectantly, but Sam didn't answer right away. And in that flicker Ruby noticed his eyes. They were glassy, on another plane. Just like Mother's when she was thinking of Walter. Ruby's stomach dropped.

"Sammy?"

"The night's grand, baby. Simply grand."

He pulled her snug and rested his chin atop her head.

"You're a light in this life, Rubes," he said, his voice vibrating against her cheek. "There's not a soul like you in all of Massachusetts. All of the world, I'd venture."

With a happy little shudder, Ruby tried to catch his eyes.

"Tonight," she said. "I'm thinking . . . tonight seems so filled with magic. So perfect and ripe. Perhaps now it all comes together."

"What comes together?" Sam asked, crinkling his forehead.

"Tonight's the ideal night to make a baby."

Ruby blinked and at once Sam's eyes went from glassy to full-out wet. Though Ruby's peepers were plenty damp themselves, she understood at once that his tears were a different type.

"What is it?" she said, trying not to snivel. "You seem . . . sad. . . . Something's wrong. Please don't rain on my parade." Ruby pointed to the harbor and then to the sky. "Either one of them!"

"Parades." Sam shook his head. "That's the whole problem, Rubes. Here we are acting jolly and carefree and an ocean away . . . Your brother is right."

"Last I remember, you two weren't exactly meeting minds on the topic. Lord almighty, can we avoid the war business for one night? One measly night?"

He gave a watery little smirk.

"Avoid the war?" he said. "An ironic request given it's Independence Day."

"Har har, very funny."

"I wasn't trying to be funny."

"Samuel Packard." Ruby drew him close, pulling his body flush with hers. "You can go back to fussing about Nazism tomorrow. For tonight, let's focus on children, and the nifty time we can have making them."

Ruby wanted a baby, a miraculous creation that was hers and Sam's alone. But there was more to her wish. A little nugget would render Sam 3-A: a man with a dependent and therefore draft-deferred. Ruby had been studying that damned chart since it came into effect days before. She was downright bedeviled with noodling out where each person she loved might fall.

"Whaddya say?" Ruby gave him a nudge. "Do we have a deal, sport?"

Sam chuckled dryly. A searchlight passed over his dark and handsome face, and Ruby felt a kick to her heart. Just like her Smith pals used to say, he was movie-star gorgeous, one hundred percent.

"Sam?" Ruby said, tentatively.

"I'd love to have babies," he said, returning his gaze to hers. "I'd love ten of them!"

"Well, now that sounds excessive. We're not Catholic."

"But we can't start a family yet. It's a scary world and I don't want to bring an innocent babe into it. Things must settle down first."

"*Settle down?!* That could take years!"

"That it could," he agreed.

"I want to start our lives *now*. Why must we wait for the outcome of some skirmish in Europe?"

"Ruby, I want a family. I do. But . . ."

Sam's words petered out and his entire body slumped. He looked like he was carrying a heavy load that only he could see.

"You're not going to enlist, are you?" Ruby said, breath clambering around her chest. "Sam, you can't. I know you want to help, and your heart is the biggest thing going, but only a crazy person would enlist. Someone who is well and truly bonkers."

"Nearly twenty million men registered for the draft last year," he said. "So it's not that crazy. Now we all *have* to register, Ruby. Every last one of us."

"Then register! But wait to be called. You don't go over there until they ask you to. Oh, God!" Ruby threw her head back. "You're going to do it, aren't you? You want to leave me for a fight."

"Ruby." Sam clamped his hands around hers. "I don't want to leave, but it feels as though I should. Like a calling."

"Then go over already," Ruby said with a sniff.

"It's not that simple. There's you, of course."

"Of course." Ruby sniffed again and rolled her eyes.

"And to be honest . . . to be absolutely frank . . . I'm not sure I have it in me to fight. I'm afraid I'm not man enough."

Ruby remained silent because, really, what could she say?

She didn't agree—Sam was the best man she'd ever known—but Ruby was hardly compelled to convince him that he was combat-ready.

So without a word, Ruby embraced her husband and then turned back around just as the first plane appeared. A second joined it. Soon birds and animals and fish began fluttering down onto the boats, restaurants, and the merry people twirling in the streets. It was literally raining good cheer but all Ruby could think was, *Damn, that'll be a wreck to clean up.*

"Don't let the cat out of the bag just yet," Mary said, an unaccustomed punch to her step as the three women walked down the road toward Sconset Casino.

It was late morning. The fog still hung round the shore; the briny air was damp and dense.

"What cat is this?" Ruby asked, cinching her coat.

"I've secured Gracie Fields for the August fund-raiser!"

"Gracie Fields, the actress?" Hattie said. "She's fab. I saw her once in Paris and twice in London. The poor woman has cervical cancer and she's hauling herself all the way out to Sconset? Good gravy, Mary. That's quite the coup. The Red Cross should be payin' ya by the hour."

"Yes, well, thank you," Mary said, as buoyed as she'd ever been. "I have truly put my full heart into the Grey Ladies but I'm not doing it for money or even recognition."

"Obviously you're not doing it for the money," Hattie said with a snort. "A Bostonian never does. You know what they say, wholesale charity and retail penury. It's not a Back Bay soirée unless you're raising money for something whilst not spending a pretty penny on yourself."

"And what do you know of it?" Mary carped.

"Oh, I know plenty. My stepmom is just your type. Swear to beetles, she's chomping at the bit for rations to go into effect. Government-ordered austerity. She's way ahead of the game with her decades of practice."

They walked a few more yards in silence. Ruby wondered if she should step in the middle of the back-and-forth but decided to keep her feet clean.

"I'm curious," Mary said with a cut to her voice. "What is it you're doing here, in Nantucket? Your family is from Boston, but you're from, where exactly?"

"Beats me," Hattie said with a shrug. "For a while, I would've told you Europe, but that's the stuff of yesteryear, courtesy of that pesky Hitler turd. Now I'm stuck at Pop's house. I guess I'm not from anywhere at the moment. Just hangin' round, seeing what's what. Getting conned into setups with handsome young Harvard men."

"Five dates!" Ruby chirped. "But who's counting?"

"I think someone is, but it's not me or Topper."

As Hattie playfully elbowed Ruby's side, Mary stopped dead in her tracks, the gravel rolling beneath her Robeez sandals.

"So let me get this straight," she said, eyes burrowing into Hattie's face. "You're just . . . *idling*?"

"That's the long and short of it, I suppose. Listen, sometimes a gal's gotta idle."

"Hear, hear," Ruby said.

"But surely you have *somewhere* to be when the summer ends," Mary pressed. "No one stays on the island save the fishermen and Quakers. You don't have a job, I presume."

"I did, at a magazine in Paris. But they canceled my contract."

Hattie chucked her cigarette into the road and reached for another, only to find she was all tapped out. She whipped out a packet of Wrigley's.

"Want one?"

She passed a stick Ruby's way.

"I don't understand," Mary said.

"Geez, back off," Ruby said. "Before this Bundles for Britain deal you weren't exactly lighting the world on fire with your industry."

"Aw, sweet Rubes," Hattie said with a cluck. "Always coming to my defense. I don't mind the question. Honestly, Mary, I haven't a clue what I'll do next. Ain't it grand? So many options to consider. Now." She clomped one foot on the ground. "Shall we proceed? The badminton fund-raiser's not gonna run itself."

She linked arms with Ruby, and even with old Mare, and together the girls continued down the road.

25

Wednesday Afternoon

After the vote, Cissy takes her disappointment and vanishes into the fog, that famous grey lady.

Bess would've worried that her mom never made it back from the meeting but, thank the Lord, there's solid evidence of Cissy's comings and goings. A swapped-out ball cap. The Young Family windbreaker discarded on a chair. Fresh bike tracks in the mud.

It's small comfort because, truth be told, Bess is pissed off. She can't even track down the woman, as Cissy is about as reliable with her phone as Palmer Bradlee. Bess calls her mother repeatedly, but the kitchen counter never picks up.

"Yes. Absolutely," Cissy said when Bess asked if she'd leave Cliff House after the vote.

Sure. After the vote. Pinky swear.

Alas, they're no closer to moving than when Bess arrived on the scene. Ninety-nine years of stuff, with only about six months of it packed. What is kept or what goes into the green Dumpster her dad ordered should be Cissy's call, not Bess's. To speak nothing of the sheer manpower needed. It'd taken Bess two full days to haul her crap out of the San Francisco place and she'd lived there five years, with one other person, and most of it she left behind.

Cliff House, on the other hand, is a veritable museum of all things Young-Packard-Codman. This "house of women" is stocked to the gills with artwork and jewelry and old clothes. There are papers and books and crystal bottles of amber-colored perfume. One drawer reveals an old camera and scrapbooks filled with articles written by a Harriet Rutter. The name is familiar. It's sprinkled throughout the book, though not in any meaningful way.

"Oh, Cis," Bess grumbles, stacking dozens of musty magazines. "You're a pill even when you're not around."

As if on cue, the front door clicks open. Bess peers around the corner to see her mother hard-charging through the foyer.

"Caroline Codman!" Bess snaps. "You stop right there. Where have you been? I was worried out of my mind."

Not exactly true, but it sounds better than "I want to strangle you with one of the twelve jump ropes I found in your closet."

"Goodness, Bess!" Cissy almost leaps out of her Keds. "You scared me. What are you doing creeping around?"

"*I'm* the one creeping around? Mother, where have you been all day? We're supposed to be packing and it's pretty crappy to make me do all the work."

"Here we go again. What a fussbudget."

Cissy tugs on her ponytail and then breezes right past Bess and on into the kitchen.

"Uh, hello?" Bess says, pattering after her.

She enters the room just as Cissy plunks a brown burlap sack onto the counter.

"What have you been doing today?" Cissy asks as she pulls groceries from the bag.

Eggs. Milk. Yogurt and cheese. Bess's stomach nosedives.

"Cissy!" she barks. "What the hell are you doing?"

"Unloading groceries. And you really shouldn't talk to your mother that way."

Cissy opens the fridge and places five large peaches inside.

Peaches!

"Please explain," Bess says, "why you've bought a sackful of perishables when we're supposed to *move*?"

Speaking of perishables, Bess thinks and glances out the window. Down on the shore, the waves break with intensity.

"We should be clearing out," Bess says. "Not adding on. The movers are coming first thing tomorrow. There are rooms for us at Tea Time."

"Oh gosh, Polly is so sweet," Cissy says, and sniffs a half-used carton of OJ. With a satisfied nod, she slides it back into the fridge. "But I'm not going anywhere."

"We can't stay," Bess says, trying not to get all shrieky and indignant.

It's maddening and aggravating, and now Bess wants to strangle Cissy for real. But none of this should come as a shock. Cissy is many things, but never hard to read. A smart person would've seen this coming a mile away, even in the Nantucket fog.

"You promised!" Bess says. "You said after the vote you'd move. I love you, Cis. And I love your fire. But, good God, we have to leave."

"Look, dear, I do hate breaking promises."

"Do you, though?"

"But there's no time for moving or packing right now. I've called for an emergency town meeting later this week and I need to prepare. After that we can talk about my temporary relocation."

"Jesus," Bess groans. "Another meeting?"

"Yes. I just had a little confab with the SBPF and one very smart attorney. You see, if this coming winter is anywhere near as bad as the last, our whole stretch of Baxter Road will fall into the Atlantic."

"I know! That's why I'm trying to get you to move!"

"Our lawyer pointed out that if this happens, the water, sewage, and electrical services that Nantucket is *legally required* to provide will get cut off."

"Didn't we go over that last night?"

"Yes, but here's something I didn't quite appreciate," Cissy says with a clap. "The selectmen were against my armoring project because of the cost."

"I didn't get the impression that it was about money."

"But if they don't do something to bolster the bluff," Cissy continues, ignoring Bess for the sake of her own argument, "and the utilities become inaccessible, then Nantucket will have to acquire new land to rebuild the infrastructure. The cost would far exceed anything spent on erosion remedies. And my staying here only strengthens this case. *What do you mean you're going to deprive the old granny at Baxter Road number one-oh-one of heating and water?*"

"Jesus," Bess says again, hot with frustration. "No one's going to buy the old-lady routine. And I don't see them changing their views on the seawall."

Bess contemplates some sort of tantrum, but knows it won't do a lick of good. Too bad Lala isn't with them. Julia Codman can move mountains—aka their mother—with one appropriately timed fit. Ah, little sisters.

"And it was voted down for multiple reasons," Bess says. "Cost aside. So what do you propose the town do in lieu of buying the land and rebuilding everything, because . . ."

"Geotubes!" Cissy trills, then spins back out of the room.

"What?" Bess calls, her voice echoing down the hall. She can almost see the smoke coming off of Cissy's heels as she hightails it into the powder room. "What the hell are geotubes? It sounds like a way to feed a pet on life support."

Cissy pokes her head back into the hallway.

"Geotubes, my dear girl, are the very things that will solve all our problems," she says. "They're what will save our beloved Cliff House."

26

Wednesday Afternoon

"I realize this is aggressively ill-conceived," Bess says, pedaling over rocks and debris. "But I didn't know where else to go."

As she loses her balance, Bess launches herself off the bike, pretending her plummet to the ground is by design. Evan stares at her and she blushes. Bess is an insecure cyclist, a sad state for even a part-time Nantucketer.

"Geez, when did Sconset get so busy?" she says, babbling, as Evan tries to puzzle out why she's there and how come she can't ride a bike. "It's almost as bad as in town. Is there a single road on this island that isn't packed with cars?"

Evan continues to say nothing.

"So, tell me, is this the biggest intrusion possible?" Bess drops her bike into the dirt. Good riddance. "Am I going to get you fired? Or are you basically in charge?"

Bess stops the runaway train that is her mouth and studies Evan's face. He stands still before her: oh so tall, oh so handsome, and oh so smirky as he tries to find a plausible excuse for her presence.

"So that's a yes?" Bess says. "Noted. And yet I remain undeterred."

He's probably thinking about Brandon and the hookers, isn't he? Damn it, why'd she tell him? There was no good reason, only bad potential outcomes.

"Anyhow, I'll see you—"

"It's not an intrusion," Evan answers at last. "I'm the boss and, as you can see, the guys are gone so we're done for the day. Thus, despite your best efforts, you're not a pain in the ass."

"Thanks a heap. And, by the by, you could've told me that five minutes ago, and saved me all the jabbering."

"I've learned to let the women in your family get everything out first. Helps a fella find his bearings, know what he's dealing with."

"The women in my family?" Bess rolls her eyes. "Don't throw me in with Cissy, please. Grandma Ruby I'll take. So, do you have a minute?"

"For you I have lots of minutes." Evan nods toward his truck. "Wanna help me load up? I can compensate you with cold beer."

"Sure, why not? I've spent my entire day moving crap. I'm already in the groove."

Bess leans down for the industrial fan on the ground beside Evan. After hoisting it up onto her right hip, she follows him toward the oversize silver truck parked at the bottom of the drive.

"So what's Cissy up to this time?" Evan asks, unlatching his tool belt.

"Refusing to budge," Bess responds as she grits her teeth.

This fan is a heavier load than she should've taken on.

"Not budging," Evan repeats. "Hasn't that been her deal all along?"

"Sadly, yes." Bess moves the fan from her right hip to her left. "But it's different this time because she promised to leave after the vote and then the vote happened and—surprise!—no move."

"Is it really a surprise, though?" Evan asks, catching Bess's eyes over his shoulder.

"You don't understand. She's gone beyond general, Cissy Codman, run-of-the-mill hardheadedness."

"I presume the two of you have discussed the hazards of staying," Evan says, and tosses his tools into the flatbed of his truck.

"Yes, we've reviewed the likelihood of death and/or dismemberment. But Cis claims that come Memorial Day every house on her stretch of road will have cars in front of it. Two doors down there's only a dining room left and apparently the entire family camps out there, like soldiers, all summer long."

"A convincing argument," Evan jokes.

"No kidding. She won't listen to me at all." She drops the fan. "I don't even know what's happening in her head anymore. This morning she mumbled something about geotubes and then went for a jog. I mean, God!"

Bess pounds at the side of his truck.

"Oops." She pats the car. "Sorry."

"I'll bill ya for that later," he says with wink.

Evan lunges into the truck bed and then pulls Bess up behind him. He clears a place for her atop a lumpy gray bag.

As Bess settles onto the makeshift seat, she presses her hands along the bag, which is weighted down by . . . something. The whole deal is reminiscent of a body bag. Not that Bess has ever seen one in person. Not yet anyway.

"Lacrosse equipment," Evan says to Bess's quizzical face. "I'm coaching some rug rats in town."

"Oh. Cute."

Evan pops open a small, red cooler and hands her a beer.

"So lay it on me," he says. "Tell me the gory details."

"I'm at such a loss. Cissy's the official problem child of the family but up until now it's been fun, part of the gag, the wonky fabric in our family quilt. She's always been reasonable, in the end, but the reasonableness ship has sailed. It's crashed, actually. Lost at sea. Meanwhile the rest of my family is useless. Christ." Bess exhales. "What even is a geotube?"

"It's essentially a large, sand-filled jute bag that looks like a burrito."

"Another erosion-control measure?" she asks. "Just like the oh-so-successful seawall?"

"Yep, though geotubes are supposedly better because, unlike concrete or stone, the sand is compatible with the existing beach. They say it's less detrimental to the downdraft beaches, too, and, best of all, isn't an eyesore like a hard armor structure would be." Evan sighs. "It's what your mother would argue, in any case."

"She *would* argue that, wouldn't she?" Bess says. "I can see why she'd be excited about geotubes, in theory, but let's be real. Isn't it too late for Cliff House?"

Evan nods sadly.

"I'm afraid it is."

"I don't get it," Bess says, picking at the label of her Grey Lady Ale. "Cissy's no dummy. She must know Baxter Road is history. Why can't she just cut her losses and leave? She's always blathering on about good New England sensibility. This isn't sensible at all."

"Come on, Lizzy C. Cliff House has been in your family for generations. It's not just a house. It's a lifetime."

"Yeah but what's a lifetime but memories and photographs? She can keep those!"

"I suppose," he says. "But memories are so much more vivid when you're in the spot they happened instead of relying on your brain to paint the picture."

"Gee thanks, that's not depressing at all."

"You know how it is," he says, and gestures to the view. "When was the last time you thought about this place?"

"Hussey House," Bess says with a smile. "Or what once was Hussey House, since you've demolished it with your greedy, money-grubbing schemes."

"I am a greedy bastard, aren't I? Imagine, wanting to eat and put gas in my car."

"Must be nice!"

"Bottom line, if you don't have the anchor, what is your memory but a ghost?"

Bess shrugs and then peels the label all the way off her bottle.

"To be honest," Evan says, "I'll be sad to see Cliff House go, too. I have my own set of memories, ya know."

"I'm sure you do. We both do. Some better than others."

Evan finishes off his beer. As he grabs a second, Bess watches two seagulls dive at each other, then flap away.

"I've never told you this," Evan says. "But my great-aunt used to work at Cliff House."

"What?" Bess says, spine straightening in surprise. "She did?"

"Yep. My grandfather's sister."

"When was this?"

"Ages ago. In the forties. She married later in life, but before that was a maid at Cliff House. My aunt said Ruby was a real firecracker."

"Really?" Bess laughs and sets down her beer. "Grandma Ruby? I find that hard to believe. She was a bit of a groundbreaker, a feminist in her way. But very much *in her way*. Stone-faced, stoic. 'Firecracker' is not a word I'd use. Cissy's a firecracker. Ruby was . . . an aircraft carrier. A battleship gliding into the harbor."

Then again, Bess frequently teased her grandmother about her very Bostonian, "low-heeler" persona. Ruby always answered with a tee-hee and a sip of gin, and so Bess took her grandmother for the very best of sports. In retrospect maybe it was because she knew otherwise.

"According to Aunt Jeanne," Evan says, "Ruby and her brothers palled around with a bevy of good-time girls and boys. Constantly getting into scrapes and shenanigans and forever winning sporting events at the club."

"Are you serious?" Bess says, laughing again. "Ruby complained about Cissy's athletic, rough-and-tumble nature. I never guessed Grandma was at all sporty."

"She was an amazing tennis player, apparently."

"That's incredible."

"My aunt might've been the help, but she adored the 'young ones at the big house.'" Evan thinks for a moment. "Although there was some European girl she didn't care for. Anyway, it all sounded like a constant party. Until the war happened, of course. Then all bets were off."

"Wow," Bess says, staring down at the flatbed and the nails discarded in the grooves. "It's weird how people change." She looks up. "Good thing I'm my predictable, same self."

"The same!" Evan says with a cough. "I can think of five ways right now that you're a completely different girl than the one who walked the stage at Nantucket High."

"Oh yeah? Name one."

"You haven't touched that beer."

He taps the open, full bottle sitting beside Bess's foot. The man, he is not wrong.

"You could match me chug for chug back in the day," he says.

"Ah. Yes. Drinking skills. One of my finer qualities. At least as determined by weaselly local teens."

"Hey!" Evan yelps. There's a hint of disappointment in his deep brown eyes. "I *knew* you had a bias against townies. That's why you won't drink my beer."

"No," Bess says, and picks it back up. "It's not that."

She studies the bottle. In holding it, she knows the beer is already warm.

"What is it then?" Evan asks. "You a wine type now? Spend your weekends in Napa?"

"Uh, no. I've been to Napa three times. I do like my wine but I like beer just as much. So, no. It's not that."

Bess peeks at her watch. It's five thirty, or two thirty back in the

Bay. She wonders if someone is trying to contact her. Right now someone could be calling her name.

"Bess?"

"If you want to know the truth," she says, "the God's honest truth is that I'm neither a wine girl nor a beer one, at least not right now. The type of girl I am is pregnant. A pregnant girl who doesn't know what the hell to do."

27

The Book of Summer

Nick Cabot
July 29, 1941
Cliff House

Tops told me to write in this book and doggone it, I shall do so.

'Allo folks, the name is Nicholas Cabot. You might know me as just plain Nick, Topper's Harvard chum. The smarter and more attractive of the duo, to be sure. Alas Harvard boys we are no more. We both dropped out. There are things to do, you see. Battles to be won. People to impress with our dash and valiance.

As for me, I'm registered straight-up class 1-A (no kids or war work to hold me back!) and will soon head out to basic training for the good ol' army. Meanwhile, Topper's farting around the island, deciding what to do. I told him don't wait to be drafted. All sails and no wind, that boy. Looks swell in the harbor but not exactly going anywhere.

I've come to Cliff House for our last hoorah. I'm not unaccustomed to Nantucket, been here a time or five. It's funny how Tops's island is not the one from my mind though. When I think of the place, my mind conjures the mansions on Main Street. Those grand homes with their heavy knockers and silver nameplates and monstrous screaming eagles above their front doors. But, lo and behold, there's a charmer of a spot called Sconset, seven miles away but might as well be a thousand. Topper's family's spread is about a mile up from its heart.

Cliff House is a stately affair, as are a few others down the lane, though most are modest in size. Little weathered boxes, many drowning in flowers. Why, it almost makes you want to chuck it all and take up a fisherman's life.

Even in Sconset, there is tennis and sailing and golfing and bowling. There are card games and dances and Friday night parties on the Cliff House lawn. Every person, every last one of us, is tanned and gay. We might be the closest point physically to Europe, three thousand miles dead ahead to Spain, but you'd never know it. Out here, you can almost pretend it doesn't exist.

Oh yes, I could stay in Sconset the rest of my days and be quite content but that's not in the cards. On Tuesday I'll thank Mrs. Young and give Tops one last pat on the back. I'll leave this place calmer, and more wistful, but with new matchbooks and memories and a clip of honeysuckle to remember it all by.

Always,
Nick C.

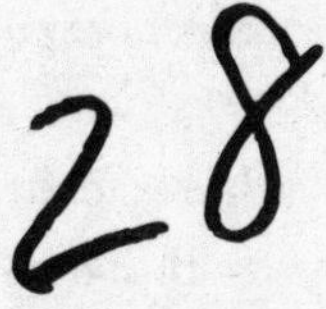

RUBY

August 1941

Not to sound uncharitable on the matter, but Ruby was damned glad that Nick Cabot character had split.

He was nice enough, if you didn't listen too closely, and you couldn't really fault a soldier going off to war. But, goodness, the man sucked up every crumb of Topper's time. With Nick around, it was as though the rest of them hardly existed, background players all.

On top of that, Nick didn't seem to like Hattie. Anyone not entirely charmed by the girl had to be several cards short of a full deck. How could he object? Unless he had a beef with beautiful, witty, continental babes who were a gas to boot. If so, then good luck.

"Selfish egoist of a girl," Ruby overheard him say one night at the casino.

She didn't so much "overhear" as he said it right to Topper's and Ruby's faces after Hattie sashayed off to find Mary. That alone told you the girl was generous to the gills. She *sought out* Mary, of all people.

"Excuse me?" Ruby said with a hard glare. "You have a problem with Hattie?"

"Okay, I was a little harsh," Nick conceded. "But there's simply nothing to her."

"'*Nothing to her*'?" Ruby steamed, glaring fiercely at her brother, who snapped his head away. "She's beautiful and brilliant and a kick and a half!"

"Beautiful, I suppose. But the rest of it? Sweets, you're reading her all wrong. Less breeding and couth and she'd be a hedonist. Only in it for the fun and gluttony."

"Gluttony. She eats like a bird. Topper! Are you going to let your friend talk about Hattie like that?"

Not meeting eyes with either one, Topper patted Ruby on the shoulder and said to his friend, "You get used to her."

"'Used to her'? What? Like a heat wave or an itchy skin condition?"

Ruby hadn't imagined there could be a person alive who didn't find Hattie Rutter incomparably charming. There must've been something darkly wrong with this Nick Cabot character. He probably kicked old ladies.

"So Nick's off to Europe," Ruby said on a glorious blue and gold afternoon as she and Topper approached the tenth hole of Sankaty Head.

Nick had been gone twelve hours and it was as obvious a statement as one could make but Ruby wanted to make it nonetheless. Since the man's departure, Topper was all gloom and blue moods. Nick Cabot's view of things still clung to her brother like a sticky, light film.

"Yes, he is," Topper said. "Off to fight the evil Axis."

With a bite of the lip, Topper teed up using one of Daddy's balls. When they ran out of this batch, that'd be it. Until the war was over, he'd make no more.

"I'm sure you'll miss him," Ruby said as Topper set up. "We all will!

Such a card to have around. But my guess is Hattie will be pleased as punch to have her beau back. She's positively thrilled you're staying the full week and not going back to Boston."

Ruby was workin' it like a pro, but "thrilled" was not exactly the shape of it.

Hattie's response had been "That's swell" when Ruby told her. Just two words: "That's swell." Of course, Hattie was not the excitable type and was hardly "thrilled" by much. A hedonist. Honestly. Hattie's unflappable demeanor was the very issue Nick took with her, no doubt. The man had all the class of an untrained Labrador. Case in point: He tromped around the upstairs in his shorts as if he were in a boys' dormitory. Even easygoing, pal-to-all Sam carped at the guy to please keep his twigs and berries in their sack.

" 'Thrilled,' " Topper said with a cough, on to his sister right away. "Really. That sounds like a Ruby word, not a Hattie one."

With an inhale, he swung and knocked the ball a clear two hundred yards off the tee.

"Well, thrilled in her own special way," Ruby clarified. "So I hear you two are going deer-spotting later?"

"As far as I know."

"That should be fun."

Ruby placed her ball on the ladies' tee and gave it a whack. It went far, though didn't come close to Topper's.

"It's a shame Daddy hasn't had the chance to get to know her," Ruby said, and flung her bag over her shoulder. They began walking down the fairway. "He'd like her, don't you think? I can't believe he came all this way for the parade but didn't stay for the ball."

"It is indeed too bad he wasn't fit to stay."

"And he's been back exactly once. In all those weeks!"

When they approached Topper's ball, he crouched down to inspect the lie of the grass.

"Poor man has been working so hard," Ruby gabbed on. "Who knew you could be a businessman and factory worker both?" She paused, hand on hip. In the distance birds tittered. "Are you going to take the shot? Or will you keep making that ball false promises with your inscrutable gaze?"

Ruby waited for Topper to react. But he didn't laugh, not a chuckle for miles. He always humored his sister, no matter how crummy the joke. But not this time. Instead he rose to standing and looked out over the fairway.

"Is everything okay . . . ?"

"You know he's not well," Topper said.

"Who? Daddy? He wasn't all roses on the Fourth, that's true. But it's only because he's been working like the devil with this gas mask venture. It's really great what he's done, when you think about it. I was skeptical at first but . . ."

Ruby let her voice trail off as she thought about the masks. There was a classification for this type of work. 2-B. Men necessary to national defense, therefore nondraftable. Daddy was too old for war, but her husband and P.J. worked at Young Manufacturing. Topper would work there, too. Ruby let loose a relieved smile.

"This isn't about any gas masks. . . ." Topper gently touched her arm. "Pops is ill, Red. You have to see that. He looks terrible."

Ruby whipped out of his reach.

"Has anyone ever told you that you're a real Sally Sunshine? He seems a tad beleaguered, like I said, but Mother would tell us if he were sick."

"Would she?"

Topper turned and took his shot, missing the green by a hair.

"Well, goddammit," he said. "Close is never good enough."

"That shot is decent and you know it. A slight breeze could nudge it into the right spot. And, by the way, Daddy is *not* sick."

"Use your eyes," Topper said. "And that precious brain of yours. Time to poke your cute head from beneath the rock. Dad is not himself. Your shot, Ruby. I recommend a seven iron."

"If I wanted advice, I'd have used a caddy."

Ruby pulled out a seven iron anyway and knocked the ball a yard from the hole.

"Not too shabby," Topper said.

He reached for his putter and, with one swift stroke, the ball plunked into the hole. A birdie. His third of the day.

"Nice one," Ruby griped.

Her second shot had been much better than Topper's, but now the best Ruby could do was to match him on this hole. All that and she'd still be twelve strokes back. Ruby was always playing from behind.

"Go to it, sis," he said.

Ruby clomped up to her ball and examined it from every angle, like Topper would, though she sorely lacked his golfing precision.

"Well, if Daddy is sick," she said, still kneeling, "then you should do something about Hattie."

Ruby stood and plinked the ball. It missed the hole by one inch wide to the right.

"What do you mean 'do something'?" Topper asked. "Come on, Red, you can putt better than that."

"Make an honest woman out of her. And, if I *could* putt better, don't you think I would?"

"That's not how golf works."

Ruby rolled her eyes and finally tapped the ball into the hole. She leaned down to pick it up.

"An honest woman?" Topper said with a cough-cackle. "We're a smidge late for that, I'm afraid."

"Don't be a worm."

"Surely you're not implying that I should propose?"

"And why not?" Ruby asked. She set her clubs down with a huff. "You and Hattie get along magnificently and you're beautiful together. She's smart and athletic, in addition to being drop-dead gorge."

"Ah, Red. Hattie's a doll and you're spot-on with all of it. But I'd say a few bang-up physical and personality traits aren't enough to start a marriage by."

Ruby was confused. Weren't those the precise things you started a marriage by?

"You know Daddy worries about you," she said. "He thinks you'll never settle down. If you're so certain he's sick, you could make him a happy man."

"He does worry about that," Topper said with a nod. "But there's nothing I can do about someone else's stress. Anyhow, if I did propose to Hattie, she'd sock me in the chin."

"See? You're a perfect match!"

"Sweet girl, I know you want the best for me. And for Hattie. But a hasty engagement is as far from 'the best' as you were from the fairway on hole five."

"Hey!" Ruby gave him a jolly punch to the arm. "That was uncalled-for."

"The truth hurts, eh?"

"And I *especially* didn't relish you snapping a picture of my failure."

"No one would believe it otherwise," he joked. "Come on, a foursome is approaching. We don't want them complaining about a girl on the course."

"I know those old toads and could beat any of them on my worst day."

"So, today then?"

Ruby growled at him.

"The man with the pipe has a fifteen handicap," she said, "but likes to think it's five."

Topper chortled and hoisted his golf bag onto his right shoulder. Then he swung it behind him, holding on with both arms. He looked like the exact kind of person Hattie Rutter should end up with. Thanks to the war, people were getting married brashly these days. Why couldn't those two join the trend?

"Her birthday's coming up," Ruby said as they approached the eleventh hole. "Hattie's."

"I think she mentioned something along those lines."

Topper held a hand over his eyes and scanned the fairway.

"I was thinking we could throw her a party. Next Friday night is free. Wouldn't that be a gas?"

"Sure, why not? I'm always game for a fiesta."

"I expected a tick more enthusiasm."

"I'm not sure what you're searching for, Red," he said, squinting at her, "but you should do it, if you want."

"But I . . ." Ruby started, though she had no real way to finish. She sighed. "Okay, maybe I will. You'd better show up."

"Of course I'll show up."

Topper removed a ball from his bag and spun it a few times before placing it on the tee.

"There's a chance, though?" Ruby said as he set up for the shot. "I mean, one day. If you keep dating and everything continues on this path?"

"A chance for what, exactly?"

"That you could propose."

"Geez-aloo, what a question."

Topper closed his eyes and waited a big thick while before finally looking at Ruby again.

"I hate to tell ya, Red. I know you have your sights set on this. But as to whether there's a chance we'll get married . . . I'm sorry, I just don't think there is."

Hattie seemed embarrassed by the fuss. As Ruby had never seen the gal rattled by a darn thing, it was a disconcerting situation.

"Do you not want a birthday party?" Ruby asked, tentatively, a few days prior. She was scared of the question, and the answer, as the wheels were already in motion. "You're twenty-five. A real milestone!"

"Lord, don't rub it in," Hattie responded and took a deep suck of her cig. She then inspected Ruby for a minute, sizing her up and a little bit down. "You know what, Rubes? Let's do it. A party sounds keen. You're fab. Absolute aces."

So there they were, on a Friday night, the orchestra playing, guests scattered across the lawn. They'd invited the Grey Ladies, as well as Hattie's friends from town. The Hulbert Avenue girls were surprised to find such grandiosity all the way in Sconset. Forget the artists and fishermen, on its cliffs stood a bona fide estate, albeit an estate built mostly with "new money," so it almost didn't count.

The party took off in a flash. The guests danced and drank champagne and told stories from college and finishing school. At one juncture a gaggle of those rabble-rouser Kennedys showed up and incited a mêlée with some of Topper's friends. Hattie managed to break the whole thing up with a slap or three. During her time in London, Hattie had known some of the boys, and one girl or another, though there was little difference between the genders in that family.

Around midnight, the evening began to wind down, though plenty of good-time gals were still jitterbugging on the patio. Couples held hands near the cliff's edge, whispering promises as they stared out across the forever. Ruby was plumb exhausted and had decided to pack it in herself when she realized Hattie was AWOL.

"Huh," she said, inspecting the grounds. "Is that her?"

She craned her neck to make out the identities of two girls roller-skating on the tennis court. Upon closer inspection, neither had the curves to suggest the birthday girl.

"Looking for someone?" Sam asked, and slipped in behind her.

"Yes. Hattie seems to be missing," Ruby said with a frown.

"She probably turned in." Sam gave her a hug. "You put on one hell of a shindig, baby. Everyone had a snazzy time."

"Oh . . . thanks. . . . Don't you think she should've stuck around? Until the last guest left? It is her party after all."

"Hmm. Perhaps. Though I'm not up on the latest etiquette and anyway this island has its own rules."

"Yes it does," Ruby said. "Nonetheless, I'm going to find her."

She was at once chafed and fighting the creeping suspicion that the party was destined for ruin, though it was mostly over. Forget decorum, the only people left would be lucky to remember their shoes.

"Are you coming?" Ruby called over her shoulder.

Sam opened his mouth as if to speak and Ruby's heart wrapped right around the sight of him. His hair was mussed and starting to curl from the briny air. He hadn't shaved since morning and so his stubble was thick and dark. Ruby smiled at her husband. Sam was too dang handsome, calamitously so.

"I love you so much," Ruby said, blurted really, as the feeling nipped at her very soul. "I'm so lucky to be your wife."

"Ah, Rubes, I'm the lucky one."

She smiled and listened as the waves broke on the shore below. Maybe this was why Hattie wasn't notably enthused by Topper. Ruby's baby brother was handsome as the sun was bright but he had nothing on Sam.

"I'm going to find her," Ruby said again. "Hattie. Make her send the remaining guests off fittingly. Care to join me?"

"Well, actually"—he blushed—"I'd planned to meet P.J. and Topper for some poker at the casino. Would you mind terribly?"

"Absolutely not," Ruby said. "But make sure you come to bed at a decent hour. And . . ." She gave him an exaggerated wink. "Please wake me when you do."

After three sweeps of the house, and a look-see from the captain's walk, Ruby couldn't rustle up even the slightest hint of Hattie. Had she gone home? Hattie stayed the night at Cliff House after most parties. Eight miles back to town was a haul after a few gin fizzes and some swings around the dance floor.

As Ruby plonked down the stairs for the fourth time, she rounded the banister toward the kitchen—called a "porch" by any Sconseter worth her salt—and stopped dead in her tracks when she heard a squeal.

"Hattie?" she called tentatively as she stepped into the kitchen.

Another muffled sound: yes, it was her friend's voice.

Ruby walked farther into the room. The noise seemed to be coming from the kitchen, but the place was flat deserted save for a dozen emptied champagne bottles and countless plates of abandoned chocolate cake. Hattie yelled something again. Her friend was in the butler's pantry.

Hattie sounded hurt, or upset, and Ruby aimed to find out why. As she pushed the door open a crack, Ruby glimpsed a flash of red. She recoiled and the door sprung back. When she pressed on it a second time, Ruby saw her pal, her newest yet dearest chum, sprawled across the carving table.

"Hattie," Ruby gasped, though the guest of honor did not hear.

Hattie was on the wood table, topless, splayed out on her back. Her knees were bent; her skirt was hiked up and crumpled around her waist. She looked like a biology frog, not a woman. Even her boobs had disappeared somewhere into her chest. With her was Topper, pants around his ankles, rutting with force.

Topper grunted as he jammed into her. With each thrust, Hattie's head smacked against a block of knives. She was grunting, too, when not bellowing out instructions using language that would make a sailor weep. Sick splashed up the back of Ruby's throat. What she was watching was animal, primal. Both were willing, but neither seemed to be enjoying it at all.

"Harder!" Hattie cried. "Fuck me harder!"

Another gasp escaped Ruby. Meanwhile, Topper bore down, ramming Hattie with ferocity. He pounded her ever more vigorously, bracing himself against her breasts as they sank farther into her chest. Ruby cringed for the pain as Hattie bucked her hips with escalating might.

God, Ruby thought, maybe she and Sam had been doing it wrong. Maybe that's why she wasn't pregnant. Nothing in their marital bed looked remotely like this.

With a sudden and staggering grunt, Topper pulled out from

inside Hattie. Ruby reeled at the sight of his member, slick and erect and grotesquely large. She made a gagging sound as Topper spun Hattie over onto her stomach and took her from behind.

As if the door were suddenly hot, Ruby let go. It swooshed several times before finally coming to a stop. She backed up, shaking her head as if that could make the scene evaporate. When she reached the hallway, she turned and scrabbled upstairs as quickly as her feet would take her.

Ruby was no authority, the sum total of her lovers exactly one, but what she saw did not check out. She couldn't explain why, but it wasn't supposed to be that way. It wasn't supposed to look like that. Not even if you grew up in France.

Ruby sat on the edge of her bed, knees tucked up into her chin, teeth chattering.

She was disgusted by what she had seen, and what she had heard. Even this very room repulsed her, with its pastel colors, the alternating walls of coral and slate blue, not to mention the pale pink wardrobe lodged in the corner. Tennis trophies, horse show ribbons, and notices of scholastic achievement surrounded her. And, God, that cutesy collection of themed salt-and-pepper shakers. The place suddenly appeared so juvenile, the room of a girl who'd never grown up. She and Sam had pushed the twin beds together, but that was the only change in ten years.

Eyes stinging in hot repugnance, Ruby stood and crept down the hallway toward the bathroom, though no amount of scouring could chase away the bitterness in her mouth.

In the bathroom, Ruby turned the faucet. As she ran her brush beneath the water, her hands shook violently.

"Hiya Rubes!"

Ruby jumped. The toothbrush flew upward, leaving a splatter of water on the mirror.

"Cripes, Hattie," she said, struggling for breath. "You scared the devil out of me. What are you doing?"

"I'm brushing the twags, same as you."

When Ruby caught her friend's face in the mirror, she saw that Hattie looked mostly the same. The hair was coiffed, falling in soft waves against her face. Her clothes were still expertly draped, hugging her body with grace, only a few new wrinkles to be found. Even Hattie's makeup was decent for that time of night. There was nothing to indicate she'd just been pillaged. Where were the marks? Where was the shame?

"Scooch over," Hattie said. She jammed her hand into her purse and extracted a toothbrush. "Move it, girl."

Hattie gave Ruby a friendly pat on the backside. Ruby jumped again, this time nearly falling through the shower curtain.

"Whatsa matter, kid?" Hattie asked around the toothbrush lodged between her molars. "You seem jumpy. Literally jumpy."

"Yeah, well, you don't seem jumpy at all, which is strange."

"Huh?" Hattie jacked up one brow. "You kill me, Rubes. You're one cutup of a dame."

She spit into the sink.

Hattie slept at Cliff House multiple times per week. If they attended a party or dinner, Hattie was almost always too pooped for the trek back to Points North. Because she stayed in Walter's old room, the two girls often met like this, in the little white bathroom halfway down the hall. How many times had Hattie come to her immediately after being ransacked by Topper?

Because that's what it was.

A ransacking. A plundering. A battering. A pounding. There were a hundred words running through Ruby's brain, not a one of them anything close to love. Topper hammered into Hattie while she bucked to meet him, angrily, determined, like waves crashing in a storm.

"So," Ruby said, and slapped a palmful of Pond's onto her face. "Did you and Topper have a nice evening? You disappeared."

"Yeah. Sure. He's a swell chap, your brother."

"'A *swell chap*'?" Ruby scoffed. "Is that all you want to say for yourself?"

"Why do I get the impression I've committed some undocumented, heretofore unknown Cliff House crime?"

"I don't know," Ruby said. "Why don't you tell me?"

"Geez, Rubes, are you cheesed at me or something? If so, spill it. No use making me guess. I'll get it wrong. I promise."

"Do you like him?" she asked. "My brother? Topper."

"Of course you meant Topper. Wouldn't be P.J. now, would it? Never mind he's already married to the matte and muted Mary."

"Just answer the question, Hattie."

"Topper's keen as can be. What gives, hon? You're angry as a cat."

"Is this a relationship?"

Ruby pictured Topper flipping Hattie over, jamming himself into the small space between her round and lifted cheeks. The girls at school discussed all manner of tips and tricks to prevent pregnancy or the loss of virginity, but no one had ever mentioned anything like that.

"Are you in it for real?" Ruby asked, trying desperately not to cry. "Or is it merely some big game for you? The girl from the Continent humoring the local Yank?"

"Is he my steady? Is that it?" Hattie asked, an amused smile playing at her lips. "Oh, sugar, we're nothing like that and, believe me, it suits your brother just fine. It's all in good fun."

"Fun?" Ruby snorted. "Yeah, looks like a real blast."

With that, she chucked her toothbrush into the sink.

"Well, Hattie, I'm gonna hit the percales. Have a good night. Sweet dreams. And don't forget to shut off the lights."

29

Wednesday Evening

Bess tells Evan about the pregnancy—every sordid detail.

It all happened so fast, she explains. One minute Bess was, if not happily married, at least unobjectionably attached. The next minute she was finding out about hookers and approximately ninety seconds after that, moving into a hastily secured rental in an undesirable part of town. By the time Bess realized her missed periods were a result of a baby and not stress, her life had already changed. She did tell her ex. A bad decision, in the end.

No, Bess hasn't been all that nauseated, just a touch "off" from time to time, no more irritable or sick to her stomach than might be expected given the prostitutes and divorce and rancid smell outside her new apartment.

And what, exactly, does Bess plan to do about the unexpected twist? Well, she missed an appointment this afternoon. If not for the Cissy problem, Bess would be in San Francisco and, as of this very moment, not pregnant anymore. So time is getting short, for Cliff House and for Bess.

"You seem completely unfazed by this revelation," Bess says after unspooling it all.

Is she glad for Evan's blank expression? Or is she concerned?

"I shouldn't have led with the whores," she adds.

Evan shrugs. "Admit it, you like saying the word 'whore.'" He cracks open a fresh beer. "Let me ask you something. If you planned to end the pregnancy, why'd you tell Brandon? I can only assume he was a total shit about it."

"Yes," Bess says with a salty sort of chuckle. "'A total shit' is one way to put it."

"So, why then?" Evan presses. "Why'd you tell him?"

"Oh. Well. It felt like the right thing."

So Bess hasn't really told Evan "every sordid detail."

Because while she plans to end the pregnancy now, she didn't necessarily have the same designs before. Not that Bess wants to be a mother under such circumstances, and she'd pity any kid forced to have Brandon for a dad. But at first Bess simply didn't know what to think. In telling Brandon she was looking for something: a sign, a hint, an outright directive. Be careful what you wish for and all that. He gave her one hell of a "sign."

"I'm pregnant," Bess had said, simple as that.

Because, while the situation was and is complex, this particular problem is quite basic. An unexpected pregnancy, the great equalizer. It's happened in every country, in every tax bracket, in every year since the dawn of time. Pretty straightforward, at least until you realize it's a total fucking disaster.

"You dirty slut" had been Brandon's reaction.

"Um, excuse me?" Bess choked out.

It was a low blow, yet also quite Brandon. He had such an aggressive, full-metal-jacket way of talking to people, followed by a heavy dose of manufactured charm. It's amazing what handsome, upwardly mobile guys can get away with. To think, Bess once considered him refreshingly direct.

"You can't talk to me like that," she'd said.

"Fuck yeah, I can. You're a complete piece of shit."

"Hey! Our marriage is ending, but I deserve to be treated like a human."

Brandon shouted something else, jumped to his feet, and then lunged toward Bess—lunged!—before remembering where and who he was. Brandon was a tech executive, a man with stature, if only in his own mind. They were sitting in a Starbucks on Sand Hill Road, only five minutes from his office. Someone might be watching.

"You dirty fucking slut," he said again, to be sure she heard.

He pulled back, then clenched his hands together.

"Jesus, Brandon, calm down," Bess answered, trembling. "The baby is yours. I haven't slept with anyone else in seven years, so you can stop with the 'slut' claptrap."

"Nice try, bitch," he said. "If you think you're going to trap me . . ."

"Trap you? No, I very much want the divorce. More than ever."

" 'More than ever,' " he said, mocking her in a girl's voice. "Ugh, you disgust me. So you want money. Is that it? You're trying to shake me down for cash?"

"What cash?"

"*Fuck. You.*"

"Listen, I don't even know if I'm keep—" Bess shuddered. "I don't want anything from you, not a single penny. Shaking you down? Please. I'm letting *you* have the house, remember? The house we bought together but with my money."

Both of their names had been on the deed, but they used Bess's savings for the down payment. Brandon's cash was all tied up in his new company, the business now dead thanks to a fight over code. This was how badly Bess wanted out. He was allowed to have everything she put into that marriage, including their home.

"So are you keeping the baby?" Brandon asked, growling at her from across the table.

God, Bess thought at the time, the things that happened in a Starbucks. Books written. Divorces decreed. Pregnancies revealed. Bess had read somewhere that meth heads frequented the private bathrooms. All of humankind, foibling in a Starbucks.

"I don't know what I'm going to do," Bess admitted. "But, rest assured, if I go ahead with the pregnancy, you won't have to contribute a thing."

"You're not keeping it."

"I haven't made a decision but, like I said, I want exactly nothing from you, should I decide to . . . proceed. I just wanted you to know."

"You're not keeping it," he repeated.

"I realize this is quite a shock and we're not exactly in a place of mutual understanding."

"You're not having this baby."

"I might, I might not," Bess said, trying to keep her voice measured and low. "But you don't actually have a say."

Eyes were beginning to make skittish glances in their direction. Bess felt like she was back in the ED, battling a patient with "chronic back pain," a patient who was desperate for oxycodone but who wasn't going to get it, at least not from Dr. Codman. Brandon had that same jittery-irate-irrational vibe, as if his pulmonary system were about to rupture.

"Listen to me, you fucking cunt."

He slammed both hands onto the table and stood.

"Hey, buddy," said a voice. "You should . . ."

Calm down?

Excuse yourself?

Shut the hell up before I punch you in the face?

Bess didn't hear what the guy said. The blood whooshing through her ears was too loud.

"Brandon!" she hissed. "Sit down."

"If you have this fucking baby . . ."

"Shut. *Up*."

"I want you to remember that thing was made when I was fucking a different whore every goddamned night."

"You're despicable," Bess wheezed.

She took a sip of coffee, thinking it was water.

"The same dick that was inside of you," Brandon raged on. "The very same dick that made that creature had been in a hundred other cunts before yours."

Bess reached under the table for her bag, accidentally knocking over her coffee along the way. She didn't bother to pick it up.

"The sperm that fertilized your pathetic egg," he said, "is the very sperm I squirted over some bitch's tits that same night. Your baby will have syphilis or gonorrhea. It will be half whore. Three-quarters whore, with you in the mix."

By then, Bess was up on her feet, heading toward the exit. Brandon kept shouting. It would be the last time she saw the man she had promised to love forever. The last time she went into that Starbucks, too. Good thing Brandon wasn't as well known in Silicon Valley as he imagined.

The next day Bess made an appointment to terminate the pregnancy. What Brandon said didn't make any biological sense. She didn't even need her medical degree for that. But Bess knew she'd never be able to stop hearing his words once she saw the baby's face. Not ever having been a mom, Bess didn't understand that the opposite would be true. A new child had a way of making the bad disappear, for a time.

"Do you still think it was the right thing to do?" Evan says now, all the way in Nantucket, on the other side of the country. "Telling him?"

Bess laughs sourly.

"Well, he called me a bunch of names," she says, the furthest into the story she'll go with Evan, or anyone else.

Not even Palmer knows the details of the coffee exchange. Maybe her cousin is onto something with the accusation of verbal abuse.

Bess doesn't know which is more reprehensible: that she can't admit it, or that part of her believes verbal isn't abuse enough to count. They should revoke her medical license for the very notion. She could give it to Palmer. Her cousin has limitless compassion and could figure out how to poke around in people eventually. That's the easy part.

"After the name-calling," Bess says, mind spinning with all she's said, and even more so with what she hasn't, "I felt pretty crappy. So the answer is no, I shouldn't have said a thing."

"You know what I think?" Evan leans back onto both elbows, his face turned toward the ocean. "You weren't sure. I think that's why you told Brandon."

"Could be," Bess says. Her body softens as her brain winds down. "But seeing him solidified my decision to end the pregnancy."

"Your decision is anything but solidified. I think it's the opposite."

"Oh yeah?" she says, squinting at him. "How's that?"

"You won't drink my beer." Evan gives a wink. "And you're never one to turn down beer."

"Good Lord," Bess says, and rolls her eyes good-naturedly. "Dr. Mayhew in session. So, if that's true, then why didn't I cancel today's appointment? Especially after I knew I was headed to Nantucket? Travel is the perfect excuse."

"You're trying to kid yourself into being *undecided*, even though you know exactly what you want."

"Yeah, well, whenever I've known 'exactly what I want' it turns out I'm dead wrong."

"Just do it," Evan says with a smile. "Have that baby."

"Oh, sure. It's so simple." Bess snaps. "New person! Appear!"

"I didn't say it's simple. But, hell, you have a life, a career. You're solid as hell."

"I'm not the least bit solid," she says. "I can't even control Cissy!"

"Pretty sure you're not expected to mother your own mom. What are you afraid of, Bess? Why can't you raise a child on your own?"

"Oh, I certainly could," Bess says with a sigh. "In theory. There are far more scandalous circumstances than a thirty-four-year-old professional, well-educated single mom. Like being a forty-year-old professional, well-educated *non*-mom."

"So what's the problem?"

"I don't . . ." Bess sighs again. "I don't know if I have it in me."

"Of course you have it in you!"

Evan's voice has always been so persuasive. Deep, powerful, as if coming from his lungs, or his heart. And those earnest brown eyes, like precious heirlooms she left behind. Bless it, Bess is falling for his old shtick. God, she hates when he does this. It's so much easier to remember Evan Mayhew as the smug jerk from high school.

"I appreciate your faith in me," Bess says, a little primly. "But this isn't some novel where a major debacle turns out for the best and they all live happily ever after."

"Why not?"

"Don't get me wrong. It's great to fantasize about," she says. "If this was a novel, and you know people *love* books set in Nantucket, but if my life were a novel, I'd chuck my ED job in San Francisco, move on-island, and become a general practitioner dealing with jellyfish stings and wacky boating mishaps."

"Cobblestone burn," Evan adds.

"Fishhook removal."

"You'd have a hard time competing with Tim, though. I can't see you doing house calls for destitute drug addicts who pay in stolen guns. Or for John Kerry."

"Dr. Lepore can have his house calls. Last time my mom went in for a tick check he was complaining that he's perennially short-staffed because no one can stand this island for long. It takes a certain kind of weirdo to be cut off from civilization year-round."

"Yes it does," Evan says, brows peaked. "The kind only found in books."

"Exactly. Anyhow, I could do the easy, in-office problems, and save the zany, contrarian cases for Lepore. Together we'd solve Nantucketers' health woes and I'd raise my baby with Cissy at Cliff House. She'd watch him, or her, while I worked. My child would write her first words in Sarah Young's Book of Summer."

"Don't forget . . . you'd also fall in love with your high school beau."

"Oh, God!" Bess says, and laughs. Her eyes at once well up. "What an idea. However, I don't think my French teacher from Choate lives around here."

"That's harsh, Codfish."

"*That's* harsh? Um, what was that personal philosophy of yours? Never make the same mistake twice?"

"Touché," he says, and shakes his head. "It's my only rule."

"Swell." Bess finds herself frowning. "Yet another reason this proposed novel could never materialize. Not to mention, Cliff House is now more cliff than house. So there's a big old hole in the middle of my plot. Literally."

Evan nods as tears glint on his lashes. Is he *crying*? Or about to? Bess pushes the thought away.

"So," Evan says, and hops up onto his feet. He brushes off the back of his jeans. "I should take you home. Any more beer for me and you'd have to drive."

"Wouldn't be the first time." Bess smiles. "But I have a bike, remember?"

She points toward the one she found in Cissy's shed, blue and rusted near the handlebars.

"You Codman broads and your bikes." Evan picks it up and launches it into his truck. "Nah. I'm driving."

"Cliff House is, like, a mile away."

"It's getting dark. Plus, now that I know you're in a delicate condition . . ."

"Why do I feel like you're going to use that against me?" Bess asks. "As if I don't have enough problems. Fine. I'll permit you to drive me home."

Bess jumps down and walks around to the passenger's side of the cab. He starts the truck, which sputters and then groans into life. Bess checks her watch. They've been at the jobsite for over an hour, probably closer to two, but Bess isn't ready to leave. She's not prepared to drive the mile to Cliff House and greet the problems looming over the bluff. So when Evan turns to her and suggests a bite to eat, Bess is quick to agree. And she is grateful that her old friend can still read her in exactly the right way.

30

Wednesday Night

"So," Bess says as they pull away from the Sconset Café and head toward Baxter Road.

They talked all through dinner—short ribs and burgers, nothing fancy—but despite topics worn to the bone and that dang growling engine, things are still too quiet in the cab for Bess.

"Any idea how I can get Cissy out of the house?" she asks. "That's why I hauled myself out to bother you at work. Am I a typical girl or what?"

"Oh, you're hardly typical."

"I went to you for advice about someone else's problems and ended up blathering about myself."

Evan smiles, tight-lipped and forlorn. "I'd say Cissy is very much your problem."

"Well, you're right about that. See? Who has time for a baby with my mother around?"

Bess gazes out the window, watching several homes pass before she speaks.

"Seriously though," she says. "What am I going to do? About my mom. It was enough of a battle when we were on the same page. Now Cissy's my antagonist. I pack up the dishes, she puts them away. I throw perishables in the trash, she digs them out or buys more. It's infuriating."

"Just take what matters, and let Cissy deal with the rest. She'll come to her senses. She always does."

"That has not been my experience. And 'take what matters'? That's Cissy! And we already know that she's not going anywhere." Bess laughs and leans into the headrest. "Oh Lord, I'm in trouble."

"You can grab the book," he says.

"What book?"

"That guest thingy everyone writes in?"

"Oh, the Book of Summer. Well, yes, that's a given. In the ranking of stuff that counts in that house, the 'guest thingy' is number two, behind Cissy. Though if she keeps acting this way, I might have to reverse the order."

"I wrote in it, you know," Evan says.

"You wrote in it?"

Bess sits upright and then eyeballs him while making a snorting-baby-piglet sound that would've caused her to blush had she not been so flippin' tired. Maybe this pregnancy is affecting her after all.

"Yup," Evan says. "I sure did. The night of your wedding."

"Okay, that's a lie. Admittedly I haven't read all of the entries, but I've read all of Ruby's and certainly every single one written around the time of my wedding."

"Not all of them."

They roll up in front of Cliff House.

"Yes," Bess says. "All of them. Twice, even. Three times."

Evan jams the truck into park and kicks open his door.

"Not mine. Because I ripped that sucker out."

Bess blinks and then hears the crunch of his work boots on the shelled drive. She slides out of the cab, eyes on Cliff House. A million memories worm through her at once.

Back in high school, Evan didn't usually drive her home, living across the street as he did. But he always walked Bess to the door. Then, later, he could frequently be seen (though never by Cissy) escorting Bess right back out of the house via the butler's pantry. Hands locked together, they'd creep past the flagpole and around the privet hedge. He'd bring Bess home sometime before dawn.

The flagpole.

Bess gapes. It's back. Damn it all to hell, Cissy has reinstalled the flagpole in the five hours Bess has been away. It is all so very Cissy Codman, this point she's trying to prove. The woman is steadfast as anything Star-Spangled to be sure.

"F'ing Cissy," Bess mutters as she tries to help Evan with the bike.

He, of course, won't allow it.

"What's that?" he says.

"What's what?"

"You mumbled something about Cissy."

"Oh." Bess shakes her head and glares accusatorially, as if Old Glory had something to do with it. "The stupid flagpole is back. Does the woman ever stop?"

"Come on, Lizzy C. You know the answer to that question."

"Right. The very minute she should throw in the towel, is the exact moment Cissy steps on the lunatic gas."

Her eyes skip back to Cliff House in time to see the grasshopper gait of Cissy scamper by a window. Bess turns toward Evan, who looks exasperatingly hot right then, standing in the fuzzy moonlight, her bike against his hip.

"So what'd you do with it?" Bess asks. "Your Book of Summer entry? I'd like to read it."

"Sorry, can't help you there."

"It was my wedding. My grand event."

And it was both of these things, but strangely enough they almost eloped.

"Cissy's driving me bonkers," Bess said to Brandon one night, or something along those lines. "Well and truly nuts."

"So let's scrap the fancy to-do," he suggested, quickly, like he'd been thinking about it for days. "Go down to the courthouse. Make it official, just the two of us, on our own terms."

He made it seem so romantic. *Just the two of us. You and me. Forever. We don't need anyone else.* She almost agreed to the courthouse nuptials but in the end wanted the Cliff House hurrah, same as her mother, same as Grandma Ruby. If she was being completely honest, Bess wanted it not merely for tradition but also for the guests who might come. She wanted it for Evan, so that he might see her on her very best day.

"You have to tell me what you wrote," Bess insists. "It's only fair. Like I said, it was *my* wedding."

"Sorry. Don't have it. And are you sure it was *your* wedding? Because I could've sworn it was your mom's."

"Ha, well, you're not wrong. Lala says she'll never get married because Cis can't figure how to be moderate. And if she eloped. Well." Bess chuckles and lets her eyes wander back to the flagpole. "Forget Hurricane Sandy. The wrath of Cissy Codman would rain down like a hundred-year storm. For Lala, it's better to live in everyday sin."

"It usually is."

Evan steers her bike through the gate, Bess dragging behind him.

"Here we are," he announces. "Delivered to your front doorstep. Don't let anyone tell you I'm not a gentleman."

"No one needs to tell me that. I already know."

"Hilarious."

Evan leans in for a hug. Bess startles as if he'd grabbed her breast. Her hands fly up and she accidentally punches herself in the face.

"Don't hurt yourself," Evan says.

"Sorry, it's just . . ." Bess tries to find the words. "Like I said. I'm 'off.' "

"Stop kidding yourself. You're more 'on' than you know. After all, you're Bess Codman."

"*Doctor* Bess Codman," she says, kidding, though it comes out sounding pompous as hell.

Thank God Evan's dad isn't around. Chappy Mayhew would use this as exhibit A as to why every single person in the Codman family is a Summer Person to the core.

"Yes, well," Evan says with a smirk. "The doctor part goes without saying."

He has enough manners to let her obnoxiousness dissolve into the gloom.

"I'm shocked you can still look me in the eye," Bess says. "After everything I've told you. I'm such a wreck."

"Everyone's a wreck," Evan says. "Most are way worse than you. Admittedly, you've been through some tough shit. But it's temporary. You'll move on from here. Bess Codman can do anything. She knows what she wants and goes after it."

"Let's agree to disagree."

"The girl I knew," Evan says. "The girl who beguiled a poor, young local with her beauty and smarts, the one who scrambled him up for years—"

"Gimme a break!" Bess chirps. "If anything, I was the one mixed up."

"The girl I knew also had a hard time figuring out when to shut the hell up and listen."

Evan gives one of his earth-cracking smiles.

"And she always understood exactly what she wanted, even when she couldn't say it."

Evan reaches out and places both hands, gently, on her shoulders. He pulls Bess in and gives her a whisper of a kiss on the forehead, another on her nose. Bess tilts imperceptibly forward, waiting and hungry for a third.

"Good night, Lizzy C.," he says, stopping at just the two. "It's great to have you back."

Bess watches as Evan returns to his car and drives away. She half expects him to pull into Chappy's drive, his old home.

Insides churning with some unsavory mix of giddiness and flat-out insecurity, Bess shuffles through the front door of Cliff House, which she'd left unlocked, secretly counting on a robbery. It'd be one way to move all that junk.

"Evan Mayhew, huh?" Cissy says, emerging in the hallway with a cocktail in one hand, a rolled-up yoga mat in the other. "That explains where you've been all night."

"Where *I've* been?"

Bess wishes her heart would stop pounding to this great degree.

"Well, Evan's not too bad," Cissy says. "At least compared to that father of his. He's crazy handsome and a real ladies' man, from the sounds of it. I'm referring to Evan. Because Chappy . . ."

Cissy makes a face.

"I'm not really interested—"

"Kinda assumed you'd gotten him out of your system in high school." Cissy sighs. "Don't get any ideas, missy. You're not permitted to marry anyone with the last name Mayhew."

"Who said anything about marriage? And anyway, nothing's going on."

"He has a fairly serious girlfriend, far as I know."

"Good for him," Bess says as her insides collapse at the thought.

A "fairly serious" girlfriend? Of course he does. But then, why should she care?

"Can it, Cissy," she says. "I'm not even divorced yet."

Also, she's pregnant by someone else. Bess can't imagine Evan Mayhew, or any other sensible male, itching to hook up with a divorced, knocked-up chick who's already eclipsed her prime.

"It's not like that with Evan," Bess prattles on. "I went to him for advice. You see, there's this very stubborn elephant I'm trying to move out of a house."

Bess tries to sweep past her mom and on down the hallway, but

Cissy springs in front of her, not dribbling a drop of booze in the process.

"Bessie, never mind those Mayhew creeps. I have terrific news. I got it!"

"Got what?"

"I got the emergency town meeting to approve the geotube installation. It's happening tomorrow night."

Bess doesn't know whether to give Cissy a high-five or dissolve into a sobbing mess. Another meeting. More straws for Cissy to grasp at. More flyers for Bess to pass out.

"You did?" Bess asks.

"Yep! The information about having to buy more land and rebuild the infrastructure, well, it really made those fogies take notice. They've realized it's better to keep what we have. Not only does it preserve Sconset's historical and aesthetic integrity, it's far cheaper. Finally, they've seen the light!"

"Or else they decided it's the quickest way to get you to zip it."

Cissy gives Bess a pinched look.

"They're lucky someone cares as much as I do!" she says. "In twenty years—in thirty—after I'm long gone, they'll be grateful for what I did. No one will remember my face or my name, but one day some soul will say, 'Hey, did you know they almost let all this fall into the ocean?'"

"Congratulations. Truly. I guess the fighting will finally pay off."

Bess makes her way toward the stairs.

"We need to discuss the big move tomorrow," she calls over her shoulder. "And why you bought a flagpole. Right now I'm too beat. I could sleep forever."

"It's not even nine o'clock!"

"What can I say? I'm getting old."

"Bessie?"

"Yes, Mom?"

She turns back around.

"You look good," Cissy says. "Pretty. Beautiful."

"Thanks."

"You should lose the glasses, though. What happened to the contacts you wore in high school?"

"Twenty years ago? I can't really say." Bess shakes her head. "You really are something else."

"Island life agrees with you."

Bess remains unmoved. It's one of Cissy's favorite mantras.

"Thanks Mom," she says.

"You've . . . I don't know. Filled out."

Cissy tries to make a shapely-woman sign with her hands, but both arms are still occupied with yoga props and vodka.

"Filled out," Bess says with a snort. "That's one way to put it."

Her mom smiles then, wide and hardy, all telltale Cissy toothy.

"There's nothing left for you back in the Bay," she says.

"Except for my job, a new apartment, a cat . . ."

"You should make this a permanent change," Cissy says, not hearing her at all.

Bess thinks of her fake novel, the one with the island practice and Nantucketer ailments and charming high school boyfriend brought back to life. She can stay here with Cissy, and eventually marry Evan. On weekends they'll play a few rounds at Sankaty Head; attend Yacht Club balls at night. It'll be sunshine and bicycles the rest of their days.

Except, of course, for all that fog perpetually hanging around.

"Oh, Cissy," Bess says with a sigh, and wraps her mother in a hug. "Stay at Cliff House? If only that I could."

31

The Book of Summer

Harriet E. Rutter
September 1, 1941
Cliff House Everlasting

That FDR is a real wet blanket, isn't he?

"Yes, we are engaged on a grim and perilous task. Forces of insane violence have been let loose by Hitler upon this earth."

Thanks, Frank. You're a real sport. A sunshine sally, to the gills.

For Pete's sake. As if we don't know a war is coming. He didn't have to tell us about it on Labor Day when we should be drinking and dancing and having a grand old time. Poor Ruby is already skulking about, pickled about this and that. Not that I blame her. She is the heart of this family, by and by. And soon all will go their separate ways. What next summer might bear, who the devil knows.

Well, dear Cliff House. This is Labor Day. A day we rest to celebrate all the non-resting from before. On the lawn, the last oysters are being shucked. A band plays near the bluff's edge. By midnight, the grounds will be littered with toppled-over champagne glasses and discarded oyster forks. That's how you'll know the party is over.

Changes come tomorrow, just like FDR said. All I can hope is that they don't come at us too fast. Is it too much to ask that we get to experience the sand of summer just a teensy bit more? Winter can be so damned long.

Until later (much, much later), I remain, yours truly,
Hattie R.

32

RUBY

September 1941

He swore he'd arrive in time for the Costume Ball, but by four o'clock it was clear that Daddy was a no-show and Mother would have to play Miner '49er on her own.

Long after the party began, Ruby sat moping on the bench outside the Yacht Club, swathed as she was in iridescent green fabric, a makeshift torch on her lap. She, the Statue of Liberty, or the saddest monument there ever was, according to Sam. He was somewhere in the ballroom, done up as Ben Franklin, kite and all. He looked swell but Ruby didn't give a fig about any of it.

She detested the rub of her own crummy attitude, it was like sand in a bathing costume but, dagnabbit, Ruby couldn't shake it away. Everything was going to seed, with her family and in the world. How were they supposed to close up Cliff House now? Shuttering the home at summer's end was like the bow atop a present to be opened later. Well, this present was a doggone mess and Ruby didn't even understand why.

"Ya searchin' for the woebegone dame?" she heard a voice say, one of the valets'. "She's on that bench."

Sure as sugar, he was talking about her. Ruby looked up to see her mother beating a hot path in her direction.

"Ruby Genevieve, enough with the sourpuss act. You get your fanny in there!"

Mother clomped up and whacked her mining pan against the very bench on which Ruby sat.

"You've got to show your face eventually," Mother said. "They're playing "The Star-Spangled Banner" and the entire orchestra is dressed in doughboy uniforms. Come on, love." Her voice softened. "All the good stuff is happening inside."

Ruby didn't respond and clamped both arms tighter around her belly. The Liberty getup was already hitting the skids. If Ruby wasn't careful, people would think she'd come dressed as the inside of a garbage can.

"Ruby?" her mom pressed. "What is it? Tell me."

"It's nothing, Mother. I just want to be alone."

"Are you . . . *hormonal?*"

"No!" Ruby said, and narrowed her eyes. "I'm not pregnant, if that's what you're asking."

"Then what . . ."

"I keep thinking he's going to come," she blurted. "He promised that he would." Ruby let out a shaky sigh. "It's the first time Daddy's ever gone back on his word."

"Oh, sweetheart," Mother said with a deep, gut-filling exhale. She sat beside her girl. "You can't be mad at your father. He'd give anything to be here."

"I'm not mad. I'm . . . worried."

"Aw, honey." Mother looped an arm around Ruby's shoulders. "You can't fret about your dad. He'd hate it. The man works hard to give you a life where worries are never had."

"Is he sick?" Ruby turned to face her. "Is there something wrong with Daddy? Because Topper says . . ."

Mother looked down at her hands.

"So he was right." Ruby let out a small gasp. "Topper says he hasn't been out because he's ill."

"He's been out some?"

"Three lousy days at Cliff House. Three! And he only spent one night."

"Oh, petal."

Ruby made a face. "Petal." The nickname was Daddy's, and his alone. Mother never used it and she wasn't one for nicknames. Already she seemed to be trying to patch some kind of hole.

"He's not been in top health," Mother said. "You've heard that nasty cough of his. The dang thing won't go away."

"*It won't go away?*" Ruby said, wide-eyed and gawping.

"That's not what I meant! He'll be fine! Your daddy is fine. He merely needed to be closer to his doctor these past weeks and didn't want to hassle with all the to-and-fro. Daddy will be right as rain by autumn!"

But autumn was just around the corner. What, exactly, was going to happen to make him "right as rain" in such a short time?

"That husband of yours has the lungs of a millworker," Ruby overheard Dr. Macy tell her mother over a hand of bridge one afternoon. "The old so-and-so hacks away like he works the factory lines himself."

It was meant to be a joke, but working the lines was exactly what Daddy did. He got down there, elbow-to-elbow, with all manner of immigrants and indigents, laboring among the grit and grime and Lord-knows. Whenever Ruby found a ball on the course she stopped to contemplate whether Daddy had touched it with his own two hands. That is, when he still made golf balls.

"How can he improve by autumn?" Ruby asked. "Summer ends in two days."

"Huh." Mother looked pensive. "I suppose it does. I don't know, Ruby. I can only tell you what I've heard. Your father is seeing his doctor, and working less, and forcing himself to rest, all things that go against his very nature. But he is determined and if Philip Young tells me that his cough will disappear, by Jove, I believe him."

Ruby nodded, unable to speak. Blasted doctors. Why couldn't they prescribe a good dose of sea air? It was said to cure anything from melancholia to tuberculosis. Surely it could remedy Daddy's run-of-the-mill (har, har) cough.

"I don't understand—" Ruby started, but was interrupted by a sudden flurry of spunk and costuming pouring out through the double doors.

"All right! Listen here, cookies!"

Hattie led the charge, with Topper, Sam, Mary, and P.J. trailing behind. Hattie was dressed as a cowgirl—a Fifth Avenue cowgirl, that is—with her mink bolero and calfskin heels. Topper was her Indian, eager to show off his "peace pipe" to anyone who cared.

"Well, lookee here," Mother said with a titter. "A welcoming party right out of Americana! I hope you aren't representing the Donner Party."

"No ma'am!" Hattie trilled. "Just a cowgirl and her band of assorted misfits, all of us intent on dragging ol' Lady Liberty onto the dance floor. You don't want Ben Franklin wandering off with some other dame, do ya?"

"I'd never!" Sam said. "Everyone knows Ben is a most loyal guy."

Ruby smiled weakly at her husband and then looked at Hattie.

"I'm not in the mood for dancing," she said.

"What kind of dingy excuse is that?" Hattie asked in a manufactured huff. "Listen here. You'd best get in the mood. You're not going to pout all night and be crowned the dullest girl at the ball. I simply won't allow it! It's the last party of the season."

"Actually there's the oyster party tomorrow night," Mary said. "At Cliff House. So not the last party, factually speaking."

"Okay, Mary Todd."

P.J. and Mary were dressed as the Lincolns, the joke being that they should've swapped roles. Mary was a dead ringer for Abe himself.

"I stand corrected." Hattie rolled her eyes. "It's the last *dance* of the season. Come on, you fuddy-duddy."

She reached a hand toward Ruby.

"Up!" she said. "Up and at 'em! You can't be this gorgeous and hide outside all night. Hip hop! To your feet! Get that hiney on the dance floor!"

Hattie snapped three times in rapid succession as Ruby continued to eye her outstretched hand. Things had been stiff between them, at least on Ruby's side, after what occurred in the pantry. Ruby recognized her own prudishness. She might have been a virgin on her wedding night, but there'd been stories aplenty at Smith. Nonetheless, the wad of revulsion lodged in her belly was difficult to pass. Yet as Ruby looked at her pal's hand, her reserve began to crackle like ice in the sun. Damn that Hattie, she could charm the gloom out of a ghoul.

"Let's go, my friend," Hattie said. "Chop-chop."

"Come on, baby," Sam said. "Where's that happy girl of mine?"

"I'll let you try my peace pipe," Topper offered.

At last Ruby smiled.

"A peace pipe?" she said, and stood. "An interesting accessory for someone so jazzed about the war."

The uncertainty and agitation began to lift from Ruby's body, like the fog off the ocean at midday. And just in the nick of time.

The summer was over and, according to Topper and Sam and the president of the USA, a war was imminent. Daddy was probably sicker than Mother let on and Topper and Hattie were . . . they were something. But Ruby couldn't let the summer end like this. Sconset had her heart and she needed to leave a piece of it there, a bookmark to hold her place until they returned.

"All right, people," she said. "Let's head inside. And I'll show you how the jitterbug is really done."

Just like that it was over.

The last drink was poured, the final cigarette ground out and left smoldering on the flagstone. The oysters had been scraped out, the shells hauled off. All that remained was a fishy scent in the air and Ruby on a chaise, blue polka-dotted frock fanned out around her.

As the caterer's van rumbled away, Ruby drained the last of her champagne and sighed. Soon she'd be back in her bedroom, in the tall brownstone near the river on Commonwealth Ave. A hundred miles away—no greater distance than the world. Ruby always felt at odds those first weeks back, even though Boston was her home and a few doors down Mother would be keeping house at number twenty-five, same as forever.

Yet the early days fit awkwardly, like a dress in the wrong size. Ruby would catch glimpses of herself in a mirror and marvel at her hair, shades blonder, and her legs, longer and leaner and tan. Even her eyes seemed to have an extra kick to their green. But by September's end, she'd fade back to her dishwater self. Everything would fit again.

Sam would do what he had all summer—it didn't change much for the men. He'd rise for work every Monday at six o'clock sharp, then toil away for the week, the chief difference between the seasons being where he dined and drank on weekends. Meanwhile, without Mother and Hattie and tennis and Cliff House itself, Ruby would need to drum up a scheme or two to fill her days. More war work, she thought with a frown. God bless it, she still wasn't sure about FDR and his big plans.

"Hey there, Ruby Red," Topper said as he tromped out onto the veranda. His shirt was untucked, his hair a sprawl.

"What's shaking?" he asked, and took a seat beside her.

"Nothing much. Just enjoying the last moments of this."

Ruby gestured toward the lawn, to where Miss Mayhew was trying to unstring lights from the trees. The woman cursed as she made it into a worse jumble.

"The ending is always bittersweet," Topper said. "But we had a helluva summer."

Did they? It was hard to tell, and so Ruby nodded as she gazed out toward the ocean. By October the grounds at Cliff House would turn gray and cold. Mother's flowers would shrivel as bayberries overtook the dunes below.

"We're lucky," Topper said, his eyes following hers. "To have this place to come back to."

"I don't want to hear nostalgia from you, Robert Appleton Young. It's going to set me in a foul mood. You're supposed to be merrier than that."

"Sorry, old gal," he said. "I'll slip back into my Topper duds by the end of the day. Just for you."

Ruby bobbed her head. They were quiet for several minutes, the wind whisking around them. As she stretched a shawl tighter around her shoulders, Ruby turned back toward her brother.

"Do you think you'll keep up with Hattie?" she asked. "After we all leave?"

"Aw, Red, not this old song. I know you envision yourself a merry matchmaker but things don't always line up as you'd please."

"I understand, okay? That's not what I'm asking."

Ruby paused.

What, exactly, *was* she asking? What was it Ruby wanted to know? That there was something between Hattie and Topper? That what she witnessed was more than two animals clawing at each other in sweaty, needful desperation? You didn't do that sort of thing for the heck of it. Or maybe you did. What did Ruby know about it, really? Perhaps European cupboards were positively packed with people doing exactly that. If so, Hitler was in for it should his aspirations pan out. An entire continent of people blind from the clap.

"You didn't answer my question," Ruby said at last. "Will you keep in touch?"

"'*Keep in touch*'?"

"Surely you're going to maintain some sort of . . . correspondence."

"Golly, dunno. Haven't really noodled on it," he said with his telltale Topper squint. "It's hard to say. Hattie's a swell gal, no matter what, and I'm grateful to have gotten to know her."

"I'll bet," Ruby mumbled.

"Of course you're the main thing we have in common." Topper gave his sister a nudge. "So without you around, who knows?"

"Without me around, who knows indeed."

"You know, we were sniggering the other day," he said. "About how much you want us to be married to each other, when we don't want that at all."

"I don't find that notably hilarious. You two make a fine couple and it's not like you haven't had plenty of time together . . . alone . . . without me. Don't tell me it hasn't been fun because I'm not buying it."

"Hattie's a blast, you know that," he said.

"I don't get it, then. She's the perfect woman!"

"Aw, hell, Red. Hattie's fab, but . . ."

"Is it . . ." Ruby stuttered. She gave him a hard stare. "Is it because she's . . . fast?"

Topper gave an uneasy laugh.

"I don't know if 'fast' is the word," he said.

"Did she give it up too easily? Is that the problem?"

"Good Lord, who said anything about 'giving it up'?" Topper's bluebell gaze suddenly went dark. "Not that it'd be any of your business if she had. Listen, Red. Fast or not, Hattie is a helluva gal but she's a different breed from you. Not bad, not good, just different. And different is all right to be. Don't let anyone claim otherwise."

Topper stood.

"I'm not sure what she told you," he said. "About us or me or anyone else. But the same prescription doesn't apply to everyone. Don't go judging her or anyone else too hastily."

"I'm not judging," Ruby said, though promptly realized that's exactly what she'd done. "Topper, are you mad? I didn't mean to . . ."

"Mad? At you? Never! Now then, I'm about three and a quarter whiskies past my limit so I'd better get myself to bed to avoid passing out in some scurrilous place. Mother will never get over having to extract me from the privet hedge the summer before last."

He bent down and kissed Ruby on the noggin.

"Go to sleep, kid. It's going to be an early morning."

Topper turned back toward the house.

As he went to open the door, Hattie materialized on the other side of the glass. She waved at the both of them.

"Speak of the devil," Topper said over his shoulder.

After a sly wink, Topper opened the door with a flourish. He took an exaggerated bow, just as he had the night of the Independence Ball, when the girls were exhausted, sun-chapped, and reveling in their tennis tournament win.

"Mademoiselle," he said. "We were just gabbing about you."

"Rats! I missed the dirt." Hattie pecked Topper on the cheek. "What's wrong, leaving so soon?"

"I'm leaving one way or another," he said. "Better to be deliberate about it. Night-o, dolls. Have the sweetest dreams."

As the door clicked behind him, Hattie plunked down beside Ruby, in the exact spot Topper had been.

"Hiya Rubes," she said. "What a shindig. Hard to believe the summer's over."

"Yup," Ruby said.

"It's been such a gas, Ruby. I'm so glad to have met ya. Who knew charity work could pay off like that? I was awfully skeptical about the whole Grey Ladies biz but it ended up being the best danged thing I could've done."

"Oh, thanks," Ruby mumbled, careful not to meet her friend's eyes.

"Look, pumpkin." Hattie placed a hand on Ruby's knee. "I know you want more between your brother and me—the rings and the gown and the luncheon for hundreds. And, Lord, Topper's a handsome guy who's a kick and a half. I can see why you love him like you do. But it's just not going to happen between or betwixt us." Hattie shook her head. "Breaks my heart to think the poor sap's gonna ship off soon. He's too sweet a guy to fight, I'll tell you what."

"Then make him *stay*," Ruby said, her voice coming out in a drawn-out whine. "He has nothing tethering him to the States. *You* be that person."

"I can't do much about the draft . . ."

"But he does defense work! He could drum up a reason to defer."

"Babydoll." Hattie squeezed Ruby's leg. "I know you don't want him to leave, and I understand entirely. But you can't keep him here, and neither can I. I'm not what he wants."

Not what he wants? He surely wanted her in the butler's pantry, Ruby had to fight herself from saying.

"Golly, Rubes! Don't look so glum. No hearts are broken, if that's what you're thinking. Topper and me, we're working from the same page. We've had a grand time but here's where it ends. Do you feel me?"

"I guess," Ruby said with a grumble, though she didn't "feel" her at all. "I thought I saw something more. Something different."

"Yeah." Hattie glowered. "I suppose you did."

"So where will you go?" Ruby asked. "From here?"

"Now, that is a story. Tomorrow I'm bound for New York City. That's right, your closest gal Hattie Rutter is going to be a true Manhattanite. Can you stand it?"

"You're going to New York? How come you didn't say anything?"

Hattie shrugged.

"Wasn't sure I'd go," she said. "But I was offered a position at a magazine in the city. *Mademoiselle*. You might have come across it."

"*Mademoiselle?!*" Ruby said, exploding into a smile, letting genuine joy lift her onto her feet. "That's amazing! The absolute tops!"

She smothered Hattie in a hug.

"Now, now, you don't want to strangle me dead before I even start," her friend said, laughing.

"Oh, Hattie, I'm so thrilled. And you'd better show me the city when I visit . . . once a month at least!"

"I'll always have a spot for you."

Just like that, any doubts Ruby had, any question as to Topper's "we had a helluva summer" proclamation, these things rolled away like they'd never been there at all. What did she care about European liberties? Ruby wasn't one to bother with others' private matters. Live and let live, she believed. Ruby had a lifelong chum in Hattie, a sister of the mind. A good thing, what with all the brothers.

In the end, those waning summer of '41 moments would be the last time Ruby and Hattie would speak face-to-face. By the next summer, Mr. Rutter would sell his island home and Hattie would morph into a New Yorker, exactly as promised.

Ruby followed her friend over the years as Hattie climbed the ranks, both professional and social. She'd see her, in a sense, years later and then not again for another twenty-five, when Ruby was in New York with her grown daughter. On that afternoon, she'd spot Hattie smack in the middle of the Rainbow Room. After catching her breath, Ruby would grab Cissy's hand and haul her onto the street.

"Geez, Mom," Cissy would gripe. "I'm getting awfully tired of being literally dragged all over this city. I don't even like shopping. I'm hardly going to need miniskirts at business school."

Ruby never explained herself. She never admitted that she'd seen an old friend, her best friend, from the last truly blissful summer at Cliff House. Cissy wouldn't have understood Ruby's reluctance to approach. Of course it wasn't the person Ruby feared, but the conversation the two women might have about the decades that had passed.

They used to say that on Nantucket every house had its tragedy, most borne of the sea. It was a ghost story, a fable, a warning to Summer People that sunshine and parties and croquet on the lawn were not the natural ways of the land.

When Ruby was young, a local boy told her about the curse of the sea. Mother scoffed at the legend as she cuddled a sobbing, shaky daughter in her pink-walled room. Those stories were for the whalers, Sarah said, and the fishermen. Her daddy dealt in rubbers and plastics. There'd be no curse with them.

The sea carried with it many misfortunes, that much was true. But man himself caused a few tragedies as well. Yes, Topper, it was a helluva summer. The parties. The sunshine. The golf. All that, and the last days of peace.

33

Thursday Morning

It's hazy, blustery. Bess again has sand in her teeth and on her skin, a sign she's at Cliff House all right. In ranking cold and windswept places, San Francisco has nothing on Sconset.

And as far as being at Cliff House goes, this morning Bess is all alone. Cissy is off rabble-rousing and pot-stirring in anticipation of the town meeting tonight. Where she is and when she might be home Bess doesn't bother to speculate. When she staggered out of bed at seven, Cissy had long since flown the coop.

After two hours boxing and bagging and tossing, Bess needed a break. Which is why she is now tromping down Baxter Road in the gloom as her face stings, her teeth chatter, and drizzle collects in a damp sheen on her windbreaker.

It's about a mile to the post office, a brisk walk, a bit of exercise, a chance to clear her mind as well as the dust from her lungs. Bess will grab a muffin at the market, or some coffee, or a breakfast sandwich from Claudette's. The weird thing about pregnancy, and residing on a cliff, is that constant sense of being simultaneously nauseated and outright famished. Half the time Bess can't decide if she's hungry or about to puke.

Despite the weather, Bess isn't the only one walking Baxter Road—she never is—and between the admiring of homes and exchanging hellos with other pedestrians, her mind stays if not fixed on Evan, at least flirting with him greatly. Never has a person been so wound up by a kiss that didn't happen on the lips.

She's thinking so much about the guy, that when Bess sees him get out of a car in front of the market, it's as though she's conjured him from the mist.

"Ev—!" she starts to yell.

A woman exits the driver's side. Bess lets out an involuntary gasp and then trips over a curb. Three quick strides later, she finds herself squatting behind a rack crammed with bikes. Bess Codman, the world's least stealthy spy. Within seconds even little kids are clucking about her behavior.

No matter. Evan and his companion haven't noticed, and so Bess retains her stakeout.

This woman, she's in a pair of skinny jeans, a red baseball cap, and a navy and gray Nantucket High School sweatshirt. A Whalers hoodie isn't exactly early-in-a-relationship attire, Bess notes with irritation. She looks to be about Bess's age, or older, and is attractive though not alarmingly so.

At first the woman's reasonable appearance is a relief. This is not the sexy Costa Rican. On the other hand—what the hell? Bess can compete with that—absent the pregnancy and Evan's stance on "repeating mistakes," of course. Why can't he be with some twenty-two-year-old scientist-model hybrid? Out of Bess's league would be much easier to take. There is exactly no justice in this world, she decides.

Not that Bess has any romantic interest in Evan Mayhew. It's all just "in theory." Another chapter for her fake Nantucket novel, her extremely fictional fiction.

Outside the market ("Fancy Groceries, Deli Meats," the sign promises), Evan puts a hand at the woman's back and leads her inside the store. This is quaint, way too quaint. Bess drops an f-bomb, much to her own surprise.

Bess waits. Her heart is thrumming. She moves when people need to retrieve their bikes.

"Just stretching my lower back," she mumbles to someone, who doesn't believe her at all.

Finally, Evan and the Ball Cap exit the store, carrying multiple bags. Bess crab-walks closer but can only make out a tube of salami, two baguettes, and what she hopes is sparkling water. The makings of a picnic, if Bess were to guess. How delightful for a Thursday morning. Don't these people need to work?

He takes the woman's bag. They've come in her car, a wagon of sorts. No wonder Bess didn't recognize it. As Evan relieves her of her load, she gives him this look, like he's just plucked a rainbow from the sky and looped it around her neck. Bess can't blame Ball Cap one goddamned bit. It's the exact way she looked at him last night.

And just like that, both doors slam shut and they drive away. A burp rises in Bess's throat. She spits on the ground.

Bess's knees crack and sting as she rises to standing. Some dude in yellow spandex scowls in her direction. She's been holding on to his bike and he makes a big show of unlocking it. Words cannot express how little Bess wants his toy. With a muttered and quarter-hearted apology, Bess turns and heads back up Baxter Road.

She's forgotten about the possible coffee and food, the things that seemed so appealing only half an hour before. Bess kicks the road as she shuffles along. She's mad at Evan, or mad at her situation, who knows. In Sconset, it's hard to remember that sometimes people get on with their lives. Tears prick at Bess's eyes, or maybe it's only the sand. Either way, it's back to Cliff House for Bess. Back to wrapping up and plowing forward. Here's to new beginnings. Here's to new mistakes.

34

Thursday Afternoon

"Forty-six," Bess counts. "Forty-seven."

Forty-seven pieces of workaday dinnerware are spread out before her. Bess suspects they hold no inherent market value, but they're her grandmother's, so what then? Everything in the whole house was Ruby's first, adding a layer of meaning to dishes and tchotchkes and everyday junk. She's starting to think there are only two answers to the Cliff House problem. Keep everything, or throw it all away.

Be reasonable, Grandma Ruby would say.

Maybe Cissy's right. Bess has lost her solid New England sense. But she's knocked up, almost divorced, and living in San Francisco, so good luck getting it back.

As she remains befuddled by the sheer amount of *stuff,* Bess's stomach roars. With the morning's ~~aborted~~ failed coffee-and-muffin mission, Bess's entire sustenance that day has consisted of two handfuls of almonds found in the kitchen. And they were stale, softer than nuts should be. She refuses to eat Cissy's peaches and Brie.

The doorbell rings. The sound is so unexpected, Bess wonders if it's merely the internal clang of her own exhaustion. Lord knows Cissy doesn't have visitors these days. Gone are the bridge games and tennis matches and drinks on the veranda. After all, it's hard to play tennis without a court, difficult to lounge on a smattering of bricks.

The bell rings again. Bess goes to answer it.

"Oh!" she exclaims, both tickled and peeved when she wrenches open the sand-and-salt-stripped door. "Evan! Hi!"

He smiles in return, a tray of coffee balanced in his left hand, a white bag clutched in his right. Suddenly she remembers that Evan Mayhew is a lefty. It's why he made a choice first baseman back in the day, according to Cis anyway. Bess just thought he looked hot in those pants.

"What are you doing here?" Bess asks.

Shouldn't he be working? Or trying to feel up some broad beneath her hoodie at a picnic lunch? Granted, the weather has worsened today. Perhaps they canceled their meal.

"You said you needed help." Evan steps through the doorway. "I'm the help. Also, I brought you coffee and lunch. Sandwiches. Chips. Sea salt and vinegar, to be exact. Your favorite, right?"

Bess ogles the bag.

"Let me guess," she says. "Leftover salami?"

"Why? Did you want salami?"

"Not particularly, no."

Evan's face tenses, like he's smelled something rotten.

"Well, okay," he says. "Then it's good I brought turkey and roast beef. You can have either. Or both. I've already eaten."

"Yeah, I'll bet."

"Is everything okay, Bess?"

"Yes." She jiggles her shoulders. "Sorry. I'm a little . . . not myself. Really. It's sweet of you to come. I *am* hungry. Starving, as a matter of fact. But shouldn't you be somewhere?"

"You mean work? Nah. We had to cut out early because of the rain. It's not a problem though as we're way ahead of schedule. Please reserve your shock. Anyway, you need more help here than my guys do over there."

"That is clearly true."

Bess glances down. She does need assistance, in myriad ways, including the fact that she's back at it with the Boston College sweatpants and free-hanging boobs. She makes Ball Cap Lady look like Nantucket's foremost leader in fashion.

"But really," she says. "I can't subject you to this mayhem. It wouldn't be polite."

"You're turning down free labor?" Evan says, and cocks a brow. "That's not smart. Especially considering." He looks around. "This house is not even minimally packed."

"True story. But going through someone else's mess? What a nightmare."

"Better than going through your own mess," Evan says with a wink. "I won't take no for an answer. Wow, this old house . . ."

Evan walks farther into the home, focus shifting from floor to ceiling as he goes. Every couple feet he knocks on a wall or runs his hand along a molding, admiring the work.

"It's so beautiful," he says. "And so much . . . the same."

"You mean the decor? Yeah, well, Cissy's too busy raising hell to bother with renovations or keeping up with trends."

"Lucky house," Evan says, and stops beneath the three-hundred-pound black iron lantern hanging thirty feet above.

They are in the center hall, the heart of the home. Whereas everything else in the place is beginning to look tired, a little shabby, definitely worn, this room steals the show. Aside from the dark wood floors, it's entirely white, the paint and wainscoting exquisitely kept. The hall is six-sided, two-storied, and has a staircase running in a spiral around its walls. Though the chandelier is daunting and grand, not to mention handcrafted in her great-grandfather's factory, it's the thirty transom windows and the Atlantic blue that illuminate the room.

"I can see why you guys refuse to move," Evan says, and meets eyes with Bess.

"Oh, I want to move . . ."

"No you don't."

Evan hooks right toward the kitchen, but not before tapping the stair above the room's entrance.

"The kitchen is different," he notes, once inside.

"Yeah, well, everyone updates their kitchen. Even Cissy."

"It looks great." Evan shakes his head. "This is such a stunning old home."

He sets down the bag, and then the tray of coffee. Bess counts three cups.

"Where should we start?" Evan asks.

He picks up his coffee, and takes a sip. Then he nods toward the other two cups.

"Help yourself. I don't think we drank coffee back in high school but I got you black. Figured it was your style."

"So you view me plain and dark?" Bess says with a small laugh.

"Strong and unaffected."

Bess blushes. Already her tenderness toward him is returning. No use punishing the poor guy. He's done precisely nothing wrong.

"So which is mine?" Bess asks. "By the way, if the other one's for Cissy, you've wasted your money. She's been gone since daybreak. Where? Who knows. Trying to write up a proposal for some sort of geotube plot, I'd assume. They're holding an emergency meeting tonight."

"Yeah I've heard. Repeatedly and with many curse words involved. Alas, both coffees are for you."

"Both?" Bess says. "Wow, the bags under my eyes must be getting worse."

"No, the two cups represent two options."

Evan points to one.

"French roast from Claudette's . . ." He gestures to the other. "Or decaf, if you'd rather."

"Oh brother." Bess rolls her eyes. "Does this relate to my, uh, revelation?"

"It does," he says with a grin.

"You're really trying to get me to commit to a decision, aren't you?"

"You've already made a decision. I only want to know what it is."

Wobbly-stomached about why, exactly, Evan might want to know, Bess reaches for the decaf but then changes her mind and grabs the French roast. She takes a sip of neither.

"I want to show you something," Bess says, and jams the French roast back into its cardboard. "Follow me."

She leads Evan into the butler's pantry.

"Ah. Your famous escape route," Evan says.

He taps on these walls, too.

"Yep. Also."

Bess gestures to a stack of yearbooks on the left-side counter. Some are Clay's, some are Lala's, but most are Bess's.

"My Nantucket High yearbooks," she says, then immediately pictures the woman's hoodie.

Was she familiar? She didn't seem familiar. Bess shakes her head.

"Isn't it wild that I still have them?" she says.

"Lizzy C., the whole reason people purchase yearbooks is for keeping."

"We bought them? I thought they were forced upon us."

Bess flips open the front cover of Nantucket High School: 1996–1997. Acting as if she doesn't know its precise location, Bess ticks through a few pages until she lands on Evan's varsity baseball team photo. He's in the back row, center. Royal-blue cap. White grin.

"Look at that guy," she says, tapping the photograph with an unexpectedly shaky finger. "He must've had all the babes after him."

"Not as far as I know. Only the babe who mattered."

Face hot, Bess claps the yearbook shut and stretches toward one of Grandma Ruby's photo albums.

"Check this out," Bess says, changing the subject if not with deftness at least with speed. She pushes the album in Evan's direction. "It's so bizarre. My grandmother saved dozens of articles written by some friend of hers and I can't figure out why this person was so important. Her name is in the book but Grandma Ruby never mentioned her *at all.*"

Evan shrugs.

"She was probably a friend from school. Nostalgia will get you every time."

"Yes it will." Bess skims a few more pages and then closes the book with a sigh. "It's like Ruby was stalking her."

Stalking and nostalgia: Both run in the family, it seems.

"I didn't know your grandmother well," Evan says. "But she didn't seem like the stalking type. She intimidated me, to be honest. I saw her as so regal and refined."

"She was both. A nice balance to the total spaz that is my mother—God love her. We bonded over the various manifestations of Cissy cuckooness."

"Your mother is a pain in the ass," Evan says. "But she's one of the greats."

"Exactly. Pain in the ass. Awesome. At the same time. That's why she'll drive you nuts."

Bess opens a box and begins sifting through it.

"You know, there's a lot to do," Evan says, scanning the room and the kitchen beyond. "I'm thinking . . . sort out the memorabilia later?"

"I know, I know," Bess says. "But first . . ."

She passes Evan a piece of paper, yellowed and thin.

"My grandfather's discharge papers from World War Two. I thought he was injured but this says he was discharged for 'psychoneurosis.'" Bess frowns. "Could be code for alcoholic."

"You're the doctor."

"We're more specific these days. We can't get away with general hysteria or run-of-the-mill batshit loony tunes."

Bess pitches the paper back into its box.

"Grandma would hate this," she says. "The packing up, the moving of Cliff House. Her mom conceived it but the house was Ruby's through and through."

"Yes, she'd hate it," Evan says. "And so do you, which is why you've done such a crap job packing."

"Hey!"

"It's true. Hell, I hate it and my own father is the demon single-handedly trying to thwart Cissy's efforts to preserve it."

"Yeah." Bess snorts. "Your father is a demon all right. We shouldn't even be in the same room."

"You miss her."

Bess looks up.

"Ruby?" she says, though the question, and therefore the answer, is clear. "Yeah. I do. I miss her a ton."

"Come on," Evan says, and grabs Bess's hand. "I have an idea."

She looks down at his fingers meshed with hers. Her insides surge.

"Shouldn't we . . . finish packing?" Bess says.

"*Finish* packing? I hate to break it to you, but you haven't even started. Let's go."

Evan slants his head in the direction of Baxter Road.

"What're a few more hours?" he asks.

"Uhhhh . . ." Bess says, her skin at once clammy. "A few more hours might be the difference between a full living room and half of one."

"So either Cliff House will be here when we get back, or it won't."

"Okay, that's not funny."

"At least you won't be in it when it falls."

"Fair enough," Bess says in a grumble. "Can I change?"

"Why are you always so worried about your clothes?"

Bess barks out a laugh.

"That is the first time anyone's ever accused me of being worried about my clothes. I wear scrubs for a job. Pajamas, basically."

Evan doesn't respond, and with a soft and careful tug leads Bess back into the kitchen and down the hall.

"I should at least put on a bra," she insists, trying not to think of her hand, or how firmly it is being held.

What would Ball Cap think?

"I couldn't rob Cissy of her hard-earned reputation for eccentricity," Bess adds.

"All right, princess."

Evan drops Bess's arm, which falls to her side and then hangs there awkwardly.

"Go find your coveted brassiere and meet me outside by the truck. This field trip shouldn't take long but it'll be worth the time."

35

Thursday Afternoon

"A graveyard," Bess says, following Evan through the Mount Vernon Gate and into the oldest section of Prospect Hill Cemetery. "To get my mind off the loss of my beloved family retreat, you've brought me to a place that is the very symbol of death?"

"Earthly demise," he says. "That's all it is. Come on." Evan takes her hand for the second time that day. "You need to tell a certain someone what's happening. And then say farewell."

They head west, toward the Soldier's Turn.

"How do you know where we're going?" Bess calls, trying to keep pace, trying not to get caught up in a bramble and find herself face-down on the final resting spot of some Eliza or Ebenezer.

"I come here quite a bit," Evan says. "So I know my way around."

"Wow . . . That's, um, odd."

Evan pauses, partway between a Joy and a Pigeon. If Bess isn't mistaken, his cheeks are slightly flushed. Probably because of the wind, which is growing stronger by the gust. According to her weather app, today they can expect gales of up to forty miles per hour.

"I like the history of this place," Evan says. "All of the island's founders are buried at Prospect Hill. Right here we have the Honorable David Joy, who was an abolitionist. And then there's Lucy Sturtevant Pidgin, M.D."

Bess leans forward, squinting. A female doctor born in 1850. She hadn't known there was such a thing.

"Across the path is Charles Robinson," Evan continues. "He was the first developer in Sconset. You know that footbridge over Gully Road?"

Bess nods. Anyone who's spent more than a day in Sconset has used it. Bess must've a hundred times. With college friends or island friends, on summer nights they'd walk the full way from Cliff House to the Summer House piano bar and back again, both ways over Gully Road.

"He built that bridge," Evan says. "Come on, let's keep going."

He directs Bess onward, past the families Luce and Cartwright and Wyer and Macy. They spy a Folger, a Murphy and, yes, a Hussey or three. DULCE ET DECORUM EST PRO PATRIA MORI, Bess sees on one headstone. Thanks to Choate, she knows her Latin and her Roman poems, too. *"It is sweet and glorious to die for one's country."*

"This poor lady," Evan says, pointing to Sarah C. Gardner. "Died soon after giving birth. She was depressed, apparently, and confined to the 'child bed.' She escaped from her nurse and ultimately drowned."

"God, how sad," Bess says, thinking of Sarah C. Gardner and the others, too.

So many women plus all those men LOST AT SEA OF LOST AT WAR. And the children and babes—in the ground before they had a chance. The ache of sorrow tightens across Bess's chest.

Soon they pass by the Starbuck Gate, two large pillars holding up a rusty scroll. Bess hesitates at one gravestone. It's thin, white, and rectangular, with clumps of moss growing beneath it.

" 'While briefly in life's book we are,' " Bess reads, " 'Death shuts the story of our days.' Well, that's cheery."

"It's also true."

"Look at this one," Bess says. " 'She was all a woman should be.' Bummer. I was planning to use that epitaph myself. I would love to know what it means. She was a good housekeeper? Aces in the sack? What?"

"Both I'd venture. Let's get a move on." Evan lengthens his stride. "I think it's about to rain again."

Bess scrambles after him. Fantastic. More weather.

"When'd you become an amateur historian?" Bess asks as they round the corner down the Macy Path. "It's very cute, and you should definitely use that factoid on the ladies, but it doesn't seem like you."

Or does it? Bess doesn't altogether know.

"Hey," Evan balks. "Who ya calling an amateur? I'll have you know that I'm the president-elect of the Nantucket Historical Society."

"What?" Bess says, gawking in surprise. "That is completely . . ."

"Lame?"

"No. Unexpected." Bess smiles sadly. "Awesome."

With each hour, Bess grows ever more glum about her fake novel that will never come to pass. Evan Mayhew is still a handsome bastard and now he's shown a snapshot of the old man he might become. Salty, quick-witted, and pestering island folk about family trees. That Costa Rican lady must've been some kind of idiot to let him out of her clutches. And Ball Cap—well, she's doing okay. Apparently.

"Ah," Evan says. "Here we are."

"What now?"

Bess shakes her head. Though she knows exactly where they stand, she is fifty kinds of lost.

"Right there," Evan says, and shows her a stone: weather-beaten, grayed, and cracked.

RUBY GENEVIEVE YOUNG PACKARD
March 10, 1919–February 5, 1994
Lived Respectfully, Loved Vastly

Bess smiles.

"Clay and I used to joke her epitaph should be: 'Stop complaining. I don't believe in it.' God, I miss her." Bess turns toward Evan. "Thanks a lot, jerk. Now I'm feeling even more 'hormonal.' "

"Hmm. Or are you just 'feeling,' period? What did you tell me last night?"

"Uh, my jeans don't fit? Don't tell Cissy I hate oysters?"

"Yes. That and you think half the problem with prescription drug abuse in this country is that people are afraid to feel stuff," he says. "Then you promptly spent twenty minutes justifying your penchant for elastic pants."

"I'm not afraid to have feelings," Bess says. "I feel all over the place. Chiefly about my sweatpants."

"Okay, you big feeler." He taps the top of Ruby's gravestone. "The two of you are due for a chat."

"But I already said good-bye."

"Not like this."

Evan takes a step toward Bess. He pushes a strand of wind-and-salt-tangled hair from her face.

"Tell her about Cliff House, and about you," he says. "Close the circle. It's the only way to move on and make room for something new."

"I don't want anything new. I like the old and the usual," Bess says. Then adds: "I'm talking about houses, obviously."

"Of course," Evan says with a smirk. "I'm going to leave you and your grandmother alone. I'll wait for you up by the Soldier's Turn. Take your time."

He gives her a gentle pat on the back and then walks away.

As she listens to Evan's footsteps fall off, Bess kneels beside Ruby's headstone. She places a sprig of zinnia, clipped from the Cliff House gardens by Evan, in the place a heart might be.

"Good thing Cissy didn't see Evan cut this," Bess says. "Or the Mayhew family would have a whole new set of problems. I think he even used an old steak knife. Oh, Grandma."

Bess sighs and shakes her head.

"Okay, this whole thing is ridiculous," she grumbles, even as tears wet her lashes. "Gram, I wish I knew how to say this."

Bess lowers all the way onto the ground, sitting Indian-style beside Ruby's marker. Yes, Indian-style, none of that "crisscross applesauce" garbage because that's what it was called when she was a kid, before it was decided an entire ethnic group might be offended by what is a pretty comfy seated position.

"I don't know what to tell you," Bess says, picking at the pebbles on the ground. "Other than things are in complete chaos. It started, well . . ." She stops. "God, it's been twenty years since we last spoke. I guess it all started just after you died, when I got kicked out of Choate. Don't get mad because, well, it was sort of on purpose."

36

The Book of Summer

Mrs. Mary Young
June 7, 1942
Cliff House

Ruby's hassled me about this book. I haven't written in it for over a year, she says. A year. It seems shorter and longer both.

"We have to keep the book going," Ruby says. "Because we're the only ones here. They've left the ship for us to captain. We need to take charge. Nothing left to chance."

Taking charge starts with this book apparently, peculiar as it's not as though the boys spent much time jotting down entries. The book seems mostly the women's, and these days Cliff House is, too.

Sometimes it hits me with might, the startling reality that we are alone and the men more than a workweek away. In past years we spent more time preparing for their arrival than actually enjoying the fact that they're here.

Even now I have to remind myself that come Saturday, they won't magically appear in the drive. It will only be the three of us: me and Ruby and of course Mama Young. What a lonely crew. My dear mother-in-law's been moony as the night sky because of it. Can't get a smile out of her to pay the postman.

Not everything's changed on the island. The boats still run from Woods Hole and New Bedford. The shops and restaurants have put away their "Closed for Winter" signs even though many speculated that after Pearl Harbor resort towns would close for the duration. Everyone is playing at business as usual despite the war raging overseas. In a week's time they'll commission the Yacht Club, and celebrate the raising of the flag.

The Grey Ladies keep up their work but is it enough? There's talk of a man from New Bedford, rescued after thirty days on a raft. He arrived battered and damaged, in body and in mind, and at half the weight as when he left. And his story is a happy one. I think of the others who would trade their souls to be found at sea in any kind of state.

I'll tell you this much, I don't have the urge to hand this stranger a blanket or some woolen socks. I want to tend his wounds. I want to do more.

Best regards,
Mary Young

37

RUBY
Summer 1942

June 4, 1942

Hi-de-ho, my darling Rubes!

Thanks for the jingle-jangle of the other night. It was a kick to hear your voice. Golly, I miss Sconset. I'll try to get out this summer, by hook or by crook. It's the loveliest place around. The rose-covered homes and dawdling summer days in Sconset are exactly why we're fighting this war.

As for me, I'm still in Sag Harbor batting off suitors. Don't get the wrong idea—these courters are of the corporate type. My stint at Mademoiselle *has come to an end. It was buckets of fun but you can only brood over fashion and frippery for so long before you go bonkers. The wrong colors, the right patterns, and all the hell they've given me for wearing slacks and not wearing a hat. I don't quite get this "style" racket. If the getup isn't your brainchild, then you can't count yourself as having panache. And that's the truth as I know it.*

Now it's off to tackle more serious endeavors. Journalistic reporting in general, foreign corresponding to be specific. A modern-day Margaret Fuller, or so I dream! Perhaps I shall pursue something more akin to Dorothy Thompson. I can't imagine an achievement bearing greater thrill than to get booted out of Germany by Hitler for being a pest. Of course I have to nab the gig first—all in due time.

I'll keep you posted, from the front lines here in Sag Harbor, which is itself more a sideline than anything.

Love and kisses,
HR

Fridays at the Yacht Club were a lot less fun with the boys gone.

It took some mettle for Ruby to get herself all gussied and glammed. If you were togged to the bricks and no one was around to see, then what? She didn't even have Hattie around, offering her review. All that and her duds didn't fit exactly as they should. Ruby was "in the club," as they said. In other words, she was pregnant.

Not that she was complaining. Ruby was thrilled to be officially on stork watch, despite the strained buttons on the blouse and the stretched fabric across her backside. At least she wasn't in E-Z-On maternity frocks just yet. But Lord did Ruby find herself constantly beat, and how. Beat and green-gilled and forever itching to take a snoozer under the buffet table. Plus, her hooves were awfully swollen for someone still able to (somewhat) squeeze into her same clothes. All that and gin tasted weird—less ginny somehow. It took most of Ruby's gumption to polish off a single glass. But she had to. How else was she to sleep?

Pregnant. Three months gone. All Ruby ever wanted was to be a mother. But a day late and all that, at least regarding the draft board. She'd been hoping for class 3-B: men with dependents engaged in war work, and therefore exempt from service. With Daddy's gas mask production Sam had the work box ticked, but their love bug was not a dependent quite yet. And so Sam joined the service.

At that very moment Sam was still Stateside, training for whatever calamitous situation Uncle Sam would throw him into. After a month or two—the timing was aggravatingly vague—Ruby's dear husband would step aboard a ship bound for a strange land and with God knows what munitions strapped to his body and stashed in his trunk. He was the kindest, most generous man to grace the mortal world and Ruby could not square with the fact that he was training to stare another human dead in the eyes and shoot.

"I'm learning to work a boat," he swore. "That's all."

It was a very Sam Packard type of lie, gentleman that he was.

And Topper, well, Topper had to top them all. He'd taken up as a nose gunner in the AAF, flying B-24 Liberators—which were built for tall pilots, he did not fail to add. The boy had always been proud of his stature. Ruby was surprised he didn't claim Liberator pilots had to likewise be certified as officially debonair. Ruby pictured the commotion he must've made with the ladies when he visited the local canteen in his uniform and sheepskin jacket.

Like Sam, Topper was neck-deep in training, which sounded preferable to war, except when her baby brother got too frank with the details. Things like unreliable fuel gauges and engines that fell plumb away. And the Krauts weren't even shooting at them yet.

"Don't worry, Ruby Red," he wrote. "The planes have four engines."

Yes, four engines. Until they had three. It was the first time Ruby realized a soldier could die before he began to fight. Thank God Sam was on a ship, which seemed safer somehow, Pearl Harbor notwithstanding. He wouldn't last two minutes with plane parts dropping off.

"Madame," said one of the Yacht Club waiters, and set a plate before Ruby. It had on it a thin slice of cake, or a facsimile of cake anyway. "Your dessert."

"Thanks," Ruby said, though she didn't have the stomach for it.

As the waitstaff bustled about, Ruby poked and clicked at her plate, scoping the room and its guests. They weren't all women. There were plenty of old fellows and at least a dozen servicemen now that the Yacht Club was open to all in uniform. Or as Mary griped the night before: "It's become a real mixed bag."

But although the dining room was chockablock with Nantucketers and off-islanders alike, there wasn't a one Ruby cared to kibitz with. She was awfully lonely in such a crowded room.

"Hello there," called a voice.

As if summoned for duty, Mary scissored up, looking ever more gray and haggard. Rationing had begun on their gilded shores, and Mary herself was like a rationed version of a normal dame. No sugar, lard, or gas with that one. The woman's new, war-friendly, rubberless girdle didn't help.

"Not that an old stick rule like Mary has anything to suck in," Ruby could very nearly hear Hattie say.

Sakes alive, Ruby missed her friend. She missed their bull sessions, likewise their tennis matches and rounds of golf. To speak nothing of all the parties and tea dances they double-starred on their calendars, all summer long. Once again, Hattie's voice clattered through Ruby's ears.

"What's with all the waltzing?" she said. "If we're going to dance, we should *dance*. How about the rumba? I could teach ya. I learned it myself during one sen-saysh summer in Cuba."

With Hattie gone, who would rumba then? It was rubber girdles and waltzes for the duration.

"How are you doing?" Mary asked, and lowered herself onto the chair beside Ruby.

"I'm okay," Ruby said, still pushing her cake around the plate. "A tad fagged out."

"What's the matter? Don't like the dessert?"

Ruby made a face and shrugged.

"Papier-mâché is best left for homecoming floats," she said.

"Well, sugar *is* under ration. Even our tongues must make sacrifices!"

Mary seemed almost giddy at the prospect of suffering all the way down to her taste buds. The woman was born to ration. Someone needed to clue her in that conserving personality and spunk wasn't going to help the war effort.

"Talk about dim-out rules," Hattie might've said.

A smirk found Ruby's lips and she covered her mouth with a napkin.

"Something funny?" Mary asked in a slight huff.

"No, not at all." Ruby cleared her throat and set her napkin back in her lap. "The rationing doesn't bother me that much."

"Then why are you sitting in a corner by yourself when there's a party going on?"

"Some party," Ruby mumbled. "Listen, Mare, it's hard to explain. It's nothing and everything at once. I'm just 'off' I suppose. Good grief, I really need to stop the bellyaching. Mother would have my head."

Not that Sarah Young was a ball of sparkle herself lately. In fact, these days Sarah Young took the sourpuss prize, hands down.

"It must be hard," Mary said, to Ruby's vast surprise. "To face this pregnancy with Sam away, when it's your first child and Mother Young . . ."

Mary wavered, plainly debating whether to release a potshot sitting at the tip of her tongue. Commiseration was dandy but you couldn't go around biting the hand that fed you.

"She's been a real crab lately, hasn't she?" Ruby said with a laugh, knowing exactly where her sister-in-law was headed.

Mary studied her before finally relenting with a resigned nod. Ruby squeezed her sister-in-law's arm, her heart at once softening to the old gal. Mary would give her left eye, or her new girdle, for the chance to produce the first Young offspring. And here was the scamp Ruby beating her to the punch. Not that Ruby's tot would be a Young in name. So Mary still had that at her hip.

"I suppose Mother's earned the right to grump," Ruby said. "With Daddy so sick and fighting her every step of the way. She turns her back and he's out the door, headed toward the office."

Ruby shook her head, feeling a little pluck of happy at the thought of Daddy acting like his normal self.

"He's a handful," Mary agreed.

"Isn't it unusual sometimes?" Ruby asked. "I know they're trying with the dances and parties and same old rigmarole, but it makes everything bleaker. Like a bad paint job on an old clunker. Why try to impersonate last summer? Or the summer before? This cake . . ."

She mashed her fork into it.

"Let's stop pretending we can have dessert," Ruby said.

Mary made a sound. Was she crying? Choking? Fighting off a seizure? Ruby went to slug her on the back, but realized it was only Mary, suffering from amusement. A chuckle, almost.

"Have you ever met such a spoiled brat?" Ruby said. "A war overseas and I'm complaining about parties that aren't up to snuff!"

"Actually, I was thinking that I quite agree. Enough with the pretending. What's that expression Topper uses? 'You said it'?"

Ruby smiled.

"The phrase you're looking for is 'You shred it, wheat.' "

"That's the one."

Ruby sighed deeply. She set her fork on the table.

"I shouldn't grouse," she said. "The boys are off saving the world, putting themselves in danger, and I'm meowing about dessert."

"But it's not about the cake, really," Mary said, astonishing Ruby with her insight. "It's the change. And you miss your friend, too. The Rutter girl."

"I do," Ruby said, one eye on Mary, who was suddenly the most changed of all. "I miss Hattie something fierce. I know you didn't much care for her—"

"Oh, she's fine," Mary lied.

"But Hattie just had a way of making everything seem gayer. She swears she'll come out soon but she's hunkered down in Sag Harbor, entertaining an offer or twenty."

"Twenty offers!" Mary yelped, grabbing at her throat.

Ruby could see it all over her face: *I knew that girl was fast . . .*

"Offers of the *career* variety," Ruby clarified as Mary managed to look relieved and disappointed all at once.

Thank God it was Ruby who stumbled upon Hattie and Topper in the pantry. Mary likely would've called the fuzz. Or expired on the spot.

"What would Hattie need with a man?" Ruby said. "She's going places. I guess that's half the problem. Don't get me wrong, I'm proud as peaches, but sometimes it's hard to be the one left behind."

Left by Hattie, and Sam, and Topper, too, as it happened. And though Ruby tried not to think about it, soon Daddy would be added to the group. He'd already outlived doctors' estimations by a good six months.

"It can be hard to be left behind," Mary said, once again displaying uncharacteristic human understanding. "But, rest assured, when a woman claims to be 'going places' it is usually in the wrong direction."

Ruby let out a cackle. So she was the same Mary, by and by. Swell to know that not everything was thrown to the four winds.

"Oh, Mary," Ruby said, still chuckling. "You do hold a curious place in my heart. And I think Hattie will do all right. She'll score some primo gig at the *Post*, then jet-set all over the world, hobnobbing with dignitaries and irritating fascist dictators left and right. What a life!"

"Yes. But you have a life as well. Two times over."

Mary gestured to Ruby's stomach, and Ruby smiled in return. Yes, a baby. Her parting gift from Sam, the lug. If nothing else, she had that—motherhood. Nothing important, mind you. Only what she'd dreamt of her whole dang life.

"Fancy a smoke, Mare-bear?" Ruby asked. "Because right about now I could use a cig and some fresh air like a rat needs his cheese."

"A rat and his cheese," Mary said, grumbling and rising to her feet. "No one would doubt you were raised with a pack of wild brothers."

"Nah. Mostly I was raised away at school."

Ruby put a ciggie to her lips and bummed a light from the chap two tables over. Folger-something-or-other. He was in uniform, another body for the cause. If Hattie were there, she'd give the man a farewell look-see of her leg, raising her hemline to midthigh to tide him over. Ruby would never do such a thing. She didn't have Hattie's gams, for one.

"Let's go outside," Ruby said, taking a puff. "The night's clear. Not a bank of fog for miles. A damned miracle."

"I'll join you but, Ruby, I have to say, when I was in Boston last I was talking with your father. And, well, he believes cigarette smoke is unhealthy. A carcinogen. He read it in some scientific journal. It made me quit cold turkey!"

"Don't listen to old Dad," Ruby said with a snort. "He also thinks they'll discover a cure for polio."

"Be that as it may, the smoking thing seems to have legs. Notably bad are the Turkish ones you prefer. You should at least switch to ivory-tipped."

"My cigarettes are French."

"Same thing." Mary slapped at the air. "Foreign, you know. I'm only suggesting you lay off on account of the babe."

She pointed to Ruby's not-quite-a-belly.

"Aw, Mare," she said. "Don't be such a nervous Nell. Smoking is a stress reliever, everyone knows. Plus, the doctor says I can only gain fifteen pounds. How else am I supposed to keep my weight down?"

"Ruby Packard, you look fantastic. I'd never know you were pregnant if you hadn't told me."

"Thanks, kid. So, whaddya think?" Ruby said, the cig hanging out the side of her mouth like a Hollywood gangster's. "Should we check out what's happening on the harbor?"

She linked her arm through Mary's. Mary gave a little jolt as though she'd been stung by a bee. But after thinking about it, she settled into the gesture.

"Sure," Mary said. "The harbor."

"All those boats," Ruby said, leading her along. "I hear there's a soirée on every one. With no gas and no go they might as well put the clippers to some use. At least these parties aren't pretending to be something they're not."

July 10, 1942

Dear Ruby,

Shoot! Shoot and a half!

I'm sorry I haven't made it out Nantucket way. Things have been dizzy-busy and I hardly have time to sit down for a meal. I hate that I missed the Independence Day festivities. And I could stab myself for not getting the telegram out to you in time. My apologies! Kiss, kiss!

I truly hope you didn't hold a place at the table for me. But you better not have gotten yourself a new doubles partner! Those Coffin girls must've been tripping over themselves when they saw you were on the tennis market. My advice: Stay away from them both. The chubby one hits forehands like she's tossing grenades that miss their mark. Listen Rubes, that is our trophy to win. Next year. Promise.

Now, on to off-island things. You might've noticed the postmark. I'm back in New York! I know you weren't too jazzed about me nosing around the front lines. Not to worry. Turns out nailing down a foreign correspondent post is no cinch. Even worse that I'm of the female persuasion.

"If we're gonna send a gal," one editor told me, "it has to be a woman who looks a little rough."

I haven't given up, though! If I have to ugly it up, then by jove, I'll do it. In the meantime, any of these diddies ring a bell?

"The Yanks shot to victory thanks to a 3-run homer by Joe DiMaggio. The Yankee Clipper walloped it far left in the top of the sixth. The swell fielding during the game helped shore up the win."

"Ted Williams was fined $250 for loafing and generally acting screwy."

"McCarthy's boys may have lost, but so did the Sox. The Boston bozos are still lagging at four games back."

Yessiree! That's right! You're pals with the latest sports reporter for the Daily Mirror*! I happened to walk into the editor's office approximately one hour after a reporter died of apoplexy while covering a game. Poor so-and-so. But good for me, as they sent me straight out on the beat! My first game was the New York Black Yankees versus the New York Cubans. Me, a real sports fiend. Can you stand it?*

Enough about my professional pursuits. What's happening at Cliff House? Do you hear from Sam or your brothers often? Are they allowed to write? I still can't believe P.J. enlisted . . . and that they'd let him in! The boy is class 5-F all the way. Physically unfit to serve due to being spineless and scarce of pulse.

Ack! Look at me. Crude and crass. I've spent too much time with ballplayers already. I realize he's your brother and Mary, you claim, is not so bad this summer. (!!!!) But them's the cards, Rubes. And don't pretend that comment didn't earn me a bit of the tee-hee, some Ruby-style cheer. The best kind there is.

Alrighty joe, off I go to cover the Yankees versus the St. Louis Browns. I'll tell you what, the world champions are on a roll and quite the gas to watch. I know your family favors the Sox, but perhaps you can come for ladies' day at the ballpark later this month?

Write soon.
xoxo, Hattie R.

Ruby crumpled up the letter and went to take it to the outside trash.

She'd chortled at Hattie's off-color gibe, but couldn't risk Mary stumbling across the note, the teeter-totter of their relationship at that second precariously balanced in a straight line. With the boys gone and

Mother and Daddy mostly absent, too, Ruby had to keep their careful kind of peace. And Mary was known to rifle through the trash, looking for scraps to refashion into something else.

Plus, it was a dang good excuse to leave the house for a breather, what with the radio on all day, bleating news from the front lines. Sam was still at the navy yard in New York, but suddenly the ocean seemed like the galaxy's most treacherous place. Especially after seeing Sam last weekend, when he was granted an unexpected furlough.

While in Sconset, Sam said nothing about his fears, but he didn't have to as they were crawling all over his face. He seemed nervous to get within two feet of Ruby, as if his jittering and jerking might knock right into their unborn child. There were moments Ruby wished Monday would hurry up and come, so Sam could get the fighting out of his system. She prayed that the navy would return her husband in the condition he'd been received.

Hattie's letter still in hand, Ruby bypassed the outside bin in favor of a quick stroll up Baxter Road. No use getting back to the house with any pep. She'd had enough ear-to-the-speaker for one day. Sure, she could disappear to other rooms, but with all the isolationist business last summer, it felt like Mary was waiting, just waiting!, for Ruby to show a lack of patriotism.

Ruby's feet rapped on the road. Between homes, she peered out at the shimmering Atlantic. Even with the war on, Nantucket twinkled like the prettiest girl at the dance. What was it Hattie said? Summer days in Sconset are why we're in this war.

True enough, Ruby decided. On-island they were rationing like the dutiful Americans they were. No gas? No problem. Let it be sailboats that fill the bay and bikes that line the streets. Nantucket was getting too crowded with motorcars anyway. Of course, biking was never as breezy as a gal might fantasize. The haul to and from town was long and the pedaling murder on the slip seams. Not to mention the hassle of painted-on "victory stockings," now that nylons were forbidden. "Mexitan" had a tendency to run.

Ruby walked a few more paces up the road toward Sankaty Head. It struck her just how on the edge of America they were. No wonder Boston chums assumed the situation was dicey in Nantucket, times two all the way over in Sconset. It was true they had the constant presence of the coast guard, who patrolled the island's perimeter dawn to dusk. But the men looked sharp and were not without their charms.

At the top of Baxter Road, after taking some appreciative ganders at the sea, Ruby turned and sauntered her way back home.

As she approached Cliff House, Ruby noticed Miss Mayhew tending to her garden across the way. Ruby smiled, for of all the domestics that'd tramped in and out of their lives, Miss Mayhew was her favorite. Hired help was another thing deemed unpatriotic these days. All the cleaning and cooking now fell to Ruby and Mary.

"Hiya Miss May—" Ruby started, but had to stop herself.

Good gravy, she didn't even know the woman's name. That was some how-do-you-do for a person considered a favorite. So much for the fleeting wish that they might be friends.

"Hello there!" Ruby warbled, trying to grin away the gaffe.

"Oh, hello, Mrs. Packard," Miss Mayhew said as she rose from crouched to standing.

"Please call me Ruby. Golly, your garden looks swell. I should have you work on ours."

Ruby blushed, realizing how it came across.

"I mean . . ."

Miss Mayhew winked, as if in on the gag.

"Perhaps," she said.

Ruby smiled at her dumbly, trying to figure what to say next. The words *Miss Mayhew, Miss Mayhew, Miss Mayhew* wound over and over in her brain. Dagnabbit, it was way too late to ask for a first name. Ruby felt like an utter boob.

"Are you headed to the navy jukebox jiggeroo tonight?" Miss Mayhew asked, saving Ruby from herself.

Lucretia? Loretta? Charlotte? Ruby shook her head. No, it was a simpler name.

"Sure," Ruby said. "I love a good jiggeroo."

Ruby dickered with the buttons on her dress. Should she return the question or was the assumption that Miss Mayhew had the option alarmingly dense? Ruby grew damp beneath her arms. She looked down to see rivulets of sweat gumming up her Mexitan.

"So, er, what are you up to the rest of the day?" she asked.

Just then a girl pedaled up on her bike, no care to the slip seams. This was a local dame, plain-faced and thick-ankled. Ruby recognized her as the woman who'd recently earned top spot as the island's most famous old maid.

"Hi there, Marg," Miss Mayhew said, and gave her friend a hug. "Margaret Hamblin, this is Ruby Packard. Mrs. Packard, this is my dear friend Margaret."

"Miss Hamblin," Ruby said, and jutted out an arm. "I'm honored to meet you."

Margaret Hamblin was big news thanks to her boyfriend, a seaman from New Bedford who'd been found on a life raft in the middle of the ocean. His unarmed freighter was bombed by a Nazi submarine and he'd bobbed along for thirty-two days before rescue.

Several started out on the raft, but expeditiously met their gruesome ends. The man's best mate, driven to lunacy by the cold and exposure, threw their food overboard before hurling himself into the deep blue. The only thing that survived, other than the man, was a picture of Margaret Hamblin.

"What a love story!" Ruby cried when she heard about it over a hand of bridge at the casino.

"I can't believe his 'girlfriend' is thirty-five" had been Mary's generous response.

It was bonkers, this war. Margaret's beau wasn't even a serviceman but they tried to sink him all the same.

"I'm so sorry about your Jules," Ruby said. "And what he endured. But I'm thrilled he's home where he belongs."

"I didn't realize news had traveled quite that far," Margaret said, eyes jumping toward Cliff House.

"Uh, er . . ." Ruby stuttered.

"In any case, thank you for your kind words."

"Well, I'll let you two be," Ruby said quickly, the air suddenly changed around them. "Nice to run into you both."

Ruby flipped around and cut a path toward Cliff House. She glanced back once more to see the girls link arms. Thoughts of Hattie hit her in the chest with a pain that was sharp and real. Ruby reached into the pocket of her dress to feel for the letter. No need to dump it just yet. She'd find a way to keep it from Mary's prying eyes.

August 23, 1942

Dear Rubes,

Oh you silly billy goat!

Don't let Mary talk you into the blue moods about my being a career gal. Working for a living is hardly a chore given the men I work with. They're all here. The ballplayers on the field, the serious types back at the paper, and, yes, the married ones, too. Don't fuss! I steer clear of those fellas, despite their efforts. I have their number and the bid is not high enough. All that to say, the war hasn't stolen all the men.

Ruby love, I might be a ways from having a ring on my finger (thank God!) but don't fret about me dying from old maidism just yet. I'm not going to end up like the dame from the life raft, or however that convoluted story went. Gotta say I didn't follow you all the way down that road but I think I sorta got the gist.

So tell me all about the island! I'm crushed that I didn't get out this year. Never mind Dad's old cottage, it's Cliff House that I miss! There's no place like Sconset on the whole damned planet. I would know. I've been to a country or twelve. Ha! I imagine it's different with the boys gone but, let's be honest, it's the gals who keep things going.

Well, my dear, off I must go. Come and visit me in the city, won't you? I know driving with gas is a no-go and every train is filled with servicemen. But you could charm any soldier off his seat. They'd be G-eyeing you left and right.

In the meantime, take care of that bean inside your tum. If it's a girl, you shall name her Harriet. If it's a boy, Harriet would suit, too. Simply call him Harry.

Farewell sweet Ruby—until next time.

Love and kisses,
H.R.

For a Saturday evening, Cliff House was unsettlingly empty.

Mary was off doing this or that with the Red Cross. She'd graduated from rolling bandages and was now permitted to dicker with actual human flesh. Hard evidence that these were desperate times.

Mother remained in Boston, the "not feeling well" number playing once more. The quintessential repeat show, a maddening encore. Sure as sugar (or not, since it was rationed), she stayed to look after Daddy, though she claimed he was doing swell. Mother always took his weaknesses as hers to bear. Ruby supposed that's what a good woman did.

"Do I need to come see him?" Ruby asked one week before.

To say good-bye, she was too terrified to add.

"No!" Mother yowled, quite snippy for her. "We're not there yet. I'll let you know when it's time. Don't stew, darling. Your father is a stubborn old mule. You stay put and look after my grandchild. I don't want you traveling about."

So with Mary and Mother gone, not to mention the permanent absence of Hattie, Ruby was bored right out of her noggin. She'd already played four sets of tennis that day and tried to chat up Miss Mayhew to little success. And wouldn't you know? Now she needed a smoke and was flat out of cigs.

Ruby checked her cigarette case and her two-in-one as well. She surveyed drawers and cupboards galore, not to mention Mary's way station for "Bundles for Bluejackets." The servicemen care packages included cigs but nary a spare could be found. Mary would never be so sloppy, which left one more option for snaffling some smokes: Topper's room. He wasn't the kind to let a butt go unused but he could be slovenly as hell.

Topper last visited Cliff House in April—over four months ago—and not body nor soul had entered his room since. When Ruby turned the knob, the door opened with a groan. She stepped gingerly on through, as if in a museum.

Glancing around at the trophies and flags and books, too many Hardy Boys to count, Ruby could almost kid herself that he'd be back soon. Except the room was too neat, too tidied and final.

With a sigh, Ruby approached his desk, which was un-Topper clean, no stray papers, golf pencils, or ball caps. No cigs either, as her luck would go. Ruby glanced up at the large crimson Harvard flag overhead.

"Come on, Topper," she said. "Help out your big sis."

Ruby jimmied open a drawer. Tops would flip his wig if he saw her mousing around like that but she needed a smoke and it didn't seem like her brother's room anymore. Or so Ruby told herself to make the situation square.

The drawers themselves were far more Topper, thank the stars. They were cluttered and jammed to the gills, a bit of him left after all. There had to be at least one loose cig somewhere.

In the bottom drawer, Ruby uncovered a stack of pictures. They featured family, mostly, though she found some friends, too. As she flicked through them, Ruby smiled. She imagined her baby brother fopping about, that camera jangling from his neck. Tops was a dang good photographer for a hobbyist. He should've gone to war for *that* and stayed behind the lines, shooting a camera instead of a gun.

Among the bundle were several of Hattie, Topper having expertly captured her beauty and light. She was at the beach in one, looking as though she were floating and not walking along.

Another was up close of Hattie's face, seconds after she stepped out of the ocean, saltwater glittering between her lashes. Ruby got the puzzling notion that Topper was the reason Hattie hadn't come out this season. Perhaps deep down it was him, not Ruby, who was last summer's featured star.

Gummed up with nostalgia and love, for Hattie and Topper and the other familiar faces, Ruby wormed her way to the bottom of the drawer. Then, something caught her eye. A photograph. Something . . . strange. And a few more just like it. Heart floundering, Ruby studied them, her mind unable to piece together any semblance of sense.

"Ruby!" shouted a voice, followed by the thumping of feet. "Ruby! Where are you?!"

It took Ruby a minute to realize the sound was not in her head.

"Mary?" she said, confused.

Ruby peeked out into the hallway, where she saw Mary stampeding her way. She had on her full warden outfit, white helmet, black armband, and all.

Suddenly, an alarm began to sound.

"There you are!" Mary said.

It was an air raid drill, which was why her sister-in-law was too wound up to question Ruby's presence in that room.

"I need to patrol the streets," Mary said.

"I'll come with you. Give me a moment to, uh, collect myself."

Ruby turned and scurried back over to Topper's desk. She dropped the photographs into their hideout and slammed the drawer closed.

"Come with me?" Mary said. "*I'm* the warden."

"I know, I just thought . . ."

"No, you need to turn off all the lights," she said over the whirring siren. "And put down the blinds. The warden's house has to be in tiptop shape."

"Okeydoke, consider it done," Ruby said, grateful for the task.

Mary left for her patrol and Ruby set to pulling down the blackout shades, all the while Topper's pictures flashing in her mind.

Those *were* Topper's pictures, yes? Or they weren't. Ruby still couldn't decide exactly what she'd seen. And so she concentrated on her duties—a good distraction for now. Alas, between the drill and the events that followed, the images would fade almost completely away. It'd be silly to worry about a bunch of pictures when, by nightfall, Ruby's entire world would transform once more.

38

Island ACKtion

GEOTUBES APPROVED!

May 23, 2013

Tonight the Board of Selectmen voted to approve the installation of geotubes along Sankaty Bluff. In a last-ditch effort to save the receding shoreline along Baxter Road, the board voted 3–2 to enter into a memo of understanding with the Sankaty Bluff Preservation Fund to support and help fund the geotube project.

"What bull*#*," says lifelong Sconset resident and commercial fisherman Chappy Mayhew. "Complete and utter crap. I can't believe those idiots voted for it."

This news comes mere days after the selectmen struck down a hard armor measure, citing it as excessively detrimental to Nantucket's shoreline. Naturally, town pot-stirrer Cissy Codman refused to take "no" for an answer. So while most of Nantucket thought Cliff House and its neighbors were down for the count,

Cissy deployed the ever-popular "we'll sue the pants off you" measure. It worked.

"I didn't threaten to sue anyone," she insists. "I simply had an attorney enumerate Nantucket's legal responsibility to run utilities to that part of the island. The collapse of the bluff would cut off plumbing and electricity to most residents on Baxter Road. But, thanks to the wise decision of our esteemed selectmen, that won't happen. I look forward to working together to ensure a successful geotube installation."

In case the indomitable Mrs. Codman hasn't gotten a hold of you by phone or by bike, geotubes are large sand-filled jute "burrito bags," which will be installed in a terrace-like fashion along nine hundred feet of bluff. They'll be held in place with anchors and covered in sand.

Proponents say geotubes not only protect the bank, but are compatible with the existing beach. As opposed to seawalls, they also minimize harm to downdraft beaches and do not adversely affect marine wildlife. What's more, geotubes aid with storm damage prevention and flood control, enhance the view, and preserve recreation trails and public access to the glorious Siasconset beaches.

That's what Cissy tells us anyway.

Shortly after the meeting, Mrs. Codman was seen at the Yacht Club drinking champagne with various cohorts including her sister-in-law Polly Bradlee. Noticeably absent was Cissy's daughter Bess, who has reportedly taken up with a local. Mr. Codman wasn't there but he never is. We here at *Island ACKtion* assume he's still alive.

Listen, I'm the last person who would rain on Cissy's parade. I don't want to end up tied to concrete blocks and rolled into the harbor. But while the geotubes sound great and all, isn't it ridiculously too late?

ABOUT ME:

Corkie Tarbox, lifelong Nantucketer, steadfast flibbertigibbet. Married with one ankle-biter. Views expressed on the *Island ACKtion* blog (Twitter, Facebook, Instagram, et al.) are hers alone. Usually.

39

Friday Morning

Bess and Palmer sit on a bench in the hallway of the casino, surrounded by the club's famed latticework. They're donning their choicest of tennis whites, as white must be worn on these courts. It's a rule.

Palmer is gently kicking at her racquet while surveying the damp red clay outside. She's in a one-piece dress, which is both retro and stunningly modern. Bess has on an old skirt and a top borrowed from Cissy. On this trip she did not pack for sport.

As Palmer sighs, Bess checks her watch for a fifth time, and then a sixth. It's been raining steadily all morning. Though the club boys stand ready by the door, poised to brush the courts as soon as the weather breaks, Bess is certain there'll be no tennis today. It isn't the worst development. She's not really in the mood for getting beaten.

"Should we go?" Bess asks. "The weather doesn't look too promising."

"Let's wait a *teensy* bit longer," Palmer says. "I'm dying to play! It's been ages. Golly I miss it."

Bess fiddles with her pullover. This she brought from California, though she originally purchased it here. A decade or so old, it bears the Sconset Casino insignia: two crossed racquets with a seagull above. SCA, EST. 1899. It's one of Bess's favorite pieces of clothing, because it reminds her of Cliff House, of Sconset, and of her family. Grandma Ruby had the same one. The girl at the reservation desk does, too. They haven't changed the style since forever.

"I guess we can wait," Bess says. "But I have a crapload to do back at the house."

"Understood. But come on!" Palmer nudges her leg. "We've barely spent any time together. What are you doing when you're not helping Cissy pack anyway?"

"Waiting for tennis courts to dry?"

Palmer rolls her eyes, an act as rare as a pink dolphin.

"No. Seriously," she says. "You can't be working all the time. I know Aunt Cissy's not!"

"You've got that right. Well, I've been doing a lot at the house. Alone. *Thanks for the assist, Mom*. And . . ." Bess pauses, she waits, she turns it over in her head. "This is kind of random, but I've also been seeing . . ."

Been seeing? It sounds wrong, like an exaggeration of what's really gone on. Of course, Bess has *seen* Evan, multiple times, when taking a very literal view of things.

"Seeing what?" Palmer asks, her interest now snagged.

"Er, I've hung out with Evan some," Bess says. "You know, my high school boyfriend? Lived across the road?"

"Of course I remember Evan Mayhew. Hotter and sweeter than a peach cobbler straight out of the oven. Whew. Lucky girl. See? What did I say? You've already found someone else. And he's quite the *someone else*. Hubba hubba."

"Hubba *hubba*?"

"Nice work, cuz. Way to get after it."

"Please!" Bess says, and whops her on the leg. "I'm not 'getting after' anything. We're friends and I live in San Francisco, remember? Plus, I'm too smart to make the same mistake twice."

Bess blushes, though Palmer has no idea she's using Evan's signature line.

"It's been fun," she adds. "Catching up. Getting advice from one of the few who truly understands my mom. And he's helped me pack."

"Helped you pack? Ooh-la-la. Sounds so very *friendly*."

"Knock it off, P."

"Whatever." Palmer blows a long, straight, wispy strand of blond hair from her explosively blue eyes.

"It's nothing," Bess insists, though Palmer didn't ask her to.

"Fine," Palmer says. "If you don't like hot guys, I really can't help you. I'm sure he has a girlfriend anyway."

Bess bristles at this borderline rude, entirely fair statement. She exhales.

"Probably," Bess concedes, though her hackles are still up. "He hasn't mentioned anyone specifically. But I saw him with some woman at the market."

"Oh, well. You should probably ask where they're registered," Palmer jokes. "First stop Sconset Market, next stop the aisle. How do you know it was a girlfriend? Were they making out in front of overpriced cheese?"

"No. Nothing like that. They weren't obvious about it." Bess recalls how they looked between the slots in the bike rack. Her knees throb as if she's still crouched. "She could be a friend. They weren't holding hands or anything. Also she wasn't that pretty."

Palmer snorts.

"Someone's jealous."

"I'm not jealous! It's just a fact."

"I'm not sure I buy that one, sweetie," Palmer says, and pops up onto her feet. "You still have a thing for him. Who wouldn't?"

She moves toward the windows. The floor moans despite Palmer's slight weight. At once Bess is filled with gratitude for this place, which most owners would've tried to update by now. It's creaky and warped and vaguely musty, last renovated ninety years ago. Only the locker rooms have changed, and not by much. Truly, the place is approaching the last stop of charmingville, refurbishtown straight ahead. Dozens of weddings are held at the casino every year, but Bess thinks there must be twice as many couples who eliminate the venue because the main room is too dark. But all that wood looks gorgeous when decked out with white tables and chairs, twinkle lights strung overhead.

"Dang it," Palmer says, peering through the glass. "More clouds are rolling in. Why don't you ask him?"

"Ask him what? If he has a girlfriend?" Bess makes a face. "I can't."

"Why not? It's an ordinary question. You get a pedicure and they bring it up fifty-seven times. *You have boyfriend?*"

"I don't know," Bess says. "I could've a few days ago but now it'd be weird. We've spent a lot of time together."

Palmer jerks her head in Bess's direction. Her ponytail flicks against the glass.

"Oh, reallllly? How much time? Do tell."

"Hours. Half a day. We've had a lot of . . . intense conversations. It'd be like screwing some dude and then asking for his name."

"*You guys did it?!*"

Palmer turns all the way to face Bess, her skirt fanning out behind her. The court-brushing boys are straining themselves to eavesdrop, albeit not owing to any interest in Bess's love life. They've likely never heard a grown woman refer to sex as "doing it."

"Shhh!" Bess says, laughing. "No we didn't *do* it. I was using a metaphor."

"Heck of a metaphor. Does he know about Brandon?"

Bess nods.

"And the . . ."

Palmer rubs her fingers together. Is she making the sign for money? Bess is perplexed. Then again, the women were paid, so . . .

"If you're referring to the hookers, then yes," she says.

"And the . . ."

Palmer makes a hammering motion.

"Construction? Tools?"

"The abuse," Palmer stage-whispers.

Bess reddens all the way to her hairline. The boys gawp and scuffle away.

"Okay, it really wasn't." Bess mimics the pounding. "I mean, not in the usual way."

"Humph," answers Palmer.

"And yes I told him Brandon was a jerk, more or less. He even knows about the—"

The words are partway up Bess's throat but she swallows them back down. Evan knows about the pregnancy. But aside from Bess and Brandon, he's the only one.

Though Palmer is her go-to confidant, Bess has to be careful what she tells her. Not because Palmer would spill a secret in a million years or for a million dollars. No, it's something else, something not even Bess fully understands. Things seem to go awry when Palmer is in on a secret. To tell her is like writing it in a journal. It doesn't become public but the mere act forces you to confront the truth. And sometimes the truth is ugly, uglier yet when compared to Palmer.

"He knows about everything," Bess says, before Palmer can press for more. "At this point it'd be odd to spring the 'do you have a girlfriend' question. That's like lame high-school-reunion banter."

"I guess." Palmer shrugs. "I'd still ask him though."

"I'm sure you would."

"Invite him tonight," she says casually, as she digs around in her tennis bag for some lip balm.

"To Flick's pre-wedding party?"

"Yeah, sure! Why not? If he has a girlfriend, he probably has plans. But what if he comes? Maybe . . ." Palmer wiggles her brows.

"Yeah, I don't think so."

Then she thinks, just as Palmer said, *Maybe*.

"Is she still having a party?" Bess says.

She can't invite him, can she? It'd be strange.

"Even in the rain?"

"It's supposed to clear," Palmer says, forever optimistic. "Anyway, a little drizzle never killed anyone."

Suddenly there's a crack of thunder. A streak of lightning shoots across the sky.

"A little drizzle?"

"Oh poo," Palmer says, glowering at the courts, which are now getting a proper soak. "I really wanted to hit!"

"It's for the best," Bess says, and stands to join her. "I need to make progress at the house."

"You need to make progress all right."

Palmer latches on to Bess's elbow and guides her toward the door.

"But it has nothing to do with that house," she says. "Let's scrap tennis. Cliff House, too. I'm taking you to town. We need new outfits for tonight. If you dress the right way, who knows, maybe you'll get to *do it* after all."

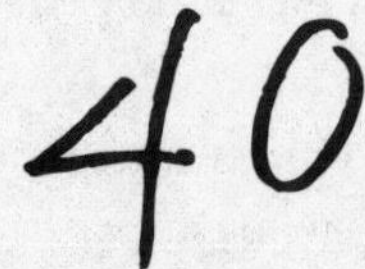

Friday Afternoon

Phone in hand, Bess taps out a few words.

She deletes them. Types a few more.

They aren't right either. Delete, delete, delete. There is nothing Bess can say that doesn't make her sound like a pathetic high school girl incapable of talking to boys. This, when she is thirty-four years old and with much bigger problems than what to do about the cute neighbor boy.

Bess shakes her head and instead writes what she really wants to say.

Hey. Party for Flick tonight. 8pm. Marina, Old S Wharf, near Slip 14. Come with? Boat parties. Like the old days.

"God, Palmer," Bess mutters, "you'd better be right about this."

She is about to end the whole pathetic deal with a winky emoticon when her phone rings, startling her and causing her to hit Send before she can exercise her better judgment.

"Shit!" Bess yelps. "Shit!"

The text has gone to Evan. What was she thinking, inviting him to her cousin's pre-wedding fête of bankers and blue bloods? She shouldn't listen to Palmer. Palmer sees the world from a very rosy place.

"Shit," Bess says a third time, for good measure, as her phone continues to ring. "Goddamn it."

DAD, the phone screams at her. DAD.

"Um, hello?"

"Bessie, that you?" her dad bellows.

He is grumpy and short of breath. Bess imagines him pacing by the picture window in his office, glaring out over the Charles River.

"Yep!" she says. "Who else?"

"How are you?"

"I'm pretty go—"

"Glad to hear it. Listen, I need you to pick me up at the airport."

"The airport?" Bess says, blinking. "What airport?"

"Nantucket! What's wrong with you? Are you drunk?"

"What? No! It's only noon! So, wait. You're coming? Here?"

The phone buzzes in her hand. Has Evan texted her back?

"Yes of course I am!" Dudley says. "It's my niece's wedding. Seriously, what is wrong with you?"

"Oh . . . right. Sorry."

It hadn't occurred to Bess that her dad might come for the event, even though Aunt Polly is his sister, Flick his niece. She's his very favorite niece, at that—his favorite in the whole family, no doubt. He likes her ambition, drive, and custom-made herringbone pantsuits. Bess should've guessed he'd show. Dudley Codman always comes through. Old Dudley-do-right-eventually.

"Um, okay," Bess says. "When? Tonight?"

"Sunday. I'm taking the late flight. Six forty-five. Cape Air. I'll be staying one night. At the Wauwinet."

"I'm happy to get you," Bess says. "But, Dad, wouldn't you rather have Mom pick you up?"

"Your mother?" He snorts. "Elisabeth, that woman once showed up at the airport on a fucking bike."

Bess laughs.

"Yeah," she says. "Been there."

"So you'll do it, okay good, speaking of your mother," Dudley says, spitting sentences like he's checking them off a list, or shooting them from a gun. "You guys 'bout packed?"

Bess clears her throat.

"Sorta?" she says.

"'*Sorta*'? Bess, you've been there a week. What the hell have you been doing if not packing? In case I haven't mentioned *you could die*."

"I know. It's just, well, some things are packed."

"Some things."

"It's been busy. Two town meetings in the past three days."

"Christ, say no more."

Bess can almost hear his eyes rolling.

"Your mother told me about the geotubes," he says.

"She did?"

"So hooray. But you gotta get that woman packed, understand?"

"Yes, but it's not that simple."

"It never is," he says. "Listen, thanks for going out there. I'm sure Cissy's been a royal pain in the ass but it's comforting to know that progress is being made thanks to you."

Bess fights a groan. Progress. Right. What's Dudley going to think when he sees Cliff House? And what will he do to Bess? With her father there are always "consequences." He might cut her out of the family. Or send her to the Sudan with Lala.

"So, um, are you going to help pack?" Bess asks, her voice coming out in a squeak.

"Why would I do something like that? Gotta run Bessie, see you later, love you, bye."

The phone goes dead.

Bess exhales. At least Dudley is staying at the Wauwinet and away from Cliff House. He won't find out that Bess is a flat liar. Sorta packed. Just like Bess is sorta married. Technically. A little bit. But not in any meaningful way.

After checking for a response from Evan (nothing, nada, zilch), Bess tucks the phone into her back pocket. Jeans this time, for the love of all that's not elastic, though the jeans are noticeably snug. Bess will have to figure out something. Soon. Sweatpants are comfy but they can't solve all her problems.

"Hey, Cis," she says, walking into the living room.

Her mother is hurricaning around the place, pulling and pushing and packing. Well, wonders never cease. There's some movement yet.

"Hiya Bess!" Cissy trills as tweenager music blares from a nearby stereo.

I'm wide awake . . .

"Wow, Mom, I didn't take you for a Katy Perry fan."

"She's cute. I like her hair!" Cissy smiles. "It reminds me of yours."

"Isn't hers blue?"

"Not always."

Cissy swipes a collection of picture frames from the fireplace mantel and plunks them into a box.

"Glad to see you're getting things done," Bess says, and perches on the arm of a floral couch at least twenty years out of style. "Packing wise, that is."

"Well, they can't move the house with everything in it! Oh, Bessie, I'm just so jazzed all of a sudden. What is it that you Californians say? I'm stoked!"

"I do not say that. Ever."

"I'm stoked on the geotube plan. Cliff House lives!"

Cissy twirls and leaps across the room, like Palmer from her ballet days, if Palmer were over sixty and mildly arthritic. Bess feels a little dizzy from all the motion.

"'I'm falling from cloud nine,'" Cissy sings, then sets about attacking an assembly of gardening and entertaining books from the eighties.

"So Dad just called," Bess tells her.

She checks her phone. No texts. No missed calls.

"He's coming for the wedding," Bess adds.

Cissy hesitates and then scowls.

"Mom?"

Cissy turns toward Bess and holds up a book. *101 Ideas for Carpeting Your Bathroom.*

"Is it awful to trash old books?" she asks.

"Not that one."

Cissy flings it into a bin.

"So yeah," Bess says, eyeing the trash. "Dad's coming, but only for twenty-four hours."

"Okeydoke," Cissy answers, wholly unfazed by the news.

Bess remembers what Grandma Ruby said, back when Bess was a little girl complaining that her dad didn't stay the entire summer.

"Oh, Bess, the men only come for the parties," she'd said. "The events. They don't have the time or stamina for the day-to-day."

"Bottom line," Bess says, and squats to inspect the box beside her. "He'll be here on Sunday."

"Fantastic."

Bess picks up a red scrapbook and tabs through some pages.

"This is from the dining room," she says. "I was looking at it the other day."

"You're welcome to have it. Otherwise, it's going in the trash."

"You can't throw this away. Grandma must've kept it for some reason." Bess turns a few more pages. "Did you know someone named Harriet Rutter?"

"Sounds familiar. I think."

Cissy checks the underside of a desk clock that hasn't worked in years.

"She was some sort of writer, apparently," Bess says. "Magazines, newspaper articles. Grandma Ruby kept everything the woman ever wrote, as far as I can tell."

"Hmmm . . ." Cissy says, moving from desk clock to candlesticks to piano bench. "She might've been a friend of my mom's from school or the club or something. Maybe she had a dalliance with Robert? I think there was a falling-out and I seem to remember the little brother was involved."

"This Hattie person had quite the journalistic repertoire. Sports stories, makeup tips, opinion pieces about the war—Second World *and* Vietnam. Also, you'll be pleased to know there are seventeen different types of dickies available for the adventurous dresser."

"I really don't know much about—"

Suddenly a slap of thunder shakes the house. Bess lets out a small cry and grips the sofa. Within seconds, rain begins battering the home.

"This weather!" Bess says.

Cissy casts a nervous glance toward the windows.

"It's fine," she says, unconvincingly.

Cissy yanks a strip of packing tape from its roll and bites it free. Ignoring the rain now assaulting the roof, Bess fishes the Book of Summer out from beneath Hattie Rutter's bizarre amalgam of press clippings.

"Aw, hello book," she says. "Not very summery today, are we?"

Bad news for Flick's party, Bess thinks. *That's why Evan hasn't texted back. Who goes on a boat in this weather?*

"Bessie, are you helping over there?" Cissy asks. "Or are you snooping?"

"A bit of both. Cis, have you ever read this?" Bess asks, holding up the book. "In thirty years, I don't think I've seen you open it once."

"Of course I have. Here and there. It's mostly just people talking about parties and hairdos. A nice keepsake but not particularly compelling."

"What?! Come on, there's so much more to it than that. Look! Here's an entry about little Cis, dated June 6, 1964. Written by your mom . . . 'We opened Cliff House today. About ten days late. Cissy had a Bobby Sox tournament. Her team lost two to one in the finals. The girls put forth a valiant effort, or so I'm told. I don't know the first thing about it. Cis is quite aggrieved by the loss.'

"Bobby Sox!" Bess says, and glances up. "How precious!"

Cissy rolls her eyes.

"Pretty slow-paced if you ask me."

"I'm delighted to learn you've had a long history of being aggrieved."

"Please. Mother couldn't tolerate any sort of 'mood.' "

"And why would she?" Bess says, returning her eyes to the page. "You had Cliff House for that. 'Our moods lifted the minute we arrived on-island. Right on time or days overdue, Cliff House gives me the same feeling every time. This is my forty-fifth summer at Cliff House, something north of four thousand days, but my stomach still somersaults with the thrill of it, the promise that our lives will change, if only for a season.

" 'The decades, the memories, only the best of these cling to the home, the bad spirited away on a swift ocean gale. Life's not been perfect here, or anywhere, but no matter what's happened, in spite of the business with Sam and all the variations of bad business before and after, my heart fills with unrepentant joy the moment the tires crunch on the shelled drive.

" 'Cliff House is a comfort. In the winter months you only need think: Well, summer's not so far away. I can last until then. Whatever happens in the real world, Cliff House remains a permanent, never-changing promise. In this big house cemented on its bluff, we can return to the people we are supposed to be.' "

"I thought you wanted me to leave the house," Cissy says, sniffling. "That doesn't help."

"Just hairdos and recipes, huh?"

Bess smacks the book shut.

"It's funny," she says. "That entry was made exactly twenty years, to the day, after D-day. I wonder why Grandma didn't mention the date?"

"Why would she?"

"Well, it's been twelve years since 9/11 and it's still a pall over the day no matter what else is going on. One of my friends got induced on September tenth just to avoid her child having that birthday."

"That's different."

"Is it?"

The thunder crashes again. Lightning rips across the sky. When Bess looks up, she sees a tall man standing in the window bay.

"Motherfucking Christ!" Bess screams.

"Bess! What in God's name?"

When Cissy spies the man, her face at once relaxes. She patters over to the French doors.

"It's just my engineer," Cissy says as she kicks open the door. "Hello, Mike. Sorry about the weather. I didn't think it'd come down like this."

A man in boots and a rain slicker stomps inside. He shakes himself off like a wet dog.

"Mike oversaw the relocation of Sankaty Head," Cissy explains to Bess proudly, as if describing how her son hit a three-run homer. "He's the best in the biz. Mike, this is my daughter Bess."

"Hi, Bess," he says in a half mumble. "Nice to meet you."

"Mike is going to move Cliff House for us!" Cissy grins. "So, what's the damage? How far back do we have to go and how much will it cost? Do you think a pool is feasible? I mean, eventually."

"Cissy, no."

"Fine." Cissy flicks her hand at him. "No pool. But the other stuff we talked about . . ."

"I'm not moving this house."

"Not you personally, but—"

"Cissy," Mike says, sternly. He must have experience in Cissy-related matters. "You're not listening."

"I *am* listening! I'm a great listener! It's one of my premier qualities."

Bess scoffs from her corner of the room. Cissy doesn't catch it, naturally.

"There's no easy way to tell you this," Mike says. "So I'll just come out with it. I can't move your house."

"Then I'll find someone else."

"No one can."

Cissy looks disoriented, like she's in a Coyote and Roadrunner cartoon and someone's tried to blast her with TNT. There are practically symbols circling above her head.

"What do you mean?" she says.

"The bluff is too far gone," Mike explains. "The soil might as well be quicksand."

"But you're testing it in the rain! It's not always like this!"

"Well, if it never rained again . . ."

"And the geotubes. Don't forget about the geotubes! Did you read that they're going to approve my measure?"

"Yes, you e-mailed it to me three times." Mike sighs. "Cissy, I really hate this."

"Listen, move the house all the way to the street. No yard? That's fine. I can hold my parties indoors. Do whatever you have to do."

"I can't move it any closer to the street."

"Take out the privet hedge! I realize that I said to keep it at all costs but if that's the cost of saving Cliff House, so be it."

"Cissy," Mike says again and takes a few steps closer.

Bess stands in place, ogling. He is a brave man to tell Cissy no.

"You can put in sandbags," he says, and gently pats her arm. "You can take out privacy hedges. You can do both of these things but the fact is that this land is unstable. A pool, you ask? I wouldn't put a bowl of good chowder anywhere on this property."

"But isn't there any way—"

"See that?" he says, and points toward the door. "My soil-testing kit outside? It's pouring rain but I'm going to walk out there and grab it. I'm afraid it won't survive the holiday weekend and I'll be out fifty bucks. Never mind the kit, though. If I were you . . ." He looks at Cissy. He looks at Bess. "I'd get out. Now. You don't have a lot of time left."

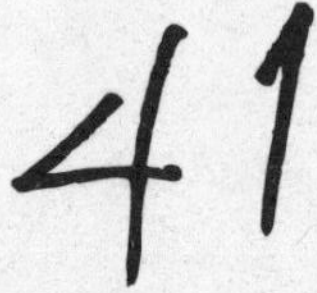

41

Friday Night

The rain has stopped, mostly, but even the lingering drizzle doesn't impede Felicia Bradlee's multiboat soirée. And why would it? Bankers and lawyers can rough it in hats and raincoats. They wear their slumming-it shoes. It makes them feel outdoorsy despite so many hours logged in conference rooms.

Bess sits on the bench of *Kip's Folly*, a glass of white wine in hand, not a friend to be found. Flick is off humoring guests with work anecdotes and her brusque, infectious laugh. Palmer and Brooks are chasing Amory around, making sure she doesn't drown in the marina. Bess checks her watch. It's already past Amory's bedtime and soon Bess will have no compatriots left at the party. The guest she invited never responded.

If that's not humiliating enough, even her mother is missing. Cissy promised to attend, RSVP'd even (unlike certain local contractors), but in the end stayed home, leaving Bess to explain her absence.

To Aunt Polly and Uncle Vince: "She's not feeling well."

To Flick: "She's being Cissy."

And to Palmer: "The engineer told her a big fat 'NOPE' on moving Cliff House so she's hunting down someone willing to give her the answer she wants."

"Cis, you have to come," Bess said earlier, as she rooted around her suitcase for something to wear.

She and Palmer picked up new tops and some "darling" wedge heels in town, but diaphanous silk blouses and slick-bottomed shoes weren't going to cut it in that weather. A gross error in judgment when the party called for the delicate sartorial balance between looking decent and keeping warm, a formula that very much defined life on-island eighty percent of the summer. It's something Bess should've remembered as the woman in the shop swiped her card. Summer People. They have no clue.

"Finding a new engineer is more important," Cissy said as Bess settled on a cashmere white-and-navy sweater. "As for the party? It was a courtesy invite. No one really wants a sixty-year-old woman there. How come Yelp won't let you expand the search to 'entire eastern seaboard'?"

"Of course people want you there, Cis. And it's rude to bail. You can't say you're coming and then not show up."

"Felicia only invited me to be nice," Cissy said. "Listen, my back is against a wall. You heard Mike. This predicament is time-sensitive. I'll attend the wedding. That's the main event. No one will miss me tonight."

"Mom, people always miss you. You add a unique dimension to any gathering of two or more."

Cissy peered out over her glasses.

"Don't be fresh."

And so Bess sits alone, on a boat, in a fog so thick she can't even pretend to gaze wistfully out toward sea. At thirty-plus she should be okay with the solitude, and she is, for the most part. But it'd be nice to not feel so out of place.

Bess takes a sip of Chardonnay: the teensiest, tiniest, most minuscule bubble of a taste. It burns on the way down—more than it should, as Flick surely bought the good stuff. A punishment, Bess decides, though she isn't sure for what. God, she is pregnant. Pregnant! Thirteen weeks almost. It's inexcusable to be that far along.

She sets down her glass (glass, on a boat, for the love of all that's logical) and glances around. Little groups of people wander up and down Old South Wharf, and Bess finds herself scanning the crowd for any meanderers of the male persuasion, approximately six foot two in height. After all, she didn't request a response, she simply asked him to show up. But people around here only walk in packs.

As Bess returns her focus to the party, she accidentally provokes eye contact with a girl standing a few feet away. The stranger offers a small wave and makes a move in her direction. Bess flinches, but it's too late to disappear.

The girl, a woman really, is in her mid-thirties, too, give or take. She wears skinny jeans and a gray cashmere sweater. Her hair is pulled back, thick and straight and blond like a horse's tail. As she approaches, Bess recognizes her from somewhere. Choate? Boston College? Definitely not Nantucket High. She's too shiny for that. Bess smiles, trying to dredge up a name, but can't get it anywhere close to the tip of her tongue.

"Hi!" Bess says brightly, too brightly.

"Bess Codman in the flesh!" she says, right out of the gate, showing off her superior facial recognition skills. "So great to see you! You look fabulous."

The woman leans down for a hug and then plants herself beside Bess.

"Gosh, thanks," Bess says. "You, too."

The woman is beautiful, though Bess doesn't know whether it's more or less so than before.

"I almost didn't recognize you," the woman says. "Did you get glasses?"

"It's not so much that I 'got glasses.' I'm just not wearing my contacts."

"Oh, weird." She makes a face. "Anyway, what have you been up to?"

The woman sips some reddish-pink concoction through a straw so as not to muddle her lip gloss.

"Uh, er, um . . ." Bess stutters. "What have I been up to?"

Choate. The woman has to be from Choate, since Flick went to Penn. Although maybe they took sailing lessons together at the club umpteen summers ago.

"Do you work?" the woman asks. "Stay at home? What?"

"Oh. Right. I work in an ED?"

The woman crinkles her nose.

"The Education Department?" she asks. "Is that in Washington?"

"No . . . no . . . the emergency . . . I work in the ER, in San Francisco."

"Oh! A doctor!" The woman claps. "That makes sense. You were a total brainiac."

"I was?"

"I work in publishing, which everyone thinks is *so cool* and *so glamorous*. People just mob me at parties, peppering me with questions, trying to tell me about some half-baked book idea." She rolls her eyes. "Everyone thinks they can write a book. It's so annoying."

"That sucks," Bess says, and looks down at her Chardonnay. She really wishes she could drink more of it.

"And, yeah, it sounds awesome and all," the woman goes on. "But what you do! You save lives! That must be such a rush."

"Um, thanks. Most of it isn't particularly exciting. It's a job, like anything else."

Who is this person? The more Bess tries to remember, the more faces from her past jumble together.

"Just a job!" the woman trills. She takes several gulps of her red-pink swill. "Just a job, she says. Please! Anyway, it's so great to see you! To talk to you like this! Hey. Whoa."

She stops jabbering for a nanosecond and grips the edge of the bench.

"Is it me or is the boat rocking like crazy?" she asks.

"I feel okay . . ."

"Anyhow, I have a confession to make."

She goes to pat Bess's leg, presumably, but misses and whacks her hand on the bench.

"I was so intimidated by you," she says, shaking out the injured hand.

"Me?" Bess snorts. "When? Why?"

Here is a gorgeous palomino with glacier-blue eyes and a foal's gait. Bess has no real objections to her own looks, she is general-population attractive and med-school smoking hot, but this girl is full-stop stunning. Bess is more along the lines of Wednesday Addams with bangs. In other words, appealing only to specific tastes.

"At school, silly!" the woman says. "First of all, you're Felicia's cousin. Her *older* cousin, which was cool in itself."

"Yes, older," Bess says. "By all of one year."

"Yeah, but I mean, it's still *older*."

"One year isn't all that . . ." Bess shakes her head. "Sorry. Go on."

How on earth could this person be intimidated by Bess when Bess was always with Palmer Bradlee, the girl who glided through life forever poised and beautiful and en pointe?

"You seemed so mature," the woman says. "So dark and exotic."

She reaches out and snags a chunk of Bess's hair, which feels like a violation though Bess isn't exactly sure why. You don't go around petting strangers at parties, right? Or perhaps such social transaction came into fashion while Bess was working weekend shifts and trying to get divorced.

"Huh," Bess says as the woman continues to grip her hair like a leash.

Though hair is nothing but dead cells, Bess swears hers is getting dank beneath this person's hold.

"Then there's the pièce de résistance, so to speak. The De Leudeville Affair."

"Oh." Bess clears her throat. "Right."

Monsieur de Leudeville. The scandal that got one French instructor fired and one student kicked out of school. It was a shocking fiasco for anyone, especially someone like Bess.

"The De Leudeville Affair," Bess repeats. "That sounds almost cinematic."

"Everyone called it that. You know you're involved in a juicy scandal when it gets its own name."

Sometimes Bess actually forgets that she didn't leave Choate so much as go down in flames. Bess can't even remember if she told her ex-husband the story. But the De Leudeville Affair wasn't an affair, not really. Yes, there was sex involved but it was more an excuse, a circumstance Monsieur de Leudeville himself walked right into. That this blond, drunk publishing person remembered Bess for him and not what happened before was the very point of the letch. And so: mission accomplished.

"He was pretty hot," the woman notes, and glugs the rest of her drink. "For an old guy anyway."

"He was twenty-seven. And into sixteen-year-old girls. So not that hot, when you think about it."

Does he have to register as a sex offender? There never was a trial, so the answer is likely no.

"Wow," the woman says. "That's scary."

"What? That he was a perv?"

"No. That if he was twenty-seven, what must *we* look like to teenagers?" She shakes her head. "Ugh."

The woman stands. She sways as she works to keep straight.

"You always seemed so badass," the woman says, going cross-eyed as she speaks. "A steamy affair and you had, like, no remorse. Zero. Felicia said they gave you the opportunity to exonerate yourself but it was like, no thanks!"

"It didn't happen quite like that. . . ."

"Can I get you another drink?"

The woman waggles her own emptied glass as Bess glances down at hers, on the bench, still full.

"No, I'm fine. Thanks though."

"Okay. Cool. I'll be back. I want to know the details. Hell, you could write a memoir. Like, unapologetic, you know?" She contemplates this. "You were taken advantage of but you liked it. Or would that send a bad message?"

"Uh. Yeah. Very much so."

"Hmmm," the woman says, wandering off. "Hmmm."

As the woman careens away, Bess reaches into her pocket, thoughts of de Leudeville evaporating at once. She checks her phone. Still no word from Evan. And why would there be? What obligation does he have to respond at all?

Bess stands, moves her glass to a nearby table, and turns to go. As she charges down Old South Wharf, the party's voices and laughter tinkle in the distance. If anyone notices Bess's abrupt departure, they don't say a thing.

42

RUBY
Summer 1942

The drill had gone as planned, which was to be expected with Mary manning the show.

Everyone in the neighborhood took cover. All blinds were drawn, no sliver of light able to sneak out. Mary checked the sum total of Baxter Road's cricks and cracks but didn't uncover a single violation, though not for lack of trying. The bird loved filing incident reports, no greater thrill than committing other people's mistakes to paper.

"Golly, Ruby," Mary said as they went through the house, turning on lights and opening curtains. "You performed aces this time around. For once you didn't treat it like a joke, or as though you have special privileges since you're related to the warden."

"Thanks," Ruby said. "I'm trying."

She did take it seriously and certainly never viewed Mary's position as anything worthy of abusing. But naturally Mary liked to think of herself in such terms. Ruby forgot to turn the radio off once and Mary harangued her about it for seven days straight.

"I can't say it enough," Mary prattled on.

Indeed, she could not.

"You're finally taking things seriously. You even seemed nervous about it! Jittery! There might be hope for you yet."

Ruby nodded reflexively, still wound up not by the drill but by what she'd found in Topper's room.

What *had* she seen? Something. Nothing. A teensy part of Ruby wanted to show Mary, get a check from another stance, but the fuddy-duddy would no doubt misread the situation entirely. Plus, Mary hated Tops's photography hobby. She deemed it unseemly for his class of man.

Hattie. Now, *she* would know what to make of it. Hell, Hattie was probably peeping over his shoulder when the Rolleiflex went click. The thought made Ruby brighten, for a spell.

"I need to tell you something," Mary said as they pulled back the living room drapes. "With Philip away, I've struggled with my place in this world. Who am I? What am I contributing? I'm not a mom. I'm barely a wife with him gone. And, so . . . well, there's no easy way to say this, but I've applied to nursing school."

Ruby's eyes bugged. She whipped around to face her sister-in-law.

"Nursing school?" she gasped.

"Yes. Down Washington way. This war looks to be long and I can do more. The government is subsidizing schools now, helping to fast-track the training. I could be with the army inside of two years."

"The army? You mean like P.J.? You've designs of joining him on the front? Mary, I understand you want to be together, I feel the same way about Sam, but you can't just—"

"No, no, no," Mary said. "This isn't about Philip. It's about me. And anyway the official posting would be with the Red Cross. If I'm accepted overseas, I'd be sworn into the army."

"Wow . . . uh . . . that's swell, Mare," Ruby said, somewhat disingenuously.

It was preposterous to envision Mary shipping out. There were already enough of them headed "overseas," thank you. Not to mention, what soldier wanted to wake up from being shot with the grim reaper incarnate hovering above his bed?

"You'd make a keen nurse," Ruby guessed, to be nice.

She really wouldn't go, would she? The idea seemed fanciful, at best.

"I haven't decided for certain," Mary said. "It'd be a big change and I'd hate leaving you alone."

"Don't worry about little old me . . ."

"And I still have to be accepted. But if I do leave, I'd like to recommend you to replace me as air warden."

Ruby gave a small chortle. Oh dear Mary. The passing of her most cherished baton. It would never happen. Mary was all talk. Not too long ago, she was brooding around Cliff House, pregnant with an invisible baby.

"Sure, sounds like a gas," Ruby said, and breezed out into the entryway.

"Good gravy, here we go again," Mary called. "Ruby, you need to get serious. I can't entrust you with this important position if you won't commit with your whole heart!"

Shaking her head, Ruby flicked on the lights of the foyer's three-hundred-pound lantern. She'd never fully get on Mary's good side, would she? Not that Ruby was much for trying.

As Mary squawked on, Ruby lifted the blackout shades. The windows were gorgeous in that room, a damned shame to have such glum housewares hooked on to them.

"Ruby, are you listening?" Mary yelled.

"Sure, sure," she mumbled.

Ruby hiked up the final shade. She turned and glanced out the windows flanking the front door. At once she spotted an arc of red over the privet hedge, the color gleaming and recognizable even in that dusky light. It was the hood of a brand-spanking-new Packard Clipper, custom edition, bought before it was no longer fashionable to spend money in such ways.

"Daddy!" she hollered, scrambling to unlock the door. "Mary! He's here!"

Without thinking, without a single notion that there could be bad news (*Pay attention, Ruby! We're at war!*), she heaved open the door and broke into a full-bore sprint, losing one shoe along the way.

"Daddy!" she yelled just as he was walking through the arbored gate.

Ruby leapt at him and wrapped both arms around his neck.

"It's so great to see you!" she said. "You look fantastic! Not sick at all!"

Wishful thinking, yes, but he did look all right. Daddy had always been reedy and pale, bowed one way or another. He was a scientist, for Pete's sake. Those types didn't come in brawny and tanned. He'd grown a tad blobsy around the middle, but who didn't at age fifty-two?

"Oh, petal," Daddy said, giving Ruby a squeeze before dropping her to the ground. "More beautiful by the day. This grandchild of mine has lit you from within."

Ruby peered up at the man, to beam in thanks, not to mention ask how long he planned to stay and was Mother in the car. She'd been a real grump lately, by the by. Ruby hadn't wanted to speak ill of her mom, but facts were facts, and there you go.

"Daddy . . ." she started.

And then she noticed the tears, the red-rimmed eyes.

"Holy Mother of God!" Ruby jumped back, waiting to be growled at for her salty mouth.

But Daddy did no such thing.

"It's Topper, isn't it?" she said, voice shaking.

Because of course it would be Topper. Dashing, handsome, reckless Robert Young. The brightest lights burned out quickest.

"No, my petal. It's not Topper. He's fine. Training, same as always."

"P.J.?" Ruby glanced over her shoulder to see Mary standing in the doorway.

"No, P.J. is . . ."

"*Sam?!*" Ruby cried.

It hadn't occurred to her, it truly hadn't.

"No, no. They are all fine," Daddy said, rubbing Ruby's arm.

"Oh praise God," she said, sending a hundred little thanks up to the heavens.

"Christ, Ruby. It kills me to do this to you. But . . . it's your mom."

"Regarding Mother, do you know she's only been out once this summer? The excuse is that she's taking care of you. But you look wonderful! I mean it. Once, Daddy! She's come out once! And I'm left to run Cliff House myself." Ruby gave another compulsory peek over her shoulder. "With Mary, but you know how she is."

She griped on because Daddy had more to say and Ruby straight didn't want to hear it.

"Ruby . . ." he said, several times, trying to stop this train. "Ruby . . ."

"Mother had better help close the house because I'm getting larger and less nimble by the day. I'm already past the halfway mark."

"Petal, I'm sorry. I hate to be the one to say this, but your mother. She's gone."

Gone. No. Whatever those words were. No. It would never happen like that.

"You're lying," Ruby said, though Daddy never did.

It could not be true. The powerful, indelible Sarah Young would not be "gone" without some seismic shift rumbling them all. "Gone" like the fog, or your ration of sugar. No, Mother was not something that could vanish while you weren't keeping track.

"That's not . . . it can't be . . ."

Ruby was nearly blinded by the tears filling her eyes. She felt Mary walk up behind her.

"Papa Young?" Mary said. "What is it?"

"My Sarah is gone," he answered, now crying himself.

Ruby's heart shattered a million times over.

"That can't be!" she said. "Mother's not even sick. She's healthy as a horse."

"It took everyone by surprise. The doctors, me, friends in Boston."

"Friends in Boston?!" Ruby yelped. "They knew and we didn't?"

"It all happened so fast. She was sick and before we could tell you, she was gone. I didn't think . . . we thought . . . I guess, when you get right down to it, we thought we had more time than we actually did. Ten years or ninety-nine. It's simply never enough."

43

The Book of Summer

Philip E. Young
August 31, 1942
Cliff House, Sconset, Nantucket

I never expected to write in this book.

It was Sarah's from the start and it feels like an intrusion, though she would not mind at all.

But really it was my dear Sarah who shaped our family. We wouldn't have Cliff House, the lookout from America's edge, if not for her insistence. I'm so glad she pried the money from my miserly hands. She will live forever in this book and in this home.

I'm not much of a writer. Or a reader. But I've enjoyed going through this Book of Summer. Sam's story about the golf match had me laughing for the first time in a while. My greatest wish is that my bright and sparkling Ruby will likewise find some cheer in a not so distant future. I should take her on a spin through our summertime history as memorialized in this book. We've had a dang great time. A shame, I've only just realized.

My petal is crushed by her mother's sudden passing, which is what I feared and expected both. I can't help but feel at fault, though Sarah would smack me at the thought. My lovely wife had breast cancer, discovered only a few months ago. That's what happens when your mind's on something else, like a sickly husband. You don't have time to worry about yourself. And here I sit, alive and hacking. It's not a bit fair, not that life ever is.

Sarah hadn't wanted to bother Ruby with the bad news so early in her pregnancy and the doctors said sweet, strong Sarah wouldn't leave us soon. We planned to tell the family after summer's end. My lovely bride couldn't fathom ruining the magic of Cliff House with news like this. Then, last Sunday, Sarah took to bed feeling poorly. She never again stepped foot on the floor.

Good-bye, dear Sarah, you will be missed more than this old scientist could rightly describe. Thank you for what you've built—a life, a family, and a house that will keep after the last of us is gone.

Signed,
Philip Young,
Husband of Sarah,
Also known as Dad

44

RUBY
September 1942

September 1, 1942

Dear Ruby Red,

It was darn aces to see you the other week, even if the reason was something less than keen. Mother gone. Can you believe it? I thought she was too reliable for any sort of illness or dying foolery. The best battleship ever conceived.

My Red, it's up to you. I hate putting on the squeeze but it's the truth. This is Very Serious Business. You're the heart of this family now, especially with the bun in that oven. Don't let your grief get in the way of your obligations.

Enough of that. Well. You asked me to write when I got "home." Wherever that is. Right now I'm at the Davis-Monthan base in Tucson, AZ. Lord, I'm ready to be done with this training but we need it, and how. Flying these B-24s is like trying to fly a damned house, a pain in the rear even for yours truly, the strongest man to ever live. (Ha! Stop rolling your eyes!) And as nose gunner, I'm the guy who drops the bombs, which means a whole added level of complexity. Sorry, I'm boring you with my woes. The boys from Harvard find these stories endlessly fascinating but you're too high-minded for such talk.

Okay Red, you keep doing your thing. Don't worry about me, or Sam, or P.J. for that matter. I saw a poster the other day outside the local watering hole—"The U.S. Needs Us Strong" it said. It was an advertisement for cheese bobbies so not exactly the thing on which hopes, dreams, or great countries are built. But the message is right, in any case.

I love you, Ruby. I can't wait until we blast Hitler to Kingdom come and the lot of us can get back to meeting up in Sconset every summer, like we're meant to. Much better than time spent in a tin coffin, hurtling through the air. Sorry, sis! It's just part of the job.

Take care of yourself.

All my love,
Your brother,
Topper

Daddy came out to Cliff House for the last weekend. Not because he wanted to, despite what he said, but because he had to.

Who else would help Ruby close it up? Mother, dead. Two brothers and one husband, in the service. No able-bodied men to hire because they were fighting, too. Even Mary was gone, training in Washington just as she'd threatened to do. Ruby hadn't thought she'd actually leave, but it seemed Mother's death was the kick Mary was waiting for.

The U.S. Needs Us Strong, Ruby repeated to herself over and over, so she didn't fall into a sobbing heap on the floor. *Red, you keep doing your thing.*

"I'm going back with you," Daddy said, three days ago, when they'd gathered at the Youngs' house on Commonwealth Ave. mere hours after burying Mother in Boston. "We'll close up the summer place together."

Ruby could almost hear Mother screaming blue murder. As good as Daddy looked a week before, he'd aged a decade in but seven days. Ruby was pregnant but nonetheless in much better shape to close Cliff House, no bones about it. Alas, without the gentle guiding voice of Mother, Ruby couldn't quite find her way.

And so Philip Young returned to Sconset with his daughter, so they could conclude the season together. On the final night, they danced at the club like it was any old summer. Dad made a good show of standing tall, though he was brittle through his suit. As the band played "Someone to Watch Over Me," Ruby bit down on her tongue to control her tears.

"Gorgeous night, eh petal?" Daddy said, trying to keep Ruby moving across the floor.

"Lovely," she answered, then clenched down harder.

"Sarah adored Labor Day Weekend."

Ruby nodded, once again hearing her mother's voice in her mind.

"What are you fussing about, Ruby?" she'd say, for Ruby was always a little boo-hoo at that last oyster party and during the farewell dance. "The *end*? Why, Ruby dear, the end is the best part. All the sugar is at the bottom of the cup."

Of course, there was hardly any sugar left in America these days.

Insides trembling, Ruby rested her chin on Daddy's shoulder so he could not see her face.

"You hear from Mary yet?" he asked.

"Not since the funeral. I'm glad things are going well for her."

Gosh darn it, Ruby missed that old gal, their favorite wet sock. Everyone needed a straight man and Cliff House had lost hers, for now. Another part Ruby would have to play. Jesus, this cast was getting slim. Ruby wondered how much more she'd have to take on.

"P.J. must be proud," Daddy said, spinning his daughter as much as his whittling strength would allow.

"We all are," she said.

Daddy spun her again and Ruby let her weary body be dragged along. Lord, was she tired. Every piece of her was heavy and untethered. Even Ruby's stomach, so often jumpy from the babe, was melancholy and still.

"And how is Sam?" Daddy asked. "Bound for the South Pacific, you said?"

"Yes, sir. Should be en route, aboard some newfangled vessel. They christened it with champagne and everything. The finest ship ever built, or so they claim. It'd better be anyway."

Funny how Ruby once regarded a ship as safer than a tank or plane. Meanwhile, the papers contained a never-ending barrage of reports about shot-up and sunken battleships. Ruby never considered that on a boat you could get pummeled from the water, shore, and sky.

"The latest and greatest is the right spot for our Sam," Daddy said. "Of course it'll be impossible to completely relax until they're all home."

Ruby sighed. Daddy was making her feel worse, the poor lug. Mother said half his sweetness was in his scientific nature, the very black-and-white of him. He never knew the right thing to say, which was aggravating but made him real and true.

"Yes," Ruby said. "Peace seems very far away."

As Daddy turned her around, Ruby caught sight of a military man standing at the edge of the dance floor. He was in a blue coat and black pants, his golden belt and buttons sparkling in the ballroom lights. With his cropped black hair and regal air, Ruby had to catch herself. For a second, she thought it was Sam, even though he would've been togged out head to toe in blue.

"Daddy, who's that fellow?" Ruby asked.

The man was strange, but not a stranger, which made it odder still. He was an army man, judging from the garb.

"What's that?" Daddy said.

"Who's that man?" she asked again. "That officer?"

As Ruby continued to stare, her brain buzzed. The stranger offered a small wave.

"Why, it's Topper's friend!" Daddy said. "That Nick fellow, from college. Come on, let's go say hello."

"Nick Cabot, you old devil," Daddy said, shaking Nick's hand with vigor, or at least as much vigor as he could muster. "Good to see you, sport. What brings you to the island?"

"Here to visit some friends before I ship out," Nick said, holding his hat against his heart. "I hoped to see Topper but haven't heard from him in a while. Hello there, Ruby. You look beautiful as always."

"Thanks," she said with a sniff, trying to work out why he made her so goosey.

What was it he'd said about Hattie? *There's simply nothing to her.* He called her an egoist—a would-be hedonist, too. As the memories came into full view, Ruby gave Nick the old side-eye and a little harrumph.

"Topper, he's . . . ?" Nick winced. "He's okay, right?"

"Far as we know," Daddy said. "The boy's still training in Arizona. Sorry he's been silent but don't take it personal. Ruby's the only one he regularly keeps up with. I go to her for all the nitty-gritty. Anyhow, I'll leave you two for a catch-up. I need to step outside."

Ruby studied him. Daddy looked peaky. His face was shiny, dribbles of sweat collecting above his brows. It wasn't even warm that night. A certain fear poked Ruby, sharp in her stomach.

"So, Ruby," Nick said, and forced a grin. "You look swell."

"Yes, you mentioned that," she grumbled.

Nick gave her a perplexed squint. He was handsome, rich, and famously lettered in every sport available at every school he'd attended. For Mr. Cabot it was probably a major twist that a gal wouldn't devour his flattery.

"I heard about your mother," Nick said. "I'm so very sorry. She was a gem."

Ruby smiled wanly and clutched her stomach. The man was giving her fits. Even her body knew the guy was shady as a cedar grove. Either that or her new girdle was screwy. It was at once too tight, or her bladder too full. This pregnancy devilry was nuts, her body changing by the hour.

Suddenly something trickled out of Ruby. Dear God. She'd been warned by women who knew, but it seemed far too early to be wetting her drawers.

After hastily excusing herself from Nick Cabot's questionable company, Ruby hustled toward the ladies' and hitched her panty girdle down. At once she wailed in pain, though dull cramps were the only physical sensation. This pain was from her heart, her hopes, and her dreams. The pain was from seeing her underwear's confident, innocent, white satin sheen completely doused in blood.

He was going to be named Robert. They planned to call him Bobby.

Ruby telegrammed Sam but for the longest time did not hear back. At first she feared the worst because this was war and the worst was surely to come. Finally, Sam answered back with one word. HEARTBROKEN.

The dreams that would never come.

45

Saturday Morning

Bess wakes up at four o'clock in the morning. She assumes that the quirks of pregnancy (indigestion, sharp pains under the rib cage) have jostled her to attention, but in fact it's all the clashing and thumping going on down the hall. Cissy, of course.

Another reason she can't have a baby. What example does she have? Bess loves that crazy woman, but sometimes she fantasizes about one of those regular homemaking, cookie-baking moms. Really though, Bess doesn't care about sweets. She'd settle for someone not risking her life for a house, someone not knocking about in the dead of night doing Lord knows what.

Bess turns onto her left side. She lies there for several uncomfortable minutes before turning onto her right. When that doesn't work, she flips faceup but then remembers that pregnant women aren't supposed to sleep on their backs. Then again, does it matter?

All spun up into a wired-exhausted state by 4:42, Bess lurches out of bed. After grabbing a robe off the pink bureau, Bess wraps it around herself with a double knot and patters out into the hallway. She's surprised to find it dead dark, all the way down to Cissy's room. The thumping has disappeared; the only sound is that of the waves breaking beyond.

Was Bess imagining things? Jacking up the volume on the home's creaks and cracks?

Suddenly she hears the front door whoosh open and then slam shut. It's not even five o'clock in the morning and the old bat is already out of her lair. Bess runs to the round window in the hall, a window now partially blocked by Cissy's ill-conceived secondary flagpole.

"Damn it, Cissy," Bess grouses with a laugh.

Although the view is obstructed, Bess has a clear shot of Baxter Road, and one Mrs. Caroline Codman scuttling across it like a blond crab. And what do you know, she's headed straight toward Chappy Mayhew's.

Bess inhales, holding the breath behind her chest until her raging heartburn intervenes and she's forced to let go. What is Cissy doing? Breaking and/or entering? Damaging property? Every possibility seems farfetched yet likely at the same time. This is how it goes with the woman, a respected town doyenne and shooter-of-Kennedys both.

Bess turns away from the window and jogs back to her room. When she fishes her phone from the depths of a Young Family Reunion windbreaker, Bess sees an unread text. It's from Evan, time-stamped 10:33.

Hey—Just got your text. Wish I could've gone to party but at LAX tourney on the cape. Keeping phone off as a good example to kids. Hope you had fun. Talk Sunday.

Bess smiles even as tears fill her eyes. She can't believe how happy she is because of a few words. He was with a bunch of kids.

You're supposed to be the good example in this scenario? she types in response. *Poor kids. JK. Travel safe.*

Bess thinks to text her mom (*I see you! Step away from the Mayhews'!*), but remembers it won't get read until sometime next week. She chucks the phone onto her bed, tosses on her ratty espadrilles, and then books it downstairs and out the front door, bedclothes and all.

Bess stalks across Baxter Road. As she gets closer to Chappy's, Bess notices there are lights on inside, which means Cissy's operations are not covert. A confrontation, possibly? Her mother wouldn't physically harm the man, Bess doesn't think.

Soon she is on the property, tramping through the yard. Rose stems prickle Bess's skin as she winds between the hedges and flowers. It's foggy. The air and ground are wet, her ankles already filthy. After lunging over three low plants, Bess sidesteps some type of open-trench situation before ultimately steadying herself on a windowsill.

Bess glances down to see scratches crisscrossing her legs. Her palms are scuffed up and her nightgown looks like she's been locked in an Appalachian barn for twenty years. But Bess will not remember the minor abrasions. When evaluating that particular night, these discomforts will prove the least of the damage.

Traumatic brain injury is nothing to joke about, but there's no other way to describe Bess's emotions after looking at the window and the appalling portrait it frames. Here is a real-life shot of Chappy Mayhew, stark naked and bucking, jamming an equally naked, very willing Cissy Codman against a wall.

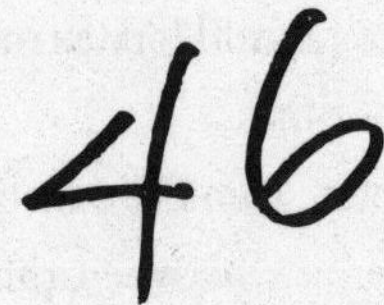

Saturday Afternoon

"You're back."

Bess stands in the open doorway as the wind sends sheets of drizzle sideways into the house.

"Yes. A day early," Evan says. "We laid a big fat egg in the tournament. I thought we'd at least make it to Sunday. I'm not sure what it says about me that I'm more upset than they are. You'd expect nine-year-old boys to be more cutthroat. Haven't they read *Lord of the Flies*? Can I come in?"

Bess stares at him. With so much to say, she doesn't know where to start.

"I hurried back," he tells her and holds up his phone. "Because of your um, slightly grumpy text. Came straight from the ferry. Is everything okay? And what is it I didn't tell you, exactly?"

"Are there multiple options to choose from?"

"Ummm . . ."

Bess looks around, though she is the only person at the house. She hasn't seen Cissy since that morning, when she saw way too much.

"Did you know?" Bess asks.

"Know what?"

"About Cissy. And your dad."

"Shit." Evan closes his eyes and lets out a small groan. "She finally told you."

"She didn't tell me crap. I *found* them. Going to town. Not, like, Nantucket Town."

"Pound town?"

"Gross." Bess scowls at him. "Not funny. But yes."

"Sorry, sorry," he says, chuckling. "Maybe it is kind of disturbing. They're usually pretty discreet. Where were they?"

"They were in his house. It was . . . I saw them through . . ." Bess shakes her head. "Never mind. It doesn't matter. Your dad and my mom are having an affair, which you were apparently aware of. We've had some pretty intimate conversations and meanwhile . . ."

"Can I come in?" he asks again.

Bess looks down. The strip of hardwood between them is now completely slick with rain.

"Fine," Bess says, and ushers him inside. "Just so you know, I'm pretty pissed off."

"Noted."

They walk toward the living room, most of it now boxed up.

"You know what I'm thinking," Evan says as he takes a seat beside Bess on the floral couch.

She promptly moves to the light blue settee.

"I was thinking," he goes on, pretending not to notice the relocation, "I'm ahead on my project on Codfish. After the holiday weekend, I can bring my guys in to help with the rest of the packing. You've done a lot but this place still feels very . . . lived-in."

"Well, yeah, because it *is* very much lived-in. I've practically set down roots." Bess exhales loudly. "Why didn't you tell me about them? Good grief. Cis's archnemesis. No wonder you thought my parents were divorced! Poor Dudley."

"I don't think your dad is being duped or anything."

"So they have some sort of arrangement? Well, that's fabulous. What a great example. I guess my divorce isn't shameful after all."

"Shameful?" Evan smirks. "As far as I'm concerned, your divorce is one of your better qualities."

"Don't be cute."

"Listen, Bess, I thought you knew. At first. And when I realized you didn't, I decided it wasn't my news to tell. Our parents are entitled to their private lives, same as we are. You've kept a couple things from your mom."

"So not the point."

Bess laces her hands together and sighs. Cissy and Chappy. Always at odds, always mired in some squabble or battle of wills. *You're an asshole, you're a bitch*. And what about the restraining order? Bess isn't the most experienced person in the world, but she knows you generally have to be within fifty yards to have sex with someone.

"So their arguments," Bess says. "They're a façade?"

"Hell no. They're like a pair of not-very-mature teenagers. Breaking up, getting back together. Screaming matches. Restraining orders. It's exhausting. But there's a load of love there. They respect each other's passion. Neither one is a pansy."

"You've got that right. God. I can't believe it."

"It's pretty sweet when you get down to it," Evan says. "Even if the last few years have been extra teenagery given the bluff situation."

"How long has this been going on?" Bess asks. "That you know of?"

Evan thinks about it for a minute.

"Fifteen years?" he says, an estimate, but close enough.

"Fifteen years!"

"Around that. It started when I was in Costa Rica."

"Costa Rica," Bess grumbles. "Of course it started when you were in *Costa Rica*."

Evan squints at her, mystified.

"Um, not really sure what you mean by that," he says. "And I don't know the details about how it began. But when I got back they were already several years in."

"So. Gross."

"You might not want to hear this, but I'm glad they have each other, broken marital vows notwithstanding. They are happy together, in their own bizarre and twisted way."

"It's so incomprehensible," Bess says. "My brain can't process . . ." She grabs the sides of her head. "It's as though you're telling me one thing, and my mind is just spitting it back out, like a wonky dollar bill in a soda machine. 'Do Not Accept.' Jesus. Fifteen years. Well, at least Cis had the decency to wait until after my grandmother died to commence the sinning. Ruby would've been horrified."

"I dunno." Evan shrugs. "I get the sense she might've understood. Don't you think she'd want her daughter happy, if nothing else?"

"No, absolutely not," Bess says. "I mean, yes, she'd want Cissy to be happy in general but not in an Oprah 'follow your bliss' kind of way. Grandma Ruby was a make-your-bed-and-lie-in-it type. I'm imagining strongly worded letters sent from the afterlife. On linen stationery."

"I guess we'll never know."

Evan slaps his hands together and stands.

"I hate to break up the party," he says. "But I must go. Lacrosse practice is in an hour and I haven't been home yet."

"Practice? Weren't they just playing in a tournament?"

"If they were still in the tournament, I wouldn't need to make them practice," Evan says with a wink.

"Wow." Bess laughs, melting toward him already.

She tried to be angry. She really gave it her all.

"You're quite the hard-ass," she says. "Isn't it raining?"

"Cissy's right, you are a Californian," he says and snorts. "*They* wanted to practice, so I agreed to a quick one for fun. Then I'm having them over for dinner and a movie."

"At your house? I wouldn't let my kid go to that at all," Bess says. "*Hey everyone! Coach is hosting a sleepover! He doesn't have a son on the team but no big deal!* Pretty sure you can get arrested for that."

"It's a barbecue, not a sleepover," he says. "And the parents are invited. I'm actually good friends with many of them."

"Smart cover."

Evan gives a brisk laugh and then surprises Bess by pulling her into a snug hold. As she breathes him in, Bess warns herself to be careful. The feelings coursing through her will not do at all. And so she wiggles free.

"Thanks for stopping by," she says, eyes sweeping the room. "And somehow convincing me that I shouldn't be mad at you. As for Cissy, my fury endures."

"I can live with that. Should I come over tomorrow?" he asks as they return to the foyer. "To pack?"

"I don't know why you'd want to, but sure. I need help and it's probably better if there's a buffer between Cissy and me so I don't strangle her."

"Where is she, anyway?" Evan asks.

"Stalking engineers? Screwing your dad?"

Evan opens the door.

"There are worse things in this world," he says, "than the romance of a couple of fogies."

"Like my situation?"

He frowns.

"That's not what I meant at all."

"I know," she says, and waves him away.

Evan gives her another hug—perfunctory this time. After exchanging good-byes, he steps onto the drive. Then he stops. He pauses before flipping back around.

"Bess . . ." he says, digging around in his pocket as he makes his way back to her. "I need to give you something."

From his wallet, Evan removes a piece of paper.

"A receipt?" Bess says, the only thing she can fathom.

"I have a confession."

"Uh-oh. You know what? That's okay. I've had enough revelations for one day."

"I remember what I wrote," Evan says, pressing on, even as Bess inches away from him. "In the book, on the day of your wedding."

"You remember? All these years later? How?"

Evan nods toward the scrap now in her hand.

"Because I've kept it in my wallet ever since," he says. "I'm sorry I didn't tell you but I didn't know what to say. I still don't. Then as I was thinking about the move, and your divorce, and everything you're going through, I decided that you should have it. It is yours, after all."

Evan bites down on his lip and then lightly pats Bess on the shoulder.

"Good-bye, Bess." He backs away from her. "I'll see you tomorrow. I promise to have you out of Cliff House within the week."

47

The Book of Summer

Evan Mayhew
August 15, 2008
Cliff House, on Elisabeth Codman's Wedding Day

Dear Bess,

It's 6:30 a.m. Dad and I are here, helping Cissy set up the stuff she doesn't trust to others. You're getting married today.

Way back a hundred years ago, I heard a rumor that you'd gone to Boston College to be near me. It only made sense because you'd been accepted at Yale and Dartmouth and a bunch of other schools besides. I hoped what they said was true. Until I realized that's not what I wanted at all.

I knew you'd break my heart. A Nantucketer might be okay on-island, hardy and handy and such, but as my dad said, you'd acquire a new taste going to school in "America."

So to save you from yourself, I went to Costa Rica, my education not in degrees but in building homes. I knew I'd fare okay in a remote outpost, having grown up in one myself. In Costa Rica I fell in love with a country and a girl. She was a great woman, one I picked because she resembled you in appearance but acted the opposite in fact. Turns out temperamental is not so fun. I like things calmer, a bit more low-key. It did not work out. Not that I ever thought it would.

The Costa Rican adventure wasn't a total waste. I became a good surfer, a decent chef, and a reputable builder of houses for wealthy Texans and Californians and people on the lam. It was all enough, for a while. But eventually the pull of Nantucket was too strong.

The night I returned, I had dinner with Dad and Cissy at the Summer House. Over Caesar salad, Cissy told me that you had a serious beau, a techie type with an MBA. A good American, just like Dad predicted.

"Sounds about right," I said nonchalantly.

According to my dad, I was not at all nonchalant and instead acted like a "pouty brat" for the rest of the meal. Meanwhile, Cissy chattered on about this or that, filling the silence as she loves to do. Whenever you're in town, I miss having her at our table. For a guy whose own mother went island-crazy and bailed before he could walk, Cissy's as close to a mom as I'm ever gonna get. A decade of Cis. Not a bad second prize.

Anyway, back to the MBA. You're marrying him.Today. And as sure as the fog will roll into Sconset, you are settling for this guy. I've met him once, though have seen him snaking around more times than that. As far as I can tell, he's a Grade-A douche. I've known a lot of douchebags, was one myself for a time, so I have some expertise. I'm sure he has a sweet résumé and a killer paycheck and those teeth could not be whiter or straighter. But like his teeth it's all veneers, whereas you're the real deal.

It kills me because the whole reason I went to a foreign land was to make sure you didn't settle for a chump like me. If I'd known this was going to happen I would've stayed. I would've loved to have been the person you settled for.

I tried to talk to you last night at the rehearsal dinner. Listen, I planned to say, scrap all this. Your friends won't care. Cissy won't care, though you might have to help break down the "set," as she calls it.

But how do you say that to someone who looks so beautiful, eyes shining with hope? How do you tell her that she's not seeing things clearly?

Hell, maybe I'm the one who has it wrong. Maybe the douche wasn't really leering at the cocktail waitress. It's conceivable he didn't yell at her later, calling her a "fucking idiot" for some minor infraction. And Lala could've been overreacting when she pulled me aside and said he "totally creeped her out." You've always insisted she doesn't understand how real people work.

Well, it's safe to say this entry isn't staying in the book. I'll help Cissy with what she needs then become invisible. At the wedding I'll try not to watch. I won't say a word to you.

I'm wishing you a lifetime of happy, Bess. And the ability to recognize if you're not. Remember, you came to Cliff House before, when you needed to start over. It's not just for summers. It stands in the bad weather, too.

Always,
Evan Mayhew

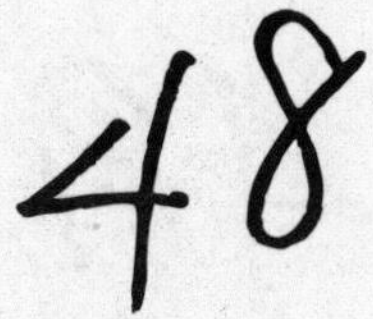

WASHINGTON, DC
SEP 13 4:43PM
MR. PHILIP E. YOUNG
25 COMMONWEALTH AVE. BOSTON

THE SECRETARY OF WAR DESIRES ME TO EXPRESS HIS DEEP REGRET THAT YOUR SON STAFF SERGEANT ROBERT APPLETON YOUNG WAS KILLED IN A TRAINING MISSION ELEVEN SEPTEMBER IN ARIZONA. CONFIRMING LETTER FOLLOWS.
J A ULIO THE ADJUTANT GENERAL

49

The Book of Summer

Ruby Young Packard
December 26, 1942
Cliff House, Sconset, Nantucket Island

It's the day after Christmas.

The island is ugly and bitter and cold. A fine match for my mood. It's taken all my grit and drive to get through these past few months. The world is different knowing Mother, Topper, and my not-quite-a-baby are no longer in it. The days as a "la-la girl" are done and over and I must press on somehow.

The U.S. Needs Us Strong.

Lately everything, every last bit of thing, from advertisements to newspapers to fliers around town, it's all "For Victory." Save for victory. Plant for victory. Smoke cigarettes for victory. As for me, the motto will be, Keep a stiff upper lip for victory. Wake up tomorrow, for victory.

Yesterday we celebrated Christmas, at least as much as two and a half broken spirits can. Daddy, Mary, and I ate our feast; a goose we weren't supposed to have but Daddy got a hold of nonetheless. A sad party: the three leftovers, and then the two. Mary darted off to Washington as soon as she set down her fork. I left soon after.

I hated to abandon Daddy, if even for a few days, but I couldn't bear Boston a moment longer. The city has grown too loud, the voices jumbled, as if everyone's speaking a different language. No ferries were running so I paid a fisherman a hundred clams and rode with him out to Nantucket. He white-knuckled it all the way, sure he was going to end up with my death on his conscience. I partway hoped it might be the case.

Oddly I find beauty in the island's drabness. Everything is the same color, even the waves crashing at the shore. The wind whispering through the walls is a dulcet song and there's comfort in the harsh cold. At least I have things left to feel.

As 1942 comes to a close, I can't help but think "damn you, you stupid year!" or a million other things besides. It's been a rotten time, filled mostly with heartbreak and hell. Mother, the baby, Topper. Back to back to back. Even all this time later, I can't pick out one pain from the other. What hurts the most? The loss of those I've loved a lifetime? Or the love I'll never have?

I'm sure Mother never dreamed something like this might go into her Book of Summer. I guess that's why I wrote it in the winter. But rest easy, dear mom, that you had this house built for comfort. And so far it's the only place where I've found the slightest hint of calm, probably because in this home the ghosts of you and Topper and my almost-child remain.

Until sunnier days,
Ruby

50

RUBY

May 1943

Ruby sat across from Mary in a heavily paneled, dank restaurant near Capitol Hill in Washington, DC. Oh but they were a heartbreakingly long way from Sconset. It was enough to make a girl weep.

"What do you mean you won't go with me?" Ruby said as she shifted anxiously in her seat.

Never mind the throb of sorrow that forever pulsed through Ruby, her entire body ached after traveling a wicked mile (or five hundred) from Boston to DC in a train stuffed with servicemen. All of them rattling toward other cities and states, new futures heretofore unknown. *Do you have any idea what you're getting yourselves into?* Ruby had wanted to scream at them. *Your good looks and bravado will turn to junk once Uncle Sam gets ahold of you!*

Just as she'd predicted, just as she'd feared when Topper and Sam announced their support of the war.

Oh, God, Topper. It'd been eight months since he died and the mere thought of him stung like a fresh cut. To think, the last time Ruby saw him was at Mother's funeral, when she was still pregnant, when faith didn't seem like something from a children's book. Almost a year out and the devastation of the losses still hung on Ruby like a heavy cloak. Now, this matter with Sam.

"I'm sorry," Mary said now, in the paneled DC haunt. "I wish I could help, but it's not a possibility."

"Mary. Please. I'm begging. I've never asked anything of you before."

Ruby hated the desperation in her voice, but desperate she was.

"I'm rather busy," her sister-in-law said simply, though it was not simple, this bad business they now found themselves in. "I can't take a whole day off from work to visit another hospital."

"You told me you go to Portsmouth all the time!"

"Yes. To provide medical aid and for training. Not on ill-advised jaunts that could land me in a bundle of trouble."

"Sam is in the hospital," Ruby said, enunciating each syllable. "A *naval* hospital. My husband is injured and you, the closest person in my life aside from Daddy and Sam himself, you can't come with me to see him?"

Ruby's cheeks burned. She thought surely—surely!—as Mary was a nurse, she would take this trip. Ruby should've gone with her first instinct, which was to ask Hattie. But in that regard she didn't want to receive four letters saying Hattie would come, followed by a telegram saying that she couldn't. Just as she had last summer. Just as she had for Topper's funeral. Ruby'd had a beast of a time forgiving her for that.

"There are others who need me more," Mary said.

"And what about me?" Ruby asked, loud enough to cause some bluster.

The people nearby cast them curious looks.

"Don't I need you?"

"Ruby, I can't. Not in my current position. I haven't even received my full qualification yet. Think of how it'd come across."

"We're family," Ruby said. "You and I, we're both Youngs, don't you see? We're supposed to help each other, especially now with Mother and Topper gone."

"I'm sorry. . . ." she said for the fourth time, or the fifth.

And Mary was sorry, truly. Though this was exactly zero consolation to Ruby.

"What you're doing"—Ruby snuffled—"or not doing. It's just . . . it's simply indefensible. If P.J. were here, he'd insist you help."

"P.J.?" Mary said, blinking like she was trying to remember the beat of some tune not heard in years.

"Yes. Your husband. Do you remember him? Because honestly sometimes it seems like you don't."

Mary shook her head. She looked at Ruby with downcast, sorrowful eyes.

"P.J. would agree with my decision," Mary said resolutely, as if she'd consulted him directly. "Once again, I'm sorry. I truly am. And it was nice to see you. The dinner is my treat."

She reached for her handbag.

"Some treat," Ruby steamed, her sadness morphed to fury.

Such quick changes were frequent phenomena these days, her emotions a real mystery prize of sentiment. Ruby never knew what might come up next.

"Ruby, don't be cross," Mary implored.

"Don't be cross? Sorry, sister, I don't see how I could feel any other way."

Seventy-five minutes. A full hour-plus of niceties and how-do-you-dos, not to mention a wretched meal of what they called steak but was canned meat. They couldn't even have coffee at the end. When Ruby asked for a cup, the waitress glared at her like she'd requested a sack of nylons. Had Ruby anticipated this outcome, she would've skipped Washington altogether and rode straight on through to Portsmouth, directly to Sam's bedside.

"I can't put myself in that situation," Mary said as she handed some bills to the waiter. "It just cannot be done."

"A nurse can't attend to a war-injured man? A naval lieutenant who's battled it out in the South Pacific for nearly a year? I don't know how they're training you in Washington, but it sounds like you might need a repeat course."

"I refuse to take offense," Mary said, "as your emotions are running high."

"You don't know the half of it."

"But as far as 'war-injured,' that is a matter of interpretation."

"You think so, do you? Well, all I know is that my Sam was sent off one way, and is currently in another state altogether. He had a physical and was deemed fit to serve. So if his health is compromised it can only be due to this war."

Mary gave a partial shrug and crammed the change into her coin purse.

"I despise that you're in this predicament," she said. "But I have no choice. Shall we go?"

"Fine," Ruby said, and stood. "I suppose good manners dictate that I thank you for my meal but I'm quite lacking in gratitude."

"I understand and was pleased to share a meal with you nonetheless."

Ruby was agog. The nerve! Mary snubbing her and acting gracious at the same time. Pick a doggone personality and get on with it already.

"Good night, Mary," Ruby said, trying to sound secure, assured, outright unbreakable despite all the cracks.

No, Ruby would not collapse. She would get through this. *They* would get through this. Her love for Sam would bolster her, toughen her once more.

The U.S. Needs Us Strong.

"I'll see you again one day," Ruby said, flip as a coin. "Presumably."

She turned to leave.

"Are you sure you really want to go?" Mary called out when Ruby was halfway across the room.

Ruby spun back around, even as her good sense told her to forge ahead.

"Beg pardon?" she said.

"What you might see and hear . . ." Mary shook her head as Ruby stepped closer. "I've visited that hospital. That ward. The very floor Sam is on."

"Well, bully for you."

Of course, Ruby already knew this. It was the first thing Mary said when Ruby called with the news, when she described Sam's condition, hoping for a sympathetic ear and some explanation as to his prognosis. Mary provided neither the ear nor the would-be nurse's impression of Sam.

"I'm only trying to tell you," Mary said, "that seeing him could change the way you view things."

"How I view things?" Ruby said with a snort. "My dear, how I 'view things' changes by the week. One year ago I had a mom, and a little brother, and a baby on the way. Nothing could change the way I view the world more than losing all of that."

Mary frowned.

"I know," she said in a whisper. "It's just . . ." Mary exhaled. "Sam is ill. Remember that, even if he looks the same to you."

May 10, 1943

Dear Hattie,

I saw your article in the Herald Tribune. It was fab! A real gumshoe piece. I didn't know the black market for food in New York City had grown so large. You must've spent scads of time chasing down the details. I suppose it's good the Yanks don't play baseball year-round!

Well, my friend, I write to you from the Hay-Adams hotel in good old Washington town. The city's a swampy pit just as promised, and the hotel (and the restaurants and people) a tad stuffy for my tastes. But there's a sense here, knowledge that, nearby, decisions are being made that will change the world.

Speaking of changing worlds, tomorrow I will venture down to the naval hospital in Portsmouth, Virginia, where Sam is recuperating, another victim of war, though compared to others he is in decent shape. That's what I tell myself. As I mentioned the other day, his injuries aren't life-threatening. Whether they are naval career–threatening I cannot begin to speculate. Mary was no help there, surprise, surprise. It's up to me to find out for myself.

Golly I'd love to see you on the ride back to Boston. Might you have a free night to step out and do the town? It's been a long time since I've had a bit of fun. Send a telegram to my attention at the Hay-Adams and let me know what you think.

Well, my friend, time to hit the percales and get some shut-eye. I trust you are well. I think of you often, always with great fondness, particularly in these dark times.

Your friend,

Ruby Packard

Ruby woke up the next morning a stitch before dawn.

It took several minutes to make out where she was. The Hay-Adams, a reservation made by Daddy so that Ruby could bypass some dreadful women's hotel like the Grace Dodge or, God forbid, the YWCA. She ran darn Cliff House without a man involved. Ruby could certainly manage an average-size bedsit.

Ruby surveyed the clothes she brought, a couple of one-piecers, and some two-piecers, before settling on a lilac rayon and wool jersey dress with sash. After securing her hair into an omelet fold, Ruby applied a light dusting of makeup and then put on a small, trim hat. She swooped up her fingertip coat and hoofed it out onto Sixteenth Street, but not before posting a letter to Hattie to be mailed out that day.

The journey used up the entire morning and a good chunk of afternoon, too. Ruby brought a book to keep her occupied—*Mrs. Parkington*—plus some magazines recommended by Hattie. In the end she only read a sentence or two in favor of staring out at Virginia's green countryside.

They rumbled up to the Norfolk station at 2:05 p.m. Ruby hailed a taxi and rode the short distance to the hospital. She read they'd doubled, or even tripled, the facility in the past eighteen months, but did not expect the sprawling, white hospital before her. Everything suddenly felt more serious.

A convoluted pathway of interlocking buildings and corridors led Ruby to Sam's ward. The place was crowded, busy, teeming with staff knocking this way and that. She didn't encounter many patients, thank God, when winding her way to the guy in charge, of Sam's health at least.

"Hello there," Ruby said brightly to a young nurse manning a desk.

She was a doll, this one, and so were the others. Mary was going to fit into this nursing gig about as well as a rotten tooth in a gleaming set of chompers.

"My name is Ruby Packard," she said as the girl smiled prettily. "I'm here to visit my husband, who's recuperating on this ward. His name is Sam Packard. *Lieutenant Packard*, that is."

Ruby didn't know if wives showed up at that hospital, as a rule. Daddy had pulled a few strings, turned a few levers, promised a few golf balls, to get Ruby so quickly on the books. Was she a common sight? Or would they be a-twitter about her presence the second she turned her back? Ruby found she didn't expressly care.

"Right-o!" the girl said, and stood with a burst. "The doctor is expecting you. Let me see if he's ready."

The nurse rapped on the door behind her, then poked her head inside, looking quite like the back end of an ostrich. Ruby tried to avoid staring directly into her tail, but the room was dang small.

"Yes, ma'am," the nurse said, her whole person returned to the room. "He can see you now." She cocked her head to the left. "Good luck, honey. Just so ya know, a lot of them recover. And you might be the perfect cure."

Ruby sat blinking at the man, trying not to seem befuddled by his words. She went to Smith for cripe's sake, even took a biology class or two. A far cry from medical school but she was no dope even though she felt like one then.

"Do you understand what I'm saying?" the man asked again, this doctor with the round spectacles and thinning hair.

"The psychoneurosis . . ." Ruby started, concentrating as she tried to decipher the word, the first she'd heard it. "The war caused it?"

"It's possible," the doctor replied. "However, often we find it's been there all along."

"All along?" Ruby said with the hint of a scoff. "Doctor, I'm sure you're a very smart man, and the folks at this facility quite well trained, but I've known Sam my entire life. We're married. I'd know if that sort of thing was . . . lurking around."

"You'd be surprised. In general, the psychoneurosis is a by-product of the underlying condition. In the unique environment of the armed forces, men with such predilections will sometimes develop psychosomatic disorders and work themselves into states of acute anxiety. This causes the psychoneurosis, and the resultant behaviors."

"So then how do these people—"

These people. Other people. But not Sam. That was not her husband. It was, as the good doctor said, a "by-product." Something to be fixed.

"How do these people get accepted?" Ruby asked. "Into the service? The exam sounded quite thorough."

"It is. The problem is that many deny their abnormalities to induction examiners because they imagine the rigors of the environment can turn them around. Others plain haven't acknowledged the truth."

"Oh," Ruby said lamely.

"In this case, based on extensive questioning and analysis, we believe your husband stretched the truth when entering the service."

"You think he lied?" Ruby said, unsure whether she wanted to cry or scream or both.

Strong, she reminded herself. *Your love for Sam will keep you strong.*

"He's never exhibited the slightest indication," Ruby told the doctor. "And I've known him since we were children."

"Yes, you mentioned that," he said. "Perhaps we're wrong and it's a temporary lapse."

"I'm sure that's all . . ."

"I have to level with you, Mrs. Packard. A year ago, he'd have been sent his papers by now. A blue discharge, as it's known. Not honorable, not dishonorable. But the lack of specificity is its own black mark. As I'm sure you're aware, all employers ask to see military service records."

"I'm not worried about Sam's employment prospects."

"Hmmm." The doctor simpered as he looked her up and down. "I suppose not. The point is, he's in a fortunate position because if we determine it's an aberration, your husband can stay in the navy. A year ago it would've been an immediate discharge and even a stint at the brig. But we don't have the luxury of squandering any borderline men who might prove fixable."

"Borderline!"

"There simply aren't enough to go around."

"So I should pray he's cured," Ruby said, jaw tightening. "In hopes that you'll be able to send him back out to fight? Another body to the war?"

"That's the short of it."

The doctor walloped his hands together and stood.

"Well, my dear, are you ready to see your husband?" he asked. "The good news is that a pretty wife is often a very reliable salve. Here. Follow me."

Mary was right, the wench.

Sam looked as he always had. A little thinner, and tanner, but given the horrors one could see in a military hospital, Sam might as well have been starring in a cigarette ad. He was handsomer than ever.

"My Sam," Ruby said, her hands cupping his face as tears ran down her cheeks. "Oh Sam, what have they done to you?"

"I'm sorry, Ruby, my love," he said through his own tears.

"No. No apologies allowed."

"Did they tell you?" Sam asked, wincing as he spoke.

"Yes. But never mind all that. This war, it goofs up people's heads. That's what happened, isn't it? The fighting? All those months at sea? It's polluting your thoughts."

Sam bowed his head, hesitating, taking a beat. At once Ruby realized the crunch he was in. The doctor said it himself. If this was a slip in character, a brief crack-up to be patched, that meant Sam could return to battle. The nightmare would begin anew.

But if it were a permanent affliction, he could go home.

"Incidentally, I don't give a fig about blue discharges or marred service records or any of that garbage," Ruby said. "If this 'condition' can send you home for good, then by God I'll accept it, a thousand times over and multiply that by two."

"No," Sam said, eyes wide with alarm. "Don't talk like that!"

Ruby glanced around. Silly girl. They were in a military hospital, for the love of jam. It was no place to admit one's secret desire to scotch the service.

"Gotcha," Ruby said with a wink and a nod—literal, that is. "I get it."

Another wink.

Sam looked at her cross-eyed.

"No, Ruby, it's not like that." He sighed. "I want to go back. This joint. It's making me bonkers."

"Of course it is!"

It was a psycho ward, after all. Naturally, Ruby wasn't eager to remind him.

"Who could blame you?" she said. "I'm jumpy and I've been here all of fifteen minutes."

"There's so much that was terrifying," Sam said, speaking more to himself than to his wife. "Beyond words."

Ruby nodded. Beyond words, except where it went into print. The papers covered the action, in excruciating detail, as much as they could give. For example, Ruby learned that last fall, U.S. naval forces had been creamed in the South Pacific. The Japs destroyed a dozen ships and took people hostage left and right. Sam's own vessel was involved but they managed to keep it floating.

This was the abbreviated tale, pasted together by Daddy, a summarized kid's version, if you please, as Ruby couldn't bear to read the reports herself. She'd stick with Hattie's black-market investigations and box scores for now. Let Daddy give her the need-to-know.

"Sweetheart," Ruby said, and took both of Sam's hands in hers. "It must've been horrific."

"It was, but even so, I miss it." Sam shook his head and bit back his tears. "Damn it, I miss the ship and the routine and the . . ."

He couldn't finish, the tears now hot and angry in his eyes.

"I want to go back," he said.

Ruby squinted at her husband. None of it seemed like a put-on, a ruse to keep the top brass happy. Ruby didn't quite know what to make of the declaration, considering Sam's state: in that bed and in that ward.

"It might sound off," Sam went on. "But the most alive I've ever felt was on that ship."

"I'll try not to take that personally," Ruby said, and attempted a terse chuckle. "And yes it does sound a little 'off.' "

"What I mean is," Sam said. "You see, I've never been filled with such drive and purpose, with such a deep sense of 'this is where I'm meant to be.' Don't you have at least some pride in me because of it?"

Ruby dropped his hands and then picked them back up so as not to send the wrong message.

"I'm very proud of you," she said. "But I'd rather you be home."

"I don't want to go home. Not yet. Please." Sam stared at her, those rich brown peepers of his wet and imploring. "Tell me that you understand."

"I'm . . . I'm not sure. I don't know how to answer."

"I want to go back."

"You've made that very explicit," Ruby said. "But how am I supposed to accept it? You going back to battle, this hospital, the events that led you here . . . You've asked me to understand but that's asking a lot."

"It *is* asking a lot. But Ruby, don't think about *here*. Believe me. I won't let that happen again. That . . . that was a onetime thing. A mistake. I promise, my love."

Ruby found she was bobbing her head as he spoke.

"That's my girl," Sam said, snuffling. "I swear to you, I swear with everything that I have, everything I am, that I'll never succumb to the vile urges that—"

"Sam, don't."

"Sometimes it's easy to forget where you are," he said, "when you're on the other side of the world."

Forget where he was? Didn't Sam say it was the very spot he was meant to be? Ruby couldn't help but think that none of this would've happened if she'd stayed pregnant, if she'd held on to that baby for the full ride. She was at least a little to blame.

"Well, Sam," Ruby said, and cleared her throat.

She kissed him gently on the forehead and felt herself fortifying. *The U.S. Needs Us Strong.*

"If you truly want to stay in the navy," she said, "then do what you need to. Just remember who's waiting for you. Remember that together we still have a home."

A heavy mist fell on Ruby as she booked it across Baxter Road. Once her feet hit the white-shelled drive, she turned and waved at Miss Mayhew. So nice of the girl to fetch her from the ferry landing. Miss Mayhew was a kind soul, not to mention sharp enough to understand that Ruby didn't have options beyond the generosity of her former hired help.

Weekender bag dangling from her left arm, Ruby struggled to unlock the front door. It always jammed in this weather, dammit. Meanwhile, Ruby's hair began to flatten as the rouge slid straight off her face. Not that her 'do and makeup weren't already in a state. She'd been traveling for eons.

Once inside, Ruby tossed her bag onto the hall table and walked to the back of the home. She'd never fully closed it up last September. Good thing, too, as she spent four weeks of winter there, trying to survive her grief. Cliff House. It would save her every time.

In the kitchen, Ruby glanced outside to where the patio furniture was strewn about, looking sad and abandoned against the brightness of the flowers blooming in the yard. Mother had planted her garden with purpose: decking it out with bright pink clematis, plus rambler, portulaca, zinnias, and their island's famous roses. In the old days, children cut flowers from their gardens and brought them to the flower stalls on Main Street to sell for ten cents a bunch. Ruby wondered if the tradition would ever resume, or if she and Topper would end up being the last children in that home.

How long did she plan to stay, precisely? An hour? A day? Ruby had her luggage, sure, but had worn most of her duds down south. To answer "how long," Ruby needed to figure out what she was doing there in the first place.

Ruby canvassed the kitchen and its pantries. Everything was bare. She'd need food if she stayed on. As she pondered what she might pick up, Ruby's eyes drifted toward the butler's pantry. Something triggered inside of her.

With a turn in her stomach and a kick to the side, Ruby beelined it toward the famous Cliff House spiral stairs and took them two at a time, straight up into Topper's bedroom. She launched the door open, heart thrashing in her chest. The room was untouched since his death, because of course it was. His death! Topper was dead! The sorrow clobbered Ruby all over again.

"Damn you, Topper," she muttered, wiping her eyes. "You were supposed to be my brother forever."

Would it always stay like this? Topper's room? With its flags and trophies of boys waiting to make that play? Mother had boxed up Walter's room lickety-split after he died, but who was going to deal with Topper? Ruby would never be fit for the task.

With a quick show of spit-shining a football trophy, not that there was a soul around to see, Ruby dropped to her knees and opened the bottom drawer of his desk.

The photographs were, no surprise, exactly where she'd left them. Ruby removed the stack and flicked past the ones of Hattie, two of Mother unawares, and on down to the bottom of the pile. And there they were, same as before. All those pretty boys.

This one, with eyelashes longer than the Nile, staring coyly at the lens.

That one, who Ruby suddenly realized was Nick Cabot himself. He was naked, or so it appeared as the frame showed only his bare torso, down to his hips, where his muscles were taut and defined and angled to some unspeakable place below.

There were others, too. One man's behind. Two male bodies, entwined, their connection unmistakable, their faces obscured. All of them godlike creatures, perfect in body and in form. Maybe that's all it was, an appreciation of art, courtesy of God.

Or was it the alternative, something Ruby never would've considered if not for Sam? It seemed preposterous what with the ladies and the swagger and the dash. Why, Ruby had seen Topper taking it to Hattie right downstairs. There was no definitive evidence formulating one conclusion or another. But there was a body of work, which sketched a certain picture.

The same picture, as it happened, the navy accused Sam of drawing. That of being queer. A sodomite.

"You're fortunate there are family members in high places," the doctor had said on Ruby's way out the door.

"My father?" Ruby asked, confused.

Daddy knew about the hospital stay, but not the nitty-gritty. Her stomach went wonky at the thought.

"No. The other offender is the son of a vaunted southern senator. He wants the whole thing swept under the rug. Count yourself lucky."

Counting luck hadn't been in Ruby's cards these days, so she hadn't been sure what to make of the so-called advice.

Photos in hand, Ruby scrambled downstairs. She scrounged up a piece of stationery, plus one large envelope, and jotted out a note.

Hattie-

Sorry I couldn't make a stop in New York. I stayed longer in Virginia than originally planned. Sam needed me. Anyhow, I found some beautiful photos of you—and a few others, too. Any idea what they mean? Give it to me straight.

Write soon.

Yours,

Ruby

She crammed them into the envelope, gave it a lick, and then, before she could think better of it, Ruby hustled outside and grabbed Topper's old bike from the shed. She hopped atop and pedaled the one mile to the post office, able to dispatch the note seconds before the postman closed the gate.

51

Saturday Afternoon

Bess is waist-and-elbow-deep in the linen closet, a misnomer of a room as it seems to include only boxes orphaned decades ago, scarcely a linen to be found aside from a yellowed tablecloth and a set of nautical tea towels.

"Yuck," Bess says with a cough as she lugs a box of themed salt-and-pepper shakers down from the top shelf.

She inspects the collection. Two bunches of bananas. A yellow iron and a black iron. Kittens wearing sailor garb. A disturbing white maid, black mammy combination. Kitschy and cute, some of them, but Bess doesn't anticipate ever needing salt-and-pepper shakers by the dozens. On the other hand, it seems wrong to sell Ruby's stuff.

Still undecided on the shakers, Bess drags a 12 × 12 × 12 box out into the hall. It is heavy, weighted down. As she goes to catch her breath, Bess reaches around for Evan's note. It remains snug against her, in her back pocket.

But how do you say that to someone who looks so beautiful, eyes shining with hope? How do you tell her that she's not seeing things clearly?

Bess doesn't know about any shiny-eyed hope, but she remembers talking to him at the rehearsal dinner as she struggled not to weep. At the time, she'd chalked it up to good old mopey-dope nostalgia. They'd had fun, the two of them. A perfect high school dream. Getting herself expelled from Choate was the best move Bess ever made, aside from attending medical school, but you really can't compare the two.

At the wedding I'll try not to watch. I won't say a word to you.

Yeah, well, Bess remembers talking to him at the wedding. He didn't exactly leave her alone, as promised.

God, Bess ignored so much, for so long. Before the marriage. The four years during the marriage. Bess was busy, a dedicated physician, aggressively head-down and toiling away just as Grandma Ruby always advised. Who needed alcoholism or drug addiction? Become a workaholic and enjoy the twin benefits of avoiding your problems and earning a paycheck.

Bess understands, for the first time, that the shame she has about the divorce is not because she couldn't make a marriage work. No, Bess's real regret is that she married him at all. She knew better. She knew she was getting a set of veneers.

With a sigh, Bess peels a strip of tape from the box, though it hardly has any stick left. After lifting the flaps, she wades through mounds of bunched-up newsprint and uncovers a carefully wrapped package. Inside are two dishes, cream-colored with silver scalloped edges, pink and yellow Virginia roses meandering about the perimeter. Grandma Ruby's china? This is something she will save.

Bess digs deeper into the box, through ever more wads of newsprint and wrapped-up dinner plates and salad plates and saucers. She even finds an empty packet of cigarettes—Gauloises, a French brand. Grandma Ruby smoked one cigarette a week. Every Sunday, five o'clock. Bess smiles at the memory.

She's enjoying the treasure hunt, cigarette trash and all, until her hand finds a strange clump of paper, distinctly urine in tone. There's a scattering of brown pellets nearby.

"Ew!" Bess screeches. "Yuck!"

A nest. Mice or rats, most likely.

"Disgusting!"

Bess wipes both hands on her jeans and then picks up the box, holding it far from her body, nose scrunched. The box doesn't smell necessarily, but it seems like it should. With previously untapped core strength, Bess clambers downstairs, through the French doors, and out onto the patio.

"Bess!" Cissy says from her spot at the bar. She's mixing a cocktail, of all things. "What on earth . . . ?"

Bess sets down the box, her arms suddenly loose and weak. She is wheezing, a little out of breath.

"Bess?"

"Rodents," she heaves and gasps, pointing. "Mice. Or rats."

A swift breeze kicks up then, goosing Bess from behind. Below her a wave crashes, and Bess's heart gives a skip. She peers over the box and sees nothing but air. Rain begins falling lightly on her head.

"Are you okay, sweetheart?" Cissy calls. "You look ghastly. Come dear, have a drink."

Cissy waves her over, smiling brightly, as Bess's eyes narrow.

"Elisabeth?"

"So, darling mother," she says, sauntering toward her. "What's new?"

"What's new?" Cissy takes a sip of her drink, vodka-whatever. "Unfortunately, not much."

"What about Mr. Mayhew? Anything new with him?"

"Chappy?" Cissy screws up her face. "Not that I know of. Other than the bastard's probably thrilled that Mike won't move the house. And neither will anyone else. I've tried everyone. Oh, Bessie. I don't know what the hell we're going to do."

Cissy's eyes begin to water, tugging on Bess's heart for a second before Bess gets her emotions back in check. She scowls to break free.

"And how would Chappy know the details?" Bess asks. "About the engineers?"

Her mother shrugs.

"It's a small island," she says. "And he lives across the road. Good grief, he's being such an asshole. Chappy, not the engineer. Although Mike's an asshole, too, seeing as how he won't do what I ask, no matter how much money I offer."

"An asshole, huh? So was it angry sex then?"

"Beg pardon?"

"What happened between you and Chappy. This morning. In the dawn's early light."

Cissy jolts. She would've dropped her highball if she wasn't holding on to it with such a fierce grip.

"I haven't a clue what you're . . ."

"Can it, Cis. You've been catting around with Chappy for the better part of two decades."

"Wherever you got that ridiculous notion . . ."

"Evan confirmed it and he always tells the truth."

Bess thinks of the Book of Summer.

"Okay, not always," she adds. "Usually. Eventually. Anyway, he'd have no reason to lie about this."

Cissy nods wearily and sets down her glass, the weight of fifteen years, the weight of ninety-nine, at once heavy upon her. She gazes out toward the horizon as thunder rumbles in the distance. The forecast calls for heavy rains.

"Well, now you know," Cissy says. "There's not much else to say."

"Oh, there's plenty to say." Bess walks under the overhang and out of the drizzle. She glances toward the box, half expecting rats and mice to come leaping out. "Like, what the hell, Mom?"

"Bess, be constructive."

"Fine. Why cheat on Dad? Why maintain such a sham of a marriage?"

"Because of you. And Clay and Lala. Even your dad. Sometimes keeping the family together under one roof is the best option. By the way, I find the word 'sham' unnecessarily harsh."

Bess makes a dramatic show of looking upward at the ceiling above them. She takes several large steps backward, out into the weather, letting her eyes travel the full height of the house.

"Hmmm," Bess says. "There's a roof. For now. But I don't see our family under it. No Dad. No Clay. And definitely no Lala. We are right now at only forty percent."

She steps back beneath the covering.

"You know very well that 'under one roof' is metaphorical," Cissy says. "And, really, I was referring to your childhood. I did what I needed to and I don't regret it." She inhales, taking a shaky, quivery breath down with her. "If it makes you feel any better, Chappy and I are done for good."

"Of course it doesn't make me feel better," Bess says. "Plus you're not 'done.' I've heard the two of you are quite prone to the back-and-forth."

"Not like this. I mean, yes, we've, um, severed relations before," Cis says, starting to tear. "But I've instigated it. I've been the one to declare 'enough.' Never Chappy. That is, until today."

"Why?" Bess asks as an unexpected surge of protectiveness courses through her. It's like she wants to go all Cissy Codman on the man and tell him to fuck off. "What'd he say?"

"That he's too old for this shit."

Bess fights a hard smirk. Indeed they are both too old for this shit.

"So there's nothing to get riled up about," Cissy says. "Because it's over. Done. All the way finished."

"I'm sorry you're upset," Bess tells her. "I really am. But you're going to have to give me a minute here. It's like someone's pushed me into a wall but, hey, no big, because I don't have an actual concussion."

"For goodness' sake, Bess."

"My parents' marriage. Fake."

"It's not fake," Cissy says, and grits her teeth. "It never has been. We know what we are to each other. And that is our concern, not yours."

"It's a little bit mine. I did live with you for a good portion of my life."

"Oh, Bess, don't be such a baby," Cissy says, sounding so much like Grandma Ruby it's like a ghost tickling the back of Bess's neck. "It's not the worst thing in the world."

"Why do people keep saying that?"

"This sort of thing happens all the time. We've always done what we believed was best for our children, and each other."

"You stayed together 'for the children'?" Bess says. "I guess that sort of thing does 'happen all the time' but I thought our family was different."

"Elisabeth, your father is difficult," Cissy says. "I recognize that I am, too, but in a completely different way. Dudley and I started in the same place but moved too quickly in opposite directions. I tried with him, even when my own mother said to let him go."

"Grandma Ruby? She would never!"

"It's true. I almost left him. I was so close." She shakes her head. "Then my mom died and I just . . . couldn't. You were still in high school and Lala was so young. The loss of your grandmother was hard enough and I didn't want this family to suffer another blow."

"I get why you felt that way then," Bess says. "But we're adults now and she died twenty years ago. Why not get divorced fifteen years ago? Seven? Last week?"

"Darling, I tell you this with great love—"

"Oh, no, here we go."

"You wouldn't understand," Cissy says.

"Right. Because I've never been divorced."

"You're lucky, Bess. You don't have kids. In your case, a divorce—not such a big deal."

"Ha!" Bess laughs, breathless in shock, as if someone's just punched her in the chest. "Too true. No big deal. What an accurate way to describe it. In fact, we've conducted all proceedings via text messages and Facebook chats. As they say in a physician's office, you'll only feel a pinch. . . ."

"I didn't mean you wouldn't understand about a divorce in general," Cissy says. "It's merely that you seem so sure of yourself. So utterly confident that a permanent split is the best course. I promise it'd be different if kids were involved. If a whole lifetime was."

"If kids were involved." Bess snorts. "Well, surprise, Cis, because—"

Bess freezes. There is a kid involved, sort of. For now. But even though Cissy is a lifelong Democrat, the ultimate bleeding heart and a women's rights drum-pounder to the core, there's no decent way to explain a proposed abortion. Not even Cissy would understand.

"Because what?" Cissy asks, pink spreading across both cheeks.

Bless it, the woman can hear the patter of potential grandbabies a mile away.

"The decision to get divorced," Bess stutters. She sniffs but then gets ahold of herself. "The decision is clear-cut, but not because we were child-free. Brandon was . . . he is . . . abusive?"

It still sounds strange, not right, like it doesn't exactly fit. No bruises, no bumps. All the bad stuff that a person cannot see.

"Abusive . . . question mark?" Cissy says, jacking both eyebrows way up into her hairline. "That doesn't sound like something you should be on the fence about."

"He was," Bess says with a nod.

Was he? He was.

"Oh, Bessie," her mother says with a sigh.

"Verbally," Bess adds. "He never hit me, though at times he seemed close. It's good that I work so much. I stayed out of the cross fire. And who knows, it could've gotten physical, eventually, if not for the hookers, who saved me in the end."

"*The hookers?!*"

It takes a lot to shock Cissy. A whole hell of a lot. But Bess has surprised her in a way no one else ever has.

"It's a long story," she says.

Bess walks over to the rusted green glider and slumps down onto it. Meanwhile, Cissy fiddles with her Red Sox hat, trying to appear unruffled while she searches for the best response.

"Well, Elisabeth," she says at last, her voice strong and assured. "I can see why you weren't keen on taking him back. I'd tell him to go fuck himself but my guess is the pervert's already tried."

52

The Book of Summer

Ruby Young Packard
July 10, 1943
Cliff House, Sconset, Nantucket Island

Oh happy days!

Sam is here, with me, at Cliff House. I can almost (almost!) pretend we're back to sunnier times. We are missing (and missing and missing) Mother and Topper. And Sam is to ship out in six days. But for now I revel in our togetherness, in our love. Not to get all gooey about it but there ya go!

Every morning we make a picnic lunch, pack up our umbrellas, and traipse across the big lawn and down the wooden stairs onto our beach. We find ourselves the perfect spot, which is any spot, really. I whip off my huaraches and wiggle my toes into the sand, my face turned to the sky.

Alas the war has changed even the beach. Uniformed men patrol at all hours, stepping over bathing beauties left and right. Stations are manned by life guardettes instead of the traditional guards. At least the island is only dimmed and not blacked out at nightfall.

In the evenings we cycle the eight miles to Nantucket Town for dinner or dancing at the club. Though we ditched the flag-raising this year. I couldn't stomach hearing the names of members who've passed.

This summer I've swapped culottes for dresses, no more meddling slips or dickering with a thorough coat of Mexitan. Bikes have taken over the whole darn island! The pleasure drivers are gone and meanwhile cheerfully painted bicycle racks are popping up everywhere, displacing hitching posts and parking spots.

At restaurants, schoolgirls now wait on customers, filling in for their older sisters who've gone to work in factories, the big sisters themselves having replaced the men off at war. It's a constant circle of replacement these days. You take from this to give to that, praying there won't be a gap in the chain.

Some things, however, cannot be replaced or swapped out and sunshiny days will be hard to come by once Sam leaves. But leaving is what he wants and therefore what I want, too. Maybe I'll tuck a pinup of me into his luggage, if I can work up the nerve.

I'm happy they judged Sam fit for service. Regardless of what happened to lead him to this spot, my husband is alive! He is recovered and he is well. Most would deem this a blessing of the highest order. I certainly plan to.

Until later,
I remain,
Ruby Packard, wife to Lieutenant Packard, U.S. Navy.

53

RUBY
August 1943

Ruby was glad they lived at the end of the street, because that was some racket outside, impossible to ignore. Which was Ruby's very problem.

She peeked out through the ruffled curtains of what was once the boys' bunk room but would be a nursery before too long. It faced the road, not the sea, because what did a baby need with a view? Ruby touched her stomach. Her monthly was almost a month overdue. She prayed that the two weeks Sam spent at Cliff House did the trick.

Damn it all to hell, though. Hattie was still down there, stomping about in her calfskin heels, looking swell as forever in a green Sunday dress with a basque top. She had a mile of pearls around her neck, bunched together and caught with a mother-of-pearl bee. Ruby wanted to ask her all about it but of course could not. Hattie didn't have a stick of luggage with her, which meant she came all that way just to talk. Well, no thank you and good luck. Ruby had her fill of

Hattie's two cents, if her words were even worth so much. She wondered how many cents that blasted magazine paid.

Though Ruby was intent on evading her former friend, she opened the window a crack, just to suss out what was what.

"I know you're up there!" Hattie called, quick on the draw. "Let me in, for the love of God! I'm on your side, Ruby!"

Because she wasn't a complete clod, Ruby did feel a crumb of guilt. To travel from New York to Boston, with a ferry at the end, was a helluva slog. Especially when only two ferries ran per day, boats so loaded with extra freight they were always an hour or more delayed.

But before Ruby got completely slushy over the girl, she reminded herself about Hattie's "investigative piece," out there for all to read. A touch of fame on the backs of people she once claimed to love. What a witch.

"You can't lock me out here!" her old friend cried. "Rubes, this is bonkers! You're the one who . . ."

Hattie paused. She shook her head, red curls bouncing to and fro.

Ruby *was* "the one who," wasn't she? She'd sent those photographs to Hattie, seeking an explanation but apparently not wanting the truth. Or Hattie's version of it anyhow.

"Topper was the best kind of fella," Hattie had said when she'd rung. "He'll be forever in my heart. But what you see is what he got, if you catch my drift. The pictures don't lie."

Hattie had spent a long time looking at them, stewing on a decent thing to say. In the end she'd decided that she owed it to Ruby to call it like she'd seen it, even if it caused some bruises along the way.

"Your brother was a remarkable person," Hattie had said. "But he was a sad, confused young man. He didn't know himself at all."

Sad? Confused? What about Topper's pranks, his wide-as-the-world grin? No one smiled or goofed around like him.

"He didn't want to be who he was," Hattie said on the phone. "He wanted to be like everyone else and so he fought it. Your brother hated being a fairy."

"A fairy? Honestly, Hattie. The two of you had . . . relations."

"*'Relations'?*"

"I saw it! In the butler's pantry!"

"Oh my," Hattie had said with a chortle. "Not a spot you'd like to spy one's brother in. Yes, we had a bit of fun together. But he never enjoyed it as much as he wanted to. He was always somewhere else. Poor guy. I tried to talk to him about it. There are communities where . . ."

"Stop. I don't want to hear any more."

And then Hattie had posed the question that'd render Ruby weak-kneed and stammering.

"Were there other photos?" she'd asked. "Anything with Sam?"

"With Sam?!" Ruby had choked, for she'd not told Hattie why he'd been hospitalized.

She'd mentioned only trauma, a brief mental . . . faltering. But Ruby revealed nothing about the senator's son, or that he and Sam were busted in the munitions room. She never used the word "pervert," as the doctor had.

"Gosh, Ruby, I thought that's why you sent the package," was Hattie's response. "Given the business with Sam in that hospital."

"No! I sent it because of Topper, obviously!"

"Huh. I wouldn't have figured you'd bring up old dirt on someone who was dead."

"Don't get all high horse on me," Ruby had snipped. "Hattie Rutter, a woman who takes it in the rear."

"Whoa, Nellie. That's a low cut, sport. You do know their history, yes?"

"Their history?" Ruby had said, addled, confused, and quite cross. "What history?"

"When the two were boys there was some . . . *experimenting.*"

"Good-bye forever, Harriet Rutter," Ruby had said before throwing down the phone. "Don't contact me again."

That was the end of their conversation, and their friendship. Ruby hadn't wanted to hear that word. *Experiment*. After all, her husband's medical records contained it, too. Sam was not queer by nature but an "experimenter" by circumstance. A "casual homosexual," if you will.

"Subject is interested in women and has enjoyed a normal heterosexual life," his file also stated, notes taken after a weeklong observation by a Red Cross nurse. "Not thought to be a confirmed pervert. Readily passed the gag reflex test, demonstrating infrequent fellatio. Official diagnosis of a psychoneurotic rather than sexual psychopath. Recommend to the board he return to duty."

And the board agreed. Stamp, stamp, stamp. A signature or two and Sam was cleared for reassignment, cleared for battle.

"Congratulations," the doctor had said when calling with the "good news" about tongue depressors and casual sodomy. "I hope you can both move on from here. I happen to believe that as with any other sick person, these types deserve compassion, not condemnation."

Ruby should've listened to Mary and never gone to Portsmouth to meddle in Sam's health. It was seeing Sam and talking to that smug doctor that sent Ruby back to Cliff House and into Topper's desk.

Why'd she send those photographs to Hattie anyway? Did Ruby really need to dig that deep? No, she did not, and the universe punished her greatly for it. Hattie did more than study the pictures. She assessed them, wrote about them, and then put them out for the world to see. Professional advancement, at Topper and Sam's expense. The photographs showed no faces, but to Ruby it was an utmost betrayal.

The doctor told them to move on, and Ruby was doing precisely that. Nothing that happened on the ship was relevant anymore. The same went for whatever occurred among puckish and exploratory boys. All that was to say: Hattie Rutter was welcome to buzz off.

"Ruby!" Hattie screamed from the Cliff House drive. "Let me in!"

Ruby backed away from the window just as Miss Mayhew approached. How much Hattie might reveal to her, Ruby couldn't guess. Harriet Rutter's wild unpredictability was a lot more of a gas two summers before, when the world wasn't shot to hell. Thank goodness

Miss Mayhew didn't run in their same circles and, having been a maid, she was already trained in discretion.

Well, Ruby couldn't worry about any of that now.

Hattie would tell her, or she wouldn't. Miss Mayhew would be surprised, or she wouldn't. Whatever the case, it was time to push forward, pick out the good scraps from the rubble and the mess. And so with fire and determination, Ruby slammed the window shut and turned away from Hattie, for once and for all.

The victory garden was coming along peachy keen.

There were no actual peaches but instead a smattering of vegetables, a right spiffy throng of tomatoes, carrots, Swiss chard, and beets. Ruby was surprised to find she'd inherited Sarah's green thumb, though she did have to knock out most of Mother's bluebells to make the room. "Deflowering for victory!" Ruby might've called it. No small number of lads would champion a sentiment like that.

"The garden looks spectacular," one Coffin sister said.

Ruby could never remember their names. It was this sister or that, the turnip or the celery stalk. The Coffins, they weren't so bad, but they did make Ruby pine for Mary's sparky beat. Yes, Mary's. The sisters were dull as wartime toast.

"Why, thank you," Ruby said, and swiped the dirt off her dungarees.

Ruby had been putting her all into that garden, her heart and her soul. There'd been too much destruction and she wanted to make the world beautiful once more. Being the number one vegetable producer on Sconset was an added kick.

"I must give credit to my sister-in-law," Ruby added. "For starting it before she left."

"Nonsense!" the Turnip said. "It's grown tenfold since then."

"Well." Ruby blushed. "With lots of help. That was an aces tip about the chard. It grows like a weed! The other veggies are doing mighty fine as well. I have quite the load for today."

Ruby planned to bike the spoils of her bounty into town later. Her production was impressive, yes, but all across Nantucket the victory gardens were exploding with produce. Come hell or high water, there'd be no food shortage there.

"I think you can supply the entire island's restaurants in one go," said the other Coffin, the Celery Stalk.

Ruby smiled. It was plumb dandy to be in on the effort, as much as she joked about the "for victory" rallying cry. Perhaps there was something more to Mary's nursing aspirations than her enthusiasm for ordering people around in an official capacity. Just like Mary said, contributing to the war effort was more fulfilling than playing tennis or honing one's golf swing. A gadabout's life now seemed grossly out of style.

"Is everything arranged for Saturday night?" Ruby asked as she began filling her basket with produce. "Any new jackpots?"

She and the Coffins had spent the last three weeks organizing a "Sell for Uncle Sam" initiative to take place at the casino that very weekend. It was a "Hard-to-Get Auction," with folks donating all the most prized rationed items, like nylons, coffee, tires, and sugar. The proceeds would go to purchase war bonds, and for one glorious night, no one would have to worry about busting a price ceiling or buying more than her fair share. For her part, Ruby had her peepers on some rubber-soled shoes. Shop for victory!

"We got ahold of one typewriter," the Turnip said. "Hardly used."

"Ohhh, we'll raise some nice dough for that," Ruby said. "I can't wait. I think even Daddy will make the trip out."

She'd also invited Mary, who responded with regret, unable to justify the odyssey from Washington. She promised to buy some war stamps in Ruby's honor, which was a nice gesture, though Ruby would've preferred the person. She'd forgiven Mary for not coming with her to Sam's bedside, an understandable refusal in retrospect. They had an unspoken agreement to never address it again.

"That's swell news about your Pops," the Celery Stalk said.

Ruby nodded and hoisted a basket of greens onto her right hip. Suddenly a stomach stitch overwhelmed her. She took in several deep breaths to chase it away. It was only her tummy pulling and stretching. Nothing to worry about, just a new baby freshly on its way. Sam had been home but two weeks and this turn of events said far more about him as a man than any medical records or stints in a mental ward. He'd done a man's job. As far as Ruby was concerned, on that ugly matter there was simply nothing left to say.

54

Sunday Morning

"So I'm here," Evan says, standing in the doorway.

"You're here."

Exactly as promised, Bess thinks. *I would've loved to have been the person you settled for.*

She wiggles away the thought of it, having already decided what can she really do? There's no getting around what happened, or didn't happen, and though she'd love to, Bess can't exactly go back and unmarry Brandon. Neither can she jettison her job, sell her possessions, and take up residence in Sconset. They'd never work in the real world. Not for a single second, a fact long since proven. Just ask Evan: They've already made that mistake.

"Put me to work," he says. "What can I do?"

He sets two cups of coffee on the round oak table between them, no spare this time. There is his cup, and there is hers, as denoted by "DECAF" scribbled in Sharpie on its side. Bess reaches for it, though she could very much stand the full caf. She is so tired her head is floating with lack of sleep. There is a gentle buzz that only she can hear.

"I brought my truck," Evan says.

"Perfect. Some of this stuff, I don't even know."

Bess points listlessly to the corner. An umbrella stand. A planter. A vase Clay cracked with an oar in a bout of teenage hijinks before he understood how to operate his gangliness.

"What do you do with an umbrella stand?" Bess says. "Or ninety percent of this junk?"

"Do you have to move it all?"

"I can't leave it here. It'd be like littering. Anyway, maybe you can start with the artwork?"

Bess gestures to a yawning seascape behind her, one of the many in the home. The painting is all large dunes and small waves, except for the shadow of a woman veering off toward the right side of the frame.

"Sure, I can move pictures," Evan says. "Even if it is a huge waste of my notable brawn."

"Ha! Don't worry about that. You've seen the glass-encased Revolutionary War flag in the foyer. It's bigger than my mom's Defender so we should probably wait until your coworkers arrive. In other words, we need some muscle."

"Ouch," Evan says, walking to her side of the table. "I'll try not to take offense. Okay, Lizzy C., whatever you need, I'm at your disposal."

Though he's going for his usual swagger and sway, Evan moves awkwardly, shuffling like a robot. What he wrote in the Book of Summer, it is the very most he's ever given Bess. Or anyone else for that matter, though Bess doesn't know this. What she does know, however, is that her heart is suddenly snagging all over the place, like panty hose after a day of med school interviews.

Bess jiggles her shoulders in order to wake up. High school loves are invariably bigger in your brain. It's sentimentality, a certain kind of homesickness, really no different from what's going on with Cissy and the house. Maybe Bess can find an engineer willing to move Evan closer to the road.

"All right," she says. Bess slaps the table to bring herself fully into the right decade. "Go to it. Rip that sucker off the wall."

"But isn't there, you know, protocol, for moving artwork?"

"I'm sure there is, but who has time for protocol? Cissy is now more concerned with being a pain in my ass than the integrity of her personal effects so I'll do whatever it takes. I need to follow Flick's advice. 'Get the shit out and be done with it.' "

"Your cousin is a smart lady," Evan says.

He goes to inspect the back of the seascape, as if it might tell him something.

"I should inform you," he says, "that Cissy's outside. On a lounge chair in some sort of gingham, whaddya call it, *tankini*."

"A tankini?" Bess gawps.

"I asked what she's doing and she said, relaxing and sunning herself. You might have noticed it's raining."

"Jesus H., that woman. Because of course she's sunning herself in a rainstorm."

"Is she okay?" Evan asks, inspecting the seascape's frame. "Because she seems a little—"

"Off her rocker? Batshit insane? Psychoneurotic?"

"More zealous than usual," Evan decides on.

"You're very polite. Cissy is not in a good place." Bess wags a finger. "Thanks, in part, to your father."

"My dad?"

"You know he dumped her, right?"

"I'm not sure he had a choice."

"Oh, there's always a choice."

The words sound biting, though Bess does not mean them to be. This is about Cissy and Chappy and their AARP love affair. Meanwhile Evan looks like someone just criticized his throwing arm. Bess would know, because she's criticized it before.

"Evan."

She rests a hand on his forearm. He glances down, warily.

"Thank you," she says. "For showing me that letter."

"You're not mad? Uh, and, I didn't mean anything by it. It just seemed like something you should have."

"Of course." Bess clears her throat but still it's closing up. "And I'm not mad at all. How could I be? Though you should've given it to me the day of my wedding. Or told me how you felt when we talked that afternoon. It would've saved heaps of grief, not to mention buckets of cash."

Bess is trying to joke, but it comes out all wrong. She doesn't give two shits about the money.

"I'm kidding," she says, smiling awkwardly, no doubt looking like someone trying to hold in a fart. "I would've married him anyway."

Would she have? Most likely. Bess was no Cissy Codman, but she'd inherited a few drips of the woman's stubbornness. It'd be hard not to, with that strong a streak.

"Seriously, though," Bess says.

Evan has turned away from her and is more or less ripping the painting from the wall. But if he leaves a hole, no matter. Only the hermit crabs will care.

"It was incredibly sweet and genuine and maybe if . . ."

Bess doesn't finish the thought. *Can't* finish the thought. Maybes are for moping and for regrets. And Bess doesn't believe in any of that.

"You're a great guy, Evan Mayhew." She thwacks him on the back, like he's just caught a forty-yard pass. "Every girl should have a high school boyfriend like you."

"Thanks," Evan mumbles, then tears the seascape down.

He leans it up against the table as he glowers, refusing to look Bess's way.

"Where are the other paintings?" he asks, so obviously done with this conversation it makes Bess's stomach dive. "The foyer? I remember something in the library."

"Wait." Although he is finished, Bess is not ready for him to leave, even if it's only into some other room. "I want to show you something."

She goes over to one of the boxes.

"Check this out," Bess says, and returns to Evan, paper in hand. "Remember the articles I told you about? The ones Grandma Ruby kept, written by that Harriet Rutter person?"

"Rutter?" Evan's eyebrows lift.

"Yep. Gram basically stalked the poor woman. Most of it's just box scores and beauty tips, the odd piece on the war. But this." She flicks the paper. "I found it in the bottom of an old jewelry box."

She passes Evan the article, which is from a magazine, the page having lost its gloss. The paragraphs are taped together, likely snipped from different places.

" 'Is He Man Enough?' " Evan reads. " 'And do we care?' "

He hands it back.

"Scintillating," he says. "But Harriet Rutter can keep her man musings to herself. I'm not really up for an education in lovemaking techniques from the forties."

"It's not what you think. In some ways, it's the opposite."

"How do you mean?"

"I don't know what to make of it," Bess says. "The article is backward and progressive simultaneously. Sometimes it's touching and other times appallingly non-PC."

"Well, it was written in, what?" Evan asks. "Nineteen forty-five? They hadn't invented political correctness yet."

"It was forty-three. Okay, listen to this. 'It used to be,' " Bess reads, " 'that the Armed Forces did not allow among its ranks a certain type of fella. You know the kind. Those with the swish and the swash, the sort of man interested in the charms of other men.' "

Bess looks up.

"She means gay," she says.

"Yeah, I got that."

" 'Heretofore Uncle Sam was choosy,' " Bess continues, " 'and enjoyed the benefit of being able to exclude confirmed homosexuals from service. Whether diagnosed by self-admission or a battery of tests—' "

Bess drops her jaw for effect. Evan remains stone-faced, confused as to why they're talking about gay soldiers from World War II.

"I mean, '*diagnosed*'?" Bess balks. "How is one diagnosed?"

"According to that article, a 'battery of tests'?" Evan says, holding up air quotes.

"And what are these diagnostic proceedings? The man must redecorate a room? Dunk a basketball? His dance skills are assessed by medically trained experts? What?"

"They gave him guy-on-guy porn and waited for a boner?"

"That," Bess says, trying not to laugh, "is disgusting."

She reads on.

" 'Whether diagnosed by self-admission or a battery of tests, a man could be precluded from enlisting simply due to his feminine nature, a lightness to his step.' " Bess looks at Evan again. " '*Lightness to his step*'? She knows they're not actual fairies, right?"

"Continue," Evan says, smirking and making a circular motion with his hand. "Sounds like you're close to the good stuff."

"It's all good stuff, in a crooked sort of way." Bess returns her eyes to the page. " 'But with a war on, things have changed and now the entire world is at stake. Men are dying and new ones are called to the front. Our fathers and brothers and friends are being drafted and each day we cast our nets ever wider. As the war bloats and our troops thin, we must ask ourselves, are we truly sending all able-bodied men? Can a person be too homosexual to serve?'

"You see?" Bess says. "I can't tell if Harriet Rutter is being compassionate, as in, hey, they're still men, why are we excluding them? Or whether it's more a matter of, as long as we're killing people, why do the queers get a pass?"

"I don't know," Evan says with a shrug. "Despite the lightness in the shoes and whatnot, I'd bet that even *suggesting* gays should serve in the military was extremely avant-garde."

"You have a point," Bess says. "Just wait, it gets better. Also worse. 'Homosexuals can presumably shoot a gun. And I've known many that are quite the sportsmen; some can even run like the wind!' Because, naturally, running like the wind is of chief importance in battle. Is she implying they'd run away screaming? Like a woman from an old-fashioned cartoon finding a mouse in her kitchen?"

"I think she's just saying they're athletic."

"Geez, you really are the nice guy," Bess answers with a smirk. "She goes on to talk about how, and I quote, 'the setting is not ideal. To send confirmed perverts to live in stressful conditions, conditions featuring communal showers and stacks of other men, seems like a recipe for sodomite disaster.' I mean . . . !"

Bess makes a gagging sound and slaps the paper again.

" 'Sodomite disaster'!" she says. "What kind of personnel handles that?"

"The Red Cross?" Evan tries.

"Harriet does quote some Red Cross friend who claims the setting is much too much for these perverts, what with the 'veritable smorgasbord of flesh.' "

Bess drops both hands, smacking the article against her thigh.

"You take issue with 'smorgasbord'?" Evan guesses.

"And the flesh! But just when I think old Harriet R. is going completely off the homophobic rails, she veers back toward 'touching.' Not like *touching, touching*—"

"So, double touching?" Evan jeers.

"Speaking of 'confirmed perverts.' " Bess shakes her head as Evan breaks into full-blown laughter. "I meant *heartwarming*, you sicko. It's actually kind of sweet. Hattie interviewed gay servicemen. She claims that despite the flesh buffet and what we imagine to be a bunch of macho, fag-hating dudes, the front lines were a *safe* place for homosexuals. She writes, 'Here's the rub. Out there it's far more accepted than it is on our own American soil. As it happens, when it comes to male-on-male lovemaking, fellow soldiers look the other way.

"'I interviewed one homosexual, a former navy lieutenant discharged after repeated offenses. He claims his proclivities were well known and he received far more guff and razzing due to his status as a half-and-half.'" Bess snorts. "An editorial note specifies this means half Mexican, not half 'Negro' as one might assume. Well, the guy told her, 'if a man could find comfort amidst such hell, the general view was: cheers to that.'"

"Aw," Evan says. "Love on the battlefield."

"Right? Apparently decades-long affairs began in these circumstances. 'Being at war,' a gay soldier told her, 'was the freest I'd ever been. The most alive I've felt was on that ship.'"

Bess sets the paper down.

"You're right," Evan says. "That is kind of sweet. Minus the half-breed stuff."

"One man she interviewed said it was hard to return to the States because it was back to hiding his true self. The article also mentions pictures, but Grandma didn't save those." Bess frowns. "Bummer."

"It's nice to think," Evan says, picking up the article, "that some people found solace in such horrible circumstances."

He studies the paper, brows crinkling.

"Harriet Rutter," he says. "That might've been the 'good-time gal' my aunt talked about. The one who palled around with your grandmother."

"They were undoubtedly close. Hell, part of me thinks Ruby had some 'undiagnosed' sexual leanings in Hattie's direction. She was unduly concerned with her."

Evan grimaces and his eyes dart back toward the article.

"What?" Bess says. "What is it?"

"It's like . . ." He shakes his head. "You know when you have that sensation? A memory trying to come out? And you can't decide if it's real or just something you made up?"

"That describes ninety percent of the time I spend at this house."

"I feel like . . ." he says. "Do you think . . . I seem to recall some rumor? About your grandfather?"

"You mean that he was an alcoholic? Yeah, not a rumor. That's true. Did I ever tell you that he died falling through a plate glass window while drunk?"

"No." Evan shakes his head. "Yes. You did tell me that. Way back. But . . ."

He taps the page.

"This might be about him. Because of him."

"Wait. You mean Sam Packard was *gay*? That can't be right."

"But you said he was discharged? Somewhat unceremoniously? The rumor was . . ." Evan squints hard. "I swear there was something about this. My aunt mentioned . . ."

"No. God no. That's wrong. I didn't know him, and he had his problems. But. No. Those weren't the issues he had."

Even as Bess says this, she wonders. An alcoholic is never just an alcoholic. He's someone with a genetic predisposition and a trigger, a reason to self-medicate. He's depressed. Injured. Suppressing some unwanted emotion. Then there were her grandfather's discharge papers. Psychoneurosis. A flimsy diagnosis, like what a 1940s doctor might say if he was too nice to call you a pervert.

"I'm probably wrong," Evan says. "I apologize for letting my imagination get away from me. Funny how long-standing family rumors eventually morph into a presumptive truth. Anyhow, you forgot Miss Rutter's seminal conclusion."

"What's that?"

Bess blinks at him, confused, unsure what to think.

"Here's how she wraps up the article," Evan says, picking it back up. " 'So if your son isn't a sporty type, and he'd rather help you shop or pick out china, don't get too comfortable having him on friendly soil. The USA must accept the truth. Homosexuals are fit to serve.' "

Something picks at the back of Bess's mind.

"And there you have it," Evan says. "What was, I'm sure, a very pro-gay and revolutionary viewpoint, courtesy of Miss Harriet Rutter."

"Evan!" Bess yelps. She clutches his arm. "China!"

"Uh, what?"

"Grandma Ruby's . . ." She shakes her head and looks outside. "I left a box of her china outside."

"Bess?"

She turns away from him and breaks down the hallway in a full sprint.

55

Sunday Morning

Bess slams through the double kitchen doors and books it out to the patio, where she finds Cissy sprawled on a lounger, clutching a highball like it's three o'clock on the French Riviera and not midmorning on Nantucket. Meanwhile, there's enough rain and bluster around them to garner a special storm name. That there's never been a Hurricane Cissy seems like a gross injustice.

"Hi Bessie-boo," Cissy says, and picks up her drink.

The wind whirls so mightily that even Cissy's iced tea is sloshing around in its glass, or what Bess *assumes* is iced tea. Cissy normally drinks vodka but you never know. Along with the drink of debatable content, Cissy has a copy of *Gone with the Wind* splayed across her legs. Gone with the freaking wind. How maddeningly on the nose.

Bess has no time for this now. She sprints to the edge of the patio, then stops short. Her heart scrambles up into her throat. The patio is smaller, yes? Closer yet. She stands shivering as the rain and sand drive sideways, prickling her face.

"The box," Bess says. "Where is it?"

"What box?" Cissy asks, and sips her drink.

Sneakers clomp out onto the patio.

"Hello there, Evan Mayhew," Bess hears her mother say. "I'd recognize those cocksure footsteps anywhere. You know, I don't say it nearly enough. Or ever. But you've turned into quite a nice young human, sabbaticals in Costa Rica notwithstanding."

"Uh, thanks?" he says.

"It's a miracle since you have no mom and the world's most obnoxious and pigheaded dad."

"Cissy!" Bess whips around. "Jesus, you'd think you were the only person in this family to ever get dumped by a Mayhew."

"Hey!"

"Mother. Where the hell is my box?"

"Hmmm." Cissy shrugs. "I'm not sure what box you're referring to."

"A cardboard box." Bess demonstrates its size, very roughly, with her hands. "I left it here last night. It was filled with Grandma Ruby's china. There were mice or something in it, so I brought it outside."

Bess retraces her steps.

"Then we started talking about the hookers . . . er, uh, about the demise of my marriage. Then it got dark—"

"Oh yeah, it got dark all right."

"*The sun set.*" Bess rolls her eyes. "We went to get dinner and I completely forgot about it."

"Strange," Cissy says with another shrug. "Sorry I can't help you."

"Are you sure you didn't move it? Maybe you don't remember?"

Cissy laughs dryly.

"I've had enough box-moving," she says, "to want to strike out on my own. But thanks for playing. It could've blown away? It's kinda breezy today."

"Breezy?" Evan says with a scoff.

"Cis, it was a box of Grandma's china. I broke a sweat carrying it downstairs. It couldn't 'blow away.' Even in this wind."

Bess toes up to the edge of the veranda and cranes her neck out over the cliff. As her stomach somersaults, Bess reaches behind her, as if on instinct, and is surprised to find Evan within her grasp. She gloms on to him to steady herself, though the very touch of him topples her off-balance in an entirely different way.

"Is that it?" Bess squints.

Her eyes sting from the wind and the sand and a million other things besides.

"Oh my God."

There it is, her box of china, scattered and cracked on the embankment. They've lost more bluff overnight.

"Cissy!"

Bess spins back around and staggers toward her mom as Evan conducts his own inspection. His hand flies to his chest and he keeps it there, as if trying to physically hold in his breath.

"Cissy, we have to leave. Now."

Bess is almost panting.

"You sucked me in," she says. "I've gotten too comfortable here. This is beyond dangerous. We're losing feet by the day!"

"What's a little patio?"

"Yes, it is now quite a little patio, that's the problem. And God knows what's happening to the foundation of the house. Cis, it's *pouring*. Are you familiar with the concept of a mudslide?"

"It's hardly pouring. By California standards, I guess. Don't be so dramatic."

"It's probably time to get a little dramatic," Evan notes as he backs up to the house.

This is a guy who climbs roofs for a living and his face has gone completely white.

"I know you're still trying to find a new engineer," Bess says. "And that's fine. I'll even help make calls! But we need to leave. The both of us. Now."

"It's over," Cissy says.

"I know it's over, that's what I'm trying to say."

"I can't get anyone to relocate our home."

"Oh, Mom," Bess says, and frowns. "I'm sorry but . . ."

"I tried to figure out if I could move it myself, but in the end it's out of reach. Oh, this poor old girl." Cissy looks up at the porch's ceiling. "She won't see a hundred years after all. Why'd my grandmother make her so large?"

Cissy Codman just cried "uncle." Bess never expected to see the day.

Everyone is quiet for a moment, no sound but the howling wind and little pieces of shell clicking against the windows. Cissy looks tired. Her eyes are sort of drifting, lolling about in her head.

"I'm sorry," Bess says at last. "I'm sorry we couldn't save the house."

"Me, too," Evan says, his voice hoarse.

"But you know what, Cis?" Bess feigns some spunk. "This will be fun!"

She walks a few paces forward and takes a seat at the end of Cissy's chaise. Meanwhile, Evan inches closer to the door. Emotional women, a deadly house. There's no decent way for this to end. And so Bess gives him a small wave, followed by a nod that says, Feel free to leave, we'll talk later.

"We'll have a grand time finding a new place," Bess says. "How about Tom Nevers? Or Polpis? I've always liked how quiet it is up there, sort of like Sconset. But you really can't beat the restaurants in town. Think of the meetings you could crash if you were only blocks away. And your charities! You haven't done anything for the Home for Aged Sailors in forever."

Bess looks up at Evan, who is partway through the door. Talk about moving a damned house. Cissy is her very own residence, a proper institution. And she was complaining about Cliff House being too large?

"I'm not leaving," Cissy says.

"Oh, for cripe's sake. We've lost a foot of bluff, at least, since *yesterday*. Frankly, I'm not staying here another night."

"Thank God," Evan mutters.

"We have to leave," Bess says again. "And I get it. This has been your home, our family's home, for all this time. It can't be easy to pack it in. I'm sad about it, too. But loss is part of life."

Bess wonders if Cissy's reluctance to leave is also about Chappy, who's lived across the street for sixty years. It must be, Bess decides. Because though he's never lived there, Chappy is part of Cliff House, too.

"It's fine to give yourself time to mourn," Bess continues. "We won't buy anything right away. You can stay at Tea Time, peruse the listings, and drive local Realtors bonkers with your crazy demands. When you're ready to pull the trigger, boom." Bess claps. "I'll be on the first flight out to help you consummate the deal."

"I'm not buying a new house."

"Mother!" Bess yells at the sky.

It's as if she's stubbed her toe and wants to scream "fuck!" a million times until the agony goes away.

"Just buy a new friggin' house!"

"I can't," Cissy says. "Because the money is gone."

"Excuse me?" Bess drops her head back down and gawks at her mother.

Poor Evan is stuck in the doorway, coming and going at the same time.

"You heard me," Cissy says with a sniff. She takes a sip of her drink.

"Your money is *gone*? I thought you had, like . . . millions or something?"

"Saving a bluff is no easy task," she says. "And not a cheap one either. I poured every last dollar of my grandfather's, and my father's, into the SBPF."

"Shit. Does Dad know?"

"Why would it be any of his business?" Cissy snaps. "That's my money."

Bess hears the door click. She looks up to see Evan still on the patio, in the wind and rain. He has officially picked a side.

"How'd you fritter away that much?" Bess asks.

"'Fritter'? You make it sound like I spent it all on wine and fancy jeans. Elisabeth. Who do you think is paying for the various studies and commissions? The geotubes that are being installed next month?"

"Aren't a lot of people contributing?" Bess says. "The city? The state?"

"All of those gave something. But I gave everything I had."

"God," Bess says.

Cissy gave it all she had indeed.

"I do have *some* money," she says. "I'm not a complete moron and I like to eat and buy clothes on occasion."

This last part is news, Bess thinks wryly. As far as she can tell, Cissy's been wearing the same uniform for half a century. Maybe Red Sox baseball caps have a quicker replacement cycle than one might expect.

"All that aside, I definitely can't afford to buy on Nantucket," Cissy says. "When did everyone get so rich?"

"Wow. You are a local after all," Evan murmurs.

"Cissy! Stop acting so cavalier!"

"Don't panic, Bess. You won't have to take care of me in my old age. I have enough to last me until I'm dead. It's not so far away."

"That's not what I'm panicked about," Bess says. "What about Dad? His firm seems to be doing, like, grossly well. His partner's wife bought a house in Vail without asking. I'm sure Dad has plenty of cash lying around, too."

"I'd never ask that of your father. I put my money where my heart is. It's not his fault."

"I get that. And I respect it, too. But you're entitled to half of the Boston house! That could easily buy you a nice place here."

"No, Bess." Cissy sighs. "I'm not going to make your father sell his home."

"He wouldn't even need to sell it! I'm sure he has fifty percent of its value in 'liquid assets' somewhere. Isn't that what people like him call cash?"

"No, Bess," Cissy says again. "I'm not taking money from your dad."

"Fine."

Bess is pretending to agree but knows exactly what she'll demand from old Dudley Codman the minute she sees him at the airport. Their marriage might be strained, or nonexistent, but he'll give his whatever-wife something fair. Dudley-do-right or Dudley-do-the-bare-minimum. He's not the warmest man but neither is he a bastard.

"Well, I can chip in," Bess suggests.

"Didn't that gigolo you married take all your money?"

"I suppose he did," she says with a bitter laugh. "What about Clay? He makes, like, embezzler-level cash."

"I'm not taking my son's money, either. No, Bessie. This is where we leave it. The last home I'll ever own. And as for Cliff House"—she takes another sip of her drink—"I'm going down with the ship."

"*What?!*"

A blood vessel pops somewhere near Bess's right temple.

"I'm not leaving this house," Cissy says, "until they drag my dead, crinkled ass out of it."

"You're acting like a lunatic," Bess says, jumping up and down, literally hopping mad. "What do you mean *they*?"

So it isn't iced tea in her glass after all. Bess glances at Evan, whose eyes are wide like windows.

"The coroners," Cissy says. "Or the geologists if they have to pick me out of the rocks and rubble."

"Jesus Christ! Cissy!" She turns to Evan. "Can you believe this?"

"I cannot . . ."

"So you're going to what?" Bess says. "Sit on this patio and wait to die? That's a spectacular plan for an otherwise healthy woman. Physically healthy, that is."

"My mental health is just fine."

"This?" Bess points to her drink and *Gone with the Wind*. "This is not grit, Cissy. This is giving up. You're giving up, throwing in the towel. The mother I know is incapable of defeat. And don't you still have a bluff to save? They're going to put in the geotubes and it *is* about the entire shoreline, right? Not just your house. Don't prove Chappy right on this one. Don't give that jerk the satisfaction."

Bess catches eyes with Evan.

"Sorry," she says with a wince.

He holds up both hands.

"Understood."

"And Grandma Ruby?" Bess says, growing screechier by the second. "She'd be hot as a fired pistol. Stop your complaining, she'd tell you. For God's sake, pull yourself together and get on with your life."

"You don't know the first thing about it," Cissy says.

Bess thinks of the articles, and what Evan told her. It's possible Ruby soldiered on with an alcoholic husband who was also a semicloseted homosexual. Then again, perhaps it wasn't soldiering on. Maybe it was stubbornness and she chained herself to that marriage, sure as Cissy has with Cliff House.

"Oh, I almost forgot," Cissy says, scooting a hand beneath her rear. She produces a phone. "Your father is looking for you. He caught an earlier flight so you'll have to pick him up. Soon, I think. Though I can't remember the details."

"Fucking hell!" Bess wails, then kicks in a few other swear words.

She's never been much of a curser but Nantucket with its wind and sea lore has brought the sailor right out in her.

"I'm so tired and I can't even . . ."

Evan walks over and puts a sturdy arm around Bess. On the chaise, Cissy wiggles to make herself comfortable. She picks up her book and begins to read.

"*Oh my God! Mother!*"

"Listen," Evan says, rubbing her shoulder. "You need to take a nap. Shake this off."

"But my mom!" Bess stomps a foot and Cissy releases a little snigger. "And my dad! Who, apparently, needs a ride from the airport."

"I'll take care of them both."

"But . . ."

"It's fine."

"But . . ."

"It's fine," he says again.

Bess thinks that he might actually mean it.

"Be forewarned, Evan," Cissy says, peering over the top of her book. "Dudley's never been a big fan of yours. So, you know, don't take offense to anything he might do."

Evan yanks Bess toward the door before she completely loses every last bit of shit she has.

"Ignore her. . . ."

"By the way!" Cissy calls, always with a final directive. "Felicia's present is on the dresser in my bedroom. Please bring it with you to the wedding since I can't be there tomorrow."

Bess makes a hard about-face, ready to charge the woman. Luckily, Evan is swift to stop her.

"Keep walking," he tells her.

"Oh my God," Bess says again, tears bubbling as he leads her inside and to the downstairs guest room.

It's the spot farthest from the ocean and all done up in white, like a cloud.

"This started as a complete catastrophe and it's gotten worse," she says.

"I know."

Evan guides her to the bed and Bess lets herself collapse onto it.

"Cissy's just fired up," he says. "It's her pattern. The Big Show before regaining her faculties. I've seen it a million times."

Either Evan doesn't have a clue or he knows exactly what he's talking about. It occurs to Bess that over the past few years he's spent more time with Cissy than she has.

"It'll be fine," he promises.

Evan kisses the top of Bess's head. She promptly comes down with a raging case of goose bumps. He notices and pulls a blanket over her.

"You're exhausted," he says. "So take a nap."

"But the cliff . . ." she says with a small moan.

"Short nap. Thirty minutes, tops. I'll get my guys over here. We'll move your stuff, including your mom. Tonight you can stay at my place."

"Your place? That'd never work," Bess says without thinking, as she is already drifting away.

Sometimes you don't know how tired you are until you actually stop to rest.

"Fine," Evan says, getting grumbly. "Stay at Tea Time. A hotel. Whatever. You're not staying here."

In the end, Evan's words will be more a prediction than an order. It's true. Bess will not go on to stay at Cliff House that night, or ever again. Neither will she stay with her cousins at Tea Time, or with Evan himself, or even with her dad at the Wauwinet. On that night Bess will sleep in a place with markedly less charm than any of these.

Bess wakes from her dark and delicious nap feeling if not better, at least not so riddled with curse words and ire. She might be able to handle Cissy without the threat of impending violence.

After a few stretches, Bess pads to the downstairs bathroom, where she runs a brush through her long, straight hair. A few of Cissy's blond, kinky ones end up on her shirt. Bess checks herself in the mirror. She looks a tad pale but otherwise not so bad. Of course, she's not wearing her glasses, so that helps.

Bess tugs down her pants, realizing just how badly she needs to pee. She closes her eyes in relief. After what feels like minutes, Bess opens her eyes and reaches for the toilet roll. Then her gaze drifts downward and Bess lets out a scream. Her formerly white jeans, bunched around her ankles, are now completely caked in blood.

56

The Book of Summer

Ruby Young Packard
June 6, 1944
Cliff House, Sconset, Nantucket Island

"Under the command of General Eisenhower, Allied naval forces, supported by strong air forces, began landing Allied armies this morning on the northern coast of France."

That's the news from the front lines today. The allies have initiated a large-scale attack, the end game the liberation of a continent. I've had the radio blasting all morning, waiting for news, listening to FDR ask the nation to join him in prayer.

I've put off food shopping for the past three days and paid the price by having to venture to the market today. At every turn people were deadly silent. What to make of this attack? We are liberating people but we'll lose so many along the way. As we passed each other, we exchanged glances of compassion, acknowledgment that on this day we all share the same mind.

How many men will perish? I've already lost one brother in this war, one brother by accident, and two babies, both male, by chance. A woman should never talk about dead babies in polite company but it is so very hard to forget them. Together these losses tell me one thing. This world is no longer safe for men.

As I write, I think of the sign in town. France: 3,000 miles. France. The beaches of Normandy. A hopeless journey. A lifetime away.

With a heavy heart,
Most sincerely,
Ruby Packard

57

RUBY

June 1944

Her little garden was suffering.

Ruby liked to think it was on account of the invasion in France, that this living, breathing thing she'd cultivated with her own two hands was showing the sympathies of the world. In truth the explanation was far more practical. They were in the middle of a drought. Ruby prayed the dying vines didn't portend things to come.

On another continent the fighting raged on. Though the Allies demolished the vaunted "Atlantic wall," there were miles left to go. Homebound nerves were frayed and fried but everybody plodded on. Citizens visited the Red Cross to donate blood and purchased war bonds at unprecedented levels, minds forever locked on the sons, husbands, brothers, fathers, and friends fighting in France. As for Ruby, she had in mind a "sister," too. Mary was now overseas, sworn into the army, same as P.J. Ruby wondered if their paths might cross.

"Any news?" Daddy would call and ask.

It was now up to Ruby to collect the bad and pass it out like sugarless cake. Daddy was sick, so very sick, his voice skinnier by the day. She'd been ginning up a plan to get him out to the island but Daddy wouldn't hear of it. He had nurses and books and a mighty fine radio, all he really needed, he claimed. Ruby wasn't comfortable leaving Cliff House so couldn't go see for herself.

"Don't stew a single second," he'd said. "You enjoy the summer in Sconset. I hear the acting colony is flourishing, the Nantucket Players at full bloom! Have fun and I'll see you back home in the fall. Meanwhile, please call me with any news."

Any news?

Not today, Daddy. Thank God. Granted, it would've been nice to have *some* word that all was nifty with her loved ones, but Ruby had to think they dealt the bad business first. She was A-OK to wait.

Ruby spent the morning in Nantucket Town, visiting shops and friends and delivering the paltry spoils of her garden. A little food was better than none but good gravy it was all a twig compared to last summer's bounty.

Despite the world-changing enormity of the invasion, Nantucket looked the same as it had months before. Bicycles were everywhere. Women helped guide boats into their slips. Every afternoon when the fishing fleets came in, people swarmed the docks, banding together to ice down the catches. The only detectable change was in the service flags in the homes.

If a family had someone fighting, they placed a flag in the window, a blue star for each person away. The blue stars turned to gold when a life was given. On Nantucket more gold cropped up every day. The Cliff House flag was still three blue, Ruby unable to make the change or changes required. Never mind the gold stars, Mary deserved a blue one of her own.

"Here's my batch of goodies," Ruby said to the man at the CDVO. "I apologize for its dearth."

It was hard to accept how much her spoils had shrunk and withered.

"It's getting worse each day," she added.

"Sure is," the man grumbled.

He had two sons in the service, Ruby recalled. She offered him a sympathetic smile.

"Hang in there," she said. "They're doing what they can and so are you. There's a lot to be proud of, all the way around."

He nodded and then signaled for the next gardener.

Ruby turned and walked back toward the Downyflake, where she'd hitched her bike. And just her luck, the Coffin sisters were lolling about, chomping on penny candies. Ruby grimaced. She wasn't keen on chatting them up but the time had passed for scurrying off.

"Hello, ladies," Ruby said, trying to kick up the tenor of her voice. "Hot as the devil's tail today, isn't it? Sure wish it would rain."

"Mmm-hmmm," they said, exchanging pointed looks.

Devil's tail. Ruby couldn't have ordered up a worse visual from a catalogue of sin.

"Will they have the Fourth of July tennis tournament this year, do you think?" Ruby asked, and lunged up onto her bike.

Buoyant was the vibe she was going for, even if it fit funny nine days out from Normandy. Nonetheless, Ruby aimed to pull out all her la-la girl tricks. It was the only way to cope.

"I've gotten out on the courts, here and there," Ruby babbled on. "But my serve is just bananas. I really need to tune my game. Anyhow, toodle-loo!"

Ruby gave the pedals a push and chugged off, glad she couldn't hear Celery and Turnip's scuttlebutt stirring in her dust.

Ruby unlocked the front door, glancing at the service flag as the latch clicked. Three blue stars. Inaccurate multiple ways and no doubt criminally unpatriotic. Truth be told, she was scared to make a change, as if righting the stars would invite ever more loss. It was silly, but Ruby wanted to hold to the losses they'd already had.

"Hello?" Ruby called, her voice echoing through the entryway.

She looked at the clock. Two hours she'd been away. Ruby's eyes skipped to the stairs, then down toward the kitchen, her feet and heart unsure which way to tread.

"Hello?" she said again.

Footsteps pattered on the wood.

"Hello, Mrs. Packard."

Mrs. Grimsbury appeared before her. The woman was back at Cliff House full-time on Daddy's insistence, even though he didn't know the half of it. Ruby protested but was pleased to have old Mrs. G. around. The woman didn't talk much, but it was less lonely knowing she was in the home.

"Hi there," Ruby said. "Sorry I'm late. I got caught up in town. How is everything?"

"Just fine. Nothing of note in today's post. I saw the Western Union man but he made no stops on Baxter Road."

"Thank God."

Ruby exhaled. That they might live another day.

"I've made some tea," Mrs. Grimsbury said. "And put out some cheese bobbies."

"Thank you," Ruby said. "And is—"

"In the library. Hasn't moved all morning. Won't give me a word."

"I'm sorry. There's no excuse for the rudeness."

"Think nothing of it," the woman said. "I understand."

Some miracle, that. Mrs. Grimsbury was a pious sort. Ruby thanked her lucky stars for the woman's mercy, for her penchant for acting like there wasn't a problem beyond stubbornness and a touch of grump.

"Thank you," Ruby said again.

She ventured toward the library, though she would've rather retreated outdoors. Oh, to spend the afternoon lounging in the veranda's shade, sipping Mrs. Grimsbury's superb tea.

At the library's threshold, Ruby rapped gently on the door frame. The room was warm, dark, and still. Ruby knocked a second time. The lump on the chaise twitched in response. Her stomach tightened.

"Sweetheart?" she said.

Sam rolled over and turned toward his wife.

"Hi there," she said with a smile.

He stared back vacantly, his face dull, his eyes glazed and bloodshot. Ruby held her lips together, her back ramrod-straight in the way of old Mary. She could not crumble. Ruby would not fall.

They'd been drilling it into their heads for years. The women needed to be strong while the men were away. And Lord, did Ruby ever try. But what the ads and the posters and Uncle Sam himself neglected to mention was you had to be doubly strong if and when the men returned.

Sam had been at Cliff House three months. He hadn't wanted to return to Boston, so Ruby brought him to Sconset.

Some ninety days ago the navy determined that Sam's transgressions were not onetime in nature, due to the definition of "one time." Sam was now a diagnosed sexual psychopath and confirmed deviant, discharged by the armed forces for good.

But Sam was home! He was safe from fire and shells and German submarines. Ruby told herself this was enough, no matter the reason behind it. There was no black-and-white in this war, no right or wrong, simply a continuum of circumstances, a million spots where a line might've been breached.

And while Ruby could hate Sam or what he'd done (again!), what good would that do? He already despised himself enough for the two of them.

"Sometimes in such hell," the doctor had said, trying to reassure, "these men succumb to their basest desires."

Ruby didn't mention what Hattie had said, that his "experimenting" went further back and these "basest desires" were what made for such a prickly relationship between Topper and him.

But, Sam didn't want to be *that* person, a fact that served as a brightness in this ugly dark. He was disgusted with himself, couldn't abide his own reflection in the mirror. Even on the ship, minutes after lying with a man, Sam would throw up from the sickness inside.

"Every time," he told his wife, who handled it like the strongest battleship ever conceived, "I wept for the person I'd become."

It would stop, Sam insisted, once he was back in their world of roses and sailboats and parties on the lawn. It was a onetime situation, which, of course, was some tough math considering that the navy caught him twice.

Because he was so repulsed by his actions and what he'd done to his wife, Sam spent his days asleep, or drunk, or both, all of it to dull the memories and the pain. Ruby endured alongside because sometimes, every once in the odd while, she'd see a spark of the man she loved. And he was remorseful, passionately so. What could Ruby do? *Forgive us our trespasses as we too forgive.*

Things remained awkward in their bed, in their house, and on their sleepy isle. Folks knew Sam was home and that he had no physical ailment, as far as they could tell. His own parents stopped coming out to Nantucket, which proved something had gone seriously off the page.

"A fairy," Ruby overheard someone say in the casino locker room.

The girl thought Ruby was still on the court.

"He's a fairy," she said. "Just like Ruby's brother."

As it happened, Topper's predilection was not the world's safest secret. Every summer he had trolled clubs and courses and watering holes, coming on to women, yes, but often trying for their brothers, too.

"Fairy." "Queer." "Sexual psychopath." Ruby resolved not to let these words provoke her. Mistakes, more than a few, but Topper was dead and Sam was regretful and no one was perfect. Ruby recalled the words she heard last summer, in Portsmouth.

As with any other sick person, these types deserve compassion, not condemnation.

A sickness. That's what it was. Ruby's job was to get him well. She loved him enough for the both of them. Especially now that a baby was on its way.

No one knew about Ruby's condition aside from her doctor, who took a cautious stance given her troubles from before. She'd lost two would-be sons thanks to a misshapen uterus. Malformed, the man called it, which made Ruby feel like even less of a woman than the nonsense with Sam.

"*Mal*formed," the doctor emphasized. "Not *de*formed."

They sounded the same to her. Either way, when her doctor delivered the grim news, Ruby broke down, devastated but also stunned to learn that she was not completely numb to loss.

Ruby withheld news of the pregnancy for now. Sam was too breakable. *They* were too breakable. All Ruby could do was be careful and, above all, hope and pray. She asked the heavens to watch over this babe, and to please make it be a girl. It was already clear that a boy could not survive such times.

WASHINGTON, DC
JUL 2 8:14PM
MR. PHILIP E. YOUNG
25 COMMONWEALTH AVE. BOSTON

THE SECRETARY OF WAR DESIRES ME TO EXPRESS HIS DEEP REGRET THAT YOUR SON CAPTAIN PHILIP E. YOUNG JR. WAS KILLED IN ACTION ON SIX JUNE IN FRANCE. LETTER FOLLOWS=
J A ULIO THE ADJUTANT GENERAL

Boston was steamy, sweltering. Ruby was pickling beneath her dress. She didn't know how anyone tolerated the summer in that city, Daddy least of all.

At the front door, Ruby hesitated. Should she ring? Go right in? It was the home she'd grown up in but she wasn't an expected visitor. She couldn't tell Daddy she was coming or he would've deduced the reason. Ruby wanted him to survive the actual delivering of the news.

Finally, Ruby pressed the buzzer. A nurse answered, her face white though she'd invited this guest. A few days before, the woman had intercepted the telegram about P.J. and sent it straight to Ruby, unsure where or how to relay the news to the boy's ailing dad.

"Do you think he's up for seeing me?" Ruby asked, this latest blow hers to deliver.

"Probably not. But he'd want to nonetheless."

The woman led her inside and to the first-floor parlor that had been refashioned into her father's bedroom since he could no longer navigate the stairs.

"Hi, Daddy," she said, slowly approaching his bed. "Surprise!"

Ruby's eyes landed on him and she gasped. *I'll see you in the fall*, he'd said. Any fool could tell he'd never make it that far.

"Oh, Daddy."

Ruby rushed to his bedside, careful not to jostle him in any way.

"Why didn't you tell me?"

"Aw, petal." His eyelids were gummy, his skin a yellow-gray. "I've been dying for so many months I wouldn't know the first thing to say."

"Don't say *that*."

"You can't fear the truth, my darling girl. It's not all bad."

"I'm not interested in that irritating practicality of yours right now," Ruby said with a smirk.

"Your mother tells me she's bored up there," he said, and lifted his gaze heavenward. "You have everything under control down on earth. She needs me more."

"That's ridiculous."

Ruby plummeted onto the bed, jostling be damned.

"There's precisely nothing on earth I'd categorize as under control," she said.

She'd planned to butter Daddy up before dropping the bomb but his bleak face told Ruby that this would be no sneak attack.

"Have you come with news?" he asked, eyes making a sweep of Ruby's left hand.

In it she held the telegram, the very one with P.J.'s full name typed in caps. Ruby brought it in case she couldn't find the words to say. A lucky thing, as that was the situation as she found it.

Ruby passed the paper to her father, hand trembling. A fresh crop of tears filled her eyes. As Daddy studied the telegram, Ruby realized the gross assumption she'd made.

"If you can't read it—"

She reached out a hand.

"No. I can still read. My vision hasn't failed quite yet. It's addressed to me."

Ruby bit down on her lip and gave a small nod.

"Tilda thought it'd be best if I read it first," she said, "I hope you don't mind."

"No," he answered, his voice a wheeze.

"See?" she said after Daddy held silent for some time. "Mother doesn't need you. She has Topper and now P.J., Walter, too. I'm the one who needs you, Daddy. Someone has to stay down here for me."

He crumpled the telegram and held it to his still-pumping heart. Ruby's own heart could've combusted with sorrow.

"Sam," he said at last. "Have you heard from Sam? Was he at Normandy, too?"

"No," Ruby said, and sighed. "He was not."

She hadn't told her father about Sam, because what was there to say? Ruby didn't even know how to speak about it herself.

"You don't sound too happy," he noted. "For someone saved from almost certain death."

Suddenly he took in a sharp inhale, and then grimaced in pain.

After a moan, Daddy fumbled about his bedside table to locate a small golden bell. With another groan, he gave it a ring.

"Can I get you something?" Ruby asked. "I'm happy to—"

A nurse materialized in the doorway, a different one this time.

"Mr. Young?"

"More pain medication," he said in a drawn-out croak.

"Right away, sir. We're almost out. I'll call the doctor for more."

The door clicked shut. Ruby turned toward her dad.

"Maybe you should . . . go slowly," she said. "With the morphine. I've read it can be dangerous."

"Dangerous?" He let out a low, wet cackle. "The risk being, what, precisely? That I might develop an addiction? Become a drug fiend? There's no use being careful, petal. Not anymore."

"Daddy, you—"

"What's going on with Sam?" he asked, and peered at her through one open eye. "Something's happened."

"Whatever do you mean?"

"Something's happened. Tell me."

"Well," Ruby said, sighing again. "Yes. I suppose something has. The truth is that Sam was not in Normandy because he's at Cliff House. That's why I haven't been able to see you. I was . . . hesitant . . . to leave him alone."

"Why's that? Is he injured?"

Daddy closed both eyes.

"In a sense," Ruby said. "Though not physically. You see, there's been a problem. A discharge. He's . . ."

Ruby steadied her breath and worked up the nerve to continue.

"Sam's done something terrible," she said. "Wicked even."

Her eyes stung as tears filled them all the more.

"He'd tell you the same," Ruby said. "I'm trying my hardest but I don't know that I can forgive him."

And just like that, Ruby tore open the little dark box in which she'd been stashing the news.

Between snuffles and sobs and the relentless parade of nurses toting compresses and drugs, Ruby told her father about Sam's indiscretions, and about his lovers, and the hospital, too. Every last miserable detail she could reveal. She left Topper out of it, though, as much to preserve her own memories as to protect her dad. Ruby refused to remember her beloved brother, her almost-twin, as anything other than a dashing figure perched on the stern of a boat, the wind and sun kissing his golden hair.

When she finally finished her vulgar tale, Ruby studied her father's face.

"Daddy?" she squeaked, for he was either dead or fast asleep. "Are you awake?"

"I'm awake," he said, and opened both eyes. "So. Is that all?"

He scooched up onto his elbows, the biggest move he'd made since Ruby tipped toes into the room.

"Is that all?" she scoffed. "I hardly think I could handle more."

"You can and you will. He's your husband. He's confessed his sins and asked for forgiveness. War plays tricks on a person's mind. The only way he'll recover is if you believe in him, if you take him at his word. Ruby Genevieve, I say this with nothing but love and adoration. But, dear girl, stop the crying. Gather your wits and march forth. At least you still have a husband to heal. There are a hundred thousand widows who'd trade places with you in a flash."

Leave it to Daddy to put it exactly like that. Oh yes, the words burned and they stung, but Ruby knew that he was right.

As she ferried back to Nantucket, Ruby's entire being soared with a renewed sense of vigor and verve. Daddy was nose on the money, same as always. It was high time to get on with this life. She was lucky she still had the chance.

You keep your spirit, she could almost hear Topper say. *You're the most special kind of bird.*

God, Ruby missed her baby brother. She missed him fiercely. And if she could forgive Topper, if she could see he was more than the sum of his sins, then she could forgive Sam, too.

And so Ruby made a promise, to Sam but also to Daddy and her brothers and Mother up above. She promised to remain strong, stalwart for them all. Cliff House was hers now, Ruby the only child left of the original four. She was determined to keep their fledgling, small family afloat.

Ruby imagined what she'd say when she swept into the library and threw open the shades (unless there was a blackout drill, in which case they'd have to stay closed). Her plan was to rouse Sam out of his awful, waking slumber. She'd tell him how she felt—that she loved him, and she loved their life together, and there was no sin they couldn't plow through. All that and she'd finally divulge that another baby was on its way.

But after Ruby exploded through Cliff House's front door, she did not find the sleeping, slumping person she'd expected. Instead she ran smack into Mrs. Grimsbury, who carried a fretful look and a very short note.

How short? Well, Sam had left. Curt as that.

In the day that Ruby had been gone, Sam had peeled himself off the furniture, packed a lone bag, and skipped town. Where was he bound? San Francisco? New York? Even Sam hadn't been sure. All he knew was that a family didn't seem like the right life. So he left home to discover who he really was.

58

Sunday Afternoon

The baby is gone.

The baby Bess planned to "terminate" (God, what a word) is no more. Evan was right; she didn't want the pregnancy to end. But in the indecision, a judgment was made on her behalf.

Was it the stress? The moving of boxes? Or simply her age? *It's not your fault,* the doctors say, which they would to anyone who looks or acts or pays taxes like Bess. She knows this because she's a doctor, too.

"I'm so sorry," Evan says, again and again.

He's lying beside her, his right arm hooked through her left. They are holding hands, both of them staring at the ceiling. She can lie on her back now. Was that the problem? Bess's nap was almost entirely faceup.

"I'm sorry, too," she whispers, and scoots an inch closer.

There's not enough room for both but Bess doesn't mind. The squished-arm, aching-shoulder position is small sacrifice for the comfort of having Evan close. Also she's high on Vicodin, so there's that.

"I'm not going to tell you that there will be another baby," Evan says. "That you're young and there's plenty of time. It'd just be insulting."

"Yes it would be insulting. Because I'm not young."

He tries to smile but is so uncomfortable he merely looks pissed off.

"How are you?" he asks.

"Physically, I feel okay. Emotionally, not so much." Bess exhales. Her insides ache. "Despite what I said, this isn't what I wanted."

"I know."

"But. It happened. I have to remind myself it's what's best for the baby. I mean . . . it would've been some kind of crap family he or she would've come into. Asshole father. A crackers grandmother who won't get off her lawn chair. And let's not get started on the mom."

"Bess, don't talk like that. Let yourself be sad. Don't explain it away or try any of that 'everything happens for a reason' crap. You would've and you will make a fantastic mother."

"My life is not exactly stable."

"No one's life is stable when they have a kid," Evan says. "That's why new parents look like shit."

Bess offers a close-mouthed chuckle and shuts her eyes.

"In that case, it would've been easier for me than most," Bess says. "To adjust. I'm already a sleep-deprived, stressed-out mess."

"There's the spirit."

Evan squeezes her hand. He doesn't agree, but all that's left to say is the wrong thing.

"Oh!" he says suddenly, using his free hand to grab his phone from the fake wood table beside him. "This might cheer you up."

He wiggles his other hand from her clutches and begins swiping through the pictures.

"God, please don't spring any nostalgia on me," Bess moans. "I can't take it. Homesickness is a disease that runs in my family and on top of everything else I'm positively infected with it."

"I know what you mean," Evan says with a snort. "And no. This has nothing to do with you. This is pure humor. Here."

He moves the phone closer to Bess, so she can see the screen.

"I had a friend take pictures for me during the lacrosse tournament. Thought it might be fun to put something together for the boys. What I found was solid evidence as to why we lost so spectacularly. I am apparently the world's worst coach. Look . . ."

He ticks over to a shot of a boy splayed facedown on the grass.

"He fell," Bess says. "How sad."

"You'll note there's exactly nothing happening anywhere in his vicinity. What's the problem, Jaden? Slippery grass? Stiff breeze?" Evan scrolls through a few more. "This kid's stick cracked in half, but I didn't even notice until the end of the game. He just ran around with it broken like that. Oh and check out this clown."

"Is he doing a somersault?" Bess asks.

"Yes. If you're not familiar with the sport, that is not a recognized move. And here's a series I like to call, 'Where Am I, and What the Fuck Am I Supposed to Be Doing?' "

"Why is everyone facing a different direction?"

"Because they can't find the ball! Ugh!"

Evan throws his head back. It clangs against the hospital headboard. Bess can't help but laugh.

"Okay," she says. "I do feel a *little* better. At least I'm not the only inept person around here."

"Can you be fired from a voluntary coaching position, I wonder?"

He swipes past several more.

"Wait!" Bess yelps, though she doesn't mean to.

She wants Evan to stop, but not for any reason Bess can admit. But stop he has, on what is a selfie, as indicated by arm position. This photo is a close-up of a lacrosse kid and *her*, the woman from the market. She's in her same hat.

"Who's that?" Bess asks, despite her better judgment.

"That kid? Oh, his name's Jack. He's my favorite, even though he can be a little shit. Maybe *because* he's a little shit? And that's his mom Grace. Cool lady. She's the one who took the pictures for me. I should introduce you guys. You'd get along great."

"Fabulous."

Bess exhales and tries not to cry. Grace and Jack and Evan. How perfectly cute. The asshole will probably make the world's best stepdad.

She's about to say something to that effect when the door pops open. And wouldn't you know, Hurricane Cissy has left her veranda and is now making landfall inside Nantucket Cottage Hospital.

"Well, Elisabeth, that was some elaborate plan to get me out of the house," she says.

"You came."

"Of course I came. Hello, Evan. Don't you think that bed should be reserved for the patient?"

Cissy has on a white cable-knit sweater, no hat. Her hair is a tumbleweed. Bess wonders about the gingham tankini. She presumes it's still on.

"You know what?" Evan says, and stands. "Why don't I leave you two alone?"

"If you want to be useful, do me a huge favor and fetch Bess's dad from the airport. She was supposed to, but . . ."

Cissy gestures dismissively toward the inconvenience that is her debilitated daughter.

"Cissy!" Bess barks. "Good grief. The guy has a life. I'm sure he has things to do!"

With Grace. Or Jack. Or both of them together.

"No, it's fine," Evan says. "I was already planning on it."

Evan kisses Bess on the head, his favorite move these days. It's sweet and egregiously friend-like—just how he prefers it, no doubt. Cissy opens her mouth to say something but Bess shoots her a look. Amazingly, Cissy backs down.

"I'll check in with you later," Evan says, slipping into his shoes. "See how you're doing. Bye, Cis, take care of our girl."

The second Evan exits the room, Cissy plunks herself down onto Bess's bed and begins to weep.

"Mother, you can't . . ."

"How come you didn't tell me?" she asks, voice quavering. "That you were pregnant? Bessie, I would've helped you in whatever way you needed."

"You couldn't help me out of this."

"But I can't imagine why you'd hide it from your—"

"I wasn't going to keep the baby," Bess spits out.

Cissy's face goes ashen, even as she clamps down on her bottom lip, trying to bite back the words she wants to say. Caroline Codman is a registered Democrat, politically obligated to be okay with this sort of thing.

"But, you changed your mind," she says, hoping.

"Not technically. I had an appointment that I missed. I kept telling myself I'd reschedule but I probably wouldn't have, to be honest. As it turns out, I very much want what I thought I did not."

As this strange, hard truth bludgeons her, Bess joins Cissy in her tears. Maybe the Vicodin isn't working after all.

"Oh, Bessie . . ."

"I'm so angry," she says. "On the one hand, I can't believe this happened. Then I think, of course it happened! The universe was like, What's that you say? You don't want to be a mom? Okay. Done."

"Elisabeth!" Cissy spanks her hand. "You can't talk like that. Miscarriages happen. Most of them are entirely random and not anyone's fault. Why am I telling you this? You're the one who went to medical school! Just think of what you learned!"

"Okay, great. I'll use the warm fuzzies of science to get me through this."

"It must be so painful," Cissy says. "But you're not alone. Your grandmother had multiple miscarriages over the years."

"She did?" Bess says, even as she remembers an entry in the book.

A woman should never talk about dead babies in polite company but it is so very hard to forget them.

"Actually, now that you mention it . . ."

"The losses hurt, but they also shaped her," Cissy says. "Ruby taught me to tie my shoes at age two. By four I was cooking dinner and shoveling snow. At eight I had a budget. FYI, it's pretty embarrassing to pay your own babysitter and tennis instructor, especially when you're not that great at math."

Bess snickers and scoots into an upright position. The story is sad but she craves more. Her connection to Grandma Ruby is strong once more.

"My mother taught me to take care of myself," Cissy continues. "In her mind, she wasn't the best shepherd of young things, given the losses. It's not the most logical thought, but motherhood is more heart than logic anyhow."

"Poor Grandma. I figured she stopped at one kid because you were too much to handle."

"Very funny." Cissy rolls her eyes. "No, I think she was more of a 'count your blessings' sort, grateful to get one out of the mess."

"That sounds like Grandma Ruby all right."

Cissy crawls into bed beside her daughter, taking the space Evan left behind. Bess glances out the window. She notices Chappy out there, pacing by his car, checking for messages on his phone.

"Cis, I'm sorry for getting mad at you about Chappy," she says. "I don't completely understand the . . . arrangement . . . but I'm glad he's made you happy. In your backward sort of way."

"I love him, Bessie. I really do. I've loved him for a long time, practically my entire life."

Cissy shakes her head and more tears slide out.

"I had such intense shame about my feelings. Sometimes I still do." She laughs dryly. "We've been together fifteen years, but I loved him for ten years before that."

"Then how come you never left?" Bess asks. "If you weren't in love with Dad? I'm trying not to be judgmental about the situation, but it's hard. Why not get divorced like a normal person?"

"Don't misunderstand, a divorce is *not* the easy way out of a marriage."

"You don't have to tell me that."

"I suppose I don't."

Cissy stares down at the bed, rubbing a corner of the thin white hospital sheet between her fingers. When she resumes speaking, she does not look up.

"My father left my mom once," she says. "When I was little. I don't remember the coming or the going, but he returned eventually. Because of me. And even though this meant he didn't get to lead the life he wanted, I'm glad for it. Even now. It's selfish and awful but I'm grateful he didn't disappear."

"I don't know the situation with Grandpa Sam," Bess says, though now she thinks that maybe she does. "But even if you got divorced, Dad would've been involved. He wouldn't have just vanished. It's different nowadays. And your situation is . . . not theirs."

"You're right. But it's the entire idea of him, and me, and you guys. 'Family' is such a powerful word. Whenever I'd be on the verge of filing papers, I'd picture all of us congregating in that big old house on Baxter Road, and it was too damned sad to imagine arriving in fragments." Cissy frowns. "I was so heartbroken after your grandmother died. And I was already heartbroken enough in my crummy marriage. Then this man came to the funeral. A navy fellow. He and my father were *very* close. For decades."

Cissy makes a face as if she might be ill.

"Anyway, I went to Chappy," she said. "And then we . . . Well.

You know. Afterward I felt horrible. I told him no way, never again, it was a onetime mistake. I spent the next five years denying my feelings, until Chappy finally called me on it."

Bess thinks about how miserable she was at Choate after Ruby passed, how she begged her mom to let her come home.

"I'm not even living in Boston full-time anymore," Cissy had said.

It was the first Bess had heard of it but she didn't have time to contemplate the new arrangement due to her vast despair.

"I don't care!" Bess had shrieked, ever the teenager. "I'll live in Sconset then!"

"You're not graduating from some rinky-dink, two-bit island school!" Cissy insisted. "So buck up! High school problems are not real!"

It was a smack in the face when Bess was so down, when she felt so far on the outside she might as well have been sitting in the street. She didn't belong at that school. Palmer tried to bring her into the fold but standing beside her cousin highlighted every ugly and unkempt part of Bess. She was a ferret to Palmer's unicorn. In trying to help, Palmer made it worse.

Despite Bess's desperation to leave, Cissy refused, and so Bess took matters into her own hands. Now she considers the possibility that her mother's veto had less to do with academic merit and more to do with Chappy Mayhew. Perhaps if Bess had stayed at Choate, Cissy wouldn't have put him on hold for all those years.

"Oh, Bess," Cissy says. "Don't give me that look."

"It's not what . . ."

"I did confess to your father, in a bumbling sort of way, but he said he didn't want to know. And he had plenty of his own . . . Listen, sweetheart, Dudley is an amazing father."

"Amazing? I wouldn't go *that* far."

"A great father. But he's a god-awful husband. I won't go into details. But you and I, we have more in common than you'd guess."

Bess nods. She thinks of everything behind the veil of cheery Christmas cards and whimsical summer homes. Long-term affairs, in one example. Hookers, in another. A lifetime spent in the closet, if what's been said about her grandfather is true.

"Cis?" Bess says. "Your father. Grandpa Sam. It wasn't just alcoholism, right? Because I heard . . . and Evan said something . . . and I saw this article . . . was he . . ."

"He had a lover, yes," Cissy says, curtly, even for her.

"And he was . . . ?"

"He was."

Bess nods again, though Cissy is not looking in her direction. Even so, they are on the same page.

As if choreographed, the two women lean into each other. They are silent for some time. In the distance a siren howls. A gaggle of voices passes by, nurses clucking about this and that. "I was, like, oh hell no!" one says. Her cohorts titter in response.

"Mom?" Bess whispers. "I love you."

"I love you, too. I'm proud of you, Bess. For so many reasons."

Bess sits up.

"I'm ready to go," she says. "Are you?"

"Sweetheart, they want you to stay the night. You lost a lot of blood. And your fever . . ."

Fever? They hadn't mentioned a fever. They must be worried about an infection.

"Oh. Okay," Bess says, slumping again.

She hadn't envisioned a night in the hospital. On the other hand, she doesn't have a home to return to. That a hospital is her best option is almost soul-crushing.

"Where are you going to stay?" Bess asks. "Not Cliff House. Promise me, Mom. I won't be able to sleep a wink. And you can't do that to me in my precarious state."

"Fine," Cissy says, and sets her mouth into a hard line. "No Cliff House. I thought mothers were in charge of guilt trips?"

"Where are you staying?" Bess asks. "I need specifics, otherwise I'll completely stress out."

"You don't trust me?" Cissy asks.

"Not one hundred percent, no."

Cissy's eyes skip toward the window, to where Chappy's truck waits below.

"Cis?"

"Oh, Bess. Don't worry about your old mom. I'll just stay across the road."

59

The Book of Summer

Mary Young
June 20, 1945
Cliff House

This will be my final time at Cliff House.

When talking bittersweet, it is admittedly stronger on the bitter end. The home is beautiful and peaceful, perched atop the cliff as it is. You can almost forget what's happened to the people coming into and out of it.

Looking back through this book, I'm almost surprised to see that I was once Mrs. Philip E. Young, Jr., and that's all there really was to me. Now I'm a second lieutenant in the army and have spent the last year moving about Europe. We deployed to France last July, my unit arriving to Normandy on the first of August, weeks after my husband lost his life. When we arrived they'd all been cleared out. The dead were buried, the severely injured evacuated to England. And so they relocated us to the Siegfried

Line, where our services were needed in devastating amounts. We've also been in Belgium, Luxembourg, and a few other places besides.

Now I'm in Sconset, a world away in a manner I couldn't have fathomed twelve months ago. My stay is temporary. I'm on furlough, here to visit the last of my former family. It's strange to think that there is nothing binding me to them. Alas, this home and the people who've lived in it will forever hold a special place in my past.

Soon I'll say good-bye to the last remaining Young, the vivacious Ruby Genevieve. That is, Ruby and a baby girl named Caroline, recently come into this world. Ruby calls her "Cissy," which is usually short for "sister." A curious thing for an only child, a sole girl, without a brother for miles.

I've come to meet Cissy, and to embrace Ruby one more time. There's nothing left for me here but sorrow and the burn of sad regret. It's best to bid the place and its memories farewell. I've asked the former Miss Mayhew to pop in on the girls every once in a while, to see that they're getting along. Though she's not a Miss anymore. You're either getting or losing a husband because of this war, all of it happening in such haste.

Well, Cliff House, you've been a treat, and you've housed a great many people and lives. Now it's up to you and Ruby to stand strong against the wind. Take care of each other, won't you?

Forever and always,
Second Lieutenant Mary Young

60

RUBY

June 1945

"Holy crumb," Mary said as Mrs. Grimsbury set the tea service before them. "She's an active one, isn't she?"

They were on the veranda. The sun was high; the clouds were sparse. The Atlantic glimmered like a blanket of blue diamonds. Meanwhile, atop the flagstone, Cissy pattered about on hands and knees, pulling up on an end table here, a piece of outdoor art there.

She was only six months old.

"Yes she's quite active," Ruby said, flushed with pride. "Gives me a run for my money all the livelong day. She's wanted to get up and go since she popped out. She has this spirit, you know? A little ball of soul. It's like she knew exactly what I needed."

As if she understood, or perhaps because she did, Cissy peered up at her mother and gave a wide, one-tooth grin as the ocean breeze kicked around her wispy white hair.

"I'm not surprised," Mary said. "Not in the slightest. You are blessed."

"She's a miracle," Ruby said. "Through and through."

Every mom believed her babe a miracle, and why not. But for Ruby it had the added punch of being true. There were the doctor's initial warnings:

"You're not equipped to carry to term."

And the later warnings, too:

"It's only a matter of time. Five months, six at the outside."

Then the blood last fall, at five and a half months in, the difference having split. Ruby was alone, no one to help, not a single person on whom to call. Never mind the absence of Sam, a hurricane bore down on New England, cutting off Nantucket and therefore Cliff House from the rest of the world. Ruby could only lock the doors, close the windows, and pray. By God, it worked.

The bleeding stopped and Ruby carried to term. Cissy was early, tiny and mighty, which would sum up not only her birth but all the days to follow.

"Are you getting by all right?" Mary asked, and took a sip of tea.

For a moment Mary closed her eyes and smiled, reveling in the respite from her life, and in tea that didn't taste like lawn clippings. This sort of escape was the very purpose of Cliff House.

"Oh sure, we're swell," Ruby said with some sway. "Mrs. G. is a big help, a saint really. And Daddy left me plenty of money. Though I maintain Grimsbury herself has been the biggest gift of all."

"I'm sorry I couldn't make it," Mary said with a sigh. "To your father's service."

"Golly, he wouldn't have minded a lick," Ruby said. "The European theater needed you more. Daddy was nothing if not practical."

"That's true, but nonetheless . . ."

"I can hear him right now!" Ruby squeezed her waist with both hands and put on a grumpy face. "What is Mary doing at my funeral? An army nurse tending to a dead body when there are plenty of live ones who need her care?"

Mary chuckled softly.

"That does sound like something he'd say."

They did not mention the other funeral she'd missed, that of P.J., her husband. Mary had only just arrived in France when his body was sent home. To secure a furlough on such short order would've been a helluva feat. But Ruby got the sense, had had the sense for a while now, that Mary left her marriage in spirit long before P.J. left in fact.

"I have to say, you do look lovely," Mary said. "Cliff House does, too."

"Thank God it survived the storm." She glanced at Cissy. "Thank God we all did. But the property's a tad ragged now. The damage isn't obvious but I find a new crack or divot every day. I swear the yard is smaller somehow."

Mary squinched toward the cliff.

"Hooey," she said. "The estate is grand as ever. And so are you. I see you're faring splendidly, just as you told me."

"Yep, me and Cissy." Ruby reached down and lifted the girl to her lap.

The gesture felt like nothing. Miss Cis was whisper-light, always a new astonishment to Ruby, given all her mettle and grit.

"And of course we have Mrs. Grimsbury, too," Ruby added. "It's funny, my entire life I was surrounded by boys, nothing but men every which way. Rough-and-tumble rascals, Wyatt and Topper and P.J., though him less so." She smiled. "Your husband was definitely the most gentlemanly of the three."

"Not a high hurdle," Mary said with a wink.

Ruby sniggered, recalling her sister-in-law's old grievances. Yes, indeed, Topper was handsome as the devil. *Acts like the devil, besides.*

"All those men," Ruby said, "and now I look around and it's only the women who endure."

Mary set down her teacup, nodding grimly.

"Do you ever talk to your old friend Hattie?" she asked.

"No, God no," Ruby said.

She wondered if Mary had seen the article. Probably not, having been overseas.

"That's quite the ardent response," Mary said as a ripple of discomfort passed over her face.

"I didn't mean it like that. She's a journalist. Hadn't you heard? Quite a success from the looks of it."

"How nice," Mary said primly. "And what about Sam?"

"Sam?"

The name was an arrow straight to the chest.

"Yes, Sam," she said. "Have you spoken?"

Mary appeared so much the same. The gray, the plainness. Ruby could almost hear her old friend-come-traitor Hattie R. *You know Mary joined the army because it gave her an excuse to wear all that beige.* Yet, somehow the gal had new sparks. Like a certain directness, a drive to get to the nut of things in one swift move.

"There's been no contact at all," Ruby answered. "Not since the day Sam left. I wouldn't even know where to find him, or what to say if I did. He has no idea about Cissy."

She thought of the items packed away. Sam's suits, pressed and wrapped and relegated to the guesthouse. Their wedding china, boxed up and shoved on to the linen closet's highest shelf. She'd stored scads of crystal and silver, too, gifted to them for parties they'd never host. It seemed cruel to throw out such considerate presents, but all those pretty things were too painful to allow among the everyday.

"Really?" Mary's eyes widened. "He doesn't know about Caroline? Don't you think he should? She's his daughter."

"Maybe." Ruby shrugged. "I don't know. He sent me a postcard, way back, after he read about Daddy's death. It was postmarked Manhattan and I came within an inch of hiring a PI to track him down. I was alone and distraught and starting to miscarry, or so I assumed. Then the storm hit and all communication went down. When we came out on the other end, I decided to let that dog lie."

"And his parents?" Mary asked. "Surely they know."

Ruby shook her head.

"They don't either. Rather, they might, depending on your view of the afterworld. Both passed in the last year."

"I'm sorry to hear that."

"Yes, it was properly awful."

Ruby didn't admit to the details. Sam's mother died of a heart attack. His father, a gunshot wound to the head. He couldn't face life as a widower, or as the father to one son killed in battle, and a second son who wasn't allowed to battle anymore.

"Would you care to contact him?" Mary asked. "Sam? Now that Caroline's arrived? Whatever he's become, he would want to meet his daughter. He loved his family. He'd love her."

"The man was not short on love, giving or receiving."

Ruby set Cissy down and grabbed a cigarette. She offered one to Mary, who waved her away.

"I quit ages ago," she said. "As it happens, smoking would be a great habit to have when you're at war. I often regret that unforeseen bout of healthfulness."

Ruby laughed.

"Are you truly ready?" Mary said. "To surrender the idea of a genuine family?"

"I'm not sure that I have a choice. And some days I *do* want Sam here, with us. Yet others I think, to hell with him. We *are* a family. She and I."

Ruby took a big old smack of her cigarette.

"A girl should have her father, if she can," Mary said.

"I don't disagree," Ruby said, thinking of her own. "But even if I wanted to find him, I wouldn't know where to look."

Mary nodded slowly and let her eyes drift out to the grass beyond.

"I've been keeping track," Mary said after some time. "Of Sam. Just in case."

"What?!" Ruby gasped.

She nearly dropped her smoke onto Cissy's head.

"Just in case," Mary repeated. "It's not that difficult to learn such things, with my position in the armed forces."

Ruby looked at her cross-eyed. What kind of dirt could an army gal gin up on a guy booted from the navy?

"I know some folks in intelligence," Mary added.

Unbeknownst to Ruby, Mary had met an intelligence officer here and there and even engaged in a brief fling with one. But most of her intelligence on Sam Packard came from a plucky news reporter in Manhattan who made it her job to keep tabs on him.

"Okay, then," Ruby said and cleared her throat. "Is he well?"

"Relatively speaking," Mary explained. "He was in San Francisco for a while, then hanging around the Seven Seas locker room in San Diego. Last check had him in New York City staying at the Sloane House YMCA and drinking—a lot—at the Pink Elephant in Times Square. 'Well' might be a subjective term, but he is alive and, er, *active* in whatever city he lands."

"Wow," Ruby said. "Wow."

She could find him. If she wanted to. Of course, whether she wanted to was the very question.

Ruby craved her old life and her old Sam, no question. More than that, she longed for a real family, since the vagaries of Ruby's woman parts meant Cissy would be an only child. And Ruby knew from experience that a life without siblings was a lonely one. The least she could do was give her sweet sprite a dad.

"Whaddya think?" Mary asked. "Want me to track him down?"

"Maybe," Ruby said, and glanced at Cissy. "Maybe. It's just too damned hard to decide."

They stood on the bright white driveway, two bags at their feet. Mary had on her full dress uniform: a light beige skirt, a darker beige jacket. A taxi rumbled on the street.

"Thanks for coming," Ruby said, and gave her a squeeze. "It means everything that you'd take a furlough just to see me."

"I had to meet little Caroline," Mary said. "She's even more precious than expected. Plus, I needed one more Cliff House hurrah."

Ruby smirked, wondering when there'd ever been a hurrah with the broad to start.

"I'll miss the old house," Mary said.

"Miss it!" Ruby quacked. "What do you mean? You can always come back. Always! When I picture this place, I see you inside. It's yours as much as mine."

The skin between Mary's brows became pinched and tight.

"But Ruby," she said in her measured Mary tone. "P.J. is gone."

"You're still family though! You're still a Young!"

"For now, though I'll likely change my name."

"You will?" Ruby balked. She shook her head. "I don't give a rip. You're still family to me."

"Aw, Ruby."

Mary patted her arm. The wet sock, dry dock back on the scene. Ruby gave her a hard glower in return. When it came to human connection the woman was a dang boomerang.

"Still family?" Mary said. "I think that's the nicest thing you've ever said to me, even including when I actually *was* family."

"And I think that's the meanest thing *you've* ever said!"

"Okay." Mary sighed. "I didn't realize . . . I didn't expect you to have this vociferous of a reaction."

"Vociferous!"

"Listen, we'll keep in touch. I'll swing by Cliff House whenever I can."

"That's all?" Ruby said. "That's all you have to say for yourself? Our relationship, everything we've been through? It ends here?"

Squinting, Mary contemplated the home, eyes skimming the windows, then following the line of the privet hedge.

"I loved your brother," she said at last. "Very much. But in the end you were the best thing about this place."

Ruby's crab shell began to crack.

"Kind or mean," Ruby said. "Pick a side."

"Lovely girl, I'll be back," Mary said. "If for no other reason than to see your face."

Mary had promised to return, but whether she truly meant it, Ruby would never know. The two women would keep in regular contact over the years, but Mary would never again set foot on the white-shelled drive.

She planned to, or so she said, but it was a great trek from France, where she eventually settled after marrying a French soldier. Then there would be kids and dogs and money stretched thin, and so in France Mary stayed. Ironic, after all the comments she muttered about the continental Hattie Rutter that summer of '41.

Before returning to Europe, Mary would make a final meddling move, an act that'd leave an indelible mark on the people who remained. Whether for good or for ill could be left to some debate. Mary believed that Sam Packard deserved to know there was a family, and so she asked Hattie Rutter to track him down one more time.

61

The Book of Summer

Evan Mayhew
May 27, 2013
The Last Day of Cliff House

Dear Bess,

I've come to Cliff House to supervise the movers and pack up the last of your things. Cissy is here, too. She seems to be preparing for departure, but since she loves to keep people guessing, I'll believe it when she's physically out of the house.

I write this from my car, parked on the white-shelled drive of the great, grand Cliff House. This will be the last entry in the Book of Summer. I won't rip it out, even though it's no less embarrassing than the first.

Do my words look strange? Stilted? Wobbly? Your mom commented that my hands were shaky. She's right, though I had to play it off. It seems a little callous to admit excitement on such a sad day. I can hardly take the hours between right now and tonight, when I get to escort you to Felicia's wedding.

A little birdie called last night. She claims you need a chaperone. You're supposed to "take it easy" and there's a better shot at following doctor's orders if someone else is keeping guard. But this babysitting bunk is not the favor she is trying to do us both.

Tonight is tonight but at this very moment my guys are guiding a piano through your front door. Behind them stand empty rooms, the ocean in the distance. It's damn near choking me up. I guess it's a good thing you haven't been in Sconset much this century. These past few days will be tough enough to shake. Deep down, I hope you stay on-island, just like we talked about in our fake Nantucket novel. But I understand why you can't, and therefore why you won't. I can only ask that one day you come home.

Well, Lizzy C., until next time, because there will be one.

Always,
Evan Mayhew

62

Monday Evening, Memorial Day

Bess is draped across a tan couch in "For Everyone Else," the cottage at the edge of the Bradlee property.

She has on wedding wear, but is struggling to gin up the appropriate wedding face. Either her bleakness sullies Flick's beautiful event, or Bess doesn't show up at all. There's no way to win tonight.

There is a knock at the door.

"Whaaaaat?" Bess grumble-moans.

Some envoy, she assumes, sent to usher Bess back among the living. No one in that family will let her get away with skulking all night, recent hospitalizations notwithstanding.

The person knocks again. Bess lets out a whimper and gives a sturdy pout. Answering seems like too much effort but you don't throw a tantrum on your cousin's wedding day. Not even Cissy would do that.

"Coming," Bess gripes, hoping the person has already decamped.

Bess shuffles across the hardwood, grains of sand sticking to her feet. With an inhale, she opens the door. On the fish-and-coral mat stands Evan. He's in a suit, carrying a reusable grocery bag.

It's a full minute before Bess can admit that it's him.

"Oh my God!" she says, heart clunking around inside of her. "What in the world . . ."

As surprised as she is, Evan is visibly gaping, too. Is it the dress? Or the presumed state of her eyeliner and hair?

"You look fantastic," he says.

"What you are doing here?"

"I'm your date. Mind if I come in?"

Evan scoots past Bess, as if she's just said yes.

"But I . . . who said I needed a date?"

"I can't tell you," he says, then grins over his shoulder. "It was Palmer."

Evan turns all the way around and Bess takes him in. His suit is light gray; he wears a white shirt and periwinkle tie underneath. A tie. The man is wearing a tie.

"Bess. You are beautiful. That dress. The necklace." He gestures. "Everything. Flick will be pissed at you for stealing the show."

"That's ridiculous," Bess says.

She put on the only dress she could tonight—a loose-cut, wool-and-silk-blend navy shift with deep Vs in the front and in the back. Thank God she'd left it at Cliff House. It was, she remembers, her backup rehearsal-dinner dress. This one would've been better than what she chose.

As for the necklace, it was Grandma Ruby's. Boston jewels to be sure, as emeralds and diamonds are far too citified for Cliff House. But somehow they seem ideal to celebrate Felicia.

"Well," Evan says. "Are you ready? Of course you're ready. Look at you."

"Evan. I don't . . ."

Bess's insides are all mixed up, stirred and shaken. He's given her the butterflies by simply walking through that door. On the other hand, is this a pity date? Shouldn't he be with Grace and Jack?

"What about . . . ?" Bess starts.

What the hell. Why ruin a good moment? She'll worry about mysterious girlfriends later.

"Hold on, let me get my shoes," she mumbles, then fishes her heels out from beneath the couch.

"You shouldn't bend over like that," he says. "Although it's a nice view."

Bess bolts to straight.

"What the hell is wrong with you?" she says.

"Sorry," he answers with a wince. "I was trying to be funny. And flirt. And it's all gone horribly wrong." Evan shakes his head. "I consider myself pretty decent at charming the ladies, but apparently I'm wrong. You're just . . . you're so damned gorgeous."

"Knock it off," Bess growls, and turns away from him so he cannot see the flush of her cheeks.

"This isn't flattery, Bess. I'm acting like a moron because I'm not used to being so far out of my league." He contemplates this. "Which is weird because I played up an age division in baseball. But I was never in the majors, which is what's going on here."

"Majors?" Bess says, slipping into her shoes. "Now you're rambling."

"I know. But it's like you've handed a sixteen-year-old a Ferrari. It's awesome as hell but he doesn't have the slightest clue how to work it."

"You seemed to have no trouble 'working it' in high school. Or now."

Bess sighs and rakes her fingers through her hair. She thinks to check a mirror, but decides she'd have to walk too far. A brief glimpse at her cell phone screen indicates that her mascara won't look too smudged in the dark or at a certain blood-alcohol level.

"Are you ready?" she asks, and tucks a clutch beneath her arm.

The purse is Palmer's and inside are two credit cards, some

twenties, and one sanitary napkin. As the purse crinkles, Bess flinches. She hasn't worn a pad in twenty years. The miscarriage already happened, but the bleeding continues because evidently the universe really likes to drive a point home.

"What do you have there?" Bess asks, swiping pink gloss across her lips.

"What now?"

"The bag." She touches the black carrier still dangling from his hand. "Do you need to buzz by the Stop and Shop on our way? Pick up some milk and toilet paper?"

"Oh!" Evan says, face brightening, perking out of its confusion. "I almost forgot. Here." He extends an arm. "The Book of Summer, delivered with the official white-glove treatment. You didn't think the suit was for the wedding, did you?"

Bess tilts her head and frowns. She takes the bag.

"Thank you." She removes the book and fans through its pages. "I can't tell you how much this means to me. In all the . . . commotion . . . I didn't check where it was."

Bess flips toward the back, though does not make it all the way to the end. The final entry she'll find at some later date, too late, she might think. After closing it again, Bess inhales deeply and then sets it on the coffee table.

"Well, let's get to it," she says, and breaks out a sad smile. "By the way, despite appearances, I really do appreciate you coming to get me. I never would've made it otherwise."

"I know what you mean."

Evan wraps Bess in a bear-cub sort of hug before they head out to his truck. Though they can easily walk from here, Bess is supposed to be lying low and Evan's vowed to make sure that she does. It's not a hard task, as she mostly feels like death.

At the Yacht Club, they leave the car with a valet and follow arrows leading them along. "Bradlee Wedding," the signs say, as if Flick's marrying herself.

On the back lawn, greeters show them to a cluster of white chairs facing the harbor. Evan takes Bess's hand and together they make their way toward the front. The ground is soggy but the rain has stopped. They find two seats on the aisle, four rows back. Soon Bess's father joins them, sitting to Bess's left. Dudley doesn't notice the hand-holding. Or if he does, he doesn't bother with his patented disapproving look.

Bess admires the setup, which is simple for two people with such vast sums of cash. The only decorations are the white chairs, the green lawn, and the harbor before them. There's not even any sort of trellis or altar. Just a minister with a piece of paper, Felicia and her almost-husband Steven, plus Palmer and some dude for witnesses. The sole flower arrangement is Flick's bouquet of Cliff House roses, which Palmer now holds.

Aunt Polly and Uncle Vince sit a few rows up, crying and beaming both. Who wouldn't be proud of Felicia Bradlee? Bess is proud and she had nothing to do with her.

Soon Felicia and Steven are exchanging humorous, loving vows. They didn't write their own—who has time for that—but they're not afraid to bastardize the usual ones. There's a lot of laughter at this wedding, and Bess suspects there will be a lot of laughter in the marriage, too. In between all the cursing about convertible debt offerings and pricing on secondaries.

Throughout the ceremony Palmer stands behind her sister, a foot shorter but with shoulders and spine so erect she looks strong enough to carry the world. Most of the guys in the audience are watching her, not Felicia. Most of the women are, too. When Bess steals a peek at Evan, she's surprised to see him focused firmly on the couple, the corners of his eyes crinkling as if he's looking into the sun.

Bess smiles to herself. In the week at Cliff House: the happiest and saddest she's been in years. Forget what's going on now or any single moms named Grace. Sleeping with that creep of a French teacher was a damned shrewd move. De Leudeville was okay, sexually speaking, not that Bess knew much about it. But it got her expelled, which was the goal after her prior attempt at a Bartles & Jaymes smuggling operation earned nothing but a warning.

"Why do you keep doing such stupid things?" Palmer had cried, after Bess's mistakes began to pile up: the Bartles & Jaymes incident, the French teacher dalliance, the noticeable decline in grades. "It's not like you!"

No, it wasn't. But Bess was "thinking outside the box."

"Are you taking drugs? I don't get it at all!"

Palmer had been too naïve and pure-minded to puzzle over the timing of Bess's "acting up," too sweet to think it might involve her, even though it very much did.

At Choate, Bess had dated Gordon Granholm for a year (a year!) and was madly in love and emoting in a way Bess Codman never did. Finally, Bess fit in at that school. All because of a guy named Gordon.

There's no explanation for teenaged tastes but love him Bess did, up until what she thought of as the Great Humiliation. First Gordon tried to feel up Palmer at a dance (boobs, twice), news that gushed through their hall like a tsunami. Then he went on to declare his love for her following a rousing 23–21 overtime football win against Deerfield.

After this second transgression, Palmer (ever honest, ever true) gave Gordon a proper upbraiding and promptly told Bess that her boyfriend was a scoundrel of the lowest order. Bess dumped him, and told people why, and in the end *her* stock went down, same as his. Only Palmer Bradlee came out of it ever more glowing and sublime. She did the right thing, but Bess was sixteen and brokenhearted and it was very hard not to hate her.

"You're going to regret it!" Palmer had warned repeatedly. "A black mark that will haunt you for life!"

Bess wasn't much interested in Palmer's advice and, as it turned out, didn't regret it at all. Among about a million other positives, she met Evan and quickly realized that dopey Gordon wasn't the main thing going. In fact, he was appealing only when thrown into a lineup of other Gordon-like fools. Evan was hardly perfect, and in many ways was the exact kind of big fish, small pond asshole you'd expect, but Bess was able to end her high school years happy. And she was able to forgive Palmer for the absolutely nothing that she did.

"Hey," Evan whispers as Palmer recites some sort of Native American blessing, the only treacle allowed at this wedding. "Have you seen them?"

Bess doesn't need to ask. He's referring to Cissy and Chappy. Bess shakes her head and glances over her shoulder. All she sees is a well-heeled mob of bankers, lawyers, and Choaties behind them.

"They're not here," Bess whispers back. "Do we need to worry . . . ?"

She leans closer in. Dudley looks at them sideways. You'd think Bess might be glad the lovebirds aren't around, with her dad seated to the left. But a public fight about infidelity is a better option than Cissy falling off a cliff. In a gingham tankini.

"I'm counting on Chappy," Bess says, "to get Cis out of there."

"Oh, brother. Not the man you should put your money behind."

Evan shakes his head and squeezes her hand. Bess shivers, head to toe.

When all vows and rings are exchanged, the crowd stands and cheers. Felicia and Steven tromp down the squishy grass aisle. Amid the seats, people trade greetings and hugs and handshakes. Through it all, Evan sticks closely to Bess's side.

As the sun sets over the water, Flick and Steve fire the golden cannon, a signal that all colors and flags in the Nantucket harbors must be lowered. The sparks from the cannon burn out, the smoke clears, and the guests stream inside. A certain weight pushes heavily on Bess's chest.

For the first time in twenty-four hours she thinks not about how hard it's been to lose that baby, or how much pain she feels in her body and in her heart. No, Bess is getting weepy, all twisted up with emotion, as she contemplates how very much it will hurt to leave.

63

Monday Night, Memorial Day

Is Bess "taking it easy" at the wedding? Not especially. But, as they say, doctors make the worst patients.

She shouldn't be dancing, at least not to every song. Granted, Bess isn't exactly smoking up the floor with her deft moves, and she's feeling better by the hour. Distance helps. Evan helps. Vicodin and one and a half glasses of Dom help, too.

The band is fantastic, playing a bit of this, a touch of that. They take requests though reserve the right to refuse Evan's suggestion of "Gangsta's Paradise." Who wouldn't want that at their wedding? It makes no sense.

"You could sing it yourself," Bess says. "Just like at prom."

"It's crossed my mind. Why do you think I've been chatting them up? I'm trying to get on their good side."

"Great. Warn me if you succeed," she says. "I'll get a front-row seat. Or leave."

"There will be no warning."

Over the course of the night, Bess detects some wonky-eyed glances in her direction, which she figures are due to how closely she's dancing with Evan.

Wait, isn't that the local boy she hooked up with in high school?

Or maybe: *Doesn't he have a girlfriend? The one with the kid?*

Whatever they're saying, Bess doesn't care. She will leave and Cliff House will come down. It's time to squeeze the last few morsels from this Sconset life while she can.

"I hate to bring this up," Evan says.

It's almost midnight. Closing time. He's holding Bess tight, they're dancing to a song that is not quite fast but not slow either. Sort of like "Gangsta's Paradise," but without the heaviness or implication of shooting.

"Have you noticed who didn't show?" Evan asks.

Bess nods. Because the only thing as conspicuous as Cissy walking into a room is when she's not there in the first place. Bess has spent the evening actively evading worry because she's had enough of that.

"I've noticed," Bess says. "But the party's not over. She could still make it."

"It's *almost* over though," Evan says, looking around. "And the fifty-plus set has all but dissolved."

It's true. Of the gray hairs, only her dad, Aunt Polly, and Uncle Vince linger. Bess hopes that Polly has consumed enough champagne to overlook the Cissy no-show. Whatever bizarre marital estrangements are happening between Polly's brother and sister-in-law, Cissy should've shown up to her niece's wedding.

"You're right," Bess says. "The elders are gone. This is going to be the toughest of Cissy's shenanigans to explain."

"Everyone's having too much fun to notice," Evan says.

"That's the dream." She smiles. "It's been a great wedding."

"The best I've been to."

"Me, too," Bess says. "And I've even had my own."

With a laugh, Evan spins Bess once and then a second time. He dips her low, though it's not at all a dipping sort of song. When he pulls her up, Bess is dizzy. She sees stars.

"You okay?" Evan asks, noticing the mixed-up eyes and clammy skin, both of which have little to do with the dipping.

"Yes. Yes. Fine," she says. "I'm getting a little melancholy though, thinking about how it's almost over. But I suppose everything ends eventually."

"Not everything."

"Um, hello? Have you seen the ninety-nine-year-old house across the street from your dad? If that can't last, what will?"

"Plenty of things," Evan says. "For example, I've felt the same about you for approximately forever."

Bess's skin erupts in goose bumps. Her breath gets short.

"Evan, don't . . ." She shakes her head. "Don't say things you don't mean."

He narrows his gaze.

"Why wouldn't I mean it?"

"What about, whatever her name is?" Bess says. She looks away to avoid meeting his eyes. "Grace."

"Who's Grace?"

Bess looks back at him. His face is baffled.

"The girl with the jerk lacrosse kid? Your girlfriend?"

He laughs oddly, uncomfortably, and with no cheer at all.

"Jack's mom? Uh, no. She's not my girlfriend. She's married to a buddy of mine who travels a lot. I try to help out where I can. Like I said, her son is a turkey. He needs the supervision. What made you think . . ."

"Never mind," Bess says, and cowers in humiliation. "It's a long, stupid story. I'm an idiot."

She buries herself in his shoulder.

"I'm sorry," she says into the warm place on his shirt. "I'm so lame."

"Oh, Lizzy C." He kisses her on the head again. "Come on. Look up. Look at me."

It takes her a minute but Bess does as he asks.

"I love you, you know," he says.

Bess shakes her head.

"I do," he insists.

"What about your whole thing?" Tears are rolling down her face now, tumbling unfettered. "Your mantra. *Never make the same mistake twice*."

"I still believe that."

"Then stop—"

"The thing is, you were never a mistake. I loved you then, I love you now, and every hour in between."

Bess smiles but can't echo the words despite feeling every crumb of them. These feelings—his, hers, theirs together—these feelings are why Bess has stayed away from her beloved Cliff House for so many years.

As they sway beneath a red anchor flag, the memory creeps up, though Bess has spent four years pushing it away. Still, she can see a younger Bess Codman pulling her wedding dress off the pink wardrobe. She hears the knock, a knock much like the one from earlier tonight.

At the time, Bess assumed it was Palmer or Lala. Dress held to her almost-naked body, Bess flung open the door to find a man standing before her instead.

"Evan!" she gasped.

He was wearing a white shirt, sleeves pushed back, and loose khakis. Sweat dribbled on his hairline.

"You can't see me like this!" she yipped.

Then Bess remembered it was only the groom who couldn't see the bride before the ceremony. Random ex-boyfriends didn't factor into the bad luck. Or did they?

"What are you doing?" she asked. "The wedding's about to start."

"Don't do it," he said. "Don't marry the guy."

"Excuse me?"

"He's not right for you. Not one bit."

"Oh, he's not, is he?"

What an intrusion. What galling pompousness. As if Bess would care what the bastard thought, a man who jettisoned her years ago in favor of an ill-advised sojourn to Central America.

"Who is 'right' for me, then?" she asked. "Someone more like you, I presume?"

Bess was being catty, purposefully rude, but some speck of her hoped that he might say "Yes." As she waited for his response, the speck began to grow.

"No," Evan said. "Not like me. We've moved on, haven't we?"

"Yes," Bess said, and gave him a hard scowl. "We have. I don't know what this is about but I'm quite comfortable in my choice."

She wasn't, not at all. But it was what had been decided, the fitting course. Anyhow, Brandon was great. Handsome. Successful. Loving and protective. Or that's how Bess regarded him then: in the best and most determined light.

"If you'll excuse me," she said. "I have to see a man about an altar."

With that, she slammed the door in Evan's face. It was the last Bess saw of him until a week ago.

"When you came to my bedroom door," Bess says now, as Evan glides her across the floor, "and said not to marry Brandon, I thought you were being difficult. Or argumentative. Until you gave me the entry, I didn't think it was because you . . ."

"Because I loved you," he answers for her. "And I still love you. I've loved you for my entire adult life, and then some."

Bess's eyes sting as the tears again form. She can't believe what he's saying to her, at this moment, in the very last second of everything.

"That's what my mom said about your dad," she tells him. "Almost verbatim."

"How cute. We could double-date. You should know, on that day Cissy told me not to stop you. Obviously I didn't listen."

"She did?"

Bess's eyebrows lift.

"Yep. I went to her, crying like a baby. It was pathetic. I had plans for some big confession, a declaration of love. She told me it wasn't fair, that I should've done it long ago and I 'had plenty of chances, sonny.' Leaving you to your day was the right thing to do. She was not wrong."

"Well," Bess says, her breath shaking in her chest. "She was and she wasn't."

The right thing to do. Bess is beginning to think that in most circumstances there's no such thing.

"And don't think I haven't noticed," Evan says. "I've used the word 'love' approximately twelve times in the last three minutes and you haven't replied once. That's okay, though, because I know you feel the same."

Bess smiles and thinks about this for a bit. *Pretends* to think about it, because the answer is clear.

"Yes," she says. "I do."

Just as Bess goes to make a joke ("If this is a ploy for sex, remember, I just got out of the hospital"), the doors suddenly whoosh open and a gale blows in. It's Cissy in a short red dress, Chappy on her arm.

Chappy! Her dad! Bess scoots out of Evan's hold and turns to look for Dudley. He is across the way, coming in from enjoying a cigar outside.

With a hard glare aimed at Cissy, Dudley takes a terse sip of bourbon. This perfect night, made even more perfect by the fact that it followed Bess's very worst day, this night is about to end in catastrophe. Damn Cissy. You don't bring your boyfriend to a wedding that your husband is already at. That's just straight etiquette.

"Fuck," Bess says.

Her father closes the door behind him and beats a hot path toward Cissy and her date. Dudley lurches at Cissy and then cloaks her in what can only be described as a friendly embrace. While Bess stands stunned and blinking, her father does the unthinkable. He shakes Chappy's hand. Proof that the world will never make sense.

The reunion breaks up. Chappy beelines toward one bar, Dudley the other (not *too* chummy, thank God). Bess turns to Evan.

"Excuse me for a minute?" she says.

He nods, unable to answer. Bess pecks him on the cheek and finds Cissy, who is standing alone at the edge of the dance floor.

"You made it!" Bess says, and gives her mom a hug. "I was getting worried."

"I had to finish packing! It's a big job."

Bess laughs and shakes her head.

"Packing?" she says. "A big job? You don't say. I'm so glad you're here, Cis. You look spectacular."

"So do you." Cissy takes her hand. "How are you?"

"Oh I'm fi—"

"No, how are you *really* doing? Don't give me the pat wedding-reception answer."

Bess considers this.

"Actually, the pat answer and the real one are not so far apart," she says with a smile. "I'm fine. Better by the second."

Cissy smiles in return and touches her daughter's cheek.

"I love you, Bessie. I'm heartbroken for what you've been through."

"Me, too," Bess says. "But suddenly it all looks so different. Like for the first time, everything might turn out fine." She snorts. "I guess because by the time you realize something truly sucks you're most of the way through it."

"That's my girl." Cissy pulls Bess in for another hug and a strong kiss on the lips. "You're a remarkable person. Thanks for being there for me. *Literally* there. In Sconset, at Cliff House. I couldn't have gotten through this on my own."

"Yeah, you'd still be on that veranda if not for me."

"Oh, I would've moved on eventually."

"You keep telling yourself that," Bess says.

Suddenly the microphone crackles. The band changes tune. A rough, familiar voice ripples through the room.

"Wow," Cissy says, and whips around, a grin erupting across her face. "Is that . . . 'A Piece of My Heart'? I'm impressed. You generally don't get Joplin at a wedding."

"Oh, God!" Bess cries, though these are happy tears.

"Oh my. Is that . . . ?"

Bess peers around Cissy's wide, wide hair to see Evan clutching the mike. His shirt is partially unbuttoned, the periwinkle tie is gone. Sweat shimmers on his face as if he's been singing all night.

"Holy shit," Bess says.

"Are you being . . . serenaded?" Cissy asks, then twists up her mouth.

"Holy shit," Bess says again as she realizes that yes, she's being serenaded.

And he's lifted the entire room to its feet.

I want you to come on, come on, come on, come on and take it . . .

The other guests flood the dance floor. Soon, the entire room is singing, shaking from the power of their voices. Evan Mayhew has brought the house down.

Chappy takes Cissy's hand and pulls her onto the floor. Meanwhile, Bess's heart flops all over the place. She is wildly charmed by the gesture, but it sure would be nice to have someone to dance with. Bess prays this won't all end in the "Macarena."

As if he can read her thoughts, and hell maybe he can, Evan turns the mike over to the real vocalist and jumps off the stage. He saunters up while Bess stands dumbed and speechless.

"So," he says. "Better than Coolio?"

"Uh. Yeah."

"I do love you, Bess," he tells her. "It's not just the night or the moment or the really good booze."

"I love you, too," she answers. Then pauses. "Although I am on Vicodin. So who knows?"

Evan throws back his head and laughs.

"Oh, Lizzy C. A piece of my heart indeed."

You know you got it if it makes you feel good.

64

The Book of Summer

Ruby Young Packard
June 1, 1948
Cliff House, Sconset, Nantucket Island

The house is open, the flags are raised, and the ferries from New Bedford and Woods Hole are running regularly once more. All that and I have three new bathing costumes, my favorite featuring blue-and-white stripes and close-fitting shorts. It's just as Mother said, the summer will always come.

They're expecting 40,000 visitors on Nantucket this season, a record by far. Folks are ready for vacation and now we're only a ninety-minute flight from New York. There's now no place on earth unreachable if you have but ten days to spare. Sconset doesn't seem so isolated anymore.

Not that the trains are suffering, not by a mile. Grand Central reported last weekend was its busiest in history. I'm sure more than a few bodies were bound our way, judging from all the gruff city voices I heard on Main Street. Admittedly I am often vexed by the tourists, even though I'm technically an off-islander myself. Not that I feel like one. Baxter Road is more my home than Commonwealth Avenue, no matter how many days I spend in each.

The roads in town are jammed with cars, from new and sporty to old-fashioned and high-slung. That the gasoline stockpiles are being released is quite evident and already biking has fallen out of fashion. Cycling is back to being a "roughing it" kind of pastime. Or as the New York Times *proclaimed, "a holiday sport suited only to those hard of muscle and with dogged determination."*

In addition to prepping the house for the season, we've spent the past few days golfing and sunning and sailing, too. I never understood my little brother's obsession with the sport until I tried my hand for real. And wouldn't you know? There is a certain splendor to sailing, to gliding upon God's great sea using nothing but rags and a chunk of wood. The simple beauty of the sport is not unlike Sconset itself, with its gray shingled homes huddled together in quiet, restrained dignity, sturdy against the winter winds.

But it's winter no more. Outside glassware clinks and the waiters scurry about. We're holding a fête tonight, the first of the summer. Our guest list tops one hundred and every single person RSVP'd "yes." Old friends and new. Nantucket and Boston and New York, even Washington town. Three cheers for summer. May it be made only of long days.

With love and hope,
Yours truly,
Ruby

65

RUBY

Summer 1948

They stood by the swimming pool, or the three-quarters pool that it was.

"It won't be done by the party," Ruby noted.

She was in her bathing costume, with a mallard-green scarf wrapped around her shoulders. Her feet were sandy. They'd just come up from the beach.

"This is not good at all," she said.

They were supposed to have 150 guests and their yard was torn to bits. Not the brightest notion to start a large construction project during the busiest season in a decade. Had Mother been alive she could've told Ruby that.

"You were the one who insisted," Sam pointed out. "The builders warned us that the timeline was too slim, that even a few hours of inclement weather could derail the whole thing."

Ruby glared at her husband over the top of her sunglasses.

"Not helpful," she said.

Suddenly an orb of yellow frenzy flashed in Ruby's periphery.

"Cissy!" Ruby barked, scuttling across the bricks and wood. "Put that down."

The three-year-old was right then dropping rocks into the gaping hole in their yard.

"Oh good grief," Ruby said, and hoisted Cissy up against her waist. "You want to help, don't you? Finish this pool yourself. I know what you're thinking, you darling scamp."

That was so like Cissy. She'd shown them exactly who she was, and straightaway. So independent, utterly take charge. Why, just that morning and out of the clear blue, Cissy took it upon herself to fold the laundry. It mostly involved slinging everything into a heap in her bureau, but the thought was there.

"You're a cute bug, aren't you?" Ruby said, and kissed her soft head. "Though a buzzy one."

Cissy squirmed to break free, right on time.

Lord, Ruby loved her little spitfire, but the get-up-and-go really wore a woman out. Sometimes there was a mighty fine line between vivacity and being a real pill.

She released Cissy to the ground and looked back at her husband. It was hard to believe that something so on the move could bind two people together in one place. When Sam showed up the year before, quite sheepish and from the oblivion, he took one gander at Cissy's round cheeks and that sassy sapphire gaze and knew at once he could never leave.

"Hey, whatcha got there, baby girl?" Ruby heard her husband ask.

"Box!" Cissy said, and crinkled something in cellophane. "Secrets!"

Ruby took three rapid strides forward and swiped the box from Cissy's hand. She chuckled. "Secrets." Or, rather, cigarettes. An ancient, emptied-out package unearthed by the workers. Ruby turned it over. Gauloises, Hattie's favorite brand. Ruby gave a watery smile of remembrance, of regret. They'd really fouled it up, hadn't they?

Though she still viewed Hattie's article as inexcusable, ultimately it was not unforgivable. And so Ruby had extended the olive branch, sending Hattie a birth announcement when Cissy arrived.

Mrs. Ruby Young Packard announces the birth of her daughter, Caroline Sarah Young Packard, on November 20, at Massachusetts General Hospital in Boston.

Ruby wasn't looking for a gift, but she didn't even get a response.

Ruby sent more letters over the years, all unanswered. She even invited Hattie to the "Salute to Summer" cocktail soirée they were holding that very night. They were raising money for the old sailors' home, and Hattie loved a good charity case. Plus, Ruby wanted to introduce her to Sam's pal, an honest-to-God congressman in the U.S. House of Representatives. John Kennedy was handsome as the devil and miraculously unattached. Ruby could tell he was a good mama's boy, not to mention Sam said he planned to run for governor! The kid was going places.

"Kennedy," Sam said with a laugh when Ruby broached the topic weeks before. "Hattie Rutter is too ambitious for the likes of Jack. He has big plans and needs a wife without too many plans of her own. Hattie would just get in his way."

Ruby didn't agree, but it hardly mattered, as Hattie obviously didn't plan to show that night or ever again. In the end, Ruby told herself it was for the best. They should leave the summer of 1941 where it belonged: in a trophy case on the highest and prettiest shelf.

"You look stunning," Sam said.

Ruby stepped out of her dressing room and into the light. She had on a gown of deep blue crepe, two daring gaps running from beneath her arms all the way down to her waist. As she walked, the accordion-pleated skirt skimmed across the floor. It was all a tad grand and chichi for Cliff House, but this was a benefit and Ruby always did her best to look the part.

"Why, thank you," she said, and took a small curtsy. "Mind helping me with my jewels?"

She walked toward the blue velvet box on the dresser. Inside was a necklace of diamonds and emeralds, a present from Sam on their anniversary several weeks before. The gift was a mite over-the-top, as he'd missed quite a few. He'd spend the rest of his life trying to make up for what he did. That is, when he wasn't picking himself up after yet another fall.

"Of course I'll help," Sam said, and approached the dresser. "It'd be my honor."

As he went for the box, his hands shook. He struggled with the clasp.

Damn it, Sam was drunk already. Ruby smelled the whiskey on him but told herself all was fine. Sam had always been a drinker and he seemed in a dandy mood. She hoped he could hold it together for the rest of the night.

"Here you go, my darling," he said, fingers clammy against the back of her neck.

"Thank you," Ruby whispered.

When he stepped away, Ruby felt for the clasp to make sure it was secure.

"Well," she said, chipper as sunshine. Ruby reached toward her husband. "Shall we?"

Sam nodded.

"We shall."

They locked fingers and exchanged wistful smiles, looks of love and appreciation, of shared history and pain. After sucking back all the bad, they walked downstairs to welcome their guests to the biggest party Cliff House had ever seen.

66

Island ACKtion

MUDSLIDE ON SANKATY BLUFF

June 7, 2013

Mother Nature's been no friend to the efforts of the Sankaty Bluff Preservation Fund. Though town selectmen okayed the geotube project, Sconset residents are wondering if it might be too late.

Never mind the storms of the past year, over the last three weeks the bluff has endured a dangerous combination of near-constant light rain and a barrage of heavy winds. Yesterday a major portion of the cliff conceded the fight. At around five o'clock in the evening, a mudslide began. The bluff lost over seven feet.

There are still homes to save and miles of shore to protect. But the woman who's been the face of this fight is waving her flag. It's hard to imagine but the fact is this. Cissy Codman's Cliff House will come down.

ABOUT ME:

Corkie Tarbox, lifelong Nantucketer, steadfast flibbertigibbet. Married with one ankle-biter. Views expressed on the *Island ACKtion* blog (Twitter, Facebook, Instagram, et al.) are hers alone. Usually.

67

June 2013

Cliff House is gone.

Most of it anyway, the parts that matter. Bess and Cissy stand on the drive, holding on to each other, as bulldozers scrape away the last bits of their home. Some of it will remain. Hunks of foundation. Plumbing and wires. Leftover bricks from the now-demolished patio. They'll do their best but the machines won't tempt or tease the bluff's edge, so they can't remove it all.

"I still don't believe it," Cissy says again and again.

Her eyes are glassy but she's past crying, having achieved that near-peaceful state that follows a hard sob.

"I really can't believe it. My mother would hate this."

Bess doesn't say anything, because Grandma Ruby *would* hate this but what more can Cissy do? She's already done everything—every last little thing. Bess is beginning to understand the unspoken expectations placed on Cissy, being the only child in a troubled home.

"Grandma would be proud of you," Bess says, as this is also true. "For fighting so hard. No one could say you didn't try."

"I tried all right."

"Good thing I came to the rescue," Bess says jokingly. "Because if not for me, you'd still be trying. You'd still be in that house instead of moving on."

"Is that right?" Cissy says archly. "Frankly, I think you needed to see the house before *you* could move on."

Bess rolls her eyes, though Cissy has a point.

Her mother smiles wistfully as she squints toward the sea. It's dazzling outside, the sun high and bright. Twenty-five years ago, on a day like this, they would've been clambering about the kitchen, pulling together food and tanning oil and hats. It'd take a full sixty minutes for someone to wrangle toddler Lala, who would no doubt be sitting buck-ass naked on a couch.

"For the love of Pete," Grandma Ruby might've said. "Has anyone thought to teach that child the benefit of pants?"

Together they'd march across the wide lawn, over the public walking path, and down their private stairs to the beach below. They'd spread out blankets and set up their chairs. Passersby would smile at the pretty family from the big old house.

"Well, Mom," Bess says at last, scowling at the spot where the kitchen once stood.

Cissy looks at her.

"I love when you call me Mom," she says. "It's quaint. Old-fashioned."

Suddenly Bess's frown loosens. She shifts her face halfway to a smile.

"Oh, Mom," she says, and sighs. "Mom. Mom. Mom. The best one there is. We should get you back to Tea Time. Clay and Lala will be there by now."

"And Sarah," Cissy says, grinning, as she thinks of her new grandchild, only a week old.

"And Sarah," Bess agrees.

"Plus you have a flight to catch."

Bess glances toward the truck behind them, which holds her luggage in its bed. The very idea of San Francisco is unthinkable. It feels like she's been gone a century. Will she even remember the route to her new apartment? Does she live on the second floor or on the third?

As they walk toward the truck, arms still around each other, they see Chappy and Evan hop out of the cab as if they're ushers prepared to shepherd them on.

"We're ready," Cissy says. "No need to get out."

"Hey." Chappy takes her hand. "Come here."

He escorts Cissy away from Bess and Evan.

"I want to say good-bye, too," Bess hears him say.

Chappy and her mother walk to the edge of the cliff. Bess can't hear their words but detects that labored breathing that accompanies a rush of tears. Maybe Cissy isn't done with the crying after all.

"What's the plan?" Evan asks, pressing his mouth into a hard line. "Airport first?"

His own eyes water.

"That makes the most sense," Bess says. "Since it's on the way. I appreciate the ride."

"Bess, don't even . . ."

"Especially since my other option is Cissy and her bike," Bess tries to joke.

Evan looks at her.

"No matter what," he says, "I'll come get you. Any time. All you have to do is call and I'll be right there."

Bess understands he's not referring only to the airport.

"You're going to be completely annoyed by how much I take you up on that," she says, and means it.

"I'll count on it."

"You know I love you, right?" Bess asks.

"I know."

"And you know that I have to leave," she says. "I don't want to but it's not really a choice. Not right now."

"I know."

"There are things I have to take care of. Real-world stuff. I can't just . . ."

"I know."

"But I'll find my way back. Somehow, in some way that will be more than it was before."

He doesn't answer. *I know,* he's said. Does he know? He doesn't. But he hopes.

"All right, you two," Chappy calls, tramping back toward the car, Cissy trailing after him. "Bess and Cissy, you gals need a final picture at the old homestead."

"Some homestead," Cissy says, trying to catch her breath.

Chappy holds up his phone.

"Let's do this," he says. "You'll hate yourself if you don't."

"Do you even know how to work that?" Evan asks.

"It's a damned phone, not a nuclear code. Cissy. Bess. Get together. One last photo taken at the head of Sankaty Bluff."

The women trade looks and shrug. Why not?

Cissy and Bess sock in together and unleash their biggest smiles as the wind whips up the sand and shells around them. In between takes they comment on the weather. It's a glorious afternoon, they agree. Finally and at last. Mark it in the Book of Summer: the first clear day.

Author's Note

This book is based on the real-life erosion of the Sankaty Bluff in Siasconset (known as Sconset), the easternmost spot on Nantucket Island. I've tried to stick closely to the facts and complexities of the erosion problem, and even the weather that's caused it, but as this is a work of fiction, I've tinkered with timelines and details for the sake of plot.

I first learned of the problem from an article in *Vanity Fair* about the gorgeous, grand homes, many passed down between generations, now falling into the sea. Though Cliff House bears the fictitious address of 101 Baxter Road, it is very loosely based on Bluff House, formerly located at 87 Baxter Road. In my mind, Cliff House is an amplified amalgam of Bluff House and the property located (for now) at number 93. These homes, real and imagined, sit high up on the Sankaty Bluff, yards away from the iconic Sankaty Head Lighthouse, which itself had to be moved owing to the faltering cliffside. Like Cissy Codman, several owners evaluated the possibility of moving their homes before finally succumbing to the inevitable.

As in the book, Sankaty lost over fifty feet of bluff during the 2012–13 winter storms. Town officials considered closing Baxter Road for good, until lawyers pointed out that they couldn't simply shut down roads or the utilities running along them. Geotubes, like the ones Cissy Codman fought so hard for, were installed in late 2013, after the Siasconset Beach Preservation Fund (SBPF), fictionalized here as the Sankaty Bluff Preservation Fund, finally gained approval from the Massachusetts Department of Environmental Protection.

These geotubes, large, sand-filled jute bags that look like burritos (as described by Evan Mayhew), are meant to keep the existing bluff intact. They are used in conjunction with a sand-replenishment program to prevent harm to neighboring beaches. According to the SBPF, as of late 2015, the time of this writing, no further erosion has occurred, thanks to these measures. The tubes currently cover about 900 feet of bluff, whereas the SBPF hopes to address the estimated 3,400 feet that are at risk.

You can learn more about the erosion, and what folks are doing to combat it, from the fund's Web site at www.sconsetbeach.org. Of course, as with all prickly topics, not everyone agrees that the geotubes have performed as promised. Those who oppose such measures say that the geotubes won't halt erosion and will instead siphon sand from the neighboring beaches and ultimately the entire island.

Van Lieu Photography has documented the erosion in memorable and evocative detail at www.vanlieuphotography.com and www.nantucketerosion.com. I've included my own (amateur) photographs on my Web site at www.michellegable.com and on Pinterest at www.pinterest.com/mgablewriter/bookofsummer. I'll leave the reader to decide which side he or she is on.

Acknowledgments

The idea for this book began with an article in *Vanity Fair*: "Coast to Toast" by Vanessa Grigoriadis. So, first and foremost, I want to thank other writers and researchers for opening my eyes and inspiring my work, not only in this instance, but in a thousand other ways.

Thank you to my agent, Barbara Poelle, the first person to believe in me, and the person who still has my back, even when I don't realize it. A million thanks (at least) to my outstanding editor, Laurie Chittenden, for forcing me to dig deeper and always finding a fix for any problem. Thank you also to Lisa Bonvissuto for all that you do!

I'm so lucky to be a part of the St. Martin's team. My covers and interior pages somehow keep getting better—thank you to Young Lim and Anna Gorovoy for wrapping this story in the loveliest of packages.

Heaps of gratitude to the world's hardest-working, smartest, and kindest publicist, Katie Bassel, and the crack marketing team, especially

Laura Clark and Lauren Friedlander. Thank you also to Sally Richardson and Pete Wolverton for your support, and to Sally for her contributions to this book.

Huge shout-out to the amazing Dr. Laura Schobitz Bauer for insight into what it's like to work in the ER, more accurately known as the Emergency Department, as my character Bess rightly points out. Thank you to Kristin Lando Parker for the knitting facts, and forcing my characters to sometimes "drop a stitch." Thank you also to Heather, Greg, and Julia Olson, for granting me use of Lala's name and nickname.

I am extraordinarily grateful to my husband, Dennis Bilski, for countless things, including the correction of my golf-related errors, not to mention his innate ability to determine when I'm "on deadline" and therefore best left in my cave. Thank you to my brilliant and funny girls, to whom this book is dedicated. Some of my happiest memories are from the time we all spent together in a house on Baxter Road.

As always, thank you to my tremendously supportive parents, Tom and Laura Gable, who make me feel like more of a star than I could ever dream to be, and to my siblings, Lisa Gable Wheatley and Brian Gable, for the ongoing encouragement. Thanks also to Bill and Suzy Gable; I so appreciate your hand-selling my books.

One of the best things about going on a book tour is seeing friends countrywide. Special thanks to my Richmond and DC crew, especially Elaine Turville Kropp, Anna Dinwiddie Hatfield, Laura Schobitz Bauer (again!), and Caryn Parlee Simpkins, and to my North Carolina pals, specifically Martha Hurst Seaman. In San Diego and always, I have the unending warmth and support of Karen Freeman Landers and Lauren Gist. Dinners, Chargers games, spa days—you two are the greatest.

Finally, thank you to the readers who show up at my events, send kind e-mails, and in general remind me how lucky I am to have this career.

Turn the page for a sneak peek at
Michelle Gable's next novel

Available May 2018

APRIL 2016
LOS ANGELES

A man sits on a patio, wrapped in a blanket and staring out to sea. It is cold in California this time of year, though much better than in New York, which is why he winters on this coast. He is old enough to do what he wants. Let someone else worry about logistics at the office, who's billing what hours, and the clients they should woo. He's sworn a hundred times he'll retire. Soon. Very soon.

His secretary comes outside. She wears a blue suit, and blue heels but in a different shade.

"Any luck?" he asks.

She frowns and extends the sealed envelope his way.

"It's the best I could do," she says.

The man turns the letter over in his hand, then tosses it onto a nearby table. He should probably ask her to type the address, as the woman's penmanship resembles that of a teenage girl. If teens wrote things by hand anymore. Oh, who cares. The destination is legible. Good enough.

"It's fine," he says, and leans into his chaise, eyes closed. "Thank you."

The secretary waits for further direction as the envelope flutters in the breeze. Before he meanders off into sleep, she has to ask.

"Do you think it's true?" she says.

At first, he doesn't answer. She assumes he's fallen asleep but, really, he's taking his time.

"We first met," he says, causing her to jump, "fifty years ago."

He opens one eye, and then the other.

"And over the decades she said many things."

He chuckles through his nose.

"*Many* things," he repeats. "Outrageous claims were made, some of which would make international news. But as to whether I believe it? I've never been able to decide. Not that my opinion matters. The only thing we can do is send the letter and wait for a response."

CRUISING CASANOVAS ARE A BAD RISK

The Boston Daily Globe, August 20, 1950

HYANNISPORT, MASSACHUSETTS

The government wouldn't deport her, she didn't think.

Alicia was unclear on the particulars, but when a person emigrates to the United States under somewhat ill-begotten circumstances, she is not particularly inclined to raise her hand. She was probably safe, because where might they send her? Alicia was no longer a citizen of Poland, and they couldn't return her to the German camp. This was, she supposed, the upside to her statelessness. To be deported, you needed a home.

For a second, Alicia felt relief. Then she remembered a story she read, about a refugee who'd spent years on a ship, circling the globe, no port willing to let him through, like a crate of damaged goods.

Alicia sent up a quick prayer—or something like it—that Irenka would come through with the job.

"I do vat I can," she'd said in her choppy, harsh accent. "But no promisink."

A risky thing, to bet it all on a maid from Poland. But she had no other options on Cape Cod.

At least she had *this* job, her part-time work at the Center Theatre. She tried to wheedle Mr. Dillon into more hours, but he was rigid as a German.

"You can help George and Dewey during peak times," he'd said. "That's all I'm able to offer."

George was the Center's projectionist, a spindly man with a swoop of black hair and oversized black-rimmed glasses. Alicia thought the person running films should have better vision, but George seemed to do okay.

Dewey was the counter clerk, though he spent most of his time taking smoke breaks behind the stately brick building, or sometimes right in front, beneath the black and gold awning.

"No more than ten hours per week," Mr. Dillon said, "and only through the Indian summer."

"How about twenty?" Alicia countered, having noted Dewey's lack of industry.

"How about seven?" Mr. Dillon returned.

"But this is the perfect job for me. The first cinema in Poland was built in my hometown, in 1899. My mother was very proud of this. She'd tell any out-of-towner who'd listen!"

When Alicia first stepped inside the Center, her heart sang, for she'd finally, after nearly a year, found something in America that reminded her of home. Though the room was empty at the time, it remained grand with its red velveteen chairs and wide, noble balconies. She could almost hear the whoosh of the curtains and the sound of her mother's laughter tumbling over time and space.

"We probably saw twenty films a year," Alicia added. "In the good years, that is."

"Listen, I don't have to hire you at all," Mr. Dillon said, unimpressed with her cinematic background.

"Ten sounds fine," she'd mumbled, accepting brisk defeat, though this did not stop her from making one last request.

"Can I display my art in the lobby?" she asked. "You see, I'm a painter—"

"Do whatever the hell you want," Mr. Dillon said. "As long as it doesn't bother the customers. Or me."

As luck would have it, Mr. Dillon spent most of his time managing the Hyannis Theatre, over on the swankier side of town. Alicia was glad she'd picked the Center. Mr. Dillon wasn't apt to let a homeless Pole display her work on the glitzy west end.

Alicia stepped behind the counter. She could probably leave, as these were hardly "peak hours." Sunday matinees rarely were. In her brain, Alicia added up the time she'd worked that week. Should she push it to eleven hours, or twelve?

Alicia crouched down and slid one row of Boston Beans flush with another. The display looked sharp, artful almost. She let herself feel proud, and wished she could show Irenka.

"You vant to clean?" her friend had shirked when Alicia showed up on her doorstep last week, fresh off the bus from Oklahoma City.

"I don't *want* to clean per se," Alicia told her, "but being a maid would tide me over . . ."

"A maid! Bah! You cannot do maid! You terrible wit cleanink!"

Maybe so, but Alicia didn't plan to sweep floorboards for the rest of her life, and she could fake it well enough, for now.

"You still selling?" asked a voice.

Alicia jumped up. She shook her head, and the room blurred.

"Oh! Yes! Sorry!" she said, the man's Boston accent prickling the hairs on her neck. "I thought everyone was inside."

When Alicia caught eyes with the guest, everything inside her body seized. Before her stood a man, tall and tanned, with mussed reddish-brown hair and an untucked white shirt. He grinned, corner to corner, eyes crinkling at the edges.

"Wow, I must've really thrown ya," the man said.

"I apologize," Alicia said, panicked. "I wasn't expecting anyone to be out here. The second showing of the movie just began. If you hurry, you won't miss a minute. It's *In the Foreign Legion*."

As if he couldn't read the marquee. Mentally, Alicia rolled her eyes.

"Yeah. I know how it works," he said. "Stahrting from two fifteen, continuous. I prefer to sneak in late."

He pushed a chunk of hair from his forehead, and Alicia found herself mimicking the gesture. He caught this, and winked, causing Alicia to jolt once more.

It wasn't the man's handsomeness. He was attractive, no question, but he was also gangly, too thin. His hair was bushy and his head preposterously oversized compared to his reedy frame. Any objective poll would place his looks well below Ty Power's or William Holden's, yet there remained something special about him, something beautiful that had little to do with actual presentation.

But, yes, okay, he was handsome, and tan, and had one hell of a smile.

"So, you didn't answer my question," he said. "Are you still open?"

"You mean for refreshments?"

He laughed.

Holy snakes, the man had intensely straight and white teeth.

"Yes, what else?" he said. "Then again, maybe you can think of another reason I might want to hang out here?"

He said "here" as if it were two syllables instead of one. *He-ah*.

"Oh, er," Alicia stuttered. "There's not much else to do, aside from order refreshments."

"You must be new," he said. "I'd surely remembah your face."

Alicia blushed furiously and reached for a cup.

"Will that be a large?" she said.

"I didn't place an order."

"Asking 'What size?' is a much better sales tactic than 'May I help you?'"

"Well, I'm a suckah for a good saleswoman," he said. "So, I'll have a large Coke, as suggested."

"You've got it."

Alicia flipped around and began to fill his cup, wondering how it'd become so hot in that room. She fanned herself with a flattened popcorn box.

"By the way," the man said. "My name's Jack. Jack Kennedy."

"Kennedy?" Alicia blurted.

He was one of *them*—the family Irenka picked up after, the family Alicia hoped would employ her, too.

According to Irenka, there were some ten, twelve of them, maybe more. The father was a former ambassador; the kids all grown. The mother was penurious, and a tad odd, though Irenka held her in high esteem.

In her letters and in person, Irenka recounted stories about this crew, and their scrapes and shenanigans. They stole cars, broke limbs, and swiped food off one another's plates. The Cape was flooded with their unpaid bills, and the house was often flooded for real, as the family seemed unable to remember when they'd left a faucet running.

They were a family of slobs, Irenka claimed. They left their towels and bathing costumes strewn about the house.

"Worse dan pigs on farm," she insisted.

But Irenka must've been mistaken. Jack was in his shirtsleeves, and his trousers hung like old drapes, but Alicia couldn't imagine that anyone would consider him slovenly.

"Aw, hell," Jack moaned, "look at that expression. And you said 'Kennedy' like it was a swear word."

Sway-er. As he spoke, Alicia realized that while Jack had a Boston accent, his was different from those she'd already heard. It was the rhythm of his speech, and how it sped up, and then slowed. Sometimes his words pushed, and other times, they pulled.

"Kennedy," said like he was racing toward something.

"Swear," like he wanted the word to last all night.

"Judging by your reaction," he said, "I assume you've had the great misfortune of meeting my brother, Teddy."

Alicia thought for a minute, mind clicking through Irenka's tales. Teddy, he was the fat one, the youngest. He was prone to problems with boats.

"Teddy," the Ambassador once said, "if you leave with the boat, you come back with the boat."

"I've never met your brother," Alicia said. "But I've . . . heard some stories."

Jack snorted.

"I'll bet. Please don't judge our entire family by that one."

Alicia smiled weakly.

"I'm sure you're all lovely," she said.

Jack threw back his head and cackled.

"Said by someone who's obviously never met us. Listen, I hate to point out the obvious, but you haven't told me your name. Sort of makes me feel like I'm doin' all the work."

"Oh. Yes." She exhaled. "I'm Alicia. Alicia Darr."

Jack grinned, wide as the heavens, and extended a hand across the counter. Alicia brought hers to meet it.

"*Enchantée,*" she said, inexplicably.

Alicia blushed yet again. French, of all things. She was at the Center Theatre in Hyannis, Massachusetts, not the damned Sorbonne. Maybe she should switch to German, to show him how many languages she knew.

"*Enchantée* indeed," Jack said. "Your accent is perfection. Where do you go to school?"

"I don't."

Jack scrunched his perfectly shaped nose.

"You don't attend school?" he said.

"I do not. The popcorn is delicious, have you tried some?"

"But you're not old enough to have graduated college."

"What's old enough?" she said. "In any case, I started out with lofty plans but didn't make it to university. The war, you know."

She looked away.

"Ah. I should've guessed. You're European."

"Am I?"

Alicia was not being coy. "European" was usually reserved for those from Paris, or Vienna, possibly Hamburg, worst case. She was from Poland, which most would regard as decidedly "Eastern Bloc."

Legally, though, Alicia wasn't from anywhere, "stateless" as her documents showed, her current home a mattress inside Irenka's closet. A person couldn't get much more displaced than that.

"So, you moved around?" Jack said with a wince. "Separated from family and friends?"

"Something like that."

He sighed, then blubbered his lips.

"Those Nazis. They were no fucking fun."

Alicia coughed out an astonished laugh, amused or deeply offended, either one.

Abruptly, Jack jerked his head toward something that'd caught his eye.

"You guys selling art now?" he asked.

"Oh. Um. Yes. It's something Mr. Dillon is trying out."

"Huh." He shrugged. "Well. Neat painting."

"Thank you?" Alicia said, craning past his (large, large) head.

He was inspecting a watercolor of Piotrkowska Street, Alicia's former home. Even though she'd created it, and studied it a hundred times, her heart sputtered as she took in the avenue's baroque buildings, and its curled lampposts, restaurants, and shops.

"You painted that?"

Jack turned her way, one brow cocked.

"I did." Alicia nodded. "It's one of the prettiest streets in Europe. It *was* one of the prettiest streets. There's no telling what it looks like now. Well, enjoy your drink and the film. That'll be thirty cents."

"Anxious to move me on, are ya?"

He narrowed his green-gray gaze and leaned farther over the counter.

"There's something familyah about you," he said. "We've met before. Have you been working here all summer?"

"No, I only started a few days ago. Do you need napkins? That will be thirty cents. As I mentioned."

"Really? A few days? Then surely you were here last summer."

He drummed his fingers on the countertop.

"You worked at the club? Teaching sailing? Tennis?"

"No, sir, not at all." Alicia wrested a napkin from its silver holder. "I've been in Hyannis less than a week. You should take one of these to your seat. Your drink will sweat thanks to the humidity. That'll be thirty cents."

"Only a week?" Jack said, appearing pinched. "That can't be right. I swear we've met before. You are so familiar and your face . . . well, it's unforgettable."

"You are mistaken," she said, staring at the floor.

Alicia could feel Jack's eyes on her as surely as she could feel the sun when she stepped outside.

"I'd like to get your number," he said.

Alicia glanced up.

"Excuse me?" she said.

"I'd like to take you out."

He reached into his pockets, but came up empty.

"You said you're new here, so I'd like to show you the Cape," Jack said, and picked up a receipt left by another customer. "Here, write down your number."

"My numbah?"

She had not meant to parrot his voice.

"I'm staying with a friend," she explained quickly.

"I'd be happy to meet her, too," he said, a glimmer in his eyes.

Alicia gave a hoarse chuckle.

"I don't know that you would be," she said. "Happy to meet her, that is."

"Wow," Jack said. "You're really making me work for it, aren't ya?"

Alicia snagged the slip of paper, and scribbled Irenka's information, hand quivering.

"It was fantastic to meet you, Miss Darr," Jack said.

He took the paper and rewarded Alicia with one last smile.

"Hope to see you again, very soon," he said.

Then Jack winked, and turned to go.

"That'll be thirty cents!" Alicia called out. "You still owe for the Coke!"

Jack spun around.

"Thirty cents?" he repeated. "That seems steep."

Alicia shrugged.

"It says right here on the sign, thirty cents for a jumbo."

"I thought it was a large?"

"I'm fairly convinced you said jumbo."

"I don't have any money on me," he said, without checking to be sure.

"Then you'll have to return the soda."

He closed his eyes and laughed.

"Don't worry, Alicia Darr. I'm good for it. You can put it on my account."

Before she could protest, or take possession of the drink, Jack vanished through the double doors. Alicia stood motionless, her body roiling with a great mixture of emotions. She was discombobulated, bewildered, and a little charmed. All that and poorer, given she was now thirty cents in the hole.